STRANGERS IN THE NIGH

There was movement again over in the corner, a shadowy form that was as black as the night.

Releasing his long sword, Oishi clenched the short blade in his hand and slithered across the room to place himself between the shadow and the corner where he had last seen Aldin.

The shadow moved again, and Oishi rolled backward, slashing at the air before him. Only a faint hiss preceded the blade that caught against his shoulder, laying it bare.

Suddenly a dagger was at his throat, and at that instant he realized that this mystery that had extended his life for a handful of days and shown him wonders undreamed of was finished at last . . ..

By William R. Forstchen
Published by Ballantine Books:

The Ice Prophet Trilogy:
    ICE PROPHET
    THE FLAME UPON THE ICE
    A DARKNESS UPON THE ICE

INTO THE SEA OF STARS

The Gamester Wars:
    Book One: THE ALEXANDRIAN RING
    Book Two: THE ASSASSIN GAMBIT

Book Two of
The Gamester Wars

The Assassin Gambit

William R. Forstchen

A Del Rey Book

BALLANTINE BOOKS ● NEW YORK

Friendship and honor are two of the rarest gifts to be found, and thus this book is dedicated to four who have shown me the value of such treasures.

For John Mina, Tom Seay, and Donn Wright. When special friends were needed you three were there. A lifetime of dedications could not repay all that you have done for me.

And for Kevin Malady, who has always exemplified for me the spirit of bushido and the honor of samurai. When a question of honor arises, it is your example I strive to follow.

ACKNOWLEDGMENTS

While researching for this book I came across the history of the Japanese Emperor Tsunayoshi and his dog decrees. Tsunayoshi was one of the first animal rights activists and placed special protection on dogs, believing them to be, and rightfully so, the most loyal and noble of creatures. I wish such laws, with the appropriate punishments for harming dogs, could be passed today to protect our canine friends, who ask only to serve and be loved.

Thus a little acknowledgment here to Tsunayoshi and to an old loyal friend, who's sat by my feet for many a book, sharing the ups and downs, always eager to see me smile, always ready to understand when I don't. A special thanks therefore to Ilya Murometz. I paid ten dollars for him a dozen years ago, the finest investment I ever made.

I hope my human friends don't mind sharing an acknowledgment with a canine and a dead emperor, but I'd also like to extend a special thanks to Tom Easton and Karsten Henckell for their help with probability theory, to Susan Shwartz and Joel Rosenberg for the right advice at the right time, and to Stephen Sterns, my always patient and understanding editor. Of course there should be a comment about Mer, but it goes without saying that without her loving support none of my books would have ever been created.

The
Assassin
Gambit

PROLOGUE

Yedo, Japan, 1702

"Come out, coward. Come out and face Oishi Kuranosuke of the Asano clan!"

"Murderer, you have no right," a voice shrieked to him from out of the darkness of the shed. "You are nothing but dishonored ronin; your master deserved the death he received!"

"Right? What do you know of right?" Oishi cried. "And of honor? You soil the very word by letting it pass your lips. Come out, Kira, you are still a lord to the emperor. Bear yourself with dignity."

"Go away," Kira screamed. "You break the emperor's law by attacking me!"

Oishi drew his long sword and, with a flourish, presented the hilt to the cornered nobleman.

"Take my sword, you are weaponless. I will face you alone then with but my short blade."

"The others," Kira shrieked. "You are the loyal league, the

1

forty-seven ronin. They are out there with you."

"But I am the leader," Oishi said softly. "Come face me one to one. If you defeat me, you are free."

"I will not soil my hands. I am a noble courtier," Kira cried, backing away from the proffered blade.

With a sigh of exasperation Oishi shifted the blade to his left hand and then drew out his second sword.

"Then if you will not fight me, take my short sword. The moment you cut yourself, before the first drop of blood has touched the ground, I will serve as your second and end your pain."

Kira's eyes grew with terror.

"I did not mean to cause the death of your lord!" Kira screamed.

Oishi struggled to control his rage, to allow this noble, even though a hated foe, the final dignity his class deserved.

"You taunted my lord Asano without mercy. Rather than help him learn the etiquette of court, you goaded him and humiliated him, until he broke the law of the emperor against the drawing of weapons at court, and raised his blade against you. You fled rather than fight him, and my lord was put to death, while you hid away and continued to hide these last two years from the family of Asano."

Oishi stepped into the shed, sheathing his short blade while holding his long sword up high. He was so close to Kira that he could smell the fear of his foe.

"It is time, Kira," he whispered.

Screaming with terror, Kira leaped at him.

Deftly Oishi stepped back and to one side. So quick and sure was the strike that Kira's body continued forward for several more steps before it finally collapsed to the ground, showering the darkened room with a river of scarlet.

Oishi bent down, picked up Kira's head, and strode out of the charcoal shed.

"It is finished," he said evenly. There was no cheer, no shouts of joy from his forty-six companions. For all had known, from the moment they had sworn to take Kira's life in payment for the death of their lord, where the path they had chosen would lead. In fulfilling the code of honor of the samurai, they had responded to a law that transcended even the decrees of the emperor—not to walk beneath the same sun with one who had caused the death of their lord. But they would now have to honor the law of the land, of their emperor, and all of them knew that there was but one response he would give to the killing of his favorite courtier—death by seppuku.

"We have played the game the fates have decreed and have faced it with honor," Oishi said. "Let us now prepare to meet our fathers."

Kirdkuh, Armenia, 1256

"My master, it is hopeless. They have gained the last gate to the inner citadel. Already they are bringing up the ram."

"Then it is time at last to face our fate," Hassan said, his dark face contorted with anger. "Tell the remaining men to retreat to the library. There we shall light our pyre."

Without a word the Refik withdrew from the audience chamber.

Hassan stirred himself from his throne and gazed about the empty room. Once hundreds had stood there to serve him, the Refiks and Dais, the higher echelons of the order, and beneath them the instrument of their policies, the sword arm of the Ishmaelites—the Hashshāshīn.

Through the power of the assassins, they had ruled a shadowy kingdom within the heart of Islam for two hundred years, a kingdom that was slipping away.

In the distance Hassan could hear the echoing boom of the battering ram that would soon force the final gate.

So here is the end of all things, Hassan thought wistfully. They had dared to defy the Mongol horde that had come out of the east. And defy them they could, their holy order entrenched atop a hundred mountain fortresses from the hills of Lebanon to the mountains that looked down upon the Caspian. But the ruler of the order, the Old Man in the Mountain, had forgotten all that their founders had taught, and in his madness had tried to negotiate with the Mongol khan Mangu.

After revealing the secrets of the order, he had surrendered their capital fortress of Alamut, and with it the lists that showed where the thousands of initiates, the hidden assassins, might be found, concealed among the vast humanity of a thousand hamlets and cities. Their greatest weapon, the fear of assassination, was thus removed, and the Mongols had then swept forward, killing the hidden agents and daring the attack no prince of Islam had ever dreamed of.

And now the last fortress was falling, and he, Hassan, the last master now that the Old Man was dead, was about to die, as well.

The Refik appeared again in the doorway, as if to hurry him along.

"There are only forty-five of us left," the Refik whispered.

"Are they ready?" Hassan asked.

"Ready to die with honor in your name and that of the Prophet."

Hassan chuckled softly. "With honor, you say?"

The Refik looked at him with confusion.

But of course, Hassan thought, this one is imbued with the dream of honor, of dying a martyr for the honor of the Ishmaelites' cause. But that was nothing but a lie, for a Refik was one who still believed, who would never have the final inner mystery revealed.

The dream of martyrdom, of sacred honor, was a narcotic for fools. Only the masters, and grand masters, had the final truth revealed, like a corpse laid open upon the table.

Honor was meaningless, the promise of paradise a tool used by the masters to entice the young, dreaming of martyrdom in the name of the Shiite Ishmaelites and the martyr Hussein, to come to them. In hidden gardens they would be drugged with hashish and live for a time immersed in the pleasures of Alamut. And then they would be whisked away, brought back from their drug-fevered dreams, and told that they had glimpsed paradise. To return forever was simple, they were told, as the knife was pressed into their hands and the victim pointed out. And so they would rush forth to die and, in dying, fulfill their true purpose—to maintain the power of those who ruled.

The inner circle of masters and grand masters knew the real truth—all that mattered was power and the terror it instilled; those who believed anything else were fools.

"Come, let us die with honor," Hassan said coldly. "Soon we shall recline amid the pleasures of paradise."

The light of belief shone in the eyes of the Refik as he

gazed upon the face of his master, not knowing the rage that lurked in Hassan's heart.

Planet Livola, Large Magellanic Cloud, 3-15-3145 C.A.

Message From: Xsarn Prime
To: Bukha Taug
Subject: Potential for Game

Received your message dated 3-14. Approve your suggestion for possible "diversion while accountants try to straighten out the mess from the Alexandrian game."

Any suggestions as to possible historical periods that could be included? Since you mention that "a question of honor to the order of Koh's was violated," I might be able to make one or two suggestions for combatants that could prove meaningful.

Join me for lunch today, we'll talk about preliminaries.

CHAPTER 1

"ALDIN, LOOK OUT!"

Oh, Gods, not again!

Aldin instinctively dived for the nearest cover, which in this case was behind a stack of wine barrels.

The first shot exploded the barrel right next to his head. Shattered wood and a shower of sparkling burgundy washed over him.

"Aldin, he's on your left!"

Aldin was blinded by the still-fizzling foam as he scrambled around the stack of crates.

Two more explosions echoed through the storage chamber, one blowing another barrel to splinters as the high-velocity round vaporized a rare selection of Halparinian muscatels, a favorite with Gaf connoisseurs.

"Yaroslav!"

There was no answer. Damn it, did they finally get him?

Another flurry of shots answered his call, touching off a chain reaction of bursting champagne bottles.

Aldin scurried across the floor, groping at last for his pistol, the plastic stock filling his hand. Somehow the weapon was supposed to make him feel more confident, but if anything, it gave him the shakes.

He backed up against a stack of crates, sank down to a crouching position, and snapped the safety off.

Five times, Aldin thought, five damn times in the last six months. Wouldn't Gablona ever give up?

But he realized that any hope for an end to this was ridiculous. To have thought that the sting pulled off in the Alexandrian game could have held up forever was absurd. Corbin Gablona had finally found out how he had been scammed out of his empire, and Aldin suddenly found himself hunted by his former employer from one end of the Cloud to the other. No, Gablona would never give up. The only satisfaction was the thought that Corbin Gablona languished in an Overseer reeducation camp, but that still wouldn't stop the contract from being fulfilled by the Gablona family retainers.

Aldin stiffened. A hand appeared from behind a stack of crates. In the hand was an Erik 10, a potent piece of artillery that punched out a 10-millimeter exploding shell that could blow through the latest set of ultramesh body armor, even the double set he was wearing beneath his clothes. Aldin brought up his own piece and waited.

The hand extended to reveal an arm, and finally a terrified eye peeked around the corner just as Aldin started to squeeze the trigger.

He let out a trembling sigh of relief. Yaroslav, his old companion and fellow conspirator in the last game, crept out to join him.

"How many?" Aldin whispered.

"Only one, I think."

"How the hell . . ." Aldin began but knew that his companion was as much in the dark as he. They had taken passage aboard this third-class tramp freighter bound for the Rafta-ne system where his old vasba companion Zergh had found a safe house for him. The ship had several hundred passengers on board, each of them a potential killer, but that was the chance he'd had to take. His days of private flying were over; the third assassination attempt had totaled his ship, and there was no way in hell he'd be able to buy another. To buy a ship meant credits, and the moment a credit check for purchase was run into the banks Gablona's boys would find out. Then again they weren't always boys—the fourth attempt had been rather enjoyable, that is, until she tried to nail him in the eye with a poison flick dart.

For two weeks he had endured the passage, hidden away in his cabin, and only minutes from docking above Rafta-ne he was jumped in the baggage hold, all for trying to lift a couple of lousy bottles of wine that a Xsarn steward had told him were being smuggled in and just waiting to be taken.

Yaroslav's eyes widened with fear. Aldin swung around, holding down the trigger, his pistol recoiling half a dozen times, wiping out more cases of wine.

The assassin popped up from behind the shattered crates.

Terrified, Aldin snapped off the rest of the clip, churning a couple of hundred gallons of the finest juice into a foaming spray. With a wild scream Yaroslav leaped up and in a two-handed stance emptied his weapon as well, the thundering shots echoing throughout the narrow cargo hull. The assassin flipped over, sprawled on the deck, kicked for a moment, and then was still.

A stream of red ooze bubbled out of the massive holes where his chest had been. Yaroslav drew up to the body while reloading. Just as he was about to kick the gun out of the assassin's hand, the man sat upright, raising his weapon. Yaroslav put his gun to the assassin's head and emptied another dozen rounds into it.

The head was gone, but still the body flopped and kicked for several seconds, until finally it was still.

Cautiously Aldin came up alongside his friend and gazed at the corpse.

"Our first shots should have killed him," Aldin whispered.

"It's a humanbot," Yaroslav replied nervously, kicking the gun out of the android's hand.

The two looked at each other wide-eyed with fear. It was bad enough that Gablona was trying to kill them, but to use humanbots . . . Replications of intelligent species were highly illegal—servobots by law were limited in abilities and, more important, had to look like bots. As killers they were even more dangerous than mere living beings, for bots knew no fear of pain, of punishment, or of dying, and as such were damn near unstoppable once programmed to kill.

Turning, the two ran for the door, trying desperately to make it out of the cargo hold and back to the main deck.

They came to the last row of cargo pallets, cautiously looking in all directions in case the bot had a friend around.

"Clear," Aldin whispered, then sprinted for the one doorway out. After grabbing hold, he yanked the barrier open and was shocked to find on the other side the Xsarn steward who had tipped him off to the wine.

Smiling, the steward was looking straight at him. Aldin gazed into the creature's eyes and knew.

"It's a trap!" Aldin cried, trying to back up but tripping over Yaroslav. The two fell to the deck as the steward pushed through the doorway, towering over them.

The Xsarn pulled from his tunic a heavy Erik 15, a weapon that could damn near blow a hole right through the side of the ship.

"A little present from some of your old friends," the steward whispered, an evil smile lighting his face. "Their only regret is that they aren't here to see this."

"Time to sleep." And pointing the gun at Aldin's chest, his finger tugged the trigger.

"Brother Corbin, time to rise."

"First of all, I'm not your damned brother, and secondly, I don't feel like rising."

The Overseer's pale bloodless lips curled into a benevolently superior smile. Floating in the air, his long robes trailing to the ground, Losa drifted into the room and hovered over Corbin's sleeping pallet.

"Ah, Brother Corbin, we are all brothers in spirit here. It's the hour before dawn and time to start your day."

"Listen, Losa, or Loysa, or however you wanna call yourself, you're talking to Corbin Gablona, see. I've had it with this reeducation shit and I'm going on strike right now."

"As you wish," Losa whispered, his features just barely flickering from the Overseers' usual holier-than-thou smile.

A faint tingling snap cut through Corbin's body. "You bastards. Why, if I didn't have this juice suit on, I'd wring your scrawny neck!"

He cursed inwardly even as he barked out his defiance. Losa raised an admonishing finger, as if scolding a defiant child.

The tingling wasn't quite painful—the Overseers could never be accused of torture with pain—but it was nearly as bad, with a sensation like ten thousand mosquitoes settling in for a feeding frenzy.

Thrashing and cursing, Corbin tore at the juice suit that fit him like a second layer of skin. It even looked like flesh, molded to fit every bulging curve and contour of his three-hundred-pound body.

He tried to hold out, but both he and Losa knew that it was only a matter of time. Some mornings he'd last for two, even three minutes. But what's the use? he thought, even as he also realized that each giving in was yet another tiny victory for them.

"All right, all right!" Corbin screamed, and instantly the maddening sensation stopped.

"Why, I'd like to—" Losa's upraised finger stopped him in midthreat.

"Come, come, my dear brother. Someday you'll thank me for showing you the path to brotherhood. We Overseers only want those beneath us to live in peace. We abhor violence and so should you. You know that our liberal, enlightened approach is far superior to your primitive warmongering, reactionary ways. Isn't that right, brother?"

Corbin glowered at him. "Yeah, sure."

"Brother," Losa said sweetly, his smile still rigid.

"Brother," Corbin mumbled as he climbed out of bed, to face the eighty-seventh day of his "reeducation." Eighty-seven days, and only two thousand nine hundred and thirteen to go—that is, if he got a sentence reduction for good behavior.

Minutes later the two went down the main corridor, Corbin walking with hunched-over shoulders behind the floating Overseer.

At least they hadn't tapped into his thoughts yet. But he knew that would only be a matter of time. They'd loosen him up for a year or so and once that conditioning was complete, they'd go for the neuro-links and get him on the inside, too.

He hated to think that no one ever beat these bastards at their game. In the end, anyone coming out of a Class One reeducation was nothing more than a simpering fool who'd debate for days on end the moral implications of eating a salad for fear that the plants might have feelings and not appreciate someone taking a bite out of them.

Damn. He had walked straight into their trap. Overseers were sticklers for the letter of the law, and Corbin figured his legal boys could so tie them up in the courts that it'd take years before he'd even come to a hearing. All he had to do was lay low so they couldn't nab him with a claim of protective custody.

But someone had squealed, and while hiding out on a pleasure barge all the way over in the Lesser Cloud, half a dozen Overseer ships had cut off all retreat and had him in a juice suit within the hour.

"What are you thinking about, brother?" Losa inquired, looking over his shoulder and fixing Corbin with his full four-eyed stare.

"Ah, you'd only juice me again," Corbin growled.

"Brother . . ."

"All right, all right, but I know you'd only juice me again, brother," Corbin snarled, placing a threatening emphasis on the last word.

"No, brother, we Overseers always want truth. In fact, I'd be far more distressed if you spoke an untruth merely out of fear. You see, brother, it is truth and total peaceful coexistence that we seek to give to you, our less-enlightened heathen natives. So do not fear, speak your heart, my friend."

"I was just wondering who squealed on me . . . brother."

"Since the truth can bring no harm, I'm pleased to tell you that it was your old rival Sigma Azermatti. His people found out where you were hiding and contacted us."

"Why, that rotten scum eater. He broke the code. He broke the damned code against squealing to you bastards."

"Brother," Losa said coldly, a flicker of disapproval crossing his features.

"Brother," Corbin quickly replied. He knew the Overseers were very squeamish about their mating rituals and legitimacy of their offspring, and smiled inwardly at the Overseer's discomfort.

"That's better. And anyhow, I must say that he did the proper thing. There's hope yet that he might find the Path to Peace. After all, Brother Gablona, you were the organizer of another one of those disgusting games, and then to our dismay you went so far as to try to cheat."

"Yeah, you come down on me for a little fun, but you guys once wasted half a dozen of our worlds in a single day. Now explain that to me, brother!"

"Come, come, Corbin, I've already been through that. We did not 'waste,' as you say, your worlds, you did. We merely put the devices in place. And we did allow the worlds to evacuate first. The explosions were set to go off only if your ancestors continued to fight. They fought, and the worlds were destroyed, thus it can be argued that you yourselves caused the destruction."

"Tragic," Losa said sadly, "but it did work—the wars stopped. We then disabled all systems for running and making devices for interplanetary conflict and have prevented you from using them ever again. Sad that there are so few of us, so that we cannot be all places. At least we've stopped your major conflicts. But it pains us when some such as you still encourage fighting among the primitives and then cheat on the event."

"Cheat, is it? I just was smarter than those guys, and anyhow, they cheated, too, and wrecked the game up good. Hell, I was only doing unto them before they did unto me."

"You are quite incorrigible, Corbin Gablona. But give us enough time, and you'll see the folly of your ways. Now, here we are for today's lesson."

The Overseer stopped and pointed toward a door, which swung open before them. In the outdoor courtyard were half a dozen servobots that looked vaguely like Overseers, who along with Losa and Overseer Vush were the entire staff of this particular reeducation center, all of them ready to work on him and him alone.

"Oh, no, not the Meeting for Peaceful Support." Corbin groaned.

"Come now, we have a full series of lectures about the Path to Peace prepared for you. It is the seventh in a series of two hundred lectures; the bots have been eagerly looking forward to enlightening you."

"Just let me out of here," Corbin suddenly whined. "I'll do anything, sign anything, but let me out of this joint, I can't take another day of this crap!"

"Now, now," Losa said, "your distress is a good sign, for it shows that you are becoming more pliable to the truth. Now go on in, it'll be good for you."

"I never trusted anyone who told me something was good for me," Corbin shouted.

Exasperated, Losa started to raise his hand, indicating that Corbin was about to get another tickle of juice. Suddenly a high piercing whistle sounded in the distance.

"Stay right where you are and don't move," Losa commanded, turning away from Corbin and beckoning to the servobots in the room.

"What's going on?" Corbin shouted as the piercing whistle increased in volume with each passing second.

"Nothing that should concern you for now."

A faint shimmer suddenly popped into focus in the main courtyard, followed seconds later by half a dozen more.

"Zergh!" Corbin roared as the first form took shape, coalescing into flesh as the jump-down beam completed its transfer.

Losa swung around to face the Gavarnian vasba who had helped to organize the Alexandrian game.

The other forms snapped into focus around the aging Gaf. Half a dozen more came in behind them . . . and all of them Xsarns, weapons pointed at the Overseer and his servobots.

"This is highly out of form," Losa said, still maintaining his composure, the faintly superior smile not even flickering.

"It took long enough to find out where you hid him," Zergh said evenly, "and a lot of time to knock out your sensing system so we could approach, but we're here for Koh Gablona."

"That's it," Corbin shouted gleefully. "Give it to him and let's blow out of here."

"I'm afraid I can't let you do that," Losa said quietly. "He's still required to spend nearly three thousand days in protective custody."

"Screw the protective custody." Gablona laughed, walking up to Zergh's side. "Blast the bastard and let's get out of here."

"You know that killing an Overseer can produce the most unpleasant aftereffects," Losa cautioned. "I'm not saying that for myself, of course, just out of concern for you, my brothers."

Corbin laughed harshly and started to reach for Zergh's weapon.

"Don't worry," Zergh replied, "we're just here for Gablona."

Without saying another word he swung his weapon around and pointed it straight at Corbin's chest.

"It's sleep time," Zergh said coldly, and he squeezed the trigger.

"Gentlemen, gentlemen, please, let us have some order. Gentlemen, please!"

The Xsarn's excitement had finally become too much, and with his last words he had the typical Xsarnian reaction to too much stress: the contents of his last meal sprayed out across the room.

The shock of the fetid spray stopped Bukha Taug from driving his balled fist into Zola Faldon's solar plexus. As one, all the Kohs stopped in midargument and, turning, started to scream imprecations at the Xsarn who was attempting to preside over the meeting.

A couple of the Xsarn's companions came up to either side of him and rose up on their hind legs.

"Either shut up," one of the Xsarns roared, "or you'll get the same treatment from us!"

That finally settled the uproar, and the assembly of Kohs backed off, most of them still mumbling threats at each other, but more softly now so that the presiding Xsarn could at last be heard.

"Gentlemen, please, may we all return to our seats. Do remember the old adage that time is money. At last count there're at least two thousand lawyers and twice that many accountants waiting in the halls downstairs, and all of them have their meters running."

Silence at last settled over the room, the only sound coming from the servobots that were mopping up after the Xsarn and cleaning the table where one of the minor Gaf Kohs had spilled a little blood during a disagreement with his neighbor.

"Good. Remember that we are Kohs, and as such should show some dignity."

The others tried to nod in agreement even as they glared at each other.

"Now, back to the bottom line of the proposal, which is in plain words that all corporate assets transferred in any way whatsoever because of what is now commonly called the Alexandrian game shall be frozen as of noon today, standard time. Each company must present its full financial records to the specially convened auditing board. This board will then work in turn with the accountants and lawyers for the previous owners to discover which assets had been stripped once it was discovered that the game was a fraud. Finally, the board shall work to retrieve those assets before company titles are returned to the original owners.

"Is that agreed?"

One of the Gaf Kohs started to stand up to speak. There was a brief flurry of curses as two or three other Gafs, led by Bukha Taug, stood up and surrounded their compatriot. The discussion was short; the group broke apart.

The Gaf who had started to rise stood with a pained expression on his face, and with a lame shrug of his shoulders he sat back down.

"Good. Then that at least is agreed upon," the Xsarn intoned. "All of you please affix your marks to the memo boards."

As one each of the group extended hand, paw, or feeler to their electronic pads and by touching the device noted their agreement.

A gentle sigh went through the room.

"That at least is the first step," Bukha said quietly. "But there is another problem."

"Another problem?" Zola interjected. "Damn it all, it will take a hundred years to sort out the first problem. First off, nearly half the Cloud's total assets were bet on that cursed Alexandrian game. Then the rumors start to fly that maybe something was amiss and the results weren't what we thought."

"And that's when all you fools," the Xsarn said coldly, forcing himself to remain under control, "rather than coming to me as director of the game, started looting the assets of any corporation that traded hands.

"This problem would have been a lot easier to solve if the freeze on all assets had been put out at once. We could have traded the companies back to their original owners and all would have been solved. But oh, no, all of you got greedy, thinking you could strip the corporations before being forced to give them back."

"A minor problem," Yarvin, one of the minor Kohs, intoned pompously.

"A minor problem, is it?" Vol, a Human who had lost heavily in the games, roared back. "My accountants report that I'll be lucky to get back half the true wealth of what I lost under false pretenses, and it was you Gafs who took the big profit."

"That's a lie," Bukha shouted, coming back to his feet again.

"Listen, if you want to make this into something more," Zola replied ominously, "then we Humans would be more than happy to comply."

An uneasy hush settled over the room. The implied threat that had been hanging over the meeting for days was at last out in the open. All suddenly realized that they stood on the edge of the abyss. Overseers or no Overseers, there was blood in the air.

"Gentlemen, please remember our stations in life, our reputations," the Xsarn said softly, extending his primary and secondary arms in a calming gesture. "We've already made the first step by agreeing to freeze all assets as of today. Accountants and lawyers from each of your houses will now have total access to the books of your previously owned companies that are held by my arbitrating firm. In short order they'll be able to report what assets have been siphoned off after ownership was transferred and return them, minus the fees, of course, to my firm."

There was almost a universal growl from the Humans and Gafs over that point, but both sides realized that without the Xsarns as arbitrators the legal tangle would be impossible to unravel.

"But the legal and accounting fees to your auditing firm, who's going to cover that?" Zola replied. "Those bloodsuckers and calculator pushers will suck us dry. Damn it, just the retainer for Leecher's House of Barristers came to an even hundred million."

"Ought to have killed all the damn lawyers back in the final war," one of the Gafs growled. "Oh, I know we need them, and I agree there should be schools for lawyers, it's just that the moment they get their diplomas they should be shot as an example and protection for the rest of society."

"Here, here, I'll drink to that," several of the Kohs cried at once, and together they all raised their glasses, finding the first grounds of agreement in many a day.

"Gentlemen," one of the Gafs interjected, "I propose a game. Let's find a planet, fill it with lawyers, bureaucrats, and politicians, and whoever strangles the other with reports and paperwork first wins!"

The others roared their approval, and for the moment a bit of calm settled over the group. The first major hurdle had been passed, and at least they had agreed in principle to rectify the damage created by their last betting spree. The Xsarn settled back on his lounger and waited for the next step.

"Before we get too self-satisfied," Zola suddenly interrupted, "my fellow Koh Bukha stated earlier that there was another problem. So go ahead, Bukha, please enlighten us."

"A simple enough question and one that I now feel is appropriate to bring up."

The other Kohs leaned forward to hear, sensing that Bukha, as usual, had held back his inner thoughts throughout the first days of the meeting, waiting for the right moment to spring.

"Go on, out with it," several of the Human Kohs shouted, smelling that something was afoot.

"What about the two Kohs not present?" Bukha asked softly.

"Gablona and Sigma, yeah, what about those bastards?" Vol seconded. "If Gablona hadn't tried to rig the game, and Sigma, finding out, hadn't then played along, all of this confusion would never have happened."

"And don't forget Aldin Larice," Yarvin added ominously. "A traitor to the code of the vasbas, that one."

Bukha settled back. He noticed the hard stare that Zola was giving him and he returned the look of inquiry with an open, innocent gaze. After all, he'd been able to prove on the first day of the meeting that it had merely been rare good luck that had guided him through the last game, and not insider information leaked from Aldin.

"Tell me," Zola asked softly, "do you perhaps know of something that the rest of us here do not?"

Bukha extended his hands and shrugged.

"Well, perhaps now would be the best time to tell you about the little solution my compatriot Bukha Taug and I have worked out," the Xsarn said quietly.

"And that is?" half the the Kohs intoned together.

"It was you who tried your brother Kohs *in absentia* and found them guilty of fraud."

The group nodded with satisfaction over that point; it was the first item of business and had taken them less than two minutes to vote upon.

"However, we must all realize that we have only three choices for punishment. We can strip them of their assets, but, gentlemen, I don't think anyone here would like to set a precedent that could be used against the rest of us later."

The economic consortiums of the Cloud, covering hundreds of planets, were the closest thing to governments. All realized that economic backstabbing and the other assorted games of fair business was one thing, but confiscation by collective force was quite another.

"For a second choice, would any of you wish to publicly turn your old comrades over to the Overseers?"

A shout of rage went up from the assembly. Any of them might tip off the hated Overseers privately, perhaps, but in public, never.

"Anyhow," Zola interjected, "there's a rumor afloat that Gablona isn't really in hiding and that the Overseers already have him."

The others muttered their outrage over that fact and thus showed their solidarity against intrusion from the outsiders.

"The third choice then is simply to kill them," the Xsarn continued.

A hushed silence fell over the room. All of them were survivors of the rough-and-tumble world of Cloud economics. After all, they were Kohs and, as such, family heads of economic syndicates. But one of the supreme rules was never to make a hit on a Koh or the members of his immediate family. Once started, they knew it could never be stopped.

"I suspect then that you've arrived at another alternative, since the first three are unacceptable," Bukha said quietly.

"Precisely," the Xsarn replied, his mandibles pulling back to reveal what he thought was a smile.

CHAPTER 2

GROANING, ALDIN LARICE OPENED HIS EYES. THE SERVOBOT by his side stared back with lifeless eyes of glass and metal, the dripping hypo still in its extended tentacle.

"Where the hell am I?" Aldin asked, sitting up and tentatively swinging his legs off the sleeping pallet.

The servobot made no reply.

Wherever he was, Aldin suspected that the situation was not to his advantage. The memories started to return. He felt for his chest; no hole, so obviously rather than an exploding slug the Xsarn had nailed him with a sleep jolt.

He had faint, dreamlike memories of semiconsciousness and then darkness again. The Xsarns must have taken him and put him on a doze unit until now, whenever now was.

The doorway swung open and two Xsarns entered the room.

"Aldin Larice, we have some friends who would like to see you."

"Oh, yeah? Well, maybe I'm in no mood to see them. First off, why the hell did you guys doze me out?"

"Would you have preferred a ten-millimeter round from one of Gablona's killers?" one of the insectoid Xsarns, wearing the red crest of a Xsarn of the Koh's house, asked in their usual polite, almost self-deprecating manner.

They did have a point, Aldin realized.

"Our agents have been trying to track you down for some time," the other Xsarn continued. "We were trying to lure you into that ship's storage area so we could take you quietly, but one of Gablona's bots got there ahead of us. We had a security net around your cabin, even took out a bot that tried to get through. We didn't know another one had been smuggled aboard and hidden with the wine. It went as we planned, however; the bot failed and we took you into protective custody."

"Yaroslav, is he all right?"

"In good health. We released him since he is no concern of ours."

"Well, thanks for the help," Aldin said, standing up, "but I think I'd rather be going now."

"Impossible. There are some friends who want to see you first."

"And suppose I don't want to go?"

"There is no sense in arguing. You will go with us."

The two Xsarns drew closer. At the very least they'd have no problem dragging him out, Aldin realized, but even worse, they might get excited in the process, with the usual unpleasant aftereffects.

"I'm coming, I'm coming."

"We're so glad you're cooperating. We have a special surprise in store for you."

Aldin didn't like the sound of that one.

"Gentlemen, I think we can all therefore agree that confiscation, murder, or turning the offending Kohs over to the Overseers is simply out of the question," the Xsarn stated, looking around the assembly for a dissenting opinion.

"Then what is the fourth possibility?" Zola asked, growing impatient.

With a nod the Xsarn turned to one of his assistants, who walked across the room to the far doorway and pulled it open.

"Aldin Larice!" Zola shouted excitedly. "You thieving, cheating scoundrel!"

Trying to maintain his bravado, Aldin looked to his two escorts and gave them a nod as if in dismissal and then stepped into the room.

If he showed fear before the Kohs, he was ruined, but suddenly his knees felt like jelly. For thirty years he had arranged games for them and thus gained access to the most powerful men in the Cloud. But after helping to arrange the sting in the last game, his one goal had been to find a quiet corner somewhere in the Smaller Cloud and simply count his profits.

With a flourish he gave a bow of acknowledgment and strode into the room. Not all the faces that turned to stare at him were angry ones; some in fact showed actual delight at his presence, and finally it was one of the Gafs who caught on.

"If the first three punishments were unacceptable choices, then the fourth must be a game!" Yarvin said with excitement.

"A game?" Zola cried, his anger suddenly diverted. "Upon my soul, I thought I'd never see one again. Damn it all, Xsarn, speak up!"

"What other solution could there be, gentlemen?" Aldin said smoothly, stepping up to the table and pouring himself a goblet of wine from one of the decanters by the Gaf end of the table. It was some of their damn muscatel but he gave them a knowing wink after downing the glass, as if he had partaken of the finest nectar in all the Cloud.

"We haven't quite discussed the details, Aldin and I," the Xsarn said staring with a jaundiced eye at Aldin, "but let me introduce the other components."

The portal on the other side of the room swung open to reveal two portly men busily shouting insults at each other.

"You thieving bastards," Vol roared, springing from his chair and starting for the door, followed a second later by half the Kohs in the room, while the more levelheaded ones sprung up to try to hold their enraged comrades back.

The two men in the doorway, suddenly aware of their enraged audience, dropped their own argument for the moment and tried to step back from the angry rush. Pandemonium reigned until finally the Xsarn called in half a dozen of his comrades, who by cajoling and various threats managed to get everyone back to their seats.

In the explosion of anger, Aldin, seeing who was in the doorway, had tried to quietly slip out of the room but was stopped and escorted back in. He had been attempting to hide from the wrath of Corbin Gablona, and now at last he was to meet him face-to-face, along with Sigma Azermatti, who Aldin realized still owed him a sizable commission and kickback.

"So I see you've got that lying thief who started this whole problem," Gablona shouted, storming into the room and pointing a finger straight at Aldin.

Another eruption was kicked off by that comment, and it was some minutes before the Xsarn finally shifted the focus of the meeting back to his original intent.

"Fellow Kohs, the first purpose of this meeting was to set the groundwork for repairing the damage that these three created with their manipulation of the game."

All three of the accused tried to respond.

"Shut up!" the Xsarn roared, and the three blanched and fell silent.

"That's better," he said quietly. He wiped his mouth clean, and continued.

"Now, of course, we all trust each other here, some company excluded—" and he nodded toward the three offending parties, "—but I think we all realize that it will be several months at least until the last arbitration is worked out between our various lawyers and accountants. Now, since this issue deals with most of your wealth, I think we've all become resigned to the fact that we're stuck here for the duration of the accounting."

A groan went up from the audience, for all of them knew that to be true. There'd be no pleasure-planet visits for some time to come, and that thought alone made them feel ugly. The banking world of Ator was the logical place for this conference, but it was famed as one of the most boring worlds in the Cloud, since, after all, it was inhabited almost solely by bankers, accountants, stockbrokers, and those who served them. The bankers of Ator were not noted for creative imaginations when it came to having fun.

"So I realized," the Xsarn continued, "that given the dreary place we're stuck in, we can handle several problems all in one nice little package and have some entertainment on the side."

"What sort of game did you have in mind?" Zola asked.

"We've agreed that the alternatives mentioned for punishing these three are out of the question," the Xsarn replied, "so let us make the fourth consideration a game to resolve the crisis."

"I object," Sigma sputtered. "I've not been consulted about this. Your henchmen interrupted me while I was on a private meditative retreat, kidnapped me, drugged me, and dragged me halfway across the Cloud against my will . . ."

"Better that then what would have happened if we had not found you," the Xsarn cut in. "We can show you the documentation later, but Gablona had a shipload of his humanbot assassins above your planet ready to pounce."

Stunned, Sigma looked at his old business rival.

Gablona could merely give him a weak smile in response.

"Let's hear your proposal," Sigma replied, looking back to the Xsarn.

"The game arrangement will be simple enough. I propose that our two friends Gablona and Sigma be set down on a planet for the duration of the legal proceedings up here. They will be allowed up to fifty guards of their choosing who must be living beings, that is the only stipulation. Once the last audit and transfer is finished up here, the game will be declared over. When final preparations for the game are made, we should know the estimated closing date for the Alexandrian paperwork, and thus set the time limit.

"Whatever you do to each other on the planet is fine with us. Live in peace if you want, or kill each other, it's all the same. Of course, a wager here and there on the outcome will help us to pass the time while waiting for our accountants to finish."

The room was silent for a moment and then the import of what the Xsarn proposed suddenly sank in.

"It's a gladiator match," Zola said gleefully. "They can do anything they want to each other while they're down there."

"Precisely!"

Savagely Gablona and Sigma looked at each other, their

mutual hatred blocking out all else. Turning to the Xsarn, they nodded their agreement.

"But there's more," the Xsarn continued. "We've all been concerned about the cost of the audits—surely it will run into the billions. Therefore it is proposed that if either Gablona or Sigma dies then his estate will be attached for the purpose of paying off our expenses."

"Fabulous idea," Zola shouted, and a universal cry of delight went up.

The two Kohs suddenly looked a little less enthused about the proposal, but both were already calculating and assuming that it would be the other who would pay.

"Then it is agreed?" the Xsarn asked.

A roar of approval went up.

"And one final point," the Xsarn said. "Aldin Larice will play in this one, as well."

There was a moment of silence. For after all, Aldin was not of the Koh class, and several of them now wondered if it would be proper to allow a mere servant to perhaps be involved in the killing of a Koh.

"It's fine with me," Gablona said, stepping up to Aldin and poking a finger into his stomach. "He'll be dead inside of ten days."

"Would you care to put a wager on that?" Bukha interjected calmly.

"Ten million katars," Gablona shouted back.

"Done!"

The side bets started to fly and for some minutes the other problems were completely forgotten. Some of the Kohs who only hours before had sworn to kill Gablona were already at his side discussing bets and sharing brandies with him.

The Xsarn looked over at Bukha and the two quietly nodded to each other. The problem of numerous possible schisms among the Kohs had, for the moment at least, been sidestepped. The diversion would unite them and keep their imaginations occupied with gaming rather than possible mayhem against their fellow Kohs.

"There are a couple of questions," Aldin said, his voice cutting through the general conversation, and the room fell silent again.

"Go on," the Xsarn prompted, figuring that it would be Aldin who would want the details first.

"You said that we can select any fifty living beings that we want."

"Precisely. Only living beings will be allowed. Our good friend Gablona broke an important law when he manufactured those humanbots for killing you and Sigma. They're strictly out of the game, and we shall find a way of disposing of them."

Gablona looked over at the Xsarn and gave a weak smile, realizing it was best not to debate the point.

"That's fine," Aldin said quietly. "And next, where is the game to take place?"

"Ah, now that's the interesting point," the Xsarn said. "You see, we'll want something close to Ator. So I felt it best to actually stage the game right in this solar system. We also need a place where security can be kept at a maximum. A place where there is limited access, so there can be no interference like last time."

The room grew quiet.

"Therefore, gentlemen," the Xsarn said quietly, "the game of the Kohs shall take place in what the locals around here call 'The Hole.'"

"You can't do that," Aldin cried, "it isn't fair!"

"But, gentlemen, the rest of us already heard the three of you agree," the Xsarn said slyly. "And anyhow, it will make the action far more lively."

A chorus of chuckles echoed around the room.

"Ten million that all of them are dead within the week," Zola said.

"I'd make it three days," Vol replied evenly.

"Well, this is certainly a fine mess. Just remember I tried to warn you fools long before you started to cook up that Alexander scheme," Zergh announced, coming through the door.

Aldin and Yaroslav looked up and motioned for their friend to pour himself a drink before coming over to join the conversation.

"Any word on what Gablona or Sigma is doing, or how arrangements are going to be made?" Aldin asked.

"The Xsarn has declared that the three of you are under

house arrest and will be forbidden to pick up the guards you elect, though you may designate a proxy to do it for you. Also, you can't meet with your people until the game begins and you start down for the Hole. I guess he fears all three of you might incite a riot if you and your designated guards have too much time together."

"Don't blame him," Aldin mumbled. "And the other two?"

"Word is that Sigma's thinking of Gavarians as guards."

"Interesting choice," Yaroslav commented, "but slow in close combat."

"Basak berserkers," Zergh continued, stirring his sparkling burgundy and throwing in a dash of anisette before coming over to join the others.

Yaroslav and Aldin looked at each other and nodded. Aldin had arranged a wager on the Basak some fifteen years back. They were noted for their fanatical bravery in battle, considering death by any means other than combat to be a disgrace that could bar them from joining their brothers in the afterlife.

"Good choice on several counts. In a straightforward attack they're damn near impossible to stop, once they get going," Aldin said slowly. "But down in the Hole, against the Al'Shiga, I'm not so sure."

"You two have been keeping me in the dark a bit too long," Zergh said slowly, and as he spoke he brought out his personal antibugger and waved it around to make sure there wasn't a tap on the room. "Isn't it time you filled me in on this? Somehow I can't believe that you're innocent victims letting the Kohs run the show. When the Xsarn gave me the orders to pick up Gablona I couldn't help but feel that there was something more to this—a game within the game, so to speak."

The two looked at him and merely smiled.

"Don't complain," Aldin said softly. "I was fingered with the last game, but my keeping quiet covered your hide and Bukha's from getting pulled in, as well. I hope you've reminded your good friends of that, and don't ask any more questions."

"At least then tell me about the Hole. It's more a concern of you Humans rather than Gafs. I've never studied it, nor had any desire to do so."

"But one of the six clans is made up of Gafs," Yaroslav said.

"Gafs we of my race would rather forget about," Zergh replied coldly. "Totally without honor. They're more like you Humans, in spite of their claim that the cult was first founded by them."

"But a most interesting cult, the Al'Shiga of the Hole," Yaroslav rejoined "founded during the first colonization wave into the Cloud. The Humans of course claim they founded it, and the Gavarnians take credit, as well, though most likely it was simply a fascinating cultural coincidence that led these two groups to share a similar historical legend. There are several other cases that some think are tied into the First Travelers, but that is pure conjecture. Anyhow, from the Human side they're believed to be liked to a radical religious tradition that nearly destroyed Human civilization in the twenty-first century."

"The Shiite Twelvers of the Middle East," Aldin interjected. "The survivors were exiled into space after the Second Atomic War."

"Yes, that was it," Yaroslav replied. "And the Hidden Taug cult among the Gafs had a similar history of causing mayhem.

"Both taught that their particular form of religious worship was the only true one. It's a cult of persecution, in which they believe their rightful place was denied them. Assassination is their path to salvation and power. They practiced it with glee, feeling it was a religious act. For a while, immediately after the Overseers imposed an end to interplanetary warfare, they were quite a force. But their numbers were small, and finally all three races banned them.

"Our ancestors were for eradicating the lot, but the Overseers stopped them, and the Al'Shiga were exiled down to the Hole, where they've stayed ever since, the technology to get off-planet having been denied them. Since the Hole is the sole source of green amber, there is some trade, but any modern devices are strictly prohibited. I must say that Hole traders in my mind are insane—most don't live a year before a Shiga takes them out. It's practice, you see, killing traders and, of course, each other."

"Practice?"

Zergh asked.

"They've broken into six rival clans," Yaroslav stated. "Assassination is a game between them, their main form of recreation, if you will. Anyhow, they believe that there will come a day when one of the clans, the purest in the cult, will rise above the others and its leader will be revealed to be the hidden Ema, the great leader who will return them to the stars."

"Ema?"

"It means 'great teacher,' the one whose coming each generation claims is just around the corner, and who will lead them back to the stars when the proper sacrifice is made."

"What sacrifice?" Zergh asked, showing his confusion over what he was hearing.

"If they knew, they would have made it by now and gotten out of the Hole," Yaroslav said, chuckling grimly.

"A force like that could cause chaos out here," Zergh said slowly.

"Exactly," Aldin replied. "And that's why the choice of the Hole for this little game hasn't struck me as all that amusing. The Al'Shiga are a bunch of murderous madmen; we have a lot more to fear from them than from each other. I still can't understand why the Hole was chosen. I figured it'd just be some primitive world, maybe even back on the Kolbard."

"It was the Xsarn's idea," Zergh replied, looking closely at Aldin after his last comment.

"Where did you hear that?"

"Through Zola."

Aldin and Yaroslav looked at each other and nodded, as if a certain event had been confirmed.

"So that can explain Gablona's choice," Zergh continued.

"Ah, yes, my dear friend Gablona," Aldin said grimly. "What's he been up to?"

"Tried to bribe the Xsarn, for starters; rumor has it he offered a hundred million to get out of the game."

"If the Xsarn leaked that one out, I wonder what the real offer was?"

"My thinking exactly," Zergh continued. "But going down to the Hole can explain Gablona's choice."

"What then?" Yaroslav asked.

"Ishmaelites from medieval Earth. I've heard you mention them before; they sound difficult to counter."

"It figures," Aldin said coldly.

"So back then to what we were talking about before you came in," Yaroslav interrupted. "Looking at what we're facing, Aldin, and Gablona's choice confirms it, you've got to find a group as treacherous as what we're facing with the Shiga, and now Gablona. Sigma's choice is also an offensive move, one aimed straight at you, I daresay. If I had my choice, I'd go with the Eytor. They're not the best in stand-up combat, but they're deadly with poison and would kill their own mothers as a joke."

"Why not the Ashantor of Gree?" Zergh interjected. "Some claim those bastards can walk through walls—some of the best infiltrators and murderers throughout the Cloud."

Aldin looked at the two as if he didn't quite hear what they were saying. "What? And be like Gablona or those damned Shiga?"

"Fight fire with fire, I say," Yaroslav replied coldly.

"You don't seem to understand," Aldin said sadly. "What was my motivation in the last game?"

"To get rich," Yaroslav replied.

Aldin could only shake his head. "Sure, that was part of it, I won't deny that. But get rich with the money that Gablona had owed me all along. To me it was a question of honor as well. My personal honor versus Gablona's greed. A hope that I could somehow retrieve the honor of my niece Tia, and also to preserve the honor of Alexander and Kubar."

"Honor." Yaroslav laughed sadly. "Honor's nothing but legend to inflame the imagination of youth to do the bidding of those who would use them."

"But I think honor can be a weapon as powerful as anything the Shiga or Gablona could offer."

"Try using honor when the Shiga come for your head." Yaroslav sniffed.

"Nevertheless it's how I see life and what makes it worth living," Aldin said grimly.

"And it's why you've been screwed by life," Yaroslav replied.

Throughout their argument Zergh sat quiet. For Gafs honor was an intrinsic part of their nature, but three thousand years of contact with Humans had tempered that somewhat with a cold realism that allowed them to live inwardly by a personal code but could justify subtle deceit against those whom they came into contact with.

"Go with the Ashantor," Zergh said grimly. "Remember you're facing Gablona."

"No, damn it," Aldin said.

"Then who will be your guards?"

"The forty-seven ronin of ancient Japan," Aldin softly, an almost dreamy look in his eyes.

"Why them?" Zergh asked, shaking his head.

"Because," Aldin replied, "in this age in which I feel so out of place, I've looked to them as an example. I discovered their story years before while still a student; a certain old friend had pointed them out to me in an ancient text," and he looked over at Yaroslav, who smiled at the memory.

"They knew there would be no reward for their loyalty. They believed there would be no praise of them, no memory of their action, only death. But honor to them was more important than life or any reward. Such men could perhaps show this age a thing or two about honor and a forgotten path to victory."

"You'll all be dead in a week, Aldin," Zergh said ruefully. "Honor can't stop a blade in the night. This isn't some damn philosophy exam, it's life and death, and I say you've got to fight in the manner your opponents will or you will die."

Aldin only smiled and shook his head as if Zergh was a child who couldn't understand.

"If his mind is made up, it's his life," Yaroslav interjected. "But let's look at the practical question in this. If you want honor and loyalty, they're fine. But if my history serves me correctly, after they finished their deed they all committed suicide in front of witnesses. Since history can't be altered, how the hell do you suggest to pull that one off?"

"The Xsarn confiscated the humanbots. Alter them to look like the men in question, and pull a switch. The Xsarn said any fifty that I want. I want them. To me loyalty is going to win this, and nothing less. I want the most loyal men in history."

"But how are you going to get such men to serve you?" Zergh asked.

Aldin looked at his old wolflike friend and smiled.

"I think I know a way," he said softly.

"If you insist," Yaroslav said, "but I think you're insane. Those men will be eaten alive down on the Hole. But I've got other things to worry about. This Hole thing I never expected. I'll have to think about it if you're going to get through this in one piece."

Aldin sat back in his chair and poured another drink for himself and his two companions.

"You know, I wonder what Zola's dreaming up at the moment," Aldin said softly. And Yaroslav chuckled at the thought.

Zergh looked from one to the other.

"I can't help but think I'm being kept in the dark," he said. "But what the hell do you mean about knowing a way to convince these samurai?"

"Trust me," Aldin said. "You'll enjoy yourself."

"All right, show him in," Zola said, and after releasing the paging button, he settled back into his chair and pushed the lift command.

The dais upon which his desk and table were set rose nearly a meter into the air, creating the illusion of a judge, or a person of great power looking down from a great height. His insecurity about his slight one-and-a-half-meter stature showed in most everything he did: the oversized pleasure ships and the gargantuan size of whatever he built; his taste in ample, towering women; and his need whenever possible to be looking down on someone.

The doorway opened and in walked a tall slender man with a narrow, ascetic face. He was pale, as if exposure to the sun happened only on the rare occasion that he emerged from some hidden room. He had the look of books and an academic life about him. In his midthirties, Kurst was no stranger to Zola. He'd employed the academic as a consultant in the past whenever questions of gaming probabilities came up, but to see him on Ator was a bit of surprise. Kurst worked at some obscure university that Zola couldn't even remember, back on the other side of the Cloud. Something must really be bothering this man for him to come this far and then to camp on his doorstep for the last twelve hours, refusing to divulge to anyone the reason for this unannounced visit.

"So, what brings you to Ator?" Zola said, not at all unhappy to see the man who'd won him some good bets in the past. "Coming to check up on some numbers just for the fun of it?"

Kurst looked up at Zola and, squinting, pushed up his glasses, which as usual were riding too far down on the bridge of his nose. Glasses had been quite a fad with the intellectual crowd a dozen years back, the popular feeling being that they provided an air of classical scholarliness.

"I've had this idea," Kurst said excitedly.

"Oh, really, an idea so important that you couldn't simply put it into a memo the way most of my employees and consultants do?" Zola asked half tauntingly.

"Oh, no, I couldn't do that," Kurst replied, shifting his feet back and forth nervously.

"All right then, out with it, but it better be worth my time."

"Zola Koh, when I have an idea, I really have an idea," Kurst said smoothly. "As soon as it came to me, I booked the first express here at great expense."

"Which you expect me to reimburse you for?"

"Well, you do know that the salary of a professor of probability theory is not all that great."

"I see," Zola said coldly. "Well, out with it, and then I'll decide."

Kurst stopped for a moment, as if he were about to burst either from nervousness or simply from excitement that he could finally talk about the idea.

"There's rumor that you and the other Kohs are going to have a game."

"Oh, really!" Zola said crossly. "From where?"

"It's been floating around for nearly a month."

"Your sources?"

"It's just that all the Kohs are assembled in one place, and there were reports of three special ships arriving here under high security. Nearly every lawyer and accountant in the Cloud is already aware of the last game and the consequences, so the gaming of Kohs is no longer a secret. Two and two always equal four, and among some of my friends the deduction started to spread that three men are to be pitted against each other on a barbaric planet. It's been on the com links now for quite some time."

"Good Gods!" Zola roared.

He turned away from Kurst. If the lawyers knew and were

chatting about it through the hookups, then the Overseers most likely knew, as well. What the hell was going on? How come the Overseers hadn't already moved in?

How come? Could it be then that the rumored encounter between the Xsarn and a representative of the Overseers wasn't a rumor after all?

He looked back at Kurst.

"Go on then," he said.

"The rumor of this game is spreading across the Cloud, and I had a tremendous idea that could turn it to your advantage."

"And that is . . . ?" Zola asked, relaxing ever so slightly.

"A lottery!" Kurst shouted, expelling the words as if they'd been pent up inside him for weeks. It really wasn't his idea, at least not initially. It had come up in a barroom conversation with a friend who'd been interested in discussing the game, knowing of Kurst's contact with Zola. The friend had commented that it could be a hell of a diversion for the masses, and after buying one more round of drinks, Kurst rushed out of the bar and booked the next flight to Ator. So, while it wasn't his idea initially, in short order he'd thought out the more fascinating permutations it could offer and thus by the time he landed on Ator he felt the idea was his, and his alone.

"What do you mean, a lottery?" Zola asked.

"A game for everyone in the Cloud!" Kurst announced triumphantly.

Zola sat silent for some seconds and then gradually the dais started to lower. Zola stood up and, stepping off, came up to confront Kurst.

"Are you mad?" he said, slowly enunciating each word savagely. "The games belong to us, the Kohs. They are not for the ill-bred rabble such as yourself!"

Kurst backed up a step, his fear obvious.

"I meant no offense to one of your illustrious class," Kurst squealed.

"Besides, it would mean that everyone in the Cloud would know," Zola said coldly. He left out mention of the Overseers, since such beings were creatures of legend to the people of the Cloud, and the Kohs never acknowledged their existence, or power that they held, to the lower classes.

"But let me explain," Kurst pleaded.

"Explain then. And when you're done taking my valuable

time, I hope you've booked your own return passage."

"As I was saying earlier," Kurst ventured, "I had a wonderful idea for a lottery around your game. Now, from what I've heard, two Kohs and a vasba are going to be marooned on a barbaric planet for a certain number of days."

He stopped as if looking for confirmation, but Zola said nothing.

"Well, knowing the refined nature of those of your class, I can well see where all sorts of interesting wagers will be set on the finer points of combat between the three, but I had something else in mind."

"Go on," Zola said.

"Let's look at it in a logical progression. You have three players. Let's call them *X*, *Y*, and *Z*. Now, there is actually a fourth element, the natives, we'll call them *N*. Starting with player *X*, there are five possible outcomes. He could be killed by the natives, he could be killed by either of his opponents, or he could be killed even by his own people. The fifth alternative is that he lives."

"I think I understand," Zola said, the faintest look of interest crossing his features.

"Fine then," Kurst replied, warming to his subject. "Now, if only one person is involved, there are five possible bets. With two people, every combination comes out to twenty-five possible results, from both of them living to both of them being killed by natives."

"And with three players, like we have?" Zola asked, growing excited.

"One hundred and twenty-five possible outcomes for the first day!"

"The first day?" Zola replied.

"That's the beauty of it. Let's go back to one example. How long, might I ask, is the game intended to run?"

Zola looked closely at Kurst. No one was sure on that yet.

"Say sixty days," Zola said softly, already starting to anticipate what Kurst was driving at.

"Good, very good," Kurst replied, rubbing his hands. "There are four probable events a day then for sixty days."

"I thought you said five."

"Living all the way to the end is simply added on, it's a nonevent otherwise. So in the end there are two hundred and forty possible outcomes plus one. Now, with three players we therefore have as a total number of probable outcomes a sum equal to two hundred and forty-one to the third power."

Zola looked at Kurst dumbfounded.

"To be exact," Kurst replied sharply, "the figure comes out to thirteen million, nine hundred and ninety-seven thousand, five hundred and twenty-one different betting potentials. You sell them like lottery tickets, with people buying bets that could read, for example, *X* dead on day three by *Y*, *Z* dead on day forty-nine by the natives, *Y* lives."

"By heavens, I should have thought of this," Zola whispered.

"Not to worry about that," Kurst replied triumphantly. "I am your consultant and that's my job."

Zola looked at Kurst, a smile lighting his features. Why, he could sell billions of such tickets. Granted, some bets were better than others, and the mob would latch on to them, but all he had to do was make the payoff low, say 25 percent, and he'd still come out on top. There were problems, to be sure. First and foremost was the Overseers, but with the profit this could offer, he'd figure out a way to deal with them.

"Sorry if I was a bit cross earlier, you know how it is with the weighty concerns of business," Zola said good-naturedly, putting his arm up over Kurst's shoulder.

"How about a good cigar and a drink?" Zola continued, leading Kurst over to a chair by his desk.

"Don't mind if I do!" Kurst replied, amazed when the Koh even went so far as to light the cigar for him.

"Where are you staying, my friend?" Zola asked.

"Oh, I've got an old girlfriend working here with the stock market," Kurst replied, slightly embarrassed.

"Ah, but of course," Zola responded, chuckling and nudging his companion in the ribs.

"I'll see you first thing tomorrow. I want to make some calls on this. See my secretary on the way out and have her call accounting. Have them draw you a retainer for, let's see, would twenty thousand be enough?"

Kurst looked at Zola goggle-eyed.

"Only the beginning, my good man," Zola replied expansively. "Why, it's only the beginning."

As the door closed behind Kurst, Zola could not suppress a

brother. Takashi caught his eyes for a moment. Both knew the other's pride in the youngster who had behaved well in their first and final fight, and both could sense the pain at what they had condemned him to.

"My lord Asano," Oishi said, bowing low before the grave, his comrades doing likewise. "I humbly beg you to accept this the fulfillment of your pledge to you."

After rising, he stepped forward and then knelt again by the foot of Asano's grave. He didn't want to release the offering, for once he had let go, it was finished, the purpose of the league completed.

His grasp lingered for a moment, and then bowing lower, he placed the freshly washed head of Kira Yoshinaka upon the grave of his master.

A sigh of contentment stirred through the empty graveyard, and for a moment Oishi was not sure if it came from his comrades or from the spirit of old Asano, satisfied that his honor was restored at last.

Oishi brought his hands together in prayer—prayer to Asano and to the ancestors of the clan that now they could rest peacefully, and prayer, as well, for himself, and for the league, so that all would face death unflinchingly. There was but one step left: to go to the head abbot of the local temple and there stay till the emperor's men arrived with the decision that all knew could only be a command to commit seppuku.

He knew he was lingering too long; it was time to act.

"Sogio, Fumio!"

"*Hai!*"

"The two of you are to go at once to the Censorate. Report to him what has transpired, and tell him that we shall present ourselves for arrest at the abbey."

The two rose up from the circle and hurried off.

"Terazaka!"

"*Hai!*"

"Leave at once, go to our lady, and inform her that the honor of her husband has been avenged."

Terazaka followed his two comrades into the darkness.

So now there were only forty-four of them, a good number that, Oishi thought wistfully.

He looked around the circle and, giving a slight nod of command, rose to his feet again, the others following.

"Are we all ready for what must be?" Oishi asked softly.

As one, his comrades nodded in reply.

He found himself struggling to hold back the tears of pride. Each knew that all he had to do was to melt into the darkness, and a populace that by and large sympathized with their cause would give them shelter and hidden passage into the countryside. But not one turned away; they had crosssed the line together and would now die together. They would force the emperor himself to pass direct judgment and set an example of loyalty and courage in this decadent age.

"Then you all understand what is to come," Oishi announced.

They looked at him in silence and nodded.

"Then let us face our destiny."

"Oishi!"

Turning, Oishi saw the look of terror on Seiji's face, a terror that cut into his own heart as well.

For a moment he stood frozen and then fell to his knees, his forehead touching the ground. A stunning glow of crystalline brilliance washed over him, and he struggled with his fear.

"Oishi Kuranosuke!" a voice out of the light intoned.

Oishi dared a glance at his companions surrounding him; they were prostrate on the ground, none daring to raise his eyes. For who would dare to do so in the presence of their lord Asano Nagamori!

Surely there could be no answer other than that the pulsing light over the tomb was their lord, come from beyond to tell them of his pleasure with their deed.

"Oishi Kuranosuke, rise and come forward."

Despite his years of training, Oishi was ashamed to realize that his knees were trembling. What would his lord think at such a sight? He could only pray that Asano would understand, that visitors from the other world could cause even a samurai to tremble.

Struggling to master his fear, Oishi gained his feet and, with head still bowed, approached the light that now fully encompassed his lord's grave.

"You may look up, Oishi."

"Yes, my lord Asano."

Oishi raised his gaze. With a startled shout he drew back.

It was not the spirit of Asano, but rather some god or, worse, a demon!

The others, roused by his cry, looked up as well, and with a shout came to their feet, some with swords already out and poised for defense.

"Silence!" the apparition roared.

The group fell quiet. The wolflike creature towered above them, his sharpened teeth glistening in the strange aura that surrounded him.

"I am not your lord Asano," the creature intoned, and then his voice fell to a whisper. "Just call me Zergh."

Zergh looked out at the assembled samurai. Damn it all, he thought, they should have sent a Human to handle this, but, oh, no, he had listened to Aldin and in the end could not refuse. He only hoped that the Xsarn crew could pull him out of here if these men decided to take offense at his presence. Aldin had assured him that the samurai of this period would hold a creature that looked similar to Earthly canines in high esteem and that they wouldn't lynch him with xenophobic delight, but he still found most primitive Humans decidedly unhealthy to be around.

"Your Emperor Tsunayoshi," Zergh said, trying to find the right godlike voice by using a small reverb mike attached to his collar, "is known even in worlds beyond for his edicts protecting all creatures that you call dogs, making it a capital crime to harm such beings. Even you, Oishi, have gained recognition for your kind treatment to such creatures. Would you and your comrades now raise blades against one who might consider such creatures to be kin?"

Startled by this statement, the samurai looked one to another. The creature was right. Some thought the emperor mad, but over a decade ago he had passed "the dog laws," which commanded all in his realm to treat dogs with compassion and forbade the harming of such creatures under the pain of death. Some thought him mad, but others, Oishi among them, saw the nobility in caring for the most loyal of all beings.

Oishi looked to his companions.

"Sheath your blades," Oishi commanded. His fear, at least for the moment, was under control, and he strived to set the example for the rest by calmly stepping forward, right to the very edge of the cone of light.

"I am Oishi Kuranosuke," he said, bowing low, giving the proper respect due a superior.

"Good, very good," Zergh replied with relief. "I wasn't sure if I was in the right place. The directions here weren't the best."

Oishi looked up at the being that stood atop Asano's grave and gave him a quizzical stare.

"You come from my lord Asano, to accept our offering?" Oishi asked, nodding first to the grave that the being stood upon and then to the head of Kira that lay before it.

The creature looked at the head and gave a slight grimace. He then gazed down at his feet, and as if realizing that he stood upon a grave, he quickly hopped off. As he did so the light that surrounded him faded and then disappeared.

"From Asano, you ask," Zergh said. "Well, not exactly, let's just say from a friend of your lord. You come highly recommended, you see."

"What friend of my lord Asano?"

"Let's just say that where I come from, beyond the heavens, you men known as the Loyal League of Forty-Seven Ronin are famous. One of the lords beyond the heavens is in desperate need of loyal men. He has asked permission of Asano for your service and Asano agreed, now that your pledge to him is completed."

"What lord?" Oishi asked, suddenly cautious, feeling that this creature was somehow hiding the full truth.

"The lord is a man of power in other heavens. He is besieged by enemies who wish his death. He needs loyal retainers, not more than fifty, and throughout the heavens it is known that the most loyal of men are the Loyal League. Your lord Asano has released you, your pledge to him is complete." And so saying, Zergh nodded to Kira's head. "Now there is another lord who needs your service."

"And his name?"

"The great lord Aldin Larice," Zergh replied, trying to keep from smirking at the thought of announcing his old pot-bellied friend in such a manner.

"Aldin Larice?" Oishi asked, stumbling over the strange-sounding name.

"I never heard of such a lord," Takashi announced, brazenly coming up to stand beside his comrade.

"A most worthy lord," Zergh replied lamely, hoping that the translator implant wouldn't convey the uneasiness he was feeling in the inflection of his words.

Takashi and Oishi looked at each other.

"I'm here with a request from the lord Aldin that you will find most interesting," Zergh quickly continued.

"And that is?" Oishi asked.

Zergh looked at Oishi and then at the other samurai who ringed him. He couldn't simply tell them that they would die if they didn't come with him. They had already decided to face such an event before his arrival. He'd have to sell them on coming, remembering Aldin's comment that the appeal of an honorable quest would be the best approach. If all else failed, he could call up to the Xsarn ship and have them snatched, but he could see that wouldn't go over too well with men whom Aldin would be entrusting with his life.

"My lord Aldin commanded me to bring him some honorable men," Zergh replied quickly.

"But we must face the emperor before we do anything else," Oishi replied grimly.

This is going to be a long night, Zergh thought to himself. How the hell was he going to explain humanbots, time travel, and a place called the Hole?

"Trust me," Zergh said, trying to smile. "I'll have you back here by morning."

Kirdbuk, Armenia, 1256

Incredulous, Hassan stood before the apparition.

"You claim then to be a jinn?" he asked.

The creature looked Human, to be sure, but was cloaked in a fiery light that blinded any who dared to look straight into it.

The men about him were on their knees, some crying ecstatically that Allah had sent this ally in their hour of need. In the distance the sound of the Mongol ram boomed louder and then suddenly stopped. They'd taken the last gate, now there was only the door to the library to stop them from the final onslaught.

"I am that what you think. I serve a prince of another land who seeks men such as you, and he has sent me to fetch you."

"Then if you are a jinn, smite our foes here," Hassan snarled.

Too long he had been a master of the inner secrets of his order. Secrets that taught that ultimately there was no Allah, no angels, demons, or jinns—merely the raw hand of power that men of reason could wield, using such legends to get others to do their commands.

"Such things are not the reason for my presence," the apparition replied coldly.

Hassan looked appraisingly about him. In another few minutes he would be dead with the last of his followers, the last Ishmaelite stronghold in the world falling before the Mongol storm. In the first moment that the apparition had appeared he had almost believed that perhaps the teachings of the inner masters was wrong. But cold logic ruled against it.

"Then if you will not fight against our foes, what shall you do?"

"My master bids you to come away with me from this place and to serve him faithfully beyond the heavens."

A look of disbelief was on Hassan's face.

"You mean you can take us beyond this?" he asked, waving his hand back toward the door through which the Mongols would burst at any moment.

"I can."

"And the price?"

"Obedience unto death for one who believes in your cause and seeks men such as you to serve him."

Hassan looked about at his surviving men, several of whom now looked up at him with hope in their eyes.

Hassan turned back to the apparition and smiled.

"I've just received word from our time-jump ship," the Xsarn announced with a dramatic flourish, strolling upright into the conference room. "It's safely made the jump-down back from Earth and will be arriving here in three days. Both sets of guards requested have been obtained. Gentlemen, I think we are going to have a most interesting game."

The Kohs stopped in their conversation and broke into polite applause.

"Sigma's guards will be docking with my gamemaster ship within the hour. According to my crews, in seventy-two hours standard the game will commence. Our legal people have given us an estimate that the paperwork from the Alexandrian fiasco will be cleared up in forty-three days. Therefore I am declaring that the exile down on the Hole will last for forty standard days. Once the other ship arrives, carrying the guards from Earth, all three teams will be awakened and they'll be transported down.

"As I explained earlier, all three contestants and their guards have had microtrackers implanted so we'll know where they are. Each tracker gives off a minute forcefield that interacts with any tracker from any opposing player. Any object touched by them picks up a slight tracer, as well, so even a poison or missile weapon can be linked back to whoever used it. Remote scanners have already been placed in the Hole, and they will register all microtrack contacts and feed the information back to the main gaming computers for cross-referencing if there is a question about a kill. Thus we'll be clearly able to register who kills whom throughout the game."

"The permutations of betting are most interesting," Vol said, standing up to address his comrades. "We can of course go for what I'd call the Trifecta bet, to use an ancient word of great tradition, that all three will die down there."

"And don't forget betting that the natives will do the job," one of the Gaf Kohs replied. "Hell, that's where I'm placing all my money."

"Of course, we can consider various weapon types, as well," Aster, another Gaf Koh, replied while pouring a brandy for his Human neighbor. "Quite a number of interesting side bets here, to be sure, such as on individual combats between, say, the samurai and the Basak berserkers."

"That's all child's play." Zola sniffed, giving the Kohs a glance of disdain. "Gentlemen, you're all being fools. There's profit to be had here, big profit."

"How is that?" the Xsarn asked.

"I have a question for you," Zola said, looking at the Xsarn.

"Ask then."

"You see, my good friend, in our previous games, there's been two sides: you either bet for or against. The bets are personal and direct between two gamers, with a gaming sponsor acting as the arbitrator and taking his cut. The same as in the last game."

"Yeah, Xsarn, just like the the last one, when you were the

game administrator," Vol interjected, and this time Zola
looked at his rival and nodded approval.

"Your point?" the Xsarn asked, growing cautious.

"It's just that the betting potentials are so complex and so
interesting that they shouldn't go to waste. Usually for betting
potentials this rich there's a house bank set up against which
gamers can gamble. Therefore we were wondering what your
plans were."

"Simple enough," the Xsarn replied. "I was going to venture my rather significant holdings as the bank. I've retained a
young vasba who's already worked out the programs and delivered the potential rates and odds on all permutations."

The other Kohs looked at each other as if the answer were
what they expected.

"I think Zola has a point," Vol responded. "You seem to be
making far too much profit of late. First, the retainer for the
Alexandrian game, next the retainer for arbitrating this conference, next the retainer for overseeing this new game, and now
we find out your bank is the house. It smells like shit to me,
my friend."

Several of the Kohs laughed at Vol's choice of words, since
what was a derogatory comment to them was in fact a high
compliment to Xsarns, but the Xsarn nevertheless understood
his meaning.

"Are you questioning my integrity?" the Xsarn asked, rising up on his hind legs.

The Kohs quickly backed up, shouting their apologies.

"Not at all," Vol cried, "not at all."

"So we'll have our little side amusements then," Zola continued. "Gentlemen, our good friend the Xsarn seems to have
arranged this little affair not just for our amusement, but also
for his profit."

"And to keep the league of Kohs from shattering apart,"
Bukha said softly.

"Oh, to be sure, most noble of him," Zola replied
smoothly. "However, I think that our good friend, in his al-
truistic concern, has ignored the far wider potential for profit,
which as Kohs should be our first and foremost concern."

"And that is?" Bukha asked.

"A lottery for the masses," Zola said.

"Are you mad?" Bukha roared. "The games are the entertainment for Kohs, not for the people. It has always been for individuals of refinement who can appreciate the subtleties of the military arts. Why, the people would turn it into... into..." And Bukha fell silent, as if grasping for the right phrase.

"It'd turn betting on warfare into a crude blood sport." The Xsarn sniffed.

"Exactly," Bukha shouted. "Lottery indeed! Now, on to the next item of business."

Zola remained silent, a thin, self-satisfied smile crossing his features as the other Kohs looked uneasily from one to the other.

"Just wait a minute," Vol said. "This is an open forum. I must say that I'm curious as to what Zola means by a lottery for the masses."

The room fell silent and as one the Kohs looked down the table at Bukha and the Xsarn.

"That's right," Aster chimed in. "We're all equals here, and I say let's hear what Zola has to say."

"Thank you, gentlemen," Zola said, not waiting for a response from the other two. "I've done a little research, you see, and have come up with the idea that we open the game up for everyone in the Cloud to bet upon."

"Madness," Bukha shouted. "First off, what about the Overseers?"

"You know how they feel about our gaming arrangements," the Xsarn replied coldly. "Noninterference or else."

"I took it upon myself to meet with an Overseer representative and told him all about it—my idea and the game that's about to be played."

"You did *what*!" the Kohs roared as one.

"This is unheard of!" Vol shouted.

For one of them to go voluntarily to the Overseers reminded many of them of Mad Duba, who nearly a century earlier had renounced his Koh status and went voluntarily to a reeducation camp. It'd caused a shake-up, for he spilled everything he knew and more than one illegal interference with a protected planet was shut down as a result.

"Perhaps we put the wrong Humans down on the Hole, but then again there's always room for a fourth," one of the Gaf Kohs growled.

"Gentlemen, gentlemen, please," Zola nervously interjected. "I merely went to tell them that I was setting up a lottery and that it was all perfectly legal. I pointed out that we were not interfering in any way with the Al'Shiga of the Hole."

"And they accepted that?" the Xsarn asked.

"Signed right here," Zola announced, and reached into his attaché case to pull out a heavy scroll, which he tossed on the table. Everyone knew what sticklers the Overseers were for legalistics, and the sight of a contract signed by them, and granting such rights, was unprecedented in the history of Overseer Koh relations.

Bukha and the Xsarn looked nervously to each other but said nothing.

"They've promised no arrests in relation to the game and noninterference in the collection of bets and payment of winnings. They've also agreed to drop their investigation and prosecutions resulting from any situation arising from the last game."

A loud murmur arose from the Kohs. They'd all been sweating out the last six months since the end of the game. Gablona had already been nabbed, and then to top it off the Xsarn had been crazy enough to arrange his being sprung. They'd all feared arrest, and now Zola, the one usually held in contempt by all the others, had gone and gotten them amnesty.

"Is this genuine?" Vol asked incredulously.

"Take it," Zola said, tossing the document down the length of the table. "The seals are all correct. Check into your system for the com line used by the Overseers, and you'll find a copy of this document there as well. The access code's in the attached paperwork."

Zola leaned back smiling. All his life they'd been looking down on him, doing cheap imitations of his falsetto voice, laughing at him behind his back. But now they owed him, and he basked in their shouts of astonishment and praise.

"Well done. Always knew you were the smartest of all of us," the Kohs cried, coming around his chair and patting him on the back.

Bukha and the Xsarn, however, did not join the rush, and Zola eyed them coldly.

"I think I speak for all of us," Bukha said, trying to gain

everyone's attention, "when I thank Zola for managing to negotiate an amnesty. After all, we're forced to be here together
for the next forty-odd days while our accountants and lawyers
straighten out the mess. Security was our biggest concern and
now we need not worry—" he paused for a moment, "—if
this document is true."

"That can be checked," one of the Gaf Kohs standing behind Zola said defensively, "but I'm not worried. Otherwise
Zola Koh would not have brought the agreement before us."

"Be that as it may," Bukha replied, "we've yet to hear of
this lottery that Zola wants."

"Come, come, Bukha," Zola said, "we're all beings of
business here, first and foremost. And like any good businessman I need to find ways to build my business. After all, the
last game you helped launch has wound up costing all of us a
lot of expense and time."

He let his words sink in, and more than one Koh, even
some of the Gafs, looked toward Bukha with a cold stare.

"The lottery is a way to help us recoup those investments
and expand our capital bases."

Zola looked out at the group and smiled. He'd assigned a
special team to explore the marketing of the game and to set
up the organization, and kept them all under the strictest of
security arrangements. If the other Kohs had found out and
had enough lead time, they could have set up their own operations, but now it was too late: the Xsarn had announced the
game and no one other than he could launch the operation in
time.

Softly at first, and then with growing excitement, he
launched into a detailed analysis of his plan, repeating what
Kurst had told him more than a week before, starting with an
explanation of how lottery tickets could be sold with players
betting on who would kill whom, and on which day. As he
talked, a look of growing astonishment appeared on the faces
of the Kohs, each of them inwardly frustrated that he had not
thought of it himself.

"Now, the Xsarn has just announced that the game will last
forty days," Zola stated, finishing up his presentation. "By a
quick calculation I see that there are over four million possible
outcomes. Now for the fun part. The game will run for forty
days, but through a nice piece of celestial mechanics, a day

down on the Hole is almost exactly one-half of a day standard, just a shade over twelve hours. Therefore, if bets are based upon days down on the Hole, we have eighty game turns. The result is an increase in possible bets by a factor of eight to over thirty-three million possible outcomes."

The Kohs were silent, looking at each other dumbfounded.

"Several other points," Zola continued. "The bet on death by one's own side might seem a weak one, but suicides, death by natural causes, and of course murder by one's own guards would all fall into that category."

"How much of a payoff?" Vol asked.

"Ah, the interesting point. Twenty-five percent. For us that would be a fool's bet, but for the mob who buy tickets on the first day it'll still be eight million katars. There'll only be one modifier. An analysis of odds would show a high probability of death by the natives, so we'll call any bets involving natives black tickets. Black tickets will pay off at half the normal rate; that'll protect us and shift bets into other areas.

"Finally, the lottery will be open till all three are dead or until there are only five days left. As each game day progresses, the mob can still buy tickets, but at a reduced payoff, of course."

"This is astonishing!" Aster exclaimed. "You're talking an average profit base of seventy-five percent, with only operating costs to deduct. There's no major capital investments other than tickets, advertising, and record keeping!"

"Why, one of my people even thought up a slogan for the ad campaign," Zola announced. "'Spend a katar and win the Cloud!'"

The Kohs looked at each other and excitedly voiced their approval.

"My psych people, in talking with my probability people, have pointed out that once this starts it will mushroom. We've been fooling ourselves if we think our games have been secret. The masses have known all along, and being allowed to play will stroke their egos."

"Play the game of the Kohs and win the stars," Vol shouted excitedly, and his friends congratulated him on his talent for thinking up a possible ad slogan.

"Very good," Zola replied good-naturedly. "That is part of

the appeal of the bet as well, and of course this is far more dramatic, a game involving Kohs in combat."

"A blood sport to them, and a loss to our dignity if we allow them to bet upon us," Bukha interjected calmly.

"Yes, indeed," Zola replied, "and the mob will love it and want part of the action. Gentlemen, the business of Kohs is business. Think of the profits we can squeeze."

Zola looked about the room in a conspiratorial manner.

"One projection model," he whispered, "worked up by my psych people runs out that every citizen of an Alpha-class world will spend a minimum of a hundred katars if the game runs a full eighty days. Now, census figures are rough as far as the ten thousand spacefaring worlds go, but I think it comes out to somewhere near two trillion katars total, with a projected profit line of one point five trillion in profits."

There was stunned silence.

"That's nearly all our personal wealth combined." The Xsarn gasped.

"It certainly is," Zola replied coolly with a smile. "Now, I'm sharing this knowledge with you because for this to go big, we must act big. We control the communication lines, the computers needed to handle the bookkeeping, the terminals to print out the tickets, and most important, the security system to record each bet so that no one can print a false ticket.

"We've got our organization structure sitting right beneath us." And as he spoke he pointed to the panoramic window that looked out over the enclosed stadium field far below. Spread out below them were acres of temporary work areas, where thousands of their accountants and lawyers had set up an office city.

"Our computer lines are all tapped in from here and out to our transjump radio hookups for instant access to the entire Cloud. From here we can run the entire game and have it up and ready to go thirty-six hours before the three contestants go down to the Hole. I've already lined up my ad people so the videos are ready to be beamed and flood every airway.

"Now, gentlemen, I've got the potential to start this game on the five hundred–odd worlds that I control, and with you or without you I plan to announce it to them within the hour. What I propose to you is simple. I can hook you into my system so that every world that we either control or have economic contact with can be part of this as well."

"What's the price?" the Xsarn asked.

"Call it an investment. You invest into it, open up your worlds for markets, and together we rake the profits. I'm selling shares in the business; each thousand-share block will cost twenty million, and that entitles you to market the game on one world. Of course, that entitles you to profits from the company as well. My friends, we'll all make hundreds of billions."

"How many shares will you hold?" the Xsarn asked coldly.

"Fifty-one percent," Zola replied evenly, "beyond the ones that I'm now offering t you."

"That means you'd get two hundred billion out of us, if you sold every share," Bukha said coldly.

"Ah, yes," Zola replied evenly. "Of course, you can refuse, but the profit sharing for all holders could run as high as seven hundred and fifty billion."

"You're selling shares?" one of the Gafs asked cautiously. "Why should we buy into yours, now that we know we could just go and run our own lotteries on our own worlds?"

"Ah, the knowledge is free, my friend, that's why I'm sharing it, but I should caution you that it'll take several weeks for you to get your game organization set up. Each day that passes means you'll lose billions in potential profits—this is a volatile market. And what's more, suppose our three friends below are so discourteous as to get themselves killed before you've started."

"This is obscene," Bukha interjected. "True, we're betting on our friends, but it was professional, weighing the skills of each, looking at the finer nuances of tactics and military strategy. You're turning it into a cheap thrill for the masses."

"You don't have to join us if you don't want to," Zola replied sanctimoniously. "But as I was saying, my system is in place, I've got the guarantee from the Overseers, and like it or not, I plan to run it. Now, the rest of you can join in the profits or not, as you see fit."

"And out of the goodness of your heart you're sharing it with us?" Bukha snarled.

"Let's just say I'm a prudent businessman. I'm spreading the risk a little. You can all buy shares, a day later the game ends and I've made a profit. If the game lasts eighty days, I wind up sharing out more than I made off of you, but still I'll make a profit. I'm covering both ends, that's all. Besides, without the rest of you, the game can't reach to all corners of the Cloud."

"I suspect," one of the Human Kohs said, "that you had this thought out weeks before and held the knowledge back from your friends so you could turn your own profit out of it first."

"Would you have shared it, if you'd thought of it first?" Vol replied evenly, coming to Zola's defense.

"But of course," the Human said, and his response was greeted with hoots of derision. To Zola's pleasure, most of the Kohs quickly voiced the opinion that old Zola only did what they would have done and he was to be respected for it.

"So that's the bet," Zola replied. "Of course, among ourselves we'll still play it out the old way, just betting on who will win based upon our knowledge as connoisseurs of military gaming."

"But of course," they all replied.

"Good then. I'll call in my people with the prospectus and we'll sign now. My technical crews are waiting below. Once you've signed, get your communications, computer, and security teams together to meet with them. By tomorrow you can be running the game out of your worlds, colonies, ships, and outposts, throughout the Cloud, and we'll fleece them blind!"

"One question first," Bukha said.

"Anything at all," Zola replied icily. Never again would he tremble before this Koh. With Sigma and Gablona gone, most likely forever, this Gaf and his Xsarn friend were already putting on the airs of running the council of Kohs, but in forty-three days, he, Zola, would be the richest man who ever lived, and then they would see where the true power lay.

"Suppose somebody buys up a large block of winning tickets," Bukha said softly. "I'm not talking about the bets made in the last days or even the last weeks when the odds are only in the hundreds of thousand to one. I'm talking about the tickets bought now, at the start. If someone has enough tickets that pay back at that rate of odds, why it'll bankrupt the entire Cloud. And you can't simply not pay, for if you did, the Overseers would be all over you. I noticed in the contract that you've drawn up that the bet must be paid off or all members of your company will be held liable."

The room fell silent, and Zola sensed the bubble might just burst. The Overseer had forced that point of the contract, but they had both laughed over it, since the odds of such an event happening were in the millions to one.

"No problem," Zola replied smoothly. "In my prospectus, which I'll now load into your computers, you'll see the analysis worked up by my master theorist of probabilities; the odds are better than a million to one against such an event."

"Still," Bukha asked, "what if it does?"

"If someone does buy a large block of winning tickets?" Zola asked, and then he started to chuckle. "We'll just have to kill him, I guess."

There was a moment of silence and finally Zola broke it by laughing out loud, as if what he had said was just a joke, and one by one the other Kohs joined in, their laughter echoing throughout the cavernous room, even as Bukha and the Xsarn strode out, closing the door behind them.

The two looked at each, even as the laughter sounded in the distance.

"The Overseers," the Xsarn said.

"So they talked to him, too," Bukha replied.

"I wonder what the hell their game is?" the Xsarn whispered nervously.

Losa looked out across the courtyard, which was his private place of meditation, and smiled inwardly.

The ambassador from the Xsarn had been the start of it all. He knew sooner or later that the Kohs would try to bribe those whom they called the Overseers, to make an arrangement to protect themselves. Oh, he had played that out wonderfully, expressing righteous consternation at their sinful ways, threatening the Xsarn with reeducation right alongside Gablona.

Then the emissary had broken the news that they wished to punish Gablona themselves, and would even help the Overseers in their task.

It had been so easy to suggest the Hole as a possible location, and then to let everyone think that Gablona had been rescued from his personal control.

The trap had been sprung, the trap he had thought about for

centuries, to end this impasse with the interlopers who had come barging into their preserve.

Oh, he knew their ways. That "punishment" was nothing but a euphemism for their disgusting games, but that was all part of his plan as well.

But this other one, this Zola, with his scheming had been unforeseen. That, however, would fit wonderfully. It could so easily lay the groundwork to distract attention away from the true intent of what he dreamed. The chaos of the Al'Shiga could go hand in glove with the chaos that Zola would unknowingly create before this was finished. The Arch Overseer would not know till it was far too late to do anything but step aside to the one who had at last solved the great problem and eliminated the intruders without violating the code in the slightest.

If Losa had possessed hands, he would have rubbed them with glee as he floated across his private chamber.

CHAPTER 4

"You're dead, Larice. The moment I see your face, my men will kill you."

Aldin looked at Gablona with disbelief. How could this man be so insane?

"Listen, Corbin . . ."

"It's Koh Gablona to you."

Aldin strode across the chamber to where Sigma and Gablona were sitting, nursing their last round of brandy and cigars before going down to the Hole.

"Gentlemen, we can talk openly here," Aldin said, the desperation in his voice obvious to the two Kohs. "I'd like to suggest that we approach this in a logical manner. There'll be enough problems with the natives as is, each of us will be lucky if we even make it to our designated safe houses. Why make the situation any worse down there than it already is? All we need do is survive our forty days, all's forgiven, and we're free."

Gablona looked at Aldin with barely concealed disdain.

"Turning coward, is that it?" Gablona sneered. "The legendary Aldin Larice is now afraid of a little fight?"

Aldin turned to look at Sigma.

The old Koh merely extended his hands in a gesture of resignation and smiled wistfully.

"As long as he's like this, I've got to be ready," Sigma said evenly, his eyes boring into Aldin's. "And how am I to know you aren't simply playing the innocent here, and that you'll engage in a little knife work in the dark once the game begins?"

"But what's to prevent us from going together to the same safe house?" Aldin argued. "We'll hole up and sit it out, that would show all of them.

"Remember, I'm a vasba. It's my job to hunt out interesting combats to wager on. But even I wouldn't go near the Al 'Shiga. They're the craziest bastards in the entire Cloud. They'll react to us like cats to a mouse. They'll play with us for a while and then finish us off, the slower and more painfully, the better. Damn it, the Hole's a place we send hardened convicts to as a death sentence. Men beg for execution rather than be sent down there. I tell you, if we want to live, we better team up."

"I'd feel safer on my own," Sigma replied.

"You'd feel safer?" Gablona snarled. "Why, you're the one that got me stuck in the reeducation center. It's me that should be worrying about you."

"Business, my friend, nothing more than business," Sigma replied.

"Well, you'll see some business from my assassins before this is done."

"Gentlemen, we're talking about survival." Aldin tried to reason.

A chime sounded through the room's intercom system and the three fell silent.

"It's time," the voice of the Xsarn intoned over the loudspeaker. "As you witnessed in the drawing of lots, Sigma will go down on the first elevator car. Your Gavarnians are waiting for you, Sigma."

The old Koh stood up and walked over to the window that looked down on the Hole. He drained off the rest of the brandy in his glass and with a flourish tossed the empty crystal into the corner, where it shattered. He gave his two companions a characteristic shrug of his shoulders and, without another word, stalked out of the room, cigar clenched between his teeth.

Aldin looked beseechingly at Gablona, but his old employer returned the gaze with murder in his eyes.

"The plan for the last game was foolproof. If you hadn't interfered, I'd be the richest man in the Cloud, and you'd be the richest vasba."

"And Alexander would have been murdered," Aldin replied quietly. "Sorry, Koh Gablona, but as a vasba, I was sworn to maintain a fair game, and fair game it was to the end."

Gablona looked at him with a hateful gaze.

"My only concern is that the Al 'Shiga will get to you first," Gablona said.

He paused for a moment and inserted a beefy finger into his mouth to pry around his teeth. After finding the source of his annoyance, he pulled his finger back out with a chunk of food dangling on the end of his fingernail. With a flourish, he licked his finger clean and looked at Aldin with a disdainful smile.

Not another word passed between the two as they waited out the long minutes until Gablona was finally called. Nervously Aldin got up and walked over to the window. The Skyhook, what the natives call the "Seda," cut a straight line down toward the planet below.

The Hole was an apt name, he realized. The entire planet was shrouded in a thick cloud cover, except for one circular region some five hundred kilometers in diameter right on the equator, which was actually an escarpment that rose more than fifteen thousand meters above the shroud-covered lowlands. The greenhouse effect below made life impossible, but above the clouds there was a warm semitropical climate year-round. It was a unique oasis of life on an otherwise dead planet.

The Seda rose straight up from the middle of the habitable region, its white surface reflecting scarlet from the dull light of the red giant that was just breaking the horizon to the east. The structure was a source of amazement to all three races that had reached the Cloud, yet another bit of evidence of the technical prowess of the First Travelers.

Why they had bothered to build it here, on what was for all practical purposes a worthless planet, was beyond anyone's knowledge. Many felt that it was the same as the ringlike Kolbard, built it seemed just for the sheer fun of building it, and nothing more.

Some even theorized that it was done for nothing more than a visual joke. From farther out, the milky-white planet with the dark round spot looked almost like a giant eye floating in space, the Hole being the iris and the Skyhook a giant needle sticking straight out of the middle.

If there was one practical advantage the Skyhook presented, it was the fact that it enabled the Hole to be sealed off with little difficulty. All ships were strictly forbidden to land. The only contact permitted by merchants to the lower world was through this one tower and the elevator cars that came up to the geosync docking port.

Security thus was fairly simple. There was a clearing station below near groundlevel to prevent any of the Shiga from trying to come up. And even if they did take over that point, they'd still have to gain control of a ship at the top of the tower, something that all three races would never allow.

The floor swayed ever so slightly beneath Aldin's feet. For a moment Aldin felt a surge of fear—the tower must be moving! And then he realized that of course it would move, shifting with the rise and fall of the solar wind, atmospheric winds down below, the gravitational pull from the planet's two moons, or from occasional seismic activity. But the First Travelers had seen to that, as well. There was another surge that he knew would be from the tower's control system to dampen the sway, which if allowed to continue unchecked could quickly build and threaten the tower's structural integrity.

"Gablona Koh, your car is ready, your men are waiting for you."

With a smile Gablona rose to his feet. "You know, Aldin, I'm actually looking forward to seeing you down there."

He dropped his cigar onto the heavily carpeted floor, grinded it out with his heel, and then he was gone.

Aldin watched as a glass car, suspended on the outside of the tower, dropped away, falling toward the planet below.

With mock gravity Aldin raised his glass in salute.

"Mind if we join you?"

Aldin turned around to see his old friends Yaroslav and Zergh standing in the doorway.

"The Xsarn said it was all right if we spent a little time together before you go down on the next car." And the two came into the room.

Aldin noticed that Zergh was no longer wearing the ceremonial tunic of the vasba but had changed instead to the robes of a samurai, with the traditional two swords belted about his waist.

"What the hell are you doing?" Aldin asked.

"Thought I'd come along for the fun."

"Damn it all, you could get killed down there."

"Ah, yes, guess I could," Zergh replied. "But those samurai kind of got to me, perhaps the first men I've ever met with a little honor to them. Now, I won't take any arguments. The Xsarn said fifty men, and since you were six short, I volunteered and he didn't object."

Aldin could only shake his head as he came up and clapped his friend on the shoulder.

"Here, I brought you this," Yaroslav said, pulling out a package that he had kept hidden behind his back.

With Zergh's help Aldin unwrapped the gift and looked at it with amazement.

"The ceremonial robes of an early eighteenth-century samurai," Yaroslav said proudly. "Took a bit of research on my part, but I think they're correct. After all, you want to impress your guards, don't you?"

"How are they?" Aldin asked.

"Good men," Zergh replied enthusiastically. "It took a little persuading, but I convinced them to come with me. Our tech folks then altered the humanbots, programmed them after doing a memory sweep of Oishi, and they were dropped down without a hitch. We sleeped the samurai as soon as they were jumped up to the ship, and they've only been awakened an hour ago. They've already received their tracking scanners and translator implants programmed for common speech and the Al'Shiga dialect. They're having some problems with the translators, claiming they're an affront to their dignity, but I convinced them that they'll need them to survive.

"For this situation, however, I'm still not sure they're the right choice," Zergh continued. "Sigma's berserkers look tough, and as for Gablona's assassins, they should fit right in down there. I'm afraid your samurai are going to stand right out. Racially for one thing—what with all your human races blending together, pure Orientals are a rarity. The other problem is their bearing. They're proud men, they carry themselves like warriors who fear nothing. It won't sit well with the Shiga."

"Do they know anything yet?" Aldin asked.

"Only what we agreed on earlier, that they've been sent to help a friend of their lord who is in trouble, nothing more."

Aldin nodded and then looked down at the bundle.

"How the hell do I get into this suit?" he asked.

Yaroslav laid the various garments out on the floor and helped Aldin to remove his coveralls. The diaperlike underwear struck him as absurd, and the three of them laughed when they finally realized Aldin had put it on backward. At last came the outer robe, which Aldin held up to admire. It was light blue in color, a white rose emblazoned on the back.

"Traditional touch," Yaroslav replied. "Your house needs a symbol, that's all."

Putting the robe on, he could not help but feel somewhat absurd, but at the same time he realized that he would gain easier approval from his new comrades if he appeared dressed as they were. With a final flourish Aldin took the long sword from Yaroslav's hand.

As a professional he had once looked upon such objects as collectables, works of art to be admired. It struck him with a cold chill that his very life might now depend upon this primitive device.

The code of the game was strict, as was the law in the Hole: only weapons powered by physical strength could be used.

As an added touch the Shiga strictly forbade any type of projectile weapon, thus bows were out. Some merchants did arm their premises with them, but if the Shiga found out, there'd be a riot. Aldin realized he could have tried to slip a microburster in by swallowing it, but the tracking scanner that had already been implanted into his body would have picked it up. Even if he got it past the scanner it wouldn't do much good. Use it once down below, and there'd be a mob of fifty thousand religious fanatics on them within the hour for having broken the rule of drawing blood only by hand. It was going to have to be swords or daggers. Or for that matter, garrotes, poison, snake baskets, the Shiga needle blade, or . . .

He tried to block it out for the moment.

Yaroslav helped him to adjust the two swords so that they balanced correctly.

"Not bad, Aldin-san."

"What?"

Yaroslav only shook his head and smiled.

The Xsarn appeared in the doorway, flanked by Bukha Taug.

"So, you two," Aldin said, trying to sound injured. "Loyal friends showing up to send off their comrade to the execution?"

"Now, Aldin," Bukha started.

"Don't now Aldin me," he shouted. "This is a hell of a note. You profited by the Alexandrian game as well as I, but now I take the fall, is that it?"

The Xsarn turned an inquiring gaze at Bukha, who extended his hands in a gesture of innocence.

"The man's overwrought," he replied coolly.

"Obviously overwrought," Zergh chimed in, the faintest of smiles creasing his features.

"It's only for forty days," Bukha said, quickly steering the topic away from any implications regarding the last game. "Get it over with, the finances here will be taken care of, and everything will be back to normal."

"Take care of yourself," Aldin said evenly, coming up to Yaroslav's side.

"Sure you don't want me to come along?" his old friend asked.

"Do you really want to?"

"Down there?" Yaroslav asked, a sheepish grin crossing his features. "Well, not exactly, not good for the health of someone like myself."

Aldin smiled and slapped his old friend on the shoulder.

"Let's get out of here," he said, looking over at Zergh. Without comment the two strode out of the room. As Aldin cleared the doorway Bukha stepped before him.

"I'm betting on you to win," Bukha whispered with a smile, his voice loud enough for the Xsarn to hear.

"Thanks for the confidence," Aldin replied coldly, and then pushed on, the Xsarn falling in by his side.

"You'll meet your guards in the lift chamber," the Xsarn stated. "Once the lift starts down you may brief them in any manner you choose. The lift will deposit you on the planet's surface in exactly four hours after departure. There, a bonded agent from the Rhee Trading Consortium will meet you once the lift is opened. His only obligation is to show you to your safe house. Once at the door of the safe house, you're on your own. Pickup will be at the tower at sundown after eighty days of Hole time. There'll only be two hours left to today, so they'll be counted in as part of tomorrow.

"The other two teams will already be down. Since there's only one entry point into the tower, it couldn't be arranged any other way, so technically the game starts the moment Sigma sets foot on the planet."

"A fine advantage for them." Aldin sniffed. "One of them could have already killed the other and then be waiting for me."

"I doubt that," the Xsarn replied.

"How come?" Aldin asked.

"You see, there's some sort of festival going on down there today. You'll see what I mean when you get there."

"Good luck," the Xsarn said, extending both right arms.

Aldin hesitated for a moment, then reaching out, allowed his forearm to be grasped.

"Never thought I'd be playing in one of my own games," Aldin said, trying to hide his fear.

"It was the only way to settle this dispute," the Xsarn replied.

"And who are you betting on?" Aldin asked, his professional curiosity getting the better of him.

"You know I can't, I'm the gamemaster."

Aldin gave him a look that said he wasn't fooling anyone.

The Xsarn drew closer.

"Sorry, old friend," he whispered, his fetid breath washing over Aldin, "but the odds are on Gablona."

"Thanks for the confidence," Aldin snapped, and he shouldered his way past.

The doorway slid open and then closed behind Aldin and Zergh. As the door clicked shut, the assembled warriors went to their knees.

"Aldin-san, we are ready to serve you in your hour of need."

Aldin looked at the men before him and the fear that had gripped him faded away. He looked back at the closed door, and thought of how all those on the other side had written him and his ronin off swept over him. Like hell, he suddenly thought.

The warriors were still kneeling, with eyes lowered.

"Oishi!"

"Yes, my lord."

"Stand up and look at me."

The samurai came to his feet, his eyes level with Aldin's.

He wrestled yet again with what he had done to Oishi and his companions. He had drafted them into almost certain death. But then again if he had not, it would not have been humanbots that had ripped their stomachs open, but these brave men. At least they had a fighting chance now.

"Come on," he said with a cold, even voice, and as the men fell in behind Aldin, they walked into the turbolifter that would drop them down into the Hole, thousands of kilometers below.

Hours had passed on their journey down, and the Hole loomed directly below them, the curve of the planet's surface spreading out farther and farther. Aldin looked straight up for a moment at the docking port they had left hours ago, which was no longer visible, and then back at the samurai. He had tried to explain the nuances of the Al'Shiga, and to explain, as well, how they had to survive not only threats from them but from two other "great lords." Somehow he felt as if the samurai had seen through him already.

They were strapped into chairs that ringed the wall of the lift car, with a clear view through the glass floor at their feet. The experience of free-fall during the descent down the side of the tower, with the destination directly below one's feet, was unnerving even for the most experienced of travelers; several of the samurai had simply fainted away, and most of the others, to their shame, had become ill.

For Oishi there had been wonders enough already. What had only seemed hours ago, he had been kneeling before the tomb of lord Asano, his task completed, ready to face the death he knew his emperor would decree.

Now they were falling out of the heavens, sliding down what looked like a great column to whatever awaited them below.

Something wasn't right, he thought. This Aldin was not his image of a powerful being from another world. If anything, he could sense fear in the man he was sworn to serve. Oishi struggled with his own fear of all that he was seeing, but at the same time he realized that for a being of the heavens there should be nothing to fear. So why did this Aldin seem nervous?

Aldin looked over at Oishi and could sense the doubt in the man. He felt a twinge of regret, knowing that Oishi had been told less than a half-truth, but for the moment he needed their unswerving loyalty, for it would be put to the test in a very short time.

How could he possibly explain all this to them? Aldin wondered, looking at the samurai. But he realized he had to say something, he could see Oishi wanted explanations.

"Everyone down there is crazy," Aldin said quietly.

"How so?" Oishi asked.

"Just believe what our lord Aldin said," Zergh interjected. "Let's just survive getting to our fortress. Stay close, don't talk to anyone, and most of all, no matter what the insult, ignore it."

Some of the samurai grumbled at this command; ignoring insults was not high on their list of proper behavior.

"Remember," Zergh continued, trying to placate them, "your lord Aldin is your first, your only concern. Your honor is pledged to protecting him. If you accept a challenge on the open street, you might suddenly face a mob of thousands ready to join in the kill. Do you understand me?"

Oishi thought for a moment and then nodded. Turning, he looked to his companions.

"You will obey," he barked, and the others were silent.

"Once we get to our safe house, we'll hole up," Aldin stated, "and then try to find out where the other two are hiding out. But for now the main problem is getting safely in; nothing else counts."

"What if we see your other enemies on the street?" Oishi asked.

Zergh looked over to Aldin.

Damn it all, Aldin thought. He now realized that he had been so preoccupied with survival on the Hole that he had not taken time to sort out any offensive strategy, an approach he was sure Gablona and Sigma had thought through.

"If we can take them, we attack," he whispered. He looked to Zergh for reassurance, and his old companion nodded with approval.

Oishi noticed the exchange of glances between the two, but said nothing. When he looked over at Takashi he saw that his brother and old comrade had noticed the exchange as well.

There was a sudden sense of weight returning. The free-fall period was over. They were starting to cut into the atmosphere and deceleration had started.

Aldin looked up and saw that already the sky overhead was starting to shift from the blackness of night into a deep, glowing red. The sense of weight increased as they crossed through one G and then pushed up to two. The samurai, unaccustomed to such a sensation, tried to hide their fear. Free-fall had been bad enough for them to adjust to; the sudden shift made several of them ill again.

Just great, Aldin thought. These men might be fighting in a matter of minutes and most of them were half sick.

Looking straight down, he started to pick out details on the surface below. Surrounding the Skyhook, a city was now clearly in view. From out of the base of the tower stretched five broad avenues that ran like ribs on a Japanese fan a quarter of the way out to the rim, and terminated in five more cities, the space in between being covered by thick, heavy growth, while the area beyond was sectioned off into orderly fields.

There was a final lurch as the descending car braked even harder and then the pressure eased off as they slowly started to drift to a stop.

With less than a kilometer to go, he felt as if he were looking down upon a writhing mound of insects that had been stirred into life. The western side of the Skyhook faced a huge open area more than half a kilometer across, and with a sickening shudder Aldin realized that it was covered with a surging mass of Humanity and Gafs, hundred of thousands of beings, seemingly locked in bloody combat.

The turbolift door opened, and all conversation was drowned out by a roaring ocean of noise.

Even as they tried to exit the car, a mad crush pushed in around them, terrified Xsarns, Gafs, and Humans, most of them dressed in the multihued garb of half a hundred different trading houses.

The samurai elbowed their way around Aldin, attempting to set up a protective perimeter, while Zergh's bellowed commands were lost in the wild cacophony of screaming chaos.

Aldin felt frightened out of his wits. Was this a real riot, or was it something perhaps whipped up by Gablona or Sigma, who had the advantage of going down before him?

A sudden scream rent the air. Turning, Aldin stood transfixed as a Gaf merchant collapsed on the edge of the circle of samurai who stood around Aldin with drawn swords. A man rode upon the Gaf's back, his right hand moving back and forth across his victim's throat with a vigorous sawing motion.

There was an explosion of scarlet. The Gaf reared back up, staggered, and then fell forward again, showering all about him with a river of blood.

The blue-robed assassin leaped from the back of his prey and held a bloody saw-toothed dagger aloft.

"Al 'Shiga of the Isma!" he screamed, his eyes wild with triumph.

"Zergh!"

Before Aldin could stop him, his old companion pushed through the protective circle of samurai.

Zergh's long, two-handed blade hissed out in a deadly arc. The severed head tumbled through the air and, driven by the impact, fell at Aldin's feet. With horror Aldin saw that the man's face was still frozen in a look of triumph.

A shout of approval went up from the samurai as several clamored to retrieve the trophy. Zergh stepped back into the ranks and could not help but grin at the admiring looks on the faces of the warriors around him.

Meanwhile, the panic-stricken merchants continued to push into the car. Several fell upon the bundle that the Gaf merchant had been carrying and with drawn daggers argued over the contents.

"Let's get out of here," Oishi roared, and leading the way, he pushed against the throng. Aldin and the rest of the group followed.

"A bad move," a voice suddenly shouted from the crowd, swarming around the encircled band of warriors.

Aldin looked up and saw a man dressed in the flowing burgundy tunic of the Rhee Consortium trying to push against the flood of refugees.

The man made it to the edge of the circling samurai and pulled back his face cloth.

"I'm Eda, with the Rhee trading group. The Xsarn contracted me to serve you," he shouted.

"Don't trust him," Zergh shouted, and as if by command, the samurai standing before Aldin snapped out their blades, ready to strike.

The man backed up a step, his hands up. With a slow, deliberate action he reached beneath the folds of robes.

Oishi, not liking the move, barked a command, and the samurai nearest to the small man thrust out, his blade stopping but a fraction from the man's throat.

Eda, as if totally detached from any possible danger, nodded his approval at the samurai's skill. Cautiously he pulled his hand back out from the tunic's fold and held up a small portascreen.

"Get it," Aldin said. His first impulse had been to simply step forward and take it himself, but his nerves were on edge. Anything could be a trap here. The portascreen could actually be a bomb or, for that matter, the handle could have a poison clip.

He watched as the samurai with the drawn sword reached out with his other hand and snatched the small dictation pad away. Aldin exhaled slowly. He had just ordered, for the first time, a man to lay his life on the line. He didn't like the feel of it; it would take some getting used to.

The samurai stepped back while one of his companions took his place with drawn sword to guard the man.

With a bow, the warrior came up to Aldin's side. Gingerly

rounded the slender Skyhook. Before them the square was jammed with hundreds of thousands of beings and for a moment Aldin feared that the mob had turned out to give him a special greeting.

The square seemed to be cordoned off into sections, a massed grouping of blue robes to the right with what looked like Gafs in red robes, followed by white-, green-, and orange-, robed groups proceeding around the tower. Around the base of the Skyhook stood a massed formation of yellows. Each of the groups was separated from the other by the broad avenues that spread out in a fan-shaped pattern from the square, with the yellows forming a ring around the base, their formation broken only by the avenues that cut through their ranks to terminate before the open dais upon which Aldin and his companions now stood.

This is going to be one very short game, Aldin thought as he looked out across the hundreds of thousands, expecting that at the sight of him the mob would surge forward and simply crush them underfoot. The eerie silence held and then suddenly a triumphant roar echoed from the white robes' section as half a dozen Gaf heads, still dripping blood, arched into the air over the avenue that divided the two groups.

A deeper growl of rage, from the assembled Gafs, thundered across the square. A contingent of half a hundred red-robed Gafs surged across the avenue toward the white robes. There was a confused flurry of action; the Gafs fell back to their comrades, bearing a struggling form. Seconds later a Human head was tossed into the air and now the Gafs howled with triumph—the riot was on again.

"Good time to move right now," Eda suggested. "The celebration is really hot and they might be too busy to worry about our passing through.

"Just tell your people to stay close, and no matter what, not to speak to anyone," Eda continued. "Your Gaf companion there's already incurred the blood debt of the Isma sect, the blue robes. Don't make it worse."

Before Aldin had a chance to reply, Eda started down the steps of the dais and onto a broad avenue that separated the Gafs from the Blues. The group fell in behind him, the samurai still forming a protective circle with blades drawn.

Aldin looked around and realized that the entire dais

around the Skyhook was almost deserted, except for small knots of Shiga, mostly yellows, who looked at them with open hatred. Few in number, they offered no challenge, but it was obvious from the way they hung just out of range that they might be willing to take an opportunity if it were offered.

One of the Shiga dressed in light blue broke away from his group of a dozen onlookers and, racing ahead of the group, disappeared into the surging mob.

"Most likely going to tell his friends," Zergh stated. With a shout of defiance he raised his sword up over his head and shook it in the direction of the blue-clad assassins who warily followed the group.

Their gestures in response were universal and readily understood.

"Nothing like calling attention to yourself. And you were worried about the samurai," Aldin commented bitterly.

As they stepped off the dais and out onto the avenue, Aldin thought that the noise, dust, and horrific stench of hundreds of thousands of unwashed bodies would simply overwhelm him. As if to somehow touch back to his normal life, he paused for a second and turning, looked straight up. It was a sight that could have held him enthralled for hours, this miracle of First Traveler engineering.

The Skyhook tower cut heavenward through the dull red sky, a perfectly straight line that soared ever upward until disappearing in a distant point of light that Aldin realized must be the first docking station thousands of kilometers above.

But the more immediate concerns pulled him back to the situation at hand. The left side of the avenue was lined with thousands of Gafs chanting and roaring. Over their heads fluttered hundreds of red banners covered with the wavery Shiga script.

On the right side of the avenue were thousands of Humans, most in blue robes, but scattered among them were occasional clumps of greens and oranges.

"Over here it's the Sutar cult, against the Isma, with some Bengada and Kuln allies," Eda roared, as if his comment would make any sense.

Eda edged over toward the Gaf side of the street, and his companions nervously followed. The middle of the street was covered with a scattering of bodies, some Gafs, but more Humans, all of them headless.

Suddenly a knot of Gafs with red bands of cloth knotted round their heads surged out of the crowd, rushing straight at the intruders. Most carried saw-toothed daggers, while several held glinting wire garrotes. Ths Japanese lowered swords, ready to meet the ance. At the last second the dozen Gafs flowed around them, barely noticing their presence except for a couple of angry snarls, and then pushed on across the street.

A wild shout went up from the Human side. The blues broke in a surging confused rush, backing away from the street, while here and there others leaped out, red cloths tied around their foreheads.

The press was so great that the mob's retreat was blocked and dozens went down, trampled beneath the confusion as the Gafs plunged into the swirling maelstrom of Humanity and disappeared from view. Awestruck, the party stopped to watch. Suddenly a Human head arched up into the air and a wild shout of triumph rose from the Gaf side. The mob surged and eddied as if it were a single living entity coiling in agony; another head went up, a Gaf's, and a cheer from the Human side greeted the sight. Suddenly the knot of Gafs broke clear a dozen meters away from their point of entry, blues scattering in every direction. Two of the Gafs held Human forms, still twisting and writhing, and they started to race back across the avenue.

The mob surged after them. One of the Gafs, obviously wounded, was swarmed over, and seconds later his head was tossed heavenward. His companions, without a backward look, pushed on across the avenue bearing their prisoners, who howled with terror.

The Humans surged after them, and for a second Aldin thought that a general riot between the two sides was about to explode with his group caught in the middle.

But at the midpoint of the avenue the chase was broken off by the masses. Shouting with triumphant glee, the Gafs bore their prisoners across the street and melted back into the red-clad ranks of their comrades, who shouted with joy at the display. The mob surged inward around them and seconds later two Human heads soared upward to be tossed back and forth like balls, while torn fragments of still-quivering bodies rained back out onto the street.

Throughout this entire display the two sides behaved as if Aldin and his entourage did not even exist. Hoping that their festival was taking all their attention, Aldin signaled for the group to catch up with Eda, who had stopped merely to let the Gaf attack party pass and was already pushing on up the street. Running after their guide, they forged ahead, staying close to the Gaf side, shifting in their path to avoid torn fragments and bloody smears that littered the length of the avenue.

At the end of the great square, Eda suddenly turned right and headed straight across the avenue toward the Human mob, and for the first time he slowed, letting the outer circle of samurai surge around him.

"This is the hard part. We got to get through this mob, our destination is on the other side," he shouted, trying to be heard above the howling madness around them.

"Couldn't we just circle around this?" Aldin shouted.

"Too far to go. Believe me, the alleys are far more dangerous than the square during the festival. Now stay close!"

Suddenly a loud, piercing whistle rent the air.

"Side shift," Eda screamed. "Brace yourselves!"

The Human side seemed to explode into a wild frenzy, while from the other side of the street the Gafs howled with joy. A small knot of orange robes came surging out of the crowd, those on the edge of the group slashing indiscriminately with their blades at any Humans not dressed in orange. A dozen or more heads were tossed up around the edge of the group. The orange ranks closed and, chanting a wild paean of joy, they surged across the avenue to the other side, where the Gafs greeted them with jubilation.

"A masterful betrayal," Eda cried. "Masterful! Now, let's move before the ranks close."

Pushing ahead, the group headed straight into the hole produced by the defection of several hundred orange robes to the other side.

They plunged into the swirling mass of warriors. The circle of samurai were up to a fever pitch of excitement with swords raised ready to slash out at any who dared to approach.

Oishi broke away from Aldin's side and darted around the inside of the protective circle, shouting for his men to remain steady.

The mob gave back defiantly, as if deeming to give serious notice to the outsiders for the first time.

After several minutes the group finally broke through the press at the far end of the square and rushed into a narrow side alley.

Eda stopped for a moment as if to catch his breath.

"What the hell is all of this?" Aldin roared, pointing back to the mass insanity just beyond the alleyway entrance.

"Festival. Happens every ten days, when the closer moon is new," Eda shouted. "All six clans live separately in their own cities. With the new moon, they all come to the great square of the Seda, to pray before the tower. Looking for a sign."

"A sign?"

"That the tower will open to them. See that?" And he pointed up to a platform that jutted out from the tower three hundred or more meters above the square.

"They call it the place of judging. Representatives from each clan enter the tower with the first car in the morning. In fact, it's a high honor. Anyhow," Eda continued, "they get to the transfer station. The servobot security system searches all the up-bound passengers. Since the Shiga don't have proper identifications and monitoring implants, they're culled out of the group. A hell of a lot of bots usually get busted up in the process. Quite expensive actually, but no one in his right mind would want the job."

"Then what?" Aldin asked.

"Why, they're taken to the platform and thrown out," Eda said matter-of-factly.

As if to illustrate Eda's point, a sudden hush fell over the crowd. A tiny yellow-robed figure appeared on the brink of the tower.

"Ema! Ema! Ema!" the hundreds of thousands started to chant.

"Ema?" Oishi asked, trying to be heard.

"The hidden teacher, the Ema," Eda replied. "A messiah figure who will liberate them. If one appears on the platform and does not fall, then he is the great Ema. Damn fool must have slipped on to the last car up. Won't these bastards ever give up?"

The yellow-robed form suddenly pitched forward. For several seconds he looked almost to be flying, his robes fluttering about him, his arms extended straight out.

The body impacted headfirst at the base of the tower.

A loud roar went up from the crowd and the rioting continued.

"Every ten days," Eda shouted, shaking his head. "Of course, no Ema's revealed, then everything degenerates from there. Each clan feels the impurity of the others prevents the hidden teacher from being revealed. Those wearing red headbands are the Mukba, the elect, and are allowed to take heads. The rules are strict, otherwise they'd have wiped each other out long ago. It's a great honor to be a Mukba, the rest are just here for the fun of it. Sort of like the running before dragons that those damn fool Daks practice. Same damn thing every week. I tell you it gets on your nerves after a while.

"I think we better get moving," Eda said, looking back toward the square.

A group of blues had detached themselves from the crowd and were now looking in their direction.

"Once outside the square, it's open season on offworlders. Those young bucks might be looking for some fun. Let's move." And the party, following Eda's lead, started up the alleyway.

"Infidels, pork eaters, nonbelievers!" the blue robes shrieked, closing in behind them. As if a signal had been given, inhabitants of the narrow, refuse-choked alleyway started to peer out from the upper floors of their squalid hovels.

Within seconds a rain of garbage and chamber-pot contents started to rain down from above, and the Japanese, now wild with rage, started to shout their defiance back.

Young children jumped from rooftop to rooftop, some of them pulling up roofing tiles to drop, while others leaned over to relieve themselves upon the foreigners.

"Just keep moving," Eda shouted, "before they can cut us off. We're almost to the foreign quarter."

Suddenly there was a sickening crunch, and with a groan, one of the samurai tumbled forward, hit squarely on the head by a heavy rock heaved from above. A shout of triumph went up from the children overhead, who danced about with joy, while the Japanese shook their fists in impotent rage as they picked up their fallen comrade. Blood was pouring out from under his helmet. Oishi rushed over to his side, bent over, and then came back up, a look of cold rage on his features.

Stunned, Aldin realized that the man was dead—the first one to die in his service. He started to say something to Oishi but then thought better of it. He looked at the man and then at his outraged comrades. With a shudder Aldin realized that he didn't even know the man's name.

"Almost there, almost there," Eda cried, the nervous strain of it all showing on him as well. "Just turn left at the next corner!"

Picking up their pace, the group surged forward, and their tormentors, sensing a growing panic, pushed in behind them, shouting abuse.

The front of the column turned the last corner and came up short.

A wall of a dozen or more blue robes stood in their way. Aldin peered over the heads of his guards and saw that the tallest one in the middle of the group was the same man who had most likely observed the killing of his comrade back by the Skyhook. Beyond the waiting blues was the gateway into the foreign quarter, the barrier open, the iron-studded doors leaning back drunkenly as if they had been smashed open, while over the street hung a low pale of eddying smoke.

Eda's cool exterior finally gave way.

"Fanatical bastards," he cried. "I'm sick of them. Just sick of them. Some of the maniacs have started a fire!"

"Well, stop whining and get us out of this," Oishi shouted, sizing up the group ahead of them. Turning, he saw that with every passing second, the group behind them was being reinforced by new recruits pouring in from adjoining alleyways. Overhead the storm of debris was turning into a veritable blizzard of tiles, garbage, and excrement.

Eda, a look of fear in his eyes, took a deep swallow and stepped to the edge of the samurai ring. "We are willing to pay blood money, so that there is no shame. We still have his head and will barter it back." And so saying, he motioned for one of the samurai to surrender the trophy, which he had belted to his waist.

"Not enough amber in the Hole," the tall one shouted.

"Barter time not now," Eda replied, nervously licking his lips. "The dead one has already been lifted to paradise and even now rests in the arms of girls ever virgin. Rejoice for him and leave us pass. Blood money will be sent to you."

"We demand the blood of a servant to go with him," the tall one shouted.

"Better move," Oishi shouted, looking back over his shoulder, "they're working up for a rush!"

Aldin looked back. There was a cry from a samurai standing next to him, and with a shove the samurai pushed Aldin to one side. There was a dull thump and the man went down to his knees, knocked senseless by a roofing tile, which shattered against the side of his head.

"Charge!" Oishi cried, and with raised sword he pointed to the blues before them.

As one the samurai rushed ahead, eager to be at their tormentors.

"No! Stop, damn it, stop!" But Eda's words were drowned out as the samurai, shouting with joy at the prospect of battle, swarmed up the filth-caked alleyway. Stunned at the sudden onset, the assassins drew back, their short daggers and garrotes no match for the long striking swords of the samurai warriors.

Blood splattered across the alleyway, bodies went down, shrieks of agony rent the air as the group waded in to the attack. Zergh, giving himself over to the blood lust, pushed to the fore, two-handed sword held high, with Aldin following in his wake. Within seconds they were through the blue-clad ranks, most of the enemy falling where they had stood, while the few survivors fled into the stinking hovels and darkened alleys that lined the end of the street.

After pushing through the shattered entryway into the foreign quarter, the group came to a stop on the other side.

Oishi barked a series of commands and the group formed up again, turning to face the threat he expected from behind. But the alleyway was quiet now, except for the moaning cries of several assassin wounded left behind by their fleeing comrades.

The mob stood silent, and in its silence it was even more threatening than it had been but moments before.

"Now you've gone and done it," Eda snarled, coming up to Aldin's side. "They were just having some fun with you, that's all."

"Fun? You call one of my men being killed fun?"

"To them it is," Eda shouted. "They were testing your nerve, that's all. It's festival day. The Mukba fight for martyrdom. It should have been a one-on-one, your stupid Gaf friend and him fighting to settle the debt. You've broken the covenants of the law and now the entire Isma, the blue robes, will kill you on sight."

"Well, why the hell didn't you tell us?" Oishi roared, coming to Aldin's defense.

"Because you panicked and didn't give me time. Look at them back there, they'll never deal with you now, it'll be kill on sight."

"Goddamn crazies," Aldin snarled, and looked over at Oishi.

"You did what was right," he said, clapping the man on the shoulder. Oishi shot Eda a vicious look for having berated his lord before the men and felt an inner sense of relief for being supported in his decision.

"Any of our men hurt?" Aldin asked.

Oishi looked around the ground and saw that they had the body of their one comrade and the prostrate form of the one knocked unconscious before the charge. He then noticed that Tomoichi, one of the youngest of the band, was sitting on the ground trembling.

He went up and knelt by the youngster's side.

Tomoichi looked up at his leader and smiled wanly.

"It's only a scratch," he whispered, and held up his right arm to show where a ragged but shallow cut had sliced his arm for several inches above the wrist. The boy started to shiver, obviously from the shock of what had just happened. Oishi grunted sympathetically. The sight of one's first wound was enough to unnerve even the bravest.

"You're a man now, Tomoichi." And he clapped the youngster on the back.

"Somebody wounded?" Eda cried, pushing through the crowd.

"It isn't much, a couple of stitches will take care of him," Oishi replied.

"A sword," Eda screamed, "give me a sword!"

Confused, Oishi just stared at the little man as if he were mad. With a wild lunge, Eda reached down to Tomichi's side and snatched up his fallen blade and raised it high.

"Stick out your arm!" he shouted. "Stick it out!"

Tomoichi looked at him wide-eyed. Oishi pushed his way in front of Eda, his own blade up, ready to strike.

"His arm!" Eda shouted again. "Cut it off now, before it's too late."

Confused, Oishi looked back at the wounded youngster. The boy was still shaking, and even as Oishi looked at him he fell over, his body wracked with convulsions.

"It's too late," Eda whispered, and, dropping the blade, he turned away.

"What's too late?" Oishi cried, grabbing Eda by the shoulder.

"Don't you know they carry poison blades here? That's why they have saw-toothed daggers. The blades are dipped in a waxy solution that sticks between the teeth. I only hope your boy there was hit with a fast agent."

Wide-eyed with horror, Oishi looked back. Tomoichi's body arched and twisted as he thrashed upon the ground. A strangled cry escaped from his lips, and then with a sigh he fell back, his features relaxing into the stillness of death.

"It was the fast agent," Eda said.

Stunned, the samurai looked down at their fallen comrade, one of the youngest of the forty-seven ronin. The silent spectators down at the end of the street had witnessed it as well, and a shouting jeer went up.

"Pig's spawn, he'll burn in hell!"

Several of the samurai, driven to the edge of reason, turned and started back toward the crowd, but Oishi pushed in front of them.

"Not now!" he barked. "We'll take them, but when we're ready."

The men hesitated.

"You are samurai," he roared. "Now obey."

His words brought reason back to the ranks, and following Eda, the group retreated up the narrow street.

Wreathed in eddies of smoke, the mob was lost to view, their shouts of defiance prodding the samurai who fought to control their anger.

"It's just around the corner," Eda said, "and then I'm done with you."

The street through the heart of the foreign quarter was empty. The shops looked like fortresses under siege. Not a single building had a window facing the street, other than narrow slits lining each floor. The single doorway into each structure was more often than not made of steel studded with heavy bolts, flanked on either side by narrow spy slits, and protected overhead by spouts out of which boiling oil or some such concoction could be poured.

As they approached the corner, clouds of smoke rolled up from the alleyway to greet them.

"I'm getting a very uncomfortable feeling about this," Zergh whispered, coming up to Aldin's side.

Trying not to appear too anxious, Aldin merely nodded in reply.

His worst fears, however, were confirmed when they reached the corner.

"Well, there it is; my contract is finished," Eda said coldly, while pointing toward the source of the smoke.

"What the hell do you mean, there it is?" Aldin shouted, coming up to the guide's side.

The building that Eda was pointing to was engulfed in flames, which shot out of the spy slits like blowtorches. The neighbors were out but were busy working the corner pump in order to throw water on their own threatened structures.

Even as they stood watching, the roof of the building caved in with an explosive roar, sending a shower of sparks heavenward into the damp air.

"That is, or should I say was, your safe house; my job is finished."

"Who the hell did it?" Zergh shouted, coming up to join the argument.

Eda merely shrugged his shoulders. "Maybe your competitors, since they got in here first. Then again, I told you killing that blue robe was going to cause problems. Perhaps his companions found out where you were staying and got there first."

"Well, now what are we going to do?"

"I've fulfilled my contract," Eda replied, his voice edged with contempt, "so it's your problem, not mine. You've made it difficult enough for me to get out of here as is, the blues might think I'm part of your group."

Feeling a touch of panic, Aldin looked around. He had thought that they'd be able to get into their safe house, barricade it, and hole up for a couple days till they sorted things out.

"Couldn't we buy your services?" he said hastily. "Look, we'll pay you what you want."

"You couldn't pay me enough," Eda said coldly. "You've got the smell of death around you. I've lived here long enough—I know it when I smell it, and I'm usually right. If I stick around, the smell will wear off on me."

"Look, back up there." Aldin pointed up toward the towering Skyhook that dominated the view. "I've got wealth, stock, I've even got my own ship."

The last part wasn't quite true, his ship was a wrecked hulk floating somewhere out in space, but neither he nor Zergh would tell it otherwise.

"Name your price," Aldin pleaded. "Just a standard day's service, that's all I ask."

Eda looked at him with contempt.

"Besides what the Xsarn's paying," he said, "I've got a hundredweight of fossil green amber. Your wealth is meaningless, and anyhow, once you're killed, your money will be confiscated and then I'm left with nothing but an I.O.U. from a dead man. You're worthless, Aldin Larice." And with a harsh laugh he started to turn away.

Oishi's blade snaked out, touching Eda on the throat. Without comment the samurai looked at Aldin, awaiting his command.

"Let him go," Aldin said, disgusted.

Eda merely smiled. "Wise. Kill me while under contract and even if you live the Xsarn will want answers."

"Get the hell out of here," Aldin snapped. "And you can tell the Xsarn for me that he can kiss my ass."

"I'm sure he'd love to," Eda replied with a laugh. "Some free advice though to you, the dying. You better find someone to let you in before dark—the Shiga love night hunts. I'll also tell you that your opponents are near, very near, perhaps hiding even on this very street, since this is the only foreign quarter in the Hole. Have fun."

With a sarcastic wave Eda turned and disappeared into the smoke and was lost from view.

"A cheery bastard." Zergh sniffed.

"Cheery all right, he's short time and getting out." Dejected, Aldin looked back at the flaming wreckage of what was to have been his safe house. "Well, I'm open to suggestions," he whispered softly.

CHAPTER 5

"MY LORD GABLONA."

Wearily Corbin looked up at the black-robed assassin who stood before him. He hadn't walked so damn far in years. His legs still trembled from the exertion of running for cover.

Damned green robes, he thought angrily, a bunch of crazy fanatics all of them, and what a stench.

He eyed the assassin closely; barbarians, as well, he thought. But at least these were barbarians in his employ.

"What is it?" Corbin barked, leaning over to rub the knotted muscles of his beefy thighs.

"The master wishes to see you."

"Well, tell him to come in here then."

Had to keep these animals in their place, Corbin thought. This was his chamber and people came to him, not the other way around. He shifted his gaze around the room. Some chamber. It still stank from the Xsarns who had inhabited it before vacating it for the purpose of the game. All the damned furniture was oversized, making him feel like a child, and was crafted, as well, for insectoids whose lower limbs articulated backward, thus resulting in some rather unusual designs for chairs and such.

"But the master wishes for you to observe something that he's noticed."

"Damn it all, why didn't you say that the first time?" Corbin said wearily, and with a groan came to his feet. He left the room located in the central core of the house and followed the assassin down a narrow corridor to the front gate. Hassan was standing in one of the narrow defense slits that projected outward from either side of the door, his eye to one of the windows.

Hearing their approach, Hassan turned with a catlike ease that Corbin found most disturbing, as if the man were ready to strike him down out of hand.

A thin smile creased Hassan's deceivingly gentle features. "I think there's something down the street that you'd like to see." He gestured for Corbin to look out one of the spy slits.

Sensing a possible trap, Corbin hesitated.

"Ah, a wise precaution," Hassan replied smoothly, not taking insult. "Rest assured, it's safe."

Corbin looked closely at Hassan. He'd only been with this man for less than half a day. Hassan had been properly correct before him, acknowledging him as his lord and commanding the others to instantly obey all commands on pain of death. The riches and titles Gablona promised seemed to have an effect at least, and Hassan had thanked him profusely, promising the best of service. The master of assassins had absorbed the briefing on the way down the Skyhook with a sharp, insightful manner, asking numerous questions about the two jinn they would be fighting and the natives that they would have to contend with. Thinking back on that, Gablona suddenly realized that the bulk of the questions had been about the beliefs of the Al 'Shiga, and several of the other assassins had displayed more than a passing interest in what they were hearing. But not one comment was made about what they had heard.

He was a cold one, Corbin realized. When he had told Hassan that failure resulting in his death would mean instant condemnation to hell, the assassin looked at him unmoving, even while the others cried aloud in dismay, babbling that they would prevent such a thing from ever happening.

There had been one curious question to be answered. Hassan had inquired as to which direction was south. He was about to ask why, but some instinct warned him not to, and he pointed off at a right angle to where the sun had risen. He finally remembered the reason behind that question when the assassins had immediately knelt for prayer, the moment they were safely in their fortress.

Realizing that the charade had to be played, Gablona had knelt with them, mimicking their actions. He remembered enough from their history to realize that being a nonbeliever would lower his status. Inwardly he cursed his people for not briefing him thoroughly on this. Now, if it had been Aldin doing the briefing, he thought almost wistfully. . .

He suddenly noticed that Hassan was still waiting for him to look where he was pointing, a gentle, almost innocent smile on his face. Corbin leaned over to look.

A low chuckle escaped from Corbin's lips as he peered down the street. So that's where Aldin's safe house was supposed to be. So now Aldin was out on the street with nowhere to hide. Pulling back, he looked at Hassan and smiled.

"Is that one of the other lords then?" Hassan asked quietly.

"That's Aldin all right."

"I thought so. You could see by the way those men around him stood in the protective circle. I've heard of such men—they come from beyond the Mongol lands to the east."

Corbin looked at Hassan wondering where in his time he had heard of samurai.

"They have some men such as us—ninja, I believe they are called. The grand master above me had dealings with them from time to time. Good warriors, but bound too much by their honor."

Corbin nodded in agreement and smiled. He liked this Hassan, he was a man such as himself. He liked him but also knew that he'd have to be controlled, for men such as himself were always a threat in the end.

"Should we try for them?" Corbin asked, realizing that he'd have to concede all tactical decisions to this far more experienced warrior.

Hassan pressed back up to the spy slit and watched for a moment. "If only we had a bow. He's not a hundred paces up the street. It'd be such an easy shot."

"What about a rush now, and get it over with?"

Hassan, his eye still to the slit, shook his head.

"No surprise. Always we must use surprise. Those look like good swordsmen, they're already on edge, waiting for a rush from any quarter. No, my lord, it is stealth, when your enemy does not expect it, that wins. First you intimidate, then you wear down through fear, then finally you kill."

"But what if they come up this way?"

Hassan still shook his head.

"Even if we rushed out, we can pass only two out the door at a time, and all their men would be there to greet us. We know where they are, but they do not know where we are. Whichever way they go, two of mine will follow. Wherever they finally hide, we shall know. Then time and darkness will be our allies.

"Besides, one of my men is already carrying the message of alliance to the lord Sigma, whom you saw moving into his hiding place on the next street. The agreement for the moment will be struck. Let him make the first move and then we shall follow up."

Hassan looked back at Corbin and smiled with a wolfish grin, and Corbin could only smile in return.

"Well, we just can't stand here," Zergh said impatiently.

"He's right, my lord," Oishi replied. "Your fortress is lost, the blue robes know where you are, and we must find shelter before darkness."

Aldin looked up at the sky and saw that the sun had shifted significantly toward what he figured would be the equivalent of west. These damn twelve-hour days were going to be difficult to get used to.

He looked up and down the street, which was now completely deserted, the neighbors having fled back inside once they realized that the fire no longer threatened them.

As if to add weight to Zergh's comment, a distant shouting echoed up from the direction from which they had come.

Oishi turned and nodded to Takashi, who leading several of the samurai, raced back up the street. After gaining the corner, they peered around the edge and then came running back.

"A mob," Takashi barked. "Hundreds of them coming up the street!"

"This way!" Oishi commanded, and without waiting to see if Aldin agreed, he started at slow trot on up into the foreign quarter.

Half a dozen samurai, Takashi in the lead, ran ahead toward the first side alley. They took a quick look around the corner and then motioned for the party to hurry up.

At a run, the group followed their lead.

Aldin kept scanning the buildings to either side, noticing the faint outlines of faces in the spy slits, sometimes Human, sometimes Gaf, and occasionally the triangular shape of a Xsarn.

Nearing the corner, they passed a house, and Aldin noticed that there were no curious faces looking out. It struck him as strange but then he pushed on. Oishi, beside him, was watching cautiously as well, ready in an instant to react to any attack, be it missile or an armed host pouring out of a building.

They reached the first corner and, turning, ran down the alley. The path was so narrow that only a thin crack of sky was visible from above, so that they ran in a dank semitwilight. One of the samurai stayed back for a moment, watching the corner they had just turned, then sprinted down after them.

"They've just turned the corner by the fire," he shouted breathlessly, coming up to Oishi to report.

The party had stopped for a moment in a small plaza with half a dozen streets to choose from.

"This way," Oishi barked, and started up a steep winding path, so that within seconds after they cleared the plaza they were lost from view. They knew the pursuit was still on though for a wild howling echoed up the street after them: the blue robes shouting their anger that the murderers of their kin had so cowardly run away and not stayed to face the hundreds wearing the red knot.

Gasping like an asthmatic in a dust storm, Aldin struggled to keep up, not wishing to accept the indignity of having some of the samurai carry him along. For long minutes they continued up the winding steps, until finally coming up short at a closed gate. It was obvious that the festivities occurring in the rest of the city were being enjoyed with particular abandon just on the other side.

"Damn, the other end of the foreign quarter," Zergh snarled. "We can't very well go back out into the main city."

"We can't retreat, either," Oishi replied grimly. Looking up and down the street, they saw no way out, other than to go all the way back down to the plaza and hope that the mob hadn't arrived there yet. But one of the samurai who'd stayed at the end of the retreating group came around the corner.

"They're fanning out from the plaza," he gasped. "Some of them are coming this way."

Oishi looked grimly around. Silently he pulled his right arm free from his robes, tucking the sleeve into his belt, thus leaving his sword arm freer for action. As one, the warriors around him followed suit.

Aldin looked at Zergh, who gave him a shrug as he pulled his two-handed sword free from its scabbard and then, with a gesture of bravado, imitated the samurai in freeing his right arm. The warriors around him murmured their approval at the sight of his powerful sword arm, not knowing that they were looking at a Gaf long past his prime.

"If it's time to die," Aldin said, his voice quavering slightly with fear, "I am honored to do so with men like you."

He knew the line was nothing but bravado, the type of thing one of his favorite generals from the past, such as Napoleon, or even Alexander, would have said to inspire the troops before battle. But what the hell, these were his troops, and this was going to be his first, and most likely his last, battle. But instantly he could see the effect.

Oishi drew in a sharp breath; a look of respect crossed his face, and quickly spread to the others around him. There was also a brief glimmer in the samurai leader's eyes, the slight twitch of a smile. Was it that Oishi had figured out that this was a game? Aldin wondered.

Oishi formed his men into three ranks, covering the street from one side to the other as the roar of the approaching mob drew closer.

"I say there," came a booming voice. "Would you lads care for a drink first before the fun?"

Aldin whirled around to find a Gaf of tremendous build standing in a narrow doorway. He was dressed like all Gafs, no matter what their home world, in the gaudiest of outfits, which in his case was a green-and-orange-checkered jumpsuit. In his hand he held a massive decanter of wine, which he held up in a friendly gesture. Several of the samurai broke free from the line and, approaching the Gaf, lowered their swords, ready to strike at the slightest provocation.

"Whoever's running this crew, would you kindly tell these fellows to point their stickers in some direction other than my belly or my friends up above might get upset."

Aldin turned his gaze away from the bizarre-looking Gaf in the doorway and saw that the narrow upper-floor windows were occupied with Gafs, while more, with swords drawn, stood behind their leader.

In the distance the shouts of the mob grew louder.

"Turn those blades aside," Aldin shouted, and he pushed through his men to come up before the Gaf. With a cry of alarm Oishi followed him, to step in front of his commander.

Aldin quickly collected his wits.

"I could use a drink," he said smoothly, extending his hand to the Gaf. If this being was one of Sigma's berserkers, he thought, then this will be over with sooner rather than later, but he had to take the chance.

With a roaring laugh the Gaf gave him the jug, which held at least two dozen liters. Aldin struggled to bring it up to his lips.

It was a Gaf favorite, their sparkling muscatel, and he nearly choked as too much of it splashed down his throat.

Aldin took a deep breath and hoped that his nose was telling him right. "Smells like a tavern in there behind you."

"That it is, and I own it. Only one on this entire stink hole. Locals round here hate them, you know. It's a sin, so I've got to keep it quiet."

"Could we perhaps adjourn our toasting each other to the inside?" Aldin asked a little too hurriedly.

The Gaf looked at him and smiled with a toothy grin that set Zergh on edge.

The tavernkeeper craned his neck to look down the street and then shifted his gaze back to Aldin. "Table fees are awful expensive."

"We'll pay it," Aldin said, trying to keep from shouting.

"Hundred katars a man," he said, surveying the group.

"My brother Gaf with you though can have his table for free."

Aldin did a quick calculation and realized that was four hundred more than the entire war chest given to them by the Xsarn.

"Ten, and that's a fair price," Zergh barked back.

"Negotiations are over," the Gaf said with a smile, and he stepped back to close the door. Oishi started to move forward, but with a warning wave of his finger the tavernkeeper pointed first up to his comrades in the windows and then to the heavily armed Gafs behind him.

"Twenty-five," Aldin cried in desperation.

"Seventy-five and it's a bargain," the tavernkeeper replied smoothly and slowly, as if he had all the time in the world.

That'd leave them more than seven hundred, Aldin thought, and was about to agree when Zergh stopped him.

"Not one-tenth of a katar over fifty," Zergh snapped back in peevish tone. "Otherwise before we die we'll kick your door down and let the blue robes come in after they've finished with us!"

Aldin shot his companion a look of anguish.

The tavernkeeper threw back his head and roared with laughter, but he was barely heard, so close was the mob in its rampaging approach.

"Sixty and not a tenth less!"

"Done!" Aldin cried, and dived for the doorway.

"Wait, wait, the color of your money first," the Gaf said, extending an open paw.

Frantically Aldin spun around and fumbled for the pouch that he had tucked into his shirt. After pulling it out, he started to count out the coins, all the time the shouts of the mob echoing around him.

Counting out the heavy coin that was the universal barter of the trading worlds of the Cloud, he found that he didn't have the right change. With a shout of exasperation he simply thrust the money into the Gaf's hand, who then hurriedly handed it back to one of his assistants.

"Your change will be returned momentarily," the Gaf said evenly, and then stepped aside.

In a mad rush the samurai stormed in, Oishi standing outside, urging his men to hurry. As the last man rushed inside Oishi leaped through the door and put his shoulder to it, while the tavernkeeper threw down the heavy steel bar.

He then pulled open a tiny peephole and offered the aperture to Aldin for a look outside.

They'd not been a moment too soon, and rather than feeling grateful he felt a maddening rage at the Gaf for having timed things so close.

The mob came storming up the street, stopping at last at the closed gate. They milled around, their angry shouts echoing in the narrow street.

"They must've have come this way!"

"Maybe they're sorcerers, as we heard," a huge Gaf wearing a blue robe roared. "And used their magic to escape."

"Perhaps they ran down one of the other streets!"

"Let's tear these buildings apart anyhow," another one screamed, and some shouted their agreement. One of them looking threateningly straight at Aldin, who realized that his eye must be visible at the slit.

Instinct told him to step back, and not a second later a narrow stiletto poked through where his eye had been.

The Gaf behind him roared with laughter at his discomfort and then slammed the steel cover port shut, snapping the blade in half.

There was an angry shout on the other side and pounding on the door. Finally the voices started to drift away as they went off to other quarters in search of their lost prey.

"Care for that drink?" the Gaf asked good-naturedly. "After all, you paid for it."

Aldin followed his host into a low-ceilinged room that stank from overripe wine, bad food, and the obvious effects consuming them had on some visitors' stomachs.

The Gaf and several of his burly assistants got behind the bar and pulled out enough mugs for his new clients. Several jugs the size of the one the Gaf still held in his hand were pulled up and uncorked.

The samurai looked around with a mixture of awe and disgust. Awe for the Gafs, whom they found fascinating. The somewhat canine look of the Gafs inspired them with the thought that perhaps these creatures were under the protection of heaven. The awe was there, as well, for the fact that the Gafs stood near nine feet in height and could obviously crush any one of them with a single blow. They had yet to realize that the strength was offset by slower speed and a coordination that in a Human would be considered clumsy.

As Japanese, the filth of the tavern repulsed them, and they made their disgust obvious by the way they gingerly picked up the heavy mugs and eyed them suspiciously before starting to pour their drinks.

All the while Oishi stood in the back of the room, watching everything, letting nothing escape his gaze. They'd been saved, to be sure, but this could still be a trap within a trap, the drink drugged to make the kill easier. He barked a single command in Japanese, overriding the speech implant.

The other samurai looked to their commander and placed their mugs down.

"Ah, poison you fear, is it?" the tavernkeeper roared, and with a laugh he went to each jug in turn and raised it to his lips, swallowing off a healthy swill.

"Come on, you paid for it," he said. Though the others could not sense it, Aldin picked up an offended tone in the Gaf's voice. The accent had the ring of Jurka to it, Bukha Taug's home world, where hospitality rites were held in the same esteem that all Gafs of the old had once honored.

He decided to take the chance.

"Most expensive cheap swill I've ever bought," Aldin said quietly, as he poured out a drink and held the mug up in salute. He looked at Oishi out of the corner of his eye, letting him know not to interfere, and then he downed the drink.

It really was what Gafs thought was a fine wine, and he almost choked on the bubbly sweetness of it.

But Oishi would not relent and the samurai sat around their tables in silence, some of them casting longing gazes upon the heavy wine jugs before them.

"As you want it," the Gaf said, "but mind you now, you've paid for them and I've provided, so I don't want to hear any complaints."

"I was wondering what else you might be able to provide," Aldin asked, coming up to lean against the bar.

"Now, I knew it was a lucky day when I saw you fellows running up the street, straight to Maladi's tavern," the Gaf said with a wink. "Customers, I said to myself, and on festival day, no less, when most folks are home quaking behind their door for fear that the celebrations might get out of hand. They kind of did this time, heard some buildings got burnt, a couple dozen merchants killed. But that's life in the Hole, we say around here."

"We could use a place to stay for the night."

Maladi's eyes sparkled with delight.

"It'll cost," he said smoothly.

"Come on and just give them a break, will you?" came a voice from the swinging doorway behind the tavern. The door snapped open and a towering woman came out.

In a coincidence that was almost uncanny, the woman looked almost identical to Aldin's first wife, so that he gave her an obvious double take. Her hair was dark, almost black, showing an early streaking to gray along the bangs that covered her forehead. Her figure was slightly plump, but definitely not unattractive in the plain shirt and loose trousers that she wore tightly belted around her waist.

If there was one difference between her and his first spouse, it was with the eyes; they were a light blue, rather than green, and did not carry a look of snakelike cunning.

She scanned Aldin's face for a moment, noticing how he was staring at her, and then took in the rest of the group.

"I'm Mari," she said evenly. "Welcome to the Pig's Kiss. I'm half owner, along with him." And she pointed at the Gaf.

"The Pig's Kiss, what a name for this place," Maladi roared. "Why, if the Shiga knew that, they'd really go wild."

"You're the game players, aren't you?" Mari said evenly, ignoring Maladi.

"Ah, so that's it!" Maladi said. "I thought it might be you. You wouldn't be Gablona, by chance?"

"No. Aldin Larice," Aldin said coldly. "Why?"

"Too bad," Maladi replied, suddenly cooling a bit. "Got my money on Gablona living—five hundred katars cross-bet twenty different ways. Damn me, I even had a couple riding on your dying the first day, too."

How the hell did this Gaf already know about the games? Aldin wondered, but realized this wasn't the time to ask.

"What about lodgings for the night?" Aldin asked, coming back to his main concern.

"Now, knowing you're the gamers sets things different. In fact, I just shot myself in my foot, I did, by letting you in.

Could say I lost my five-hundred-katar bet, seeing how Gablona's first rival would be a smear out on the street by now if I hadn't."

"I'll make good on your lost bet," Aldin said wearily.

"Ah, now that's the spirit. Now, beyond that your lodgings will cost—"

"Five hundred will buy 'em lodgings for the week," Mari snapped. "And that's still twice the going rate. Anyhow, you only bet a hundred, and fifty of that was mine."

Maladi turned on Mari with an evil look, but she stood her ground.

"I already heard what you charged them for their first drink."

"Business, purely business."

"Look at it this way," Mari interjected. "They're the gamers, you'll have the ringside seat and the inside track on the betting if they stay. They leave, and you lost out on the information you could sell."

Maladi suddenly broke into a grin again.

"Knew I went into business with you for a reason," he roared good-naturedly. "Second round of drinks and dinner are on me for tonight." And with a laugh he kicked the swinging door open and disappeared into the kitchen to get the cooks working.

Aldin could only shake his head. The money that was supposed to last them for the full eighty game days was almost gone in the first four hours.

The woman was the only one left as Maladi's guards followed their boss into the back, and she drew closer to Aldin.

"That was generous of him throwing dinner in," he said sarcastically.

"You could still be out on the street," she shot back.

Yes, he realized, he certainly could be.

"Let's just hope that he doesn't realize for a while that when your enemies make a move on you, this establishment might be in the way." And a conspiratorial smile flickered across her face and then disappeared.

Aldin found that he was still staring at her, completely unnerved by her resemblance to his ex.

"Something about me bothering you?" she asked evenly.

"Well, ah, you see . . ."

"It's just you look a lot like his damnable ex-wife." Zergh laughed, coming up to Aldin's side.

"Does that bother you?" she asked coldly.

"Ah, no. Well, actually, yes," Aldin said, fumbling for an answer.

"Reminiscing about your loving wife is all fine and good," Zergh interrupted. "First, though, how do you know about the game?"

"Why, everyone around here knows," she replied as if it were a fact they should have been aware of.

"This certainly screws the situation." Zergh cursed quietly. "If the money's running on Gablona, then it will be to everyone's interest to help him out."

"Were you aware of this?" Zergh asked, looking over at Aldin. "I was with the samurai the whole time and completely out of touch with what was happening."

"How could I? I was locked up the whole time you were away. Yaroslav must have known, but damn it all, he didn't say a word."

"Well, it's common knowledge around here," Mari replied, pouring herself a drink. "Most likely even the Shiga know about it, the way the foreign quarter was buzzing."

"And there's another thing," Aldin said quietly. "Maladi really spilled it when he called it a game. Oishi must have heard, and that sure as hell doesn't match up with what he's been told about this fight. He thinks I'm fighting mortal enemies, and then that loud-mouthed Gaf tells him it's a game. It's still a mortal conflict for us, but somehow knowing the details might not settle well with him."

Aldin looked over his shoulder and saw that Oishi was looking straight at him, as if reading his thoughts.

There was only one thing to do, Aldin realized, and that was to come completely clean and tell the whole thing out.

"It can wait for now," Zergh responded. "Let's get some food in us first, secure the guards, and then take a closer look at this place."

"Some advice," Mari interrupted. "Don't think about trying to doublecross Maladi about paying just 'cause you have all those armed ruffians. He's not a bad sort and usually keeps his word, but if he smells a double cross, he'll have more friends here than you can whistle up in a year, and they'll turn your heads over to the Shiga as a payoff to keep them from bothering us."

"Well, that's a nice way of putting it, but I've got a question for you," Aldin replied.

"Go on then. But I already know it. The reason Maladi brought you in was the profit. My reason for giving you a place to stay? Well, let's just call it profit as well—business's been slow lately. Something's been stirring with the Shiga, and most of the merchants have gotten out of here over the last couple of weeks. It's that simple," she said evenly, holding Aldin's gaze the whole time she spoke.

Aldin could only nod in reply.

"I hope the food's better than the wine," he said dryly, realizing it was best to shift the subject, even though his curiosity was aroused concerning this woman.

"It should be, I'm the head cook for this dump." And with a smile she turned and went back into the kitchen.

Aldin turned and motioned for Oishi to join him at a grease-covered table in the corner of the room.

The samurai sat down by Aldin's side, his back to the wall. Nothing was said, but Aldin could feel the tension.

"I have some explaining," Aldin began lamely,

"I have not asked," Oishi replied formally.

"But I owe you the truth. I've lied too many times, to too many people. I'm not going to now. I needed men with honor, men I could trust, and that is why I wanted you."

"But to a samurai life is honor, and honor the reason for living."

"That is why I wanted you. It is true some men are calling this a game. I shall tell you about that when time permits. But to me it is more than that. I've studied you, Oishi; I've studied warriors throughout history. If there is one thing positive I can say about some of them, it is that those who reached true greatness did so because they cherished honor.

"The men I face are without that. They believe that it is cunning, that it is deceit that brings power. True, it can, but it is a power that is chimerical, for in the end their deceit is revealed, and then their power fails. The friends of some of those men think what we are going through here is a source of amusement, a game, if you will, for them to bet upon.

"But there is more to this, Oishi. Far more. For me this is a question of honor. Can men of honor win against men of deceit? If there is a game in all of this, then that is it. A test to prove that we can triumph."

Zergh, who was sitting at the same table, could not help but give a snort of disdain. "Then explain how men of deceit usually win. You're an idealist, Aldin; that's why I came along, to protect you from your own idealism."

Oishi was silently watching the two.

"Then if this is a game," Aldin replied, "let this be the testing of it. I'm talking about the broader sweep of history, Zergh. There are times of darkness when deceit does win, but I'm convinced, as well, that the tide of Human, or Gaf, or even Xsarn nature wins out, and sets things back onto a path of progress, throwing down those who win by deceit.

"I want to prove that to those bastards up there watching this."

Aldin shifted and turned back to Oishi. "There's a lot more to explain about those who are watching this contest. But know for now that I chose you because I wanted men of honor around me, and in turn know that I will not deceive you."

He held Oishi with his gaze. For a long quiet moment the samurai stared at Aldin, probing, looking to see if there was a different answer hidden within.

"We'll need to talk yet more, my lord," Oishi said quietly.

"Something's up!"

Aldin looked up to see Takashi standing by the table. "What is it?"

"There's a Gaf outside who wants to talk to you, and to you alone."

"Who is it?" Oishi barked, coming to his feet.

"Claims to be an envoy from the lord Sigma and wants to arrange a meeting."

"How the hell did Sigma know where to find us?" Aldin asked.

Takashi could only shrug his shoulders, while behind him the doorway swung open and Maladi came strolling out to check on his guests.

Aldin and Zergh looked at each other.

"Word travels fast," Zergh observed dryly.

"I'll see to it. Then we'll talk more later," Oishi said, coming to his feet, and strode off to meet with the envoy who was still out in the alleyway.

Zergh looked at Aldin and leaned across the table.

"Looks like you're on probation," he said evenly.

And what if I fail? Aldin thought nervously.

CHAPTER 6

"He is unarmed," Oishi said, "but still I don't trust him, my lord. I've seen curious weapons here, and he might have something hidden on his body."

"He's right," Zergh replied. "A Gaf like that one—" and he pointed over to the messenger in the corner of the room "—could crush a man with a single blow. Remember, Sigma has berserkers; those warriors are convinced that dying in battle is the final glory."

"But he won't give you the message?" Aldin asked, looking back at Oishi.

The samurai shook his head. "Insisted that it must be to you alone."

"We could force it out of him," Zergh responded, his voice cold.

Aldin looked over at his friend. Zergh still surprised him at times. When need be, he could display an absolutely deadly cunning.

"If we tie him down, will you do the torturing?" Aldin replied. "Remember, we're no longer talking theory and academic questions of war, this is cold hard reality."

"If need be," Zergh replied, but to his relief Aldin could hear the doubt in his old comrade's voice.

"Zergh has just given the answer," Oishi replied, and with a bow he turned and walked away.

Minutes later Aldin came up to the table in the corner of the tavern and sat down. Across from him sat one of the legendary beserkers of Basak, perhaps the finest individual warriors in Gaf history, who were trained from childhood in the belief that the only moment of reality was the moment of death and the taking with you of servants to do your bidding in the next world. If the manner of death was considered exemplary, their comrades would sacrifice additional servants to go with them before their funeral pyre. Thus they actually had a rudimentary rating system classifying one's death as a one-servant death, or higher, depending upon how dramatic the comrade's departure.

Knowing the proper approach, Aldin stared at the warrior with a full display of teeth.

"You shall crawl before me, when I go to my ancestors," Aldin opened.

The Gaf spat on the floor and as he did so the samurai, who'd drawn back, reached for their blades, ready to avenge the insult. But Aldin motioned them to be still.

"In the next world you shall eat my spoors and consider it an honor."

Aldin laughed in reply and, pulling up a chair, sat down across from the messenger.

The Gaf's hands and feet were bound. At first he'd almost refused, roaring that he would be at their mercy, until Aldin had finally pledged to serve him in the next world if he was betrayed. But he could see the berserker was still nervous with the arrangement.

"You've agreed to much," Aldin said, "to allow yourself to be thus bound."

"I swore oath to Taug Sigma to bring the message; if I failed, then there was but one choice left."

"A pity to waste your life on suicide with no servants to

wait upon you, your siblings to be shamed that their brother had failed in the leaving of life."

"The Gaf was silent.

"What is the message then?"

"Taug Sigma has charged me to arrange a meeting between you and him."

Aldin sat back. Sigma, as usual, did not waste time. But why the hell hadn't he talked before they came down, unless it was because there was no way they could hold a coversation without Gablona being present.

"And has he met with the other Taug, the one called Gablona?"

The Gaf only looked across at him and smiled.

"Foolish of me to ask a man sworn to die for his Taug."

"I expected you to be a fool. Your guards are puny; many of them will serve us before long."

"We shall see," Aldin replied evenly. "Tell Sigma that he is welcome to come here to meet with me at any time."

The Gaf leaned back and gave a short bark of disdainful laughter. "Rather you should come to meet with him."

"I am not that simple to fool," Aldin snapped. "Sigma knows that."

"Sigma is willing to arrange several alternate meeting places."

"Unacceptable. If he can select, then he can prepare the trap."

"Then we must have an intermediary," the Gaf replied.

Aldin sat back.

Of his two opponents, he trusted Sigma more than Gablona, and he suspected that Sigma felt the same. An alliance at the start would be to their advantage. He had to meet with him face-to-face in order to work out the arrangements though. He couldn't let this chance be passed up. And besides, Sigma already had a tactical advantage: he knew where Aldin was hiding but Aldin did not know Sigma's location.

"All right then, we'll meet," he said cautiously. "We'll let someone else select the place."

"Who then?" the Gaf replied.

Aldin realized immediately that the Gaf's ready agreement meant that Sigma had foreseen Aldin's thinking and had ordered the Gaf to agree. Could this be a trap within the trap?

He hesitated for a moment, and then realized that this game was for real. It was no longer mere risks on money, he'd have to weigh the odds on every decision and then gamble—with his life.

Aldin looked back over his shoulder. "Zergh, go back in the kitchen and bring out Mari."

Aldin turned back to look at the Gaf. After upturning two mugs, he poured a drink out for the both of them. The Gaf eyed the drinks suspiciously.

"Tell me which one to take first," Aldin replied politely, and the Gaf pointed out one of the mugs, which Aldin brought up and then drained off. The Gaf reached out with his bound hands, clumsily grasped the mug, and finished his drink in turn.

"Did Sigma ever tell you what this was really all about?" Aldin asked cautiously as he poured another drink.

"What?"

"Why we're fighting."

"Ah, he told me about the gods who set him down to be tested against you and the other evil demon."

Aldin could only laugh.

"Did you want something?" a voice interrupted, and Aldin turned to face Mari, who stood before him with a slightly sardonic smile lighting her features.

"You are now ambassador extraordinaire," Aldin announced with a pompous tone.

"You've been drinking too much," she replied sarcastically.

"Ah, just like my ex," Aldin responded. "We need a go-between, a neutral who will select a meeting spot."

"A Human woman?" The Gaf sneered.

Mari shot him an evil glance.

"Then we'll ask her boss to work on this as well. The two of them will decide on a place in secret. She'll go with you to inform Sigma. He and six guards will then proceed to the meeting place, while Maladi over there," Aldin said, pointing to the hulking Gaf who was sitting behind the bar eyeing them curiously, "Will guide us. Two of your guards and two of mine will first enter and agree the place is secure and then we shall meet. The woman will go with you, and the tavernkeeper will go with me."

"Why the hell should I go rather than Maladi?" Mari

asked. "Not to say I'm willing to be part of this thing anyhow."

"Because I trust you more than I trust him. He could go with this messenger and arrange a double cross if he saw enough profit in it."

The Gaf looked at him, a slight smile crossing his lips. "My Taug said you were crafty. All right then, it is agreed."

Aldin smiled inwardly, for through Mari he'd be able to find out Sigma's hiding place.

"You've agreed, but I sure as hell haven't," Mari snapped. "The blues are tearing the streets apart looking for you. It's dangerous out there."

"I'll make it worth your while," Aldin replied.

With a snort of disdain Mari turned and stormed off, but Maladi stopped her before she got back into the kitchen and after a brief exchange the tavernkeeper took her by the arm and led her back over to the table.

Aldin felt himself bristle at the Gaf holding her like that, and thought the reaction strange.

"Ah, my noble guest," Maladi started, "so my services are needed. Surely my partner and I would be more than happy to serve you."

"If we do, it's an even split," Mari snapped back.

"But of course," Maladi said offhandedly. "But my services will be steep for such a dangerous task. Shall we say, five hundred katars."

Aldin groaned, but after several minutes of spirited debate he got the Gaf down to two fifty.

"Of course, the fee is split," Aldin finished up. "I'll give Maladi his half, and Sigma will pay you before the meeting starts."

Aldin looked over at the berserker. He knew that talk of money to their class was considered dishonorable, but the Gaf did have to come back with an arrangement, and the berserker growled an agreement.

"Then we meet in one hour. My men will untie you, those two will privately decide on a place, and then you can be on your way."

"In the next world you shall lick the ground before me, so that it is clean for my boot to step upon," the berserker snarled.

"Your brothers and you as well shall carry me upon your backs and cry out that they are thus honored to be my servants," Aldin snapped in reply.

"You're all crazy," Mari growled, as the two spat on the ground by each other's feet.

"You know the blues are rampaging through this quarter looking for you," Sigma said, a cheery smile lighting his features.

Aldin settled back into his chair and looked around the narrow candle-lit room. The approach to the amber merchants' warehouse, owned by a customer of Maladi's, had been a nervous one. All his guards except two left behind to hold the tavern had started out and then been dropped off at an abandoned building a block away, while the six primary guards had pushed on to the place Maladi had designated.

Unfortunately Mari had not made it all the way to Sigma's hiding place, but instead had been held in the street by several Gaf guards until Sigma had returned with the rest of his followers. After a hurried conference he agreed to follow her to the meeting.

But Aldin realized she'd most likely be able to make some fairly good guesses as to where Sigma's fortress was located.

"And I suppose you've thought of selling me to the blues and currying their favor," Aldin replied.

Sigma leaned back and examined his manicured fingernails. Even while in captivity waiting for the game to begin he had somehow arranged to have his hairdresser, masseurs, and body scrubbers attend to him. Aldin wondered how he'd look after forty standard days on the Hole.

"With you gone in the first day, Gablona would turn his attention on me. I prefer you as the buffer."

"And I prefer you as the buffer," Aldin replied.

"Come, come, Aldin, you're only a vasba, and might I add a vasba who's made a lot of citizens angry over the last year. With the wealth and connections Gablona and I have, we can arrange certain advantages down here that you cannot. So, as a betting man, I'd put you on the low end of bets worth taking."

"On the planet of the Al'Shiga," Aldin replied smoothly, "I doubt that."

"With the right promises of money, Gablona and I will be able to buy support."

Aldin could only laugh. "Remember, Sigma, as you've just pointed out, I'm the vasba and you are not. It's my job to arrange fights and to have a superior knowledge of military history. The Al 'Shiga frighten me, and they should frighten you as well. They are perhaps the most potent political movement in the Cloud—if ever they obtained spacefaring capabilities, they could tear us apart."

"Ridiculous. The Skyhook security system prevents that, and that is why all the Kohs who trade here pay a heavy premium to provide security for this world."

"Don't underestimate them," Aldin warned.

"They're all insane animals," Sigma replied disdainfully. "I don't know what was going on when you came down, but it was sheer insanity when my people came through. That tossing of heads, really quite disgusting. Can't understand why they haven't wiped each other out ages ago."

"From what I could see today," Aldin stated, "the killings follow a complex ritual, otherwise they'd all run amok and wipe each other out in a couple of days. That's the curious part of it all. They're all on the razor's edge of mass murder, but somehow their leaders keep them in check.

"Most likely not more than a hundred or two died today. Thus in a typical year maybe five or six thousand die. Add in another ten or fifteen thousand killings a year, to keep their skills in practice, and you could call it social Darwinism if you like."

Aldin sat back in his chair and looked closely at Sigma. It was a shame, he thought, that they were being pitted against each other. Of all the Human Kohs, he had the most respect for this one. Many an evening they had sat like this, debating some point of military history. Sigma was not one of the true connoisseurs who had acquired a master's knowledge in one particular subfield—his sense of business kept him from that, for unlike many of the Kohs, Sigma still believed in having his hands on the family business rather than delegate it to underlings. Thus he didn't have the time that, say, Zola or Vol could devote. To him the games were an interesting hobby, when time allowed it.

"My point is," Aldin continued, "that the Al 'Shiga are to me a terrifying power. Our information about them is quite limited, actually. No outsider has even gotten into their ranks. Hell, I didn't even know about this festival business till I got down here. It's one of the most closed societies in the Cloud. I did read though that for them assassination is a daily part of life. Every move, every action is taken either to complete a kill or in defense against it. Do you realize that when one is accepted as an initiate of the knife, he is given the name of a stranger from another clan? Nothing but the name, no photo, no vid, nothing. He must then find his prey and stalk him."

"To kill?" Sigma asked.

"No, that's the interesting thing. If he kills him outright, then he is still an initiate. If it was organized any other way, then half of all their people would be dead. Remember as well that I'm talking both male and female on this world. So it would be against the logic of survival for a group to have such a system that killed women before they bore the next generation.

"But anyhow, once he receives his ceremonial knife and endures the naming ceremony, the game, so to speak, has started for him. The initiate might spend years trying to track down his target—in fact, many never do, for the concealment of identity is obviously to one's advantage. But if successful in finding the target, the game has only started, for he must isolate his target. If he can succeed in catching his target, he is allowed to perform a single slash with a nonpoisoned blade on the victim's body and then must escape. Only then is one a full member of the clan."

"Madness," Sigma grumbled.

"Genius," Aldin replied sharply. "The body of the clan does not lose anyone, but all the stealth and training for the kill has been brought to bear. Also, if someone is thus struck, they may never be a master. And if they are a master, they lose their rank. Thus it is a ritual with serious connotations of rank and prestige. The game has its deadly side to it. One can defend to the death, and if a witness is present they can kill out of hand. Finally, if a master is cut, he can regain his honor and rank only by assassinating the initiate who took away his honor. Killing of foreigners is viewed as a side action. We're beneath their dignity as far as the games go, but if they feel the urge to try their garrote out some evening, then the attitude is 'boys will be boys.' That's why this place is so deadly. In self-defense, we might kill one of them, and since we are outside of the clans, then everyone in a clan turns against us, as I've so unfortunately already discovered.

"Killing of foreigners is practice to them." Aldin lowered his voice so his guards wouldn't hear. "The same way my own samurai would test their blades on convicts, to make sure the cutting edge was good."

Sigma looked over at Oishi and the other guards who stood by one wall of the room and saw the drawn swords glinting wickedly in the candlelight. He quickly looked back over his shoulder and gathered some reassurance by the sight of the Gaf berserkers with their massive axes drawn and ready if Aldin was considering a double cross.

"It's tied up in their worship of the Seda as well," Aldin continued.

"Yeah, that struck me as strange. Here they worship that thing, and yet only we can go up and down it."

"Precisely," Aldin replied. "It is their holy of holies. According to their tradition, when they were cast down from heaven, it was by us, the demons who took wrongful possession. But it is also their belief that we won because they had allowed themselves to be impure. They believe that those of us who come down do so in part to taunt them."

"So why do they allow it?" Sigma asked.

"That's just it. Because they feel they are not yet ready to return to the Cloud. They need this Ema, who they believe is in hiding. He'll come when one of the clans has purified itself."

"Purified how?"

"Through the proper blood sacrifice. However, we don't know when that will be. It's one of their hidden secrets."

"But what about this red headband business?" Sigma asked, still curious about the Al'Shiga. He realized that this conversation was essential and that, if anything, Aldin was giving away valuable information that could only help.

"I saw them slashing at anyone with glee," he said.

"The highest honor both for killer and victim," Aldin replied. "The festivals are a safety vent, a release, and wearing the red band means you can kill anyone with impunity. It is given to each master and the religious leaders, called ullas, during the thirty-odd festival days. Everyone turns out to see how many heads are taken. It's an honor, as well, if you're cut by a red band but escape. Sort of like the masculinity rituals of Lentra, where the Xsarns jump into the serpent pits and run before the vipers to prove their virtue, or those damn fool dragon runners we see on the vids.

"These people, Human and Gaf, might seem mad," Aldin concluded, "but look at what they've set up. It's a vast training ground for warfare through assassination. They're all promised paradise if they die with blade in hand. To us it seems illogical, because all that killing is turned against themselves, but consider if they were ever taken and turned outward, with modern weapons put in their hands. They could shatter the social system of the Cloud in short order."

"You sound paranoid, Aldin Larice."

"When I look at the Al'Shiga, I have every reason to be. We allow contact because of the trade in precious ancient ambers, which they alone control. They understand the secret that warfare can be fought through other means and that one man can get to his target with enough skill and determination. If anyone, or any system, ever turned them loose on us, we'd be destroyed."

"But that's foolish," Sigma replied. "Besides the Overseers, it's our mutual understanding that conflict hurts business, which has held the peace between the various Kohs. Granted, we wage war against each other, but it is economic war, and all of us benefit in the end. If anyone was so foolish as to use the Al'Shiga, then we'd all suffer, and whoever used them would see that terror turned against him as well."

"But I wonder about the Overseers," Aldin said quietly, keeping his voice down to a whisper. "Why have they allowed us to use this place for our little conflict? Let's not fool ourselves. Setting up a game out on the edge of the Cloud, on the Kolbard, for instance, is one thing. But the Hole is damn near in the middle of the Cloud, with half a dozen major trade lanes intersecting in this solar system. The world where the monetary conference is taking place is in the same system. You know damn well that the Overseers must be aware of this. I can't help but wonder why they're sitting back. And I can't help but wonder, as well, if they might have something to do with the Al 'Shiga movement."

"Just like you." And Sigma gave a snort of derision. "Here you are, facing me, Gablona, and those crazies out there, and you worry about something that doesn't even affect you. If I were you, I'd be thinking about how to survive till tomorrow, and to hell with the Overseers. Why, if anything, I'm praying the Overseers come in and break this game up so we can get out of here."

Aldin was silent.

"Enough of this," Sigma replied. "My guards are most likely hungry—" he dropped his voice to a whisper, "—and their leader has already told me that they can be most disagreeable if they don't get four full meals a day. Let's finish our business so we can get a good night's rest."

"Are you then proposing an agreement?" Aldin asked cautiously.

"If I didn't have that in mind, I wouldn't have asked you to come out and meet me," Sigma replied.

"What are the terms then?" Aldin asked.

"Nonaggression for the duration."

"Do you already have the same agreement with Gablona?" Aldin asked.

Aldin watched Sigma's eyes, but there was no waver. But he knew Sigma was too much of an old hand to give himself away.

"With that madman? You heard the threats he shouted at me before we came down."

There was no way he'd know for sure, but to be on the safe side Aldin had to assume that not only had there been an understanding, but that Sigma might be setting him up as well.

"Just nonaggression then?" Aldin asked. "I was thinking of shared information and daily contact between two of our representatives for the latest updates on Gablona."

"But of course," Sigma said.

Aldin settled back in his chair and eyed Sigma coldly. "For thirty years I've deferred to you, since you were a Koh, but there's no title, no rank down here. I'm going to give you a blunt warning. First, I won't come for you as long as you don't come for me. I think you know me well enough to know that I'm speaking the truth. But if you do come for me, then I'll not stop till I've taken you out."

Sigma bristled at the threat but didn't reply.

"And secondly," Aldin continued, "if you've made a deal with Gablona, I'll be betting on your being the first to die, and it will be by his hands. He wants you almost as much as he wants me. Don't trust him."

"I can imagine if I had met with him, he'd be saying the same about you," Sigma replied.

"No doubt, but the difference is I think you know who is the more believable."

There was a second of hesitation, but then the same dispassionate smile returned. And in that second Aldin knew that this meeting was a setup to lure him out.

"I think it'll be best if I leave now," Aldin said sharply, and he rose from the table. "And beyond Gablona, don't underestimate the Al'Shiga. Their part in this game, I fear, is more than just simple madness."

He motioned for his guards, who fell in around him. Maladi and Mari joined the group as well. Oishi stepped out first, checking the street, and then motioned for the party to follow.

The foul, filth-encrusted alleyway was silent as the party slipped out. One of the samurai stood by the door, acting as rear guard, while the group continued on up the path to where the rest of their guards waited.

It was Mari who suddenly grabbed Aldin by the sleeve, holding up her hand for silence, and pointed.

Oishi, noticing her move, started for her, suspecting the worst, but then, following where she pointed he froze as well.

The next alleyway up, and across the street, was as dark as the others, but somehow there was a feeling that a particular threat lurked there.

"Alarm!"

The shout echoed down the street, and at the same instant there was a faint flash in the dim light. One of the samurai leaped before Aldin even as he tried to back against the wall, in a desperate attempt to hide. There was a dull thump and a slight gasp of pain.

From up the street dark forms came surging out. For a

moment Aldin felt a wild panic, then in the starlight he saw the flowing robes of the samurai, blades drawn, racing down the street toward the party. Oishi ran up the street, shouting a command, and some of the party turned into the side alleyway. Seconds later they reemerged and came back to surround Aldin.

But Aldin did not notice. Crouched over a body, he sat in stunned disbelief. The samurai lay before him, the hilt of the blade in his chest rising and falling spasmodically as life drained away. The blade became still.

Zergh pushed his way through the crowd and then saw Aldin.

"Thank the heavens," Zergh cried softly. "I thought it was you."

"No," Oishi replied, "it was only one of mine." And Aldin looked up to see the bitterness and rage on the samurai's face.

"He didn't have to." Aldin groaned. "He stepped right in front of it."

"He did what his honor demanded, what he would have done for any lord, at least for what he thought was his lord," Oishi replied coldly.

Aldin came to his feet and looked closely at Oishi, and then with a growing sense of shame he turned away.

"Definitely not one of the blues," Zergh said matter-of-factly, having not even noticed the bitter exchange.

"How can you tell?" Oishi asked, kneeling down alongside the body.

"If I may?" Zergh asked, and then without waiting for permission he pulled the blade out of the corpse and handed it to Aldin.

"Earth origin," Aldin whispered. "Looks to be medieval Persian."

"Gablona," Zergh said quietly.

Zergh took the blade from Aldin's hands and tucked it into his belt.

"If I may interrupt," Maladi said, his voice edged with nervousness. "You may discuss the worth of the blade when we're back at the tavern; I can even put you in touch with a collector hereabouts, but let's get off the street. You've just lost a man, the slayer is still loose, your friend Sigma's guards are not far away, and there are the blues, and your other rival, to think about as well. For reasons of health I think it best to seek a better climate."

With a grunt of approval Oishi came back to his feet and directed some of the men to help carry their fallen comrade home, and the party set off.

The group arrived at the tavern several minutes later without incident, the relief evident on all their faces when the door was safely bolted.

"Who called the alarm?" Oishi asked, once they were back in the taproom. "It was good work."

The room was silent.

Aldin looked over at Zergh, who sat in one corner examining the blade. He shrugged without replying.

"No one?" Oishi asked.

"We heard the shout, and that was when we charged out," Seiji replied. "We thought it was you calling."

"Then who?" Oishi asked, looking over at Aldin.

The attempt was by Gablona, that was obvious, so he was out. The locals certainly wouldn't have intervened, and Sigma wouldn't have warned him either. If there wasn't anyone left, then who had? Mari had helped, to be sure, but still there was someone else out on the street who had stopped him from being killed. If someone wanted him to live, who was it, and why?

CHAPTER 7

"I'M GLAD YOU WANTED TO MEET WITH ME," KURST SAID, AS he came in through the door. "I've had some great ideas since we last met."

Zola couldn't help but smile at his probability analyzer. This man had made him tens of billions in just the first day of the game. The Kohs had begged for the stock in the gaming business, and now five days into the match, shares had nearly doubled in value as the full impact of the game started to take hold. Considering his own fifty-one percent share, the doubling in value had earned him yet billions more. He had every reason to feel expansive.

Behind him a bank of vids was monitoring the messages that were being flashed from one end of the Cloud to the other, and even on into the smaller Magellanic. The ad people had cost a bundle, over a billion up front, but within hours their campaign had swept every tech world within reach by transjump link. Ads designed to every species, culture, and eco-standing had filled the airways almost nonstop now for days, pitching the game and posting every move of the three players.

The pitches had to be tailor designed for each market. Mistakes could be costly. On the world of Ilm a single mistake showing a Gaf of the Obe class standing within a hundred meters of one from the Jiil class would have triggered revulsion and destruction of every vid transmitter that had dared to show such sacrilege.

The Ophet system required special care, for the covering of one's genitalia was considered a disgusting practice designed to draw attention. Religious leaders would be sure to howl at such sexually provocative material. Each of the worlds therefore had to have a system set up to match the particular cultural mores, and the ad execs were sharp with their calculations, for all could see that this was a short-term account that needed immediate and massive exposure.

Then there was the printing of tickets. This was the first major difficulty and had become acute, causing a serious paper crisis throughout the Cloud as tickets were printed out in the tens of billions every hour. On several worlds paper stocks had been completely depleted, triggering riots that had killed thousands when no more tickets could be issued.

Riots broke out, too, as lines, sometimes kilometers in length, formed up for the gambling opportunity of the millennium. Sales offices had been set up through the management firms, agencies, and government stations controlled by the various Kohs. But still there were not enough locations to handle the flood of buyers who were bombarded nonstop by the advertising campaign.

In some areas, those who successfully purchased tickets would be set upon the moment they left the office and torn apart by the mob, who'd yet to realize that just holding the ticket was useless. For to avoid fraud and the printing of bogus tickets, an elaborate system had been established whereby each ticket purchased was identified, and the purchaser's personal identity number printed on the stub, with the information stored in the local computer. Twice a day the local information was uploaded to the main systems on Ator, which created another crisis. So much data was flowing in that the systems were hopelessly overtaxed. The main offices were simply swamped with the backlog, and as a result, no one even bothered to run a betting analysis.

Then there was the crisis of computer capacity, which resulted in the sudden purchase of massive memory and data-handling systems. They had to be plugged in even while the system was running, all, of course, at triple overtime pay by the high priests of the industry, whose mysterious jargon was always a guarantee for yet higher prices.

There were other factors, as well, that the Kohs had not anticipated. For one, the commerce of the Cloud had suffered tremendously over the last five days. Billions of employees from their various business ventures were calling in sick, so they could stand on line to buy tickets. Millions of others had to be pulled off their regular duties in order to manage the game.

Ships were not being loaded, passengers and crews were staying close to the nearest betting gate, ready to place the next day's wager as the odds changed. It was not serious enough yet to start an economic panic, but the trend was disturbing. But for the moment Zola didn't care, as the man who first thought of it all pulled up a chair and accepted the brandy and cigar that he now took without asking—as was his right.

"Have you seen the latest reports?" Zola asked, waxing enthusiastic.

"It's already topped two point two trillion on the eighty-day tickets," Kurst shouted. "Considering the lag time on the machines and communications systems, I'm willing to project that by the end of this week ten trillion tickets will have been sold!"

"Ten trillion in the first ten days," Zola whispered, awe-struck by what had happened. More than a hundred and fifty for every citizen of the Cloud.

"When I get an idea, I get an idea," Kurst said in a self-satisfied tone.

"Glad the three bastards lived this long," Zola replied. "If one of them had been so impolite as to have died, it would have screwed the odds and perhaps ruined our game. I almost feel as if someone were looking out for them."

Kurst looked up at Zola, hoping for some insider news. He'd been trying to crack into the com links that were carrying the raw information coming up from the Hole, but the

Kohs had realized that any such information could affect the bet flow and had been sure to keep the insider news confidential. There'd been a flurry of action the first four days, with four known attempts on Aldin's life and two on Sigma. But somehow, as if someone had been watching over them, all attempts had failed and the stockholders had breathed a sigh of relief at the end of each day. For if one died, the odds would drop dramatically.

"Do you see any leveling off of bets?" Zola asked lazily.

"After about ten days the odds and the payoff are down by a third. I expected we'd see a dropoff by now. The key thing is a death by around the midpoint or so. It'll stir up the action —the psych people believe that a sensory overload will be setting in by then and interest will be diminishing. One death, and they'll flood the ticket agents again up till the cutoff point."

Zola listened closely and smiled while pouring another drink for his brilliant find.

Kurst smiled in turn. There were some other permutations as well, but that could wait for the moment. After all, there was the idea his girlfriend, a broker in the stock and futures market, had come up with, but that was a deal best left outside of Zola's control.

"So, tell me about your ideas," Zola asked, and Kurst, looking across at the Koh, smiled openly.

"But how could you have bought in with him?" Bukha said wearily. "You've got an uncle on one side, and your family head on another, fighting to the death, and you throw in with that Zola who's turned it into a cheap blood sport for the mob. Being a Koh should carry more dignity than that; loyalty to blood should come before anything else."

"Blood has nothing to do with it," Tia replied. "The technicality of my being a Koh is a flimsy one at best. My dear uncle Corbin, if he lives, will be sure to eliminate me."

Bukha sat back with a sigh.

"I always thought a little bit better of you," he said, shaking his head. "Figured that some of Aldin's teaching would rub off on you."

"I learned from him," Tia said evenly. "Learned that nice

guys finish last when it comes to living with Kohs, or anyone, for that matter."

Bukha looked closely at the girl. Was this a bluff, an angry retort, or had she really hardened to such an extent that the Gablona blood was coming to the fore?

"So why have you decided to get together with the two of us?" the Xsarn asked, stirring from his couch in the corner of the room.

"Just wanted to see a couple of old friends," Tia said evenly, "who've been sulking by themselves while everyone else is busy chasing profits."

"When the Xsarn and I figured this game out," Bukha replied sadly, "we thought it'd be a damn good lesson to those three." As he spoke he looked over to the Xsarn, who sat in the corner, noisily sucking on a feeding tube.

"And you were all so innocent," Tia replied sarcastically. "Or was the bet that wiped out Gablona based on playing on a little inside information yourself?"

Bukha looked at her evenly and did not reply.

"As I was saying," Bukha continued, "we never figured they'd truly get to each other, that their fear of the Al 'Shiga would cause them to hide away until the forty days were up. The betting then between us Kohs would be a minor amusement to help ease the tension of our accountants and lawyers fleecing us blind, and might help pay some of the expenses as well. I never should have let the three choose their own guards. Gablona threw the whole thing off balance when he pulled in some of the best assassins in history. It was a move completely for the offensive and he was out for blood."

"Come on now, do you really expect me to believe your plea for innocence?" Tia replied sarcastically. "You knew that this game would be ugly, and Corbin would grab hold of it with a vengeance. And besides, if one of them did die, it would help to defray the costs of the accounting as well."

Tia stopped for a moment and looked at the two closely. "And another thing, exactly why did you two pick the Hole? Or should I ask why did you agree to the Overseer's suggestion to use it?"

The two were silent, looking back and forth to each other like two conspirators fearful that someone else already knew.

Finally Bukha broke the silence. "It was suggested to us." He hesitated and looked over at the Xsarn.

"It's none of your damn business," the Xsarn snapped, coming to his feet.

"Curious, that's all," Tia replied smoothly. "No need to get excited."

The three settled back, eyeing each other cautiously.

"Well, anyhow," Tia said after a long, uncomfortable moment, "my other reason for dropping by is that I thought you might find a little piece of information rather interesting."

"And that is?" Bukha asked.

"Well, I was taking a close look last night at the incoming reports, and I noticed something rather unusual coming out of the Livollen Consortium of worlds."

"I own the Consortium," Bukha snapped. "Some of Vol's agents set up ticket sales through their trading representatives, but I'm not involved with the selling, if that's what you're wondering about."

"I know that," Tia replied. "It's just that there's been a dozen large blocks of tickets bought. Twelve people have each purchased five million tickets all on the third day of the game. Each in a different city, and each purchaser did so with cash."

"Incredible!"

"Just the thought of that much money in hundred-katar cash coins is staggering," Bukha said. "And the printout. It must have taken hundreds of machines to churn out the mountains of paper."

"Caused several riots," Tia said, chuckling. "One whole province's betting system was clogged for the entire day just to handle it, and no one else could bet."

"Who were they?" the Xsarn asked.

"I don't know. I've got their ID numbers, but they're citizens of your world, so we don't have any records."

"Five million each, you say."

"Almost to the katar. I've quietly asked one of my people to run an analysis, but it'll take days. But just a quick random check of several hundred bets from each purchaser shows that so far there is no cross-lapping of bets."

"So you think they're working together."

"Just an educated guess, but I think so. I never would have even caught it, our system wasn't designed to flag such a thing, but the data came in on the riots so I called up the reports and saw that our line from that world was feeding in bets full-tilt. The bets coming in from each locale all had the same ID number assigned to them. If I hadn't thought to check, it would have been folded in with the trillions of others and never noticed.

"This whole damn game was set up on such short notice, no one ever thought to program for or even to look at trends other than the gross numbers. Trying to sort through trillions of bets looking for patterns is damn near beyond us. It was just a lucky accident, I guess, but it just doesn't feel right."

"First off," Bukha said, "you know and I know that the whole thing is a sucker's bet. Anyone with enough sense to own that much money wouldn't be laying it all out. Sure, the average mark'll buy five, ten, maybe even five hundred tickets if he's a complete idiot, but five million?"

"My thoughts as well," Tia replied. "You know, at first I thought it might be one of the Kohs, figuring to fix events with the game and then get the payoff. But that wasn't the case."

"Communications for the game both in and out are strictly under my control this time." The Xsarn sniffed. "If any Koh wants to go down there himself, let him, but I don't think anyone is crazy enough to even think about that."

"So why are you telling us this?" Bukha asked, looking over at Tia.

"Just thought you might be curious," Tia replied airily, but Bukha could see that the information had been troubling her and she definitely wanted it checked out.

"It's your lottery, not mine," the Xsarn replied coldly.

"They're your worlds," Tia snapped. "I think something's afoot here. I'm thinking, as well, that you're more involved in this game than you'd like to have known."

Bukha almost started to bristle at the accusation, but realized that it was useless. He was about to respond when a soft paging chime cut in.

"The latest game report," the Xsarn said, his voice showing his excitement.

Tia came around to the side as he punched the information up on his desk scanner.

He looked out of the corner of his eye and could see the concern on Tia's face as she scanned the report.

"FOR STOCKHOLDERS ONLY, GAME DAY FIFTEEN—ATTEMPT ON LARICE CURRENTLY IN PROGRESS, BY GABLONA. IMPLANT UNITS FLAT-LINED FOR THREE GUARDS WITHIN LAST FIVE MINUTES; GABLONA, TWO FLAT-LINES ON GUARDS."

There was a pause as the real-time data link waited for any changes.

The screen flashed again and Bukha felt Tia's hands digging into his shoulder.

"LARICE INJURED, NO REPORT IF BLADE POISON . . ."

Bukha looked up at Tia, a tight grimace creasing his face.

"This could be it," he said softly.

Damn it all, she thought, and she turned away. That fat fool, why the hell wasn't he more careful?

"Worried for your uncle? Or the effects on the bet flow?" Bukha asked coldly.

"You bastard," she snapped, whirling around.

He raised his hand up.

"All right then, all right," he said softly. "I just had to be sure. So, you're playing something inside of this as well, is that it? Aldin Larice isn't just a number then, a bet to be won."

She stood eyeing him defiantly.

"You don't have to say anything more." He looked back at the screen.

"I'll check out those bets for you. It'll take a while to track them down, but my curiosity is aroused," he said quietly. "Perhaps there's someone who knows more about this game than we'd care to think. And if they do, then it affects Aldin as well."

The terminal started to flash again, and yet another report started to scroll across the screen.

* * *

"We're getting reports that it's absolute chaos out there."

Losa floated from the corner of the room, where he'd been meditating, and looked at the messenger.

If it was possible for an Overseer to feel emotion, then this must be it, he thought inwardly. He thought about the last such time, when the subject Gablona had escaped, or thought he had escaped. For a moment he had actually felt something; he was not sure what, but the look of malicious joy on the one called Gablona when he thought he was being rescued had stirred something within. It had taken days to purge out the turmoil that had brought about.

The Overseer looked at Vush. He could see that the younger, slightly rotund Overseer was clearly excited by what was happening. Most disturbing, all of this. Were the intruders somehow polluting them, after all? Was their desire for a finish to the charade in fact a defeat rather than the victory hoped for?

"Go on then," the Overseer said softly.

"Information is coming in about an attempt at termination," Vush responded.

"And?"

"It has triggered absolute chaos. Their economic activity has all but ceased, everything is at a standstill. Reports are indicating that within minutes after the first report, productivity started to curve downward. There are already reports coming in from agents of riots, as mobs attempt to buy tickets before this particular event affects the betting."

Losa nodded. "And is the situation covered?"

"Of course, in either direction," Vush replied. "I made sure of it myself."

"Then it is acceptable," Losa replied softly and, turning away, he floated back to the corner of the room to continue with the meditation of Inward Searching.

So disturbing, all of this, he reasoned, but, after all, it was a most cunning idea that he had created, and if he could allow himself to feel anything, it would be pride at his ingenuity.

"Takashi, behind!"

His old companion whirled in a blur of motion. There was the faint hiss, the sound of a sword arcing on a deadly path, and the soft thump as the blade cut through cloth and flesh.

Oishi sat crouched in the darkness, watching from the

corner of his eye. Was it Takashi or the assassin who had just been hit? But his thoughts had to be elsewhere, for there was the faintest of flickers in the darkness to his right, a motion more felt than seen. It had to be another one. Darkness was their enemy now. If only he could get to one of the lamps and start it up again to see if Aldin was still alive.

The attack had been totally without warning. Aldin along with half a dozen guards had been up late; the rest were asleep in the converted barracks rooms upstairs. It had been a habit of Aldin's since their arrival to sit up into the night, plotting strategy with Zergh, or talking with Mari, staying awake for a day and half of game time then sleeping for one night.

Oishi had warned him to vary every pattern to his life, to never sleep in the same room twice, to do everything different, at all times. But Aldin had laughed in his usual self-deprecating way.

Oishi could only thank the gods that some inner sense had stirred him from his sleep and brought him downstairs to check, for just as he had stepped into the taproom, half a dozen black-clad forms had burst out of the kitchen. Three had made straight for Aldin, and then the single lantern in the room had gone out, even as he leaped to Aldin's defense.

There was the movement again, while over in the corner where Takashi had dived he could hear the sound of labored breathing and struggle. The doorway to upstairs was closed, with the sound of fighting behind it. He was tempted to head for it and try to free the staircase for his men, but he had to get to Aldin first.

Again there was the flicker of motion, a shadowy form that was as dark as the night.

After releasing his long sword, he clenched the short blade in his hand and slithered across the room to place himself between the shadow and the corner where he had last seen Aldin.

The shadow moved again. There was a bounding leap. Oishi rolled backward slashing the air before him, even as he fell over.

Only a faint hiss preceded the blade that caught against his shoulder, laying it bare. The shock of the unexpected blow set him back.

The shadow was above him slashing, jabbing.

Oishi cut out with his foot, short quick jabs that hit nothing. He kicked again and felt bone smashing beneath his heel. There was a grunt of pain. The attacker dived forward, driving his blade into the floorboard within inches of his throat. Oishi slashed with his own blade, striking flesh, and then a desperate hand clamped over the blade, slamming it to the floor. A hot sticky spray splashed across his eyes as his opponent tried to twist the blade free with his bare hand.

Oishi drove his free hand up, catching his opponent in the throat. There was a terrible crack as he smashed the man's windpipe, and then a sickening gurgle. The hand on the blade loosened. With a quick even motion Oishi raised the sword and slashed with a horizontal motion. A river of blood washed over Oishi's face as the body above him went limp.

Suddenly a dagger was at his throat, and at that instant Oishi realized that death was upon him. This mystery that had extended his life but for a handful of days and shown him wonders undreamed of was finished at last. He would go into death and the realm where all should be as it should be, and the confusion of this strange world be left behind. He waited in that single extended moment for the cold kiss, but the dagger held.

"Samurai?" a voice whispered next to his ear. It was Aldin.

For a split second Oishi felt a towering rage. How the hell was he to protect this man, if he wouldn't protect himself? A proper lord would have simply cut, taking no chances. If a guard was killed by mistake, then that was the price paid to preserve the lord's life. Yet having stared in that second into the abyss and now to have it close, at least for the moment, caused a strange sense of release to wash over him.

"Oishi," he whispered, and he felt the blade draw back.

Oishi pushed aside the still-bleeding corpse above him, and Aldin crawled up to his side. Gently, so as not to frighten him, Oishi brought his hand up to Aldin and placed it over his mouth to signal that he wasn't to speak. Aldin nodded in reply.

Ever so slowly Oishi led Aldin back into the corner. The fighting on the staircase continued. In the darkness, he wasn't sure how many assassins had made it into the room, and for that matter, the door to the outside could still be open and another wave of attackers already infiltrated into the building.

"Oishi, don't move." It was Takashi speaking in Japanese. So, he'd gotten his man. Stealthfully Takashi rose up, his form barely visible. He started for the door that led up to the barrack rooms. Oishi was about to call a warning even as Takashi reacted. His blade hissed out again, this time cutting the body completely in two, and Oishi heard the grunt of satisfaction as his companion snapped his blade back, to slash the upper part of the body yet again before it had even hit the floor.

Takashi reached the door and with a wild scream yanked it back.

A shaft of light flooded into the room, and with a roar, Takashi charged up the stairs, striking the enemy force from the rear. A wild cheer rose up from the samurai fighting downward. Oishi ached to join the fray, but knew that he had to stay with Aldin. From the light produced through the doorway, the rest of the room was dimly visible. He could see several of his men, dead in pools of blood, the enemy that he had killed sprawled out on the floor not an arm's length away.

He looked over to Aldin, who sat with his back to the wall, an assassin dagger in his hand, stained to the hilt with blood. And for the first time Oishi saw the river of blood pouring down from Aldin's scalp. The man was still alive, and if the blade that hit him was poisoned, there was nothing he could do now. Suddenly Aldin's features grew tense and he came up to a fighting crouch.

Oishi looked back. One of the assassins had gotten by Takashi and for a split second was poised in the middle of the room. Oishi was about to spring, but then realized that though he could see the assassin, the assassin could not see him, for he'd been fighting in the light, and in the dim room his night vision had not yet adjusted. He had to stay next to Aldin, in case there was yet another attacker in the room.

The lone assassin turned and fled for the door back into the kitchen. Seconds later there was a gurgled cry and the door was flung open again. Oishi braced to receive another rush, but there was only a lone form staggering out, the man who had just escaped the moment before. A butcher's knife was plunged to the hilt into his chest, the point of the blade sticking out of his back. He staggered and then ever so slowly, collapsed against the bar.

Behind him Mari came walking out, her right hand stained with blood, a look of grim satisfaction on her face.

"You better secure the back door," she said calmly. "I've been holding those bastards off for the last ten minutes while you children have been playing in here."

Incredulous, Oishi came to his feet. "Takashi, sweep this room first, then every inch of the building. Assign your men."

As his lieutenant shouted commands, Oishi turned to check Aldin.

Aldin came slowly to his feet. Oishi quickly wiped the blood from the man's face and saw the fresh flow pouring down from a wound that had nicked off part of his left ear and cut a sharp line from the back of his head down to his cheek. It looked ugly but as far as he could tell, it wasn't serious. He watched closely, fearing the start of the convulsions but nothing came.

Aldin stood looking at him as if in shock.

"This room is clean," Seiji shouted, and then, leading a group of men, he stormed into the kitchen, while other guards came up to circle Aldin. Zergh, who had stepped out of the room only moments before to relieve himself in the basement, came storming through the pack of men and up to Aldin's side. At the sight of blood he stopped, stricken with terror, but Oishi nodded reassuringly.

"It was obviously Gablona," Mari said, coming up to Aldin's side.

Aldin looked around at the bodies in the room. Five assassins were dead, along with three of the samurai who had been laughing with him only moments before. Slowly he walked over to the staircase and looked up. Two more of the enemy were dead up there.

"Why only seven?" he wondered out loud.

"Eight," Mari interrupted, and Aldin and the samurai turned to look at her. Taking his arm, she led him into the kitchen, where the eighth body stood, pinned to the wall with a carving knife.

"Who did that?" Oishi demanded.

"I took care of the bastard," Mari replied evenly, and she then nodded over toward a dead Gaf. It was Maladi, facedown in a bucket of grease, his throat cut from ear to ear.

"You killed him, too?" Aldin asked, incredulous.

"What? My own partner?" she cried, insulted at such an accusation. "I thought it curious that he gave his bouncers the night off. I was in the taproom keeping an eye on you when I heard three knocks, then three more. That set me on edge, so I slipped back into the kitchen and hid in the corner. Maladi was opening the door. The first eight assassins slipped in and Maladi closed the door behind them, and I thought, 'Uh-oh, Mari girl, this is it.'

"I couldn't give the alarm, they were between me and the door out to the taproom. It was then that one of your samurai must have suspected something and came into the kitchen.

"Well, then everything happened at once. They killed the man and seven of them charged in. The eighth turned on Maladi and, as easy as can be, he cut him an extra mouth. I heard the fighting going on in the next room, and that eighth fellow went to open the door again, I guess to let more of his friends in. So it was simple self-preservation, and I felt it best to sheath my carving knife in the source of my problems."

Even as Mari spoke she walked over to the corpse, gave him a curious sort of look, as if she were about to ask him a question, and then pulled the blade out of his back. The corpse slumped to the floor, and she wiped the blood off on her apron.

"I bolted the door shut again," she continued matter-of-factly. "They were sure mad out there, you could hear them hollering and yammering in their gibberish from one end of the quarter to the other."

"You saved us all," Oishi replied, his voice full of admiration. "If you hadn't bolted that door shut again, they would have overwhelmed us."

"They'd have had my throat cut like Maladi over there, that's why I killed the other one, too. I figured if I didn't, he'd get me, it was as simple as that," she said smiling.

The samurai stood around the woman open-mouthed with amazement. She talked about killing two of the dreaded assassins as easily as if she had been dispatching pigs in the basement. Even Takashi, who had just killed several in hard-fought combat, was shaking his head in amazement.

"I guess that means I own this dump now," Mari said

quietly. "Maladi never did have any relatives; sometimes I thought nobody would be so stupid as to admit it for fear he'd hoodwink them out of something. I might as well tell you that I suspected he was playing you out against the other two for profit. But I couldn't prove anything, so I kept my mouth shut. Anyhow, I loaned him money more than once out of my own savings when he fell on hard times over some bad bets. So I guess you could say this dive was my collateral."

Oishi eyed her closely and then looked over at the dead Gaf in the corner, and then back to Mari. She merely smiled at him. Was it possible? he wondered.

She patted Oishi on the arm, as if to say that they were now sharing a little secret, and then stepped back into the taproom with the rest of the group in her wake.

"What a bloody mess," she said, looking around the room. The three dead samurai had been moved to the corner of the room, where their comrades prepared them for interment in the basement, since a pyre was not possible.

Mari came up to Aldin's side as he slumped into a chair and looked at him with concern.

"So what are you going to do?" she asked quietly, her hand slipping over Aldin's.

"Survive," he said bitterly, and then he looked over at Oishi, who sat next to the bodies of his fallen men. "Survive and outthink, outfight my enemies, so that my men survive. That's what it's all about. It's not causes, it's not bets, it's simply surviving so your friends can survive as well.

"It was Gablona who did this," he said coldly, motioning to the corpses of his men in the corner. "I was willing to sit back, to leave him alone, even after those other attempts that failed. Funny how I got warning on each of those, but not tonight. If my men are to survive, then it'll have to be Gablona who's eliminated, or kept so off-guard that he'll not be able to do this again. That Koh is still playing at war; it's time he learned what the reality truly is. If I don't teach him, Oishi and those who serve me will continue to die like this."

Aldin came back up to his feet, and Oishi watched him closely as if searching for his inner thoughts. The samurai came to his feet and then walked over to Aldin's side.

"We go for Gablona," Aldin said quietly.

The samurai looked at Aldin closely and realized that at

last this man understood and felt the true essence of what it was to be samurai. For the first time Oishi felt, as well, that there might be a chance of surviving this after all.

"You should have killed me in the dark," Oishi replied. "You did not know if it was me or another attacker."

"I was willing to take the chance."

The faintest of smiles crossed Oishi's face. This man was not the typical lord, but in the end he might be one worth serving after all.

"So, the doorway was blocked before the second detachment could get in?"

"That is right, my lord."

Hassan looked the man over with disdain. In former times the answer would have been obvious. The two dozen who'd been sent would either have succeeded or not returned. But their numbers were too few, far too few. Thus he had made the one mistake in his plan. He'd not completely trusted the tavernkeeper's offer to open the door.

In his suspicion that it was a trap, he had ordered that eight men were to first go in and secure the back room and only then were the rest of his precious men to be committed. Perhaps it was a trap, but he doubted that. Something must have gone wrong once the first group got inside.

"Dismissed. And as you lay upon your pallet tonight contemplate the pleasures of paradise that your far more worthy comrades now enjoy."

The door closed behind him.

So the fat one would not be pleased. Hassan gave a snort of disdain. Let him. For the moment it was to Hassan's advantage to serve him. But that time would pass. That the fat one thought him to be such a primitive as to believe in gods above was insult enough. If this Gablona was truly an initiate into the highest orders, then he would know the truth as Hassan knew it, that there were no gods, there was no Allah, there was only one thing—and that was power, unalloyed by sentiment or fear.

For that was the secret of secrets. He, too, had once risen through the ranks. As initiate, as Refik, as master, and then finally to grand master.

But as a master he was shown that religion was but a sop

for the masses. That there was but one supreme rule, and that was the rule of power through fear and lies. A power he fully intended to seize yet again on this world made as if to his order.

He had wandered disguised in these strange streets, and had learned what the fat one had not told him, for the city was hot with rumor and beneath the rumor, truth, which any man of wisdom could divine.

At first his senses had reeled with the shock. The world he had known did not exist except in legend. Nearly two hundred generations of men had passed since his age. If Gablona was near godlike, then it was in the fact that he and his kind had somehow mastered the ability to race across time. The shock had almost overwhelmed his mind, that for a moment he doubted his own teachings, for surely only a god could do such a thing.

But in watching the fat one he had seen nothing but a man. A man consumed with lust, greed, and the desire for vengeance.

He had heard, as well, the other rumors, the truth about what this battle was about. A merchant from the tower in the sky had showed him blocks of paper, covered with strange script, and offered to sell them, claiming they were part of the game.

Hassan smiled at how easily he played that one. Drawing out the questions, even buying some of the paper, while the merchant had rattled on about the odds and how thousands of worlds were betting on the outcome of what he, Hassan, was now playing such an intimate part.

Then he had returned again to the city and the people who were a thread back into his own time. Though the translating device compensated for the different language, the words were sometimes strikingly similar to his native tongue; the rituals were hauntingly familiar as well, even to the bowing to the Seda. And he knew that these people looked to the first Old Man of the Mountain, Sabah, though they did not know his name, as their first teacher of the truth about power.

Then at last he had met Ulsak, the leader, and the groundwork for the plan started to form in Hassan's mind.

But to this Ulsak he revealed nothing. He spoke not a word of how he was a destiny, it was that he had come forward to lead these people to their greatness, and the fat one would be his path to that dream. First there would be victory for his master of the moment, but later power far beyond the worthless rewards Gablona babbled about. For Gablona could not give him the one thing that he truly wanted: the power of life and death over others.

The door swung open behind him.

Hassan smiled to himself; the fat one was angry.

Fixing his features, he turned.

"I know," he said softly.

"That cuts our strength by nearly a sixth," Gablona snapped.

"And theirs as well, most likely," Hassan replied evenly. "My men don't sell their lives cheaply. But remember that you sneered at these men who carry the long swords and said they would fall easily. I think now that it is proven that they are good fighters. Let us not underestimate them again."

"This gives Sigma the advantage," Gablona shouted, not even realizing that Hassan had put the blame on him. "We haven't attempted him yet, planning to take out Aldin first. Sigma had promised to try for Aldin as well."

"Obviously he did what a prudent leader would in such circumstances, and has waited for us to eliminate each other." Hassan replied, the tone of reproach in his voice growing more evident.

"Are you saying that I didn't plan this correctly?" Gablona snapped. "After all, you approved it."

"For it was your plan," Hassan said. "And coming from such as you, I assumed it to be infallible."

Gablona glowered, not sure if Hassan was mocking him or simply showing the proper respect.

"So, now what do you suggest?" Gablona asked, realizing that he desperately needed this man, but in his heart feeling the first tug of fear, his inner sense that had always saved him in all his dealings with dangerous men.

"Take out Sigma now."

"Why?"

"Because for the moment he is the more powerful, and since he hasn't attacked Aldin as planned, we must assume that he has betrayed you. We can also assume that Sigma might very well be planning a strike against you. Therefore, strike first."

"But what about Aldin? Our attack might have stirred him to strike back."

"The blues are still looking for him," Hassan said evenly.

"I don't trust that rabble," Gablona said. "They could turn on us just as easily."

"I'll take care of that," Hassan replied smoothly. "I already know where Sigma is hiding. The rest can be planned out in several days."

Gablona hesitated for a moment.

"Trust me," Hassan said, a gentle smile lighting his features.

Sigma looked across the table to the head of his berserkers. The week had been quiet. The only problem had been simply feeding the Gafs under his command. He found that in a strange sort of way he was actually growing fond of these big, lumbering warriors.

They kept him up most every night, what with their shouting and brawling, but he did have to admit that when all fifty of them surrounded him and marched down the street, he did not feel the slightest fear, for even the Al 'Shiga drew back at their approach and only pelted him with offal from afar.

Now, if only Aldin had the sense to have hired such guards. What a fight that would be. Why, he'd almost be tempted to arrange a set match, a hundred Gaf berserkers smashing it out. It would have been like the betting days of old.

It was too bad about Aldin, Sigma thought, shaking his head sadly. He had heard the report on the assassination attempt. He assumed it came from Gablona, and if it had, Aldin's forces were most likely weakened by the effort. And if that was the case, there was only one answer.

Aldin might be the more trustworthy, but Gablona was definitely the more cunning, thus the harder to take out. Most likely the old Koh had simmered down a bit by now and was ready to listen to reason. He'd offer him part of his Sulli Conglomerate as a payoff. After all, Gablona had wanted that particular venture for years. A deal would be struck, and they could sit out the game and then go home. After all, Kohs could talk to each other. In the end it was profit that counted more than vengeance.

But he'd have to make a good-faith gesture first. And Aldin was indeed nothing more than a tradesman, a vasba, when one got right down to it.

"I think it's time that you boys had some action," Sigma said evenly, and the expressions around the table lit up.

CHAPTER 8

"Blackie, it's remarkable," Kurst exulted. "Simply remarkable what you've done."

Sisa Black leaned over and with a playful gesture ruffled Kurst's heavy mane of tangled brown hair. Like his glasses, his shoulder-length hair was also a dozen years out of fashion. Most likely Kurst hadn't even noticed the latest trend of quarter-inch cropping, with long bangs in front.

Her job required that she be smartly turned out, so she always followed the latest trend, which for this year was ankle-length dresses with a bustle and a neckline that plunged almost to her belt. Kurst and she had been students together years before, and, though never making their arrangement permanent, the relationship had held, even though separated by a thousand light-years of space. Professorships were hard to find on Ator, and Sisa had no desire to give up her job as president of a futures brokerage to live out on some provincial planet.

"Any word on hits brewing?" she asked softly, while pouring out her fifth caffeine jolt of the day.

"Looks like something's moving down there. I'm keeping close to Zola, and the moment I hear..."

The two looked at each other and smiled.

His fascination with what they were doing took hold, and after getting out of his chair, he walked over to the vid display that dominated one of the office walls.

The market was in full swing, and she came up to his side to watch.

"When we get an idea, my dear, we certainly get an idea," she whispered while nibbling on his ear.

The floor that she ran, which had once dealt in amber and precious metal futures, was now given over solely to gaming futures. It was a highly classified venture; no knowledge of it had yet to reach the Kohs. For they would be sure to muscle in, and besides, Zola would discover who the major inside contact was.

So it was trading on the sly, but trading that way was quite lucrative indeed. The tickets kept their original registrations, to be sure, but contractually any winnings were signed over to the current holder of an option.

Blocks of tickets purchased by investment firms would be bid upon. The final outcome was not important at this date, rather the potential of future outcomes is what mattered. Therefore, any tickets that had not called for a death before the fourteenth game day was now a valuable commodity with a potential of winning, and as such held a potential value, calculated on the various current odds.

Options could be purchased to hold tickets for as little as six hours, one-half of a day down on the Hole. Of course, if during those six hours an event occurred that the tickets did not cover, then the buyer was wiped out. But if the tickets were still viable after six hours or, even better, an event had occurred that the tickets did cover, then their value would soar.

The big board that filled one wall of the trading floor started to light up with buy orders, and the market, sensing a trend, started to go wild.

"Looks like buy orders for a Gablona hit on Aldin,"

Blackie said. "We've got some of those in our portfolio. What do you think?"

Kurst was awed by the power that he now held. In a matter of days he had come from being a forgotten professor in the outback to a financial advisor playing with millions, and all because of a barroom conversation with an old friend.

"I don't think so," he said softly. "Put out a sell order on those. Aldin survived the last hit attempt. I think if anything he'll be going for Gablona and not the other way around."

Sisa tapped into her phone link and in seconds the sell order went out.

Kurst laughed with glee as he saw tens of thousands of tickets changing hands every second. The potential profit of it all was staggering to contemplate. What had started out only days before as a venture involving tens of thousands of tickets now saw hundreds of millions of tickets changing hands every hour. Sisa had told him how only this morning a whole new trading consortium from one of the Gaf worlds had bought into the market, doubling their volume within the first hour.

Sisa's sell order was on the floor, and the trend kicked off as a Gaf consortium started to snap up all tickets dealing with a Gablona hit on Aldin.

Her pager rang and she tapped back into her floor dealers, spoke what sounded like a code, and then looked over at Kurst.

"We just cleared a profit of two hundred and fifty thousand on that sell order," she said, squeezing Kurst's hand. "My dear, I think we're going to be very rich before this is all over."

For a moment he wondered about that. They had to keep security on this little venture. If the Kohs ever found out and his insider leaked, there'd be hell to pay. But the big board was flashing like a machine gone berserk, and Kurst giggled as he watched.

The streets were empty. It was festival time again and the foreign community was in hiding, while the natives were busy over in their quarter whooping it up and trading heads.

Feeling that this was to be an all-out effort, Sigma decided to commit his entire force to the attack and not leave half his men behind as guards.

Stealthfully, as stealthfully as fifty heavily armed Gaf berserkers could be, the contingent wound its way up the narrow street to Aldin's hiding place.

The forward guard came back around the corner and motioned that all was clear.

Ura, the berserker leader, looked back at Sigma, who merely nodded.

A dozen Gafs surrounded each of the two heavy beams and picked up the knotted rope ends that extended out from each of the battering rams.

Ura raised his hand and then with a bellowing roar brought his arm down.

With a wild shout the berserkers hefted the rams and started out. The first group turned up a side alley leading to the back entrance, while the second group, with Sigma at the rear, charged up the main street.

The lead Gafs stormed up to the spy holes on either side of the door, slamming up heavy wooden shields to block attack from inside.

The battering team slowed for a second as they turned and positioned the ram and, then with a shout, they ran straight for the door. The beam hit with a bone-shattering impact, the wooden and steel frame cracking and groaning.

Again Ura roared.

The attackers backed up and slammed the ram in again.

Peering around the arm of one of his guards, Sigma watched the building. At any second he expected Aldin's defenders to appear, but there was no response.

Again the ram hit the door still blocking their way. With a roar of rage the Gafs backed up and charged yet again.

As they started forward, the door was suddenly flung open from the inside. One of the Gaf warriors, who had broken in through the back door, filled the narrow entryway, the ram coming straight toward him.

With a terrified squeal he fell backward, the heavy ram coming through the doorway like a bolt fired from a bow. The dozen Gafs running with the ram suddenly found no resistance as the ram shot through thin air where the door had been only seconds before. The mass of warriors went down in a roaring tangle as one after another they slammed into the doorsill to either side, each warrior's four hundred pounds of flesh and armor piling into one confused heap.

Ura shouted with rage at the tangle and, raising his heavy battle-ax, he ran straight for the heap of warriors, leaping over them, and charged on into the building.

Sigma's guards, inflamed with the prospect of battle, left his side and, screaming with delight, stormed on into the building, leaving the Koh standing alone on the street except for the dozen dazed rammers.

Beneath the head of the ram Sigma saw the Gaf who had opened the door, struggling weakly to lift the hundreds of pounds of dead weight off his body, even as his companions leaped onto the log in their mad clattering push to get into the building.

Sigma suddenly realized that standing out on the street alone was the height of madness. With a running leap he raced for the door, and jumped onto the log. There was a groan of protest from underneath, but he pushed on into the darkness.

It was roaring confusion inside. Peering into the gloom, he saw his warriors lumbering about the main taproom, shouting and growling for their foes to show themselves.

There were no Humans in sight.

Sigma actually felt a surge of excitement. What a story this would make once he got back with the other Kohs! A charge of sweaty Gaf berserkers, chanting their battle cries, he at the forefront. How the others would envy this.

Ura came up to Sigma's side and saluted, his anger visible. "The filthy cowards have all run away. The place is empty."

"What? But this is the right place," Sigma said, suddenly angry that the heroic nature of the raid had been ruined by Aldin not complying by being around.

"Kolda led the charge on the back door; it broke on the first strike, the beam was not in place. That's how the front door was opened for us. The place is empty. They've all run away, the miserable cowards," he said dejectedly. "And we were there'd be a good fight today."

The Gafs around him, who'd been worked into a fighting frenzy, were now venting their rage by shattering the tables with axes and chopping the bar apart in a shower of splinters. Several berserkers were already behind the bar, smashing off the tops of Maladi's horde of muscatel and draining the huge jugs off, half the contents spilling down their armor, while others eagerly snatched and growled for their share of the loot.

"You better get them under control," Sigma shouted in exasperation. "The last thing I need is a lot of drunken guards."

"Ah, let them have their fun. It'll take their minds off the disappointment of not finding servants," Ura replied happily. "You've kept us cooped up, what with your hiding and all. The lads need a little fun. Otherwise, they might vent their rage at missing a good fight in a manner you might not appreciate."

Ura looked over at Sigma, a strange glow in his eyes, and Sigma realized it was best not to argue.

"And don't worry," the Gaf said, slapping him on the shoulder with a blow that made Sigma's knees buckle. "If that enemy of yours isn't here, then he'll be back or we'll just go out and look for him. Anyhow, my warriors fight best after they've had a couple of drinks."

Sigma, shaking his head, walked over to the corner of the room and settled down, realizing there wasn't anything else he could do. Ura came over to the table and slammed down a jug of muscatel.

"Good stuff this," the Gaf roared. "Have a drink, you look like you need it!"

Sigma pulled the cork out of the jug, sniffed it, and wrinkled his nose with disgust.

"Too strong for you?" Ura asked, laughing at this strange Human's discomfort, and then, turning, he went back to join his comrades at the bar.

Sigma looked about the darkened room. The Gafs were getting louder with every passing moment. Several of them chanted their bizarre minor-key death songs, stopping for a moment to upend a jug before passing it on to their comrades.

There'd be no hope of surprise if Aldin and his samurai should come wandering back in, Sigma realized. But if Aldin wasn't here, and had left his place abandoned, the old Koh suddenly wondered, then where in hell was he now?

"It doesn't feel right," Oishi whispered, drawing away from the window slit that faced Gablona's fortress across the street.

Aldin came up and crouched by the samurai's side.

For several days they'd planned this move. Now that Maladi was gone, Mari had proved herself invaluable once again.

Within a day after he had asked, she returned with the information as to Gablona's hiding place, and had already purchased a small warehouse directly across from Gablona as a base of operations. To Aldin's shock it'd only been several blocks away from Sigma's, and not a block away from the original safe house assigned to him.

She also told him about the catacombs beneath the city where it was believed the Al'Shiga buried their dead. It was a secret few outsiders knew; even Maladi had been in the dark about that. Unfortunately there were no entrances which connected the tavern to the warehouse, so they'd have to risk traveling above ground.

Aldin swore a silent oath. "Should we try for it anyhow?" he asked.

Oishi looked at him. There was a time for caution, but not now, he thought. Perhaps the enemy had been forewarned, but to withdraw would be bad for the morale of his men, who were aching to avenge the deaths of their comrades. Neither would it have the desired effect on the morale of the foe, who so far had struck with impunity.

"Do you want to withdraw?" Oishi asked, curious about the answer.

Aldin looked at him grimly.

"Let's try to get this damn thing over with," he said coldly, and his answer was greeted by the slightest of smiles on Oishi's face.

Oishi looked at the other men in the room and nodded.

The two crossbow catapults were small ones, rigged together by several of Oishi's men.

The samurai strode over to the closed doorway and, reaching down, picked up the first bottle. It was quite a remarkable weapon, Oishi thought, an idea mentioned by Aldin and the potential of which he realized at once. It was in violation of the Al'Shiga custom, but since they were all attending the festival, Aldin reasoned that the risk would be worth it. Taking the candle, Oishi lit the rag wick at the end of the bottle and then nodded to the two catapult crews to fire.

As he yanked the door open, the two machines fired, slamming their bolts across the street, the shafts disappearing through the two narrow watch slits to either side of the door. Oishi threw the bottleful of distilled alcohol, which shattered a quarter meter away from the intended window, the liquid igniting nevertheless and flowing down the wall like a river of flame.

Several more samurai stepped to the door, throwing in turn. The second and third bottles disappeared into the building, the men around Oishi barely able to suppress a cheer when they could see the crackling flames ignite within.

Two more bolts slammed out, sweeping into the upstairs floor. Within seconds half a dozen bottles had slammed into the building. In a moment of reckless abandon, Takashi dashed out of the door, three bottles in his hands, their wicks burning. Standing in the middle of the street, he aimed them for the upper floor; two of the three sailed through the narrow slits above, where they shattered into flames.

But nothing happened. No response or defense was offered.

Takashi stood in the street as if daring the enemy to strike. With a dramatic flourish he drew his sword and waved it over his head.

"We are the forty-seven ronin!" he cried in Japanese.

Then with a quick dash he ran up to the nearest spy slit and looked inside. A second later he dashed to the next one, and then the next. Turning, he raced back to his companions.

"It's a furnace in there," he shouted, coming through the door.

Suddenly from around the corner came Hideo, a short, extremely thin samurai who had been in command of the watch set on the back entry to Gablona's fortress, with his three companions racing behind him.

"Nothing," he shouted with disgust. "We tossed our bottles right in, even looked in the slits; there's no one there."

"It's empty," Aldin said quietly. "Somehow either Gablona knew or he has gone off elsewhere."

"For what?" Takashi snapped, his blood up for the confrontation.

"To hit either Sigma or myself," Aldin replied.

"I don't care where he is," Mari suddenly interjected, "but I think our welcome as the new neighbors has just worn out."

From out in the street came shouts of anger. Aldin went up to the window slit with Mari at his side. Across the street the building was a roaring inferno. But above the crackling flames could be heard a gathering roar of angry shouts. On either side of the building the neighbors were pouring out, some with large contingents of armed guards. More than one was pointing at the small warehouse and shaking their fists. Aldin noticed, as well, a scattering of blue robes suddenly starting to appear.

"You've broken the taboo down here on any weapon other than one that can be held or thrown by hand. You've got the Shiga going as well."

"Time to leave," Aldin said, looking back at the samurai, who nodded in reply. Several of the men started to pick up each of the catapults.

"We can build more. If you're seen on the streets lugging those things, then we're really in trouble."

Seiji, who had helped with the building of the machines, patted his catapult affectionately and then fell in with the others and started for the back door.

Weaving down side streets to throw off any pursuit, the group pushed on as twilight started to descend around them. Aldin struggled to get up to the front of the group where Oishi and Mari, as guide, were leading.

Nearing the block where Sigma's fortress was located, the front of the column slowed. Aldin pushed forward to where Oishi stood peeking around the corner, his hand held back in a gesture of warning.

As Aldin came up to his side, he could hear the sound of drunken yelling. Surprised, he realized that it was Gafs.

"What the hell is going on?" Aldin whispered.

The next street over was boiling over with Gafs, obviously drunk and roaring their defiance. And then he saw Sigma, not fifteen meters away.

Oishi looked at Aldin, who was completely taken aback by this sudden turn of events. To take out Gablona was one thing, but with Sigma it was not quite the same. Still, he was the enemy now as well, like it or not.

He had to decide, and quickly. Sigma was out in the open, his guards scattered up and down the street. Somehow it was almost ludicrous, the small, portly man surrounded by the giant, hulking warriors.

It was a question of honor to him. Somehow he found it hard to order an attack on the man who had yet to openly raise a hand against him. Would Sigma do the same if the opportunity was offered? In his heart he knew the man would.

He looked back down the street to where Sigma stood, and then to his astonishment the Gaf closest to the Koh staggered as if the alcohol had finally laid him low. But as the berserker fell, a river of scarlet flashed out from where his throat had been only seconds before.

Sigma had finally convinced Ura that with the uproar they had created, any hope of surprise was now lost. For a moment they had debated whether they should hide and wait for Aldin's return, but the approach of twilight had made Sigma feel uneasy. A trap could easily be turned on him as well. Their own fortress was far more secure than the now thoroughly destroyed tavern, and the party finally decided to leave.

One of the Gafs talked about burning the place, but no one had thought to bring along a striker, and fumbling about, looking for a means to become arsonists, they quickly grew frustrated and simply gave up on the idea.

The return was far less stealthful than the approach. If anything, the Gaf's blood was now so thoroughly worked up that they were almost aching for a fight.

Sigma walked in the middle of them, lost in thought. Had Aldin been warned? he wondered. He knew that the implant they all carried could locate them on the scanning systems in the Skyhook right down to the very centimeter. He could not help but wonder if the implant had a double purpose: to monitor not only his vital signs, and that of his companions, but also to pick up every spoken word as well. If so, could Aldin have gotten the information?

His musings were interrupted by a loud cry of delight from one of the Gafs by his side. Sigma looked up.

A crowd of green robes stood at the end of the street blocking the approach to his safe house, all of them wearing the red headbands of the Mukba.

"I think we're going to have some fun," one of the Gafs growled, raising his axe and testing its edge with his thumb.

Sigma's pulse quickened. Could this be a trap? But he also felt a rising curiosity to see how his berserkers would perform pitted against some of the locals.

The Gafs, laughing with drunken joy, started to spread out in the narrow street, tossing aside the remaining jugs of liquor. Their shouts echoed and reechoed.

Sigma watched the green robes carefully. There was something about them that just didn't fit. They remained still as the berserkers started to approach, until the two groups were only a couple of dozen paces apart. Suddenly one of the green robes gave a universal gesture of contempt that was understood by any being.

With a roar, several of the Gafs raised their battle-axes high and started into a lumbering charge. Their comrades around them caught up in the spirit, rushing to join in the fun.

The green robes broke and, turning, fled back up the street. A Mukba wouldn't break, Sigma realized. Hell, they fought Gafs on this planet every festival day. The berserker's charge rushed straight past the safe house and kept on going.

Sigma turned to look for Ura to order him to call the guards back. But Ura was gone, rushing ahead with the rest of the mob. He suddenly felt a sense of foreboding.

"Ura!" Sigma shouted, his high, thin voice lost in the uproar of the Gafs.

A bellow of rage sounded next to him, and Sigma turned to see one of the few remaining guards around him stagger forward.

And then Sigma saw the blood.

The Gaf twisted and squirmed by his feet. Stunned, Sigma backed up from the dying warrior. There was another scream of pain. A guard on the other side of the street collapsed, a throwing dagger sticking out of his open mouth.

Confused now, Sigma turned in a circle. What was happening?

The safe house, he had to get in. He started for the door and saw that it was being pulled open. His guard on the inside, he thought.

Another Gaf on the street went down.

The door now swung wide to reveal Human men dressed in loose, flowing robes of black.

Gablona's assassins had taken his house while he was away!

Several of the Gafs who had started with the charge now saw the threat pouring out from behind as a swarm of assassins leaped through the doorway and out onto the street.

Sigma backed up against the far side of the street. One of his guards rushed past him, battle-ax held high, his death chant filling the air. An assassin headed straight toward him. The Gaf swung low in a deadly sweep. With almost mocking disdain, the assassin rolled under the blade, came up behind the Gaf, and with one swipe of his scimitar cut the Gaf behind both knees, sending him tumbling to the ground.

The assassin did not see another Gaf coming up behind him, and as if splitting a log, the berserker's axe cut down, slicing the man nearly in half with a single blow.

In spite of his terror, Sigma doubled over, retching at the sight of the man's entrails spilling out in a steaming pile onto the pavement.

But the assassins had seen their target, and nothing would stop them now. The Gaf who had cut down the first assassin went down seconds later as a black-robed attacker hit him from behind, driving his blade into the berserker's back, cutting the spinal column.

Sigma looked up and saw two men coming straight toward him. One more Gaf tried to intervene, leaping before the two. He caught one on a downward blow, cutting him from shoulder to hip, but the other leaped past, driving straight for his target.

With a squeal of terror Sigma turned blindly, running up the street.

How could Gablona do this? They were fellow Kohs, they had an arrangement! And, after all, it was only a game!

Sigma barely saw the loop of wire as it snaked over his head.

There was only the cold shock as the razor edge of the garrote dug through flesh, severing tissue and nerves.

An explosion of light filled his sight.

It was only a game! And then he fell into the darkness.

Sickened, Aldin turned away. If only Sigma had turned up the alley instead of going the other way, he most likely would have sent his men out to save him. He had been tempted to intervene anyhow. But he knew that in doing so some of his own men would die, with little if any hope of success, so sudden had been the attack.

He looked up at Oishi.

"That's one less," Oishi said coldly, and numbly, Aldin could only nod in return.

Hassan bolted the door shut as the last of the attackers slipped back in. One of the acolytes stood before him, panting for breath, a bloody garrote in his hand.

Gablona came pushing through the crowd at the door and could tell by the look on Hassan's face what the news was.

"Who did it?" Gablona asked, and Hassan pointed to the wide-eyed youngster who held up the gory instrument of destruction for his inspection.

Gablona looked at Sigma's blood as it slowly dripped off the handles tied to either end of the wire.

"Good," he mumbled, as if to himself, and then without another word turned and walked away.

The plan had worked just as Hassan said it would. One of the assassins had managed to creep onto the roof of Sigma's building and had overheard the Gaf's excited talk about their attack. Suspecting that Sigma would strike with everything he had against Aldin, they had simply waited until the attack was launched and, after taking the fortress, had simply settled back and waited for the return. The ruse of dressing up some of his own as green robes had worked better than planned, scattering Sigma's guards from one end of the street to the other.

Just before the attack had come word that Aldin had attempted to take him and destroyed his hiding place in the process. He could only laugh now at Aldin's discomfort. Hassan had second-guessed that one as well.

They now had Sigma's hiding place and supplies. Next it would be Aldin's turn, and then they could wait out the remaining days and return up the Skyhook in triumph.

Out in the street the Gafs howled with rage. The green robes had disappeared, easily outrunning the heavier warriors. Ura quickly realized that the cowards had no intention of fighting, and as he slowed, he heard for the first time the screams of combat behind him.

It was a trap! Turning, he called for his warriors to follow. Together they had raced back down the street and turned into the alleyway that led to their fortress. A score of his comrades were down, two or three still fighting with a knot of assassins that were withdrawing back into what was supposed to be their hiding place.

Bellowing with rage, Ura charged, but the door was slammed shut in his face. He and his comrades slammed on the door, trying to chop it down with their axes, and for several seconds he was oblivious to the fact that yet more Gafs were dropping around him as the assassins poured hot oil out of the murder hole above the door, while long spears were shoved out of the side windows.

Screaming with rage, Ura drew back and his comrades followed, the taunting jeers of the assassins ringing in their ears. It was then that Ura suddenly wondered what had happened to the one he was charged with protecting.

He scanned the street and spied several warriors standing in a circle farther up the street, looking somewhat mournfully at the ground.

It was Sigma.

Ura came up by the old man's side and knelt in the gutter. The slash mark of the garrote had cut clear to the spinal column and the Koh's head lolled back obscenely. Ura threw back his head and howled with rage.

For a Human, one without hair, he had found the old man to be tolerable, almost amusing with comments about battle and his obvious discomfort with the rough ways of the Basak. It was a wound to his pride that he had agreed to protect him and then failed. Ura looked at the body for a moment and then came back to his feet.

"Now what are we going to do?" Kolda snarled.

Ura looked around the group that had gathered. He looked back at their former hideout. And as he looked, yet another bitter taunt was hurled at the group.

More than half his comrades were dead. So thorough had been the surprise, many of them had been struck from behind as they pushed on up the street, oblivious to the threat from behind.

There was no place to hide now, and darkness was setting in—the time when mobs of Al'Shiga wandered the streets of the foreign quarter looking for victims. To rush the fortress was suicide, but he could see no other way. Raising his axe, he started to turn back toward certain death. At least then he could see the hairless one in the next world and apologize.

Kolda smiled as his leader walked away. At least this was one assignment that he didn't have to risk his life for. Maybe the one called Zola would pay him nevertheless. Then again, he realized, the game was still young, and perhaps there would be another chance to earn the riches that had been promised him.

"Come on," Oishi hissed, "let's get moving."

The last of the samurai slipped across the alley; in the darkness they were not even noticed by the knot of Gaf warriors standing over Sigma's body.

But Aldin, and Zergh standing by his side, did not move.

"They'll all be dead before morning," Zergh said quietly.

"There's not much we can do about it," Aldin replied grimly, still shocked at how vicious Sigma's end had been. There was a time when that man had been the most powerful Koh in the Cloud, and now he lay dead in the gutter, a victim of the so-called fun of combat.

"There is something you can do," Zergh said.

"Look, I know what you're thinking," Oishi interjected, ready to argue.

"And it's a damn good idea," Mari snapped quickly. "Those lumbering giants are fools on the defensive, we just saw that, but they would be murder to face in tight quarters on the attack."

Zergh came up close to Aldin.

"Let me do it," the old Gaf said. "They're savages, but honest savages.

"And besides," he said softly, "they're Gavarnians."

Aldin was about to stop him, but before he could say a word, the old Gaf broke free from the group. Oishi swore softly beneath his breath.

From out of the twilight Ura saw a shadow emerging. For a second he was ready to strike and then, to his amazement, realized that it was an aging Gaf, and not one of the Shiga, for this one wore a wonderful outfit of flowing robes, with two swords belted at his waist.

"I'm here to make an offer," Zergh said straightforwardly.

"What?"

"I'm a comrade of Aldin Larice."

With that several of the berserkers snarled and raised their axes, but Ura held them back.

"It was the other one, the fat one called Gablona that did this, not my man. We share the same enemy; we can share in his killing."

Ura hesitated. He was a fighter, not one to talk parley.

Zergh looked back at where Gablona and his men were now cloistered, and the taunts of the assassins could be plainly heard.

"You are good warriors," Zergh said. "Charge that fortress, and you'll die good warriors."

"We are not afraid of death, old one," a berserker snarled.

"Of course not," Zergh continued, "but all of you will die without taking a single one of them with you. You will go before your brothers without any servants to wait upon you in the afterworld. Your brothers will say that you are brave, to be sure, but that you died without bringing servants to honor them."

Several nervous minutes passed and then Aldin saw the Gafs coming back up the street, Zergh at the lead. Oishi swore even louder now.

"If they get into our midst and turn on us, it'll be difficult," Oishi snapped.

"But with them we have more numbers than Gablona," Mari argued.

Aldin looked at her and realized that for the first time she was speaking as if part of the group, rather than merely an outsider. She saw his look and shrugged her shoulders.

"We can barrack them in the basement," she continued, "and keep a guard up until we're sure. They just lost their leader, they're on a strange world—I think it's worth the chance."

Zergh came up to Aldin's side. "They'll join us. I think we can trust them, but it'll take a little time for their blood lust to calm down."

Together the two groups set off into the night, the Gafs being kept to the rear. At last the tavern was sighted. With a cry of alarm, Mari stopped at the sight of the back door, which had been torn clear off its hinges.

Oishi ordered Takashi and two others to rush the building. They entered and came out shortly thereafter and signaled that the tavern was empty.

The group rushed in, and with a cry of rage Mari surveyed the wreckage of her property. Lamps were finally lit, and while the group stayed in the kitchen, teams of samurai were first sent out to look for any deadfalls or traps.

"Who could have done this?" Mari shouted. "Look at this mess, just look at it!"

"Gablona perhaps?" Oishi ventured.

"I doubt it," Zergh said. "It would have been booby-trapped from one end to the other."

"It couldn't have been the Al'Shiga, the attackers were drinking like fish from the looks of it," Mari shouted, kicking the broken remains of emptied wine jugs.

Suddenly they all fell silent and turned to the Gafs, who still stood out in the narrow courtyard.

"Well, we were angry when you weren't here for a good fight," Ura said, a look of pained embarrassment on his face.

CHAPTER 9

Out of breath, Kurst turned the last corner at the run. Blackie was already there to meet him.

He looked up and down the corridor—it was empty.

"Come on, let's move!" he shouted, grabbed her arm, and raced for the nearest lift that would send them up the two hundred stories to the hidden exchange office.

He punched the buttons, and the elevator kicked up, rocketing them skyward.

"What is it?" Sisa gasped, still trying to catch her breath. She'd been in her office when the personal com link that tied her to Kurst clicked on, telling her to meet him by the back service elevator.

Kurst looked around the elevator wide-eyed. It could be bugged. The information was so hot that he didn't even dare to call it in over their private link from Zola's offices across the street. It had been an incredible stroke of luck that he had been with Zola in the com center when word came up through the scramble system and then been decoded while they were in the room. With a shout of triumph Zola had raced from the center, leaving Kurst to fend for himself. And fend he had, covering the half kilometer to Blackie's office in what he felt must have been record time.

Damn, why hadn't he thought of a code?

Desperate, he fished in his pockets for a slip of paper and a pen and then started to dash off a note.

Sigma dead 20 min ago by G; 10 min, info goes public!

The door slipped open.

Blackie grabbed Kurst by the arm, and together they ran to her office.

"Stay here," she snapped. "You can watch through the hookup."

Blackie raced out of her office and down the corridor to the trading floor.

The big board was still going wild, the last hour's report having announced that Sigma had hit Aldin's hiding place. Odds had shot up for one of the two to be dead by the other before the day was out, and trading had been frantic.

Kurst adjusted the vid link and saw Blackie slowly and deliberately walking on to the trading floor, her traders and agents coming around her in a circle.

The group broke apart and within seconds the buy and sell orders went up for a primary kill/day buy, meaning that they were centering in on options for a particular event for a particular day, in this case for Sigma to be killed by Gablona on game day thirty-one, while at the same time unloading blocks of tickets that called for Sigma to live. Kurst felt a moment of panic. When the news hit the floor within the next five minutes, her jumping the market would be just too obvious.

But then he breathed a sigh of relief when he saw that she was masking the buy, mixing it in with other orders that would, in fact, be worthless.

Within minutes she had closed out on nearly a quarter of all tickets bearing the critical information regarding Sigma's death. However, several other firms still held the rest, steadfastly refusing to sell at any offer, and were now competing with her in frantic bids to snap up the blocks held by a number of the smaller firms. Among the hundreds of traders on the floor, this drama was but a minor scene in the far wider frenzy.

A siren sounded in the background. The hundreds of traders on the floor fell silent.

The big board, quoting the various options, went blank, and in two-meter-high letters an announcement started to scroll across.

CONFIRMED REPORT JUST ANNOUNCED BY GAMEMASTER XSARN TO ALL COM LINK SERVICES. SIGMA AZERMATTI DEAD DAY FIFTEEN, GAME DAY THIRTY-ONE, BY CORBIN GABLONA.

Pandemonium broke out. Only moments before there were still over seven million possible outcomes to the game. The number had now dropped to just under forty thousand. Over 99 percent of the options that moments before were worth billions were now nothing but worthless scraps of paper. The first cut in the market had been made.

Traders ran franticly, screaming. White-robed medical crews that had been waiting days for this moment came out onto the floor. Half a dozen traders were already down with cardiac arrests, mixed with a sprinkling of strokes and various fits. In a far corner there was the crack of an Erik 10, but the user had not been thoughtful, and after the bullet smashed through his head, it took out two other traders. Many others, however, had taken the far more customary path for such a moment. Swarms of traders raced off the floor to call their lawyers so that defenses could be prepared, since more than one innocent investor in mining shares off Oseabond would soon discover that his broker had looted the stock for "temporary working capital."

Ninety-nine percent of the market was gone, but there were still tens of millions of options on tickets that had increased a hundredfold in value.

Blackie finally managed to break free of the floor and slipped back up to her office.

"That was a close one," she said, slumping into a chair.

"Do you think it was too obvious?" Kurst groaned, now very nervous over what they had just pulled off.

"Discounting the bad tickets we bought as false leads, we still increased our investment by at least ten thousand percent. We can pay back the investments that I sort of, how shall I say, borrowed from, and the profit is all ours! I think that was worth the risk:"

Kurst shook his head in amazement. The fear of being found out by Zola was washed away by the incredible wealth the futures market was creating.

"Besides," Blackie boasted, "I can out-con any con in the business. Hell, I got my start selling polyester futures to Gafs. Now let's set up that coding information so we can jump the next kill as well."

"They did what?"

With a shout of rage Ulsak, the Master Ulla of the yellows, rose up from the silk divan, a long-bladed knife poised in his hand, and strode across the room to confront the trembling messenger.

"Now repeat what you've just told me," he said evenly. All who served Ulsak feared these moments when a message came that was contrary to his given orders and plans.

"All three tried to kill each other," the messenger, a young ulla, said slowly, staring past Ulsak as if he did not exist.

"And?"

"The one called Sigma was slain by the one protected by the dark robes."

Ulsak stood silent for long seconds, the dozen lesser ullas about him silent as well.

"And the men assigned to cover this moment?"

"They weren't there," the messenger replied, a slight tremble in his voice.

"They weren't there?" one of the ullas cried. "That was their assignment, and you were responsible!"

"Some blue robes came into the foreign quarter during the festival, a fight started, and my men left their posts to aid their brothers," the messenger replied weakly.

"Damn. Damn all the fools!" In his rage Ulsak was about to say more, and then, remembering that others were present, he turned away.

"Leave, all of you leave. And wait out in the hall," Ulsak roared.

He heard the door creak shut behind them.

Returning to the divan, he wearily sat down. He could understand in a way how it happened. All of the lower orders viewed the other clans with suspicion. It was as it was planned to be—constant training and warfare that only those of the inner order of ullas and masters understood. But nevertheless, this one foolish mistake could cost him everything that he had planned.

Rising up again, he went into the private room behind the audience chamber and pulled down a book of holy writ. As he opened the bound volume, several sheets of paper fell out. Taking them in his hand, he gazed upon them for a moment. They were of a texture never before seen on the Hole, pearly white, almost translucent, unlike the rough parchment used for the holy writings. Holding the sheets up, the memory of that moment of fear had come back.

Nearly forty days past, he had stepped alone into the Seda. The messenger had come in the morning, identical to the messenger that had come a half-dozen times before to speak of a plan so stunning that he at first had refused to believe it.

But the words of that first messenger had gradually weaved a spell, until he had finally spoken what had been hinted at throughout the previous meetings.

"It is the time for the hidden Ema to reveal himself," the stranger had whispered.

Those words had come to him as if the messenger had somehow looked into Ulsak's dreams. Dreams that had tormented his nights, and in recent years had danced at the edge of his every waking thought.

Could he, in fact, be the hidden Ema? The one promised to at last unite the Al'Shiga, to end their exile and return them to their destiny among the stars?

So the whisperings of the messenger had worked their way, until at last the stranger had offered him proof of his greatness.

"Come with me to the Seda, rise upon it into the heavens, and there meet with the archangel that shall give the Keys of the Cloud to you."

He had slain the man, in a wild moment of fear. In fact, the man had challenged him to do so as proof of what he said. So, drawing his blade, he had cut him apart. But strangely the man had not died, even with belly open. At last Ulsak had decapitated the creature, and, to his horror, still the severed head had whispered those words to him.

"You shall be the Ema. But first you must rise up to heaven to receive your mandate."

The next night another messenger had come, knowing all that had happened to the previous one and saying that still the archangel waited. But if he did not come, then another of the master ullas would answer the summons to greatness instead.

So at last, in the middle of the night, Ulsak had followed him to the base of the Seda. He felt somehow that he was going to his doom, for surely any of the Al'Shiga who dared to ascend the tower to the first level fell back to their death. But he knew in his heart that if he did not attempt this, he would be forever tormented in his mind, wondering if what the messenger said was truth.

Alone, they had stepped into the ball of glass and rose heavenward. The glass room slowed at what he knew was the place of falling, but strangely it did not stop, and then suddenly it raced upward with such speed that he had cried aloud with fear, for it felt as if his body were being crushed in upon itself.

As a master, Ulsak knew that such things as archangels, such things as heaven, were merely legends to feed to the masses, but as the Hole fell away beneath him and the stars shined with piercing coldness above, he feared for a moment that he might have been wrong.

At last the crushing eased and the room of glass slowed, rising into what appeared to be a great building hanging on the side of the Seda. Attached to the building was a strange shape, and then he realized that for the first time in two thousand years, one from the Al'Shiga was looking upon a ship that sailed the stars. And then the door from the glass room opened.

For the first time in his life Ulsak knew a moment of true terror. If there was such a thing as archangels, then he was gazing upon one.

The creature hovered before him, with long robes trailing to the floor and what he supposed were eyes gazing upon him with cold intensity.

"I am Losa," the creature had whispered. "Do my bidding and through me you shall be called the Ema."

The memory of that moment still struck fear into his heart. He had come to realize that what he had seen was no angel of the Unseen One, no being tied to the legends of holy writ. But at that moment all that he knew had been washed away in awe and terror.

He turned away from the memory, for even in the privacy of his inner musing Ulsak found it impossible to admit to himself that he was capable of fear. For in the end, had not this creature merely been part of his own plan and shown him the path to the Ema? The path that he had known in his heart was rightfully his.

He let the book of holy writ drop to the floor, and taking the sheets of paper, he walked over to the single lamp that illuminated the hidden room.

After opening the sheets, he spread them out upon the table. The instructions of Losa had been clear. The creature had been wise in that he had stated that not all events might be controlled. There were certain things that would be allowed to happen, but he must guarantee that specific proscribed events could not happen.

Ulsak scanned the notes upon the paper, and coming to the thirty-first day, he saw what was listed—and sighed with relief.

Turning through the sheets, though, he saw what would be allowed afterward and started to form his plans. There had been one mistake, but there could not, for any reason, be a second.

He would be the Ema. Was not the prophecy of his coming correct? All of this was no coincidence. Had not this Losa come in preparation of the Great Darkening that would occur in but five more festivals? The day before the messenger had first come, the sky watchers had told him of the coming celestial event with hushed awe. The soothsayers and shamans had whispered that the Great Darkening would be the proper time for the Ema to reveal himself. The masses were not yet aware of the portent, but he would declare its coming when the moment was right.

He scanned the sheets of paper yet again and smiled. The strange offworlder in the dark robes would have to be told now what to do, and Ulsak would find a way to work upon the other offworlder as well.

After returning to the bookshelf, he picked the book up off the floor, placed the papers inside, returned it to the shelf, and walked out of the room.

"Return to my presence," he shouted, coming back into the audience chamber.

The door out into the hall swung open and the ullas filed in.

"This shall not happen again, for I command it, and as I command, so it shall be written and done, for every word that I speak shall now be written as law. Soon the Great Darkening shall be upon us and then I shall be revealed," Ulsak said evenly, fixing each of them in turn with his gaze.

Nervously the ullas looked at each other. Only one could ever say that his words would be written as law—the one who would be the Ema, the one who would lead them back to the Cloud.

Ulsak looked at them and smiled.

"And I shall remember which ullas served me well in the days before my revealing," he said.

"There is a message to be sent," he continued. "Send in my writer, and one to carry the note. You may leave me now."

The ullas nervously looked to each other.

"And the one that failed me," he said softly, and the ulla who had brought him the message stopped and turned back to hear his fate.

"You shall go to the temple of our fathers where . . ." Ulsak stopped for a moment, staring into the man's eyes. He always felt a strange delicious chill when he gazed into the eyes of one he was about to kill.

". . . You shall impale yourself," Ulsak whispered.

The man's features went ashen.

He watched the eyes widen into terror. Some would cry out now, or even throw themselves to the ground, screaming for mercy. Ulsak waited.

The man started to sway, and then collapsed.

"Get him out of my sight," Ulsak snarled, disgusted with the display.

The door closed and he was alone.

Chuckling softly, the one who dreamed of being the Ema

turned to the side table and, cutting a fragment of his favorite delicacy, contemplated what needed to be done.

"It's chaos out there," Bukha said, looking out over the stadium field at the thousands of lawyers and accountants working on the financial tangle of the Alexandrian game. Wild shouts echoed up from the open field, which had been sectioned off into thousands of office cubicles. Several in the crowd were already being taken away by the medical crews, and Bukha could only wonder if they would still be billing their services at eight hundred katars an hour even as they lay in the hospital.

Tia looked over at the Gaf.

"Ticket sales have skyrocketed again, just as Zola predicted," she stated even as she stirred the drinks and then offered one to Bukha.

"So, your stock is going up as well," Bukha replied.

"Zola just announced a doubling of shares, so of course I'm happy. Hell, I've just made more than a billion on paper in the last hour."

"On paper, and on the blood of Sigma," Bukha replied sharply.

"It was you and the Xsarn who thought it up," Tia snapped back in reply.

"I know, I know," Bukha said, throwing up his hands in a defensive gesture. "But at the time it was still just a game. Granted, a game with some danger to it, but I never thought it would come to this," he growled, pointing out to the thousands below who were still running about in a frenzy.

"Anyhow," Tia said, putting a hand on Bukha's arm in a gesture of reconciliation, "you sent me a message saying you'd learned something."

"Right, well, I managed to track down two of the individuals in question."

"And?"

Bukha left his perch by the window and settled in behind his desk. With a flip of a switch, the window overlooking the stadium was sealed off and the faint hum of an anti-bugging static field switched on.

"Can't be too careful," Bukha said.

"Then you're on to something," Tia said, coming up to sit across from Bukha.

"We're still hunting through the records for the others. Damn difficult. The ID numbers are valid, cross-referenced with retinal scan and printing at birth, but who they are now has been buried through name shifts and such. Most of my own security people go through the same procedure. But anyhow, we think we've got a lead on two of them. One of them is a Heta drone, so wiped on the juice he's a scramble. His story is that he won the cash in a massive gambling binge, bought the tickets, then sold them out to a dealer to buy more juice."

"Five million katars of juice! Who's he kidding?"

"Claims he got jumped and lost the shipment."

"Xsarnfood," Tia snapped.

"Exactly."

"So that leaves us nowhere. The juicer was a front, and we still don't know for whom."

Bukha shook his head slowly, and for the first time Tia saw a look of fear in the Gaf's eyes.

"The second buyer is a juicer as well, same story, but there's one key difference: his last job was working as a liaison officer for the Alma Consortium."

Tia's eyes grew wide with astonishment. The Alma was a board set up by the Overseers to coordinate the few business transactions that would from time to time arise between the Overseers and the other inhabitants of the Cloud.

"Then the Overseers are in the game!"

Bukha nodded his head in reply.

"But if they are, then what the hell for?"

It'd been an uneasy night for all of them. The Gaf berserkers had finally been convinced by Zergh that the basement was the best place for them, so that both sides could get a good night's sleep, and in the end he had agreed to go down with them.

The doors were another problem. The Gafs in their enthusiasm had smashed the front barrier to pieces and, before leaving, had torn the back one off its hinges. There was nothing to do but pile shattered tables and debris against the openings and post triple guards of samurai on each.

The brief night of six hours finally passed, and the Gafs were let up from below.

"It can't go on like this," Oishi whispered impatiently, as the hulking warriors barraged into the kitchen, bellowing for food, while Mari shouted back that the damn fools had destroyed most of it the day before.

"Well, we've taken them in, for better or worse," Aldin replied wearily, still yawning from lack of sleep. "If we try to turn them out now, we'll have twenty-six more enemies ready to tear us apart. And besides, how the hell are we going to get them out anyhow?"

"They can be useful," Takashi interjected.

Oishi looked at his old friend with a jaundiced eye.

"Remember what our emperor said about dogs—and to my thinking they're nothing but overgrown fighting dogs."

"Don't let Zergh hear you say that," Aldin mumbled.

"They've got traits to admire: bravery in battle and absolute disregard for self, to begin with," Takashi argued.

"Along with loudness, brawling, and drunkenness," Aldin started.

"If we could only be sure of their absolute loyalty to you," Takashi continued, "they'd be worth the trouble."

Aldin sat back in his chair. If only Yaroslav were here. Yaroslav had been an absolute encyclopedia of arcane knowledge about such things. With such beings, to simply go up and ask what would command their loyalty would be a loss of face.

He tried to cast back through his memory. There were the territorial rituals of dogs, which involved holding the lesser creature by the throat or urinating on territory or even the body of the lesser being, but he didn't think that would go over too well.

"I wish we had some sake right now," Takashi said wistfully. "It'd clear my head for some action."

Then the memory came back to Aldin, from what seemed ages ago when he was still a student and Yaroslav was lecturing on the similarity of Gaf social customs across thousands of primitive worlds that were prefeudal, even though they'd been cut off for centuries.

Aldin caught Zergh's eye and motioned for him to come over, even as he gagged on the thought.

The circle of Gafs stood before Aldin, a look of reverent awe on their faces. Even the samurai were impressed and mumbled to themselves in the background. Ura was the last to finish, and coming up to Aldin, the Gaf raised the two-handed beaker up to where he stood atop the shattered bar.

Aldin looked inside and struggled to stop the churning of his stomach. If only pissing on their territory could have been the answer, he thought wistfully. He had to do it; to back out now would be the worst possible rejection imagined, and certain to trigger a fight to the death.

He closed his eyes and brought the beaker to his lips, and then raised it up. The hot liquid hit his lips. He forced his mouth to take it, and the salty taste made him want to gag it all back up.

Finally he swallowed. It had to be done. He swallowed again and then again, but still the beaker was only half empty.

The warm liquid coursed down his throat. He tilted the beaker up higher, cheating a bit as some of the liquid poured out either side of his mouth and ran down his robes. At the sight of it, however, the samurai let out a cheer of approval and the Gafs joined in, beating their axes on the floor, raising a shower of splinters.

The cup was getting lighter. He gulped again and then tilted up to the vertical so that the last splash of liquid washed over his face.

He opened his eyes and looked out at the Gafs. As one they raised their axes on high, bellowing their approval. Aldin smiled, and looked about the room. Even Oishi was impressed, shaking his head, a bemused smile on his face that turned to a wince of pain when Ura came up to the samurai's side and clapped him on the shoulder in a show of comradely spirit.

"You have taken part of our spirits into your flesh, Aldin Taug," Ura roared, "now we shall serve without question.

Even our last lord had not offered to do such, to mingle his soul with ours."

Aldin heard that bit of news with astonishment. He assumed Sigma would have done so, but then realized that the old Koh, who had merely dabbled in primitive anthropology as a hobby related to the games, would not have picked up such an arcane bit of knowledge.

"Then hear me," Aldin said sharply. And the Gafs stopped their celebration.

"It is true I am a hairless one, and am honored that warriors such as you would agree to fight for me."

The Gafs roared at this, making ribald comments about how they would put hair on him one way or another.

"But you let your last master die, even if he was only a master of coin for you."

The Gafs fell silent, not wishing to be reminded of their failure.

"I say this not to shame you," Aldin said quietly, "but to promise you honors and the souls of many servants. But there is only one way you can win those honors."

He fell silent, playing a typical trick of oration, and the Gafs went for it, calling out for an answer to his riddle.

"You will listen to me, even in the heat of battle, and if not me, then Oishi or Zergh. Even if the enemy is before you and we say fight not, then you will not fight."

The warriors started to mumble, but Aldin held up the cup he had just drained, and at the sight of it they fell silent again.

"By what I have just done, I have taken in a small part of each of your souls, some of your strength and your wisdom. Trust me, turn aside from the small meaningless fights when I tell you, and in the end I shall give you the greatest fight that you have ever dreamed of as reward."

With that, the Gafs again roared their approval. Aldin stepped down from the bar and, with a ceremonial flourish, strode out of the room and into the kitchen, with Mari and Zergh following.

"What big fight at the end?" Zergh asked.

"I had to promise them something," Aldin said, "so I promised them what they wanted most."

"But if there isn't any fight at the end, then they'll be real problems, for one who has drunk of them cannot lie."

"I'll worry about that later," Aldin said weakly, desperately looking around the room. Then seeing what he was looking for, he sped to the far corner of the room and, leaning into the sink, promptly vomited back up the half gallon of Gaf blood he had downed only minutes before.

"So, the Overseers are into the game," Yaroslav said, as if it were knowledge that he was already familiar with and wasn't any cause for concern on his part.

"You act like you already know," Tia replied sharply.

"But of course, my dear. But of course."

Tia looked across at the old man, not sure if she should be angry at him for not saying anything before. She wasn't quite sure why she had even bothered to come see him. Since Aldin's departure, he had seemed to have withdrawn from all involvement with the game, or the possible negative effect it might have on his old friend.

"I thought you'd at least have some concern for Aldin."

"But I do," he replied evenly.

"Well, you certainly aren't showing any. He's been down there for seventeen days, and what have you done but sit here in this lousy one-room flat and read your damn journals on the com link?"

"What else can I do?" Yaroslav said quietly. "Research keeps me busy."

"Well, you could try to help Aldin."

"How?"

She couldn't find an answer for that, and exasperated, she sank into the one empty chair that graced the shabby little room.

"You really do care for him, don't you?" Yaroslav said softly, looking across at the girl.

"He may be the only thing I've got left," Tia replied, her eyes starting to brim over with tears. "I've been such a bitch to him. He tried to warn me about Gablona, and I thought he was just being an old prude. He's the only man that's ever shown me any kindness."

Yaroslav sat back in his chair and sighed. "You're lonely, dear. But it'll pass."

"I don't think so," she said. "I can't trust anyone. If any

man shows an interest, I think right away that he's after me because, technically, I'm a Koh, or that I was once the mistress to that pig Gablona and might still have influence."

She spat the name Gablona with hatred.

"Remember, you're a Gablona as well," Yaroslav replied. "Your tie to the Gablonas is with blood; Aldin's only your uncle through marriage."

"But he's the only one that showed any interest in me for who I am."

Tia looked away for a moment, struggling for control. When she turned back again, the cold exterior was back.

"I just wish," she said softly, "that I'd never gotten involved in this whole thing."

"It was the only way," Yaroslav replied. "Corbin would have hunted Aldin down sooner or later. We had to bring it to a head where Aldin would at least have a fighting chance for survival. It's just that certain unforeseen things seemed to have come into play."

"You mean the Overseers."

Yaroslav smiled, and standing up, he shut down the com link system.

"I think I've found what I was after this morning," he said. "Had my suspicions from the beginning. I was presented with only half of a puzzle, you see. That's why I stayed behind. I couldn't tell Aldin, it'd just give him something else to worry about."

Yaroslav walked over to the one closet in the room, and, pulling open the door, he stepped back as clothes, books, and stacks of papers came tumbling out. A white, mangy-looking cat with mismatched eyes of blue and green leaped out as well, took one look at Tia, and then leaped back into the closet. Yaroslav stepped over the pile, waded into the jumble, and started poking around.

"I'll be going on a little trip, my dear," he shouted from out of the darkness.

"Where?"

The old man stuck his head back out of the closet and smiled. "Rather not say. Things might be getting a little heated before the end, and the fewer that know, the better. Just do me a favor. Drop by here occasionally and feed little Tanya for me. Found her or, should I say, she found me the other day, and we've become quite good friends.

"Oh, and by the way," he said almost as if by an after-thought. "When you get a chance, check up on any of your family's shipping firms. I have my suspicions—might be nothing, then again it might be everything. It's what I've been hunting for. That's why I've got to leave, make sure that certain things don't happen."

"What are you talking about?" she replied.

"Just a hunch, the other half of the puzzle, if you will. You'll know it when you see it."

A moment later Yaroslav reemerged from the closet, and shouldering a weather-beaten pack, he gave Tia a quick kiss on the cheek and headed out the door.

"When will you get back?" Tia cried, following him out into the dank, foul-smelling hall.

"Who knows?" he said, and turning, he disappeared down the hall whistling an off-key tune.

CHAPTER 10

"THIS IS SHEER INSANITY," OSHI GROWLED, LOOKING WARILY from side to side. The north gate of the foreign quarter was behind them now, and as they turned the corner, it disappeared from view.

"We need food, we need other supplies, and most of all we need information. I plan to go the Seda," Aldin replied.

"But you shouldn't be out like this," Oshi pleaded. "It's too dangerous."

"The Gafs are sworn to me," Aldin whispered. "I've got to demonstrate to them that I'm willing to take the risks as well."

Oshi fell silent at the response, not willing to admit to the logic of what Aldin was saying. The argument was far too true; he knew that his old lord Asano would have done exactly the same. Asano was no daimyo to hide within his fortress; if there was a crisis, he would stride forward to meet it head-on.

When Aldin had casually announced that he was going out on the trading venture as well, the Gafs had shouted their approval, and Oishi had seen his own men look one to the other and quietly nod their approval.

The addition of the Gafs was already paying off. Thirty of the samurai under Takashi had stayed behind to guard the tavern and work on defense, leaving eight men and all the Gafs to go with Aldin.

Not being festival day, the streets were crowded with Al'Shiga going about their daily business. Young men and women, dressed in their distinctive tight-fitting robes, wandered by in small groups, eyeing the passing strangers with open hostility. Mari stuck close to Aldin's side, guiding him and his followers toward the Seda.

So mysterious had the Al'Shiga been to Aldin that he had assumed that the city would somehow be like a badly made vid, with knife-welding assassins lurking in deserted alleyways, the streets empty except for furtive forms sneaking out of dark hiding places rushing to secret rendezvous.

But even on such a world as the Hole, people still had to fulfill the mundane tasks of living, no matter how exotic their beliefs might be.

Open-air market stalls lined the street, merchants selling a wide variety of wares. Finely woven carpets were spread out for display next to delicately worked silver jewelry, furniture carved from exotic woods, pottery, and finely painted prayer cards that, when burned, served as votive offerings.

Being a restricted primitive world, there were no tech devices, and Aldin found the change to be refreshing. Here were products still made by individuals who obviously took pride in their skills, and eagerly shouted to the passing offworlders to come and buy.

Heading down toward the main thoroughfare, the group passed the food markets, and Aldin was reminded that there were some negative aspects to primitive worlds as well.

They plodded through rotten castoffs, for when the produce had spoiled to the point of no longer being sellable, the merchants simply swept the refuse off their tables and into the streets.

The Shiga taboo against meat meant that only vegetable products were available out in the open. There was a wide variety of tropical fruits and grain products from the cultivated fields beyond the cities. Some of the offerings were mushrooms and fungi grown in the geothermal-heated caves that honeycombed the world beneath their feet. Some of the growths looked truly gruesome in the daylight. One species and its dealers caught Aldin's attention, for he'd heard mention of it even before coming down to the Hole, and he slowed to take a closer look.

The fungi being offered was a huge bud nearly several meters across that looked like a decaying human corpse, known appropriately enough as "the rotting man." The plant had an elongated central pod with five tendrils, one rounded where a head would be, the other four corresponding to arms and legs.

The closer the plant looked to human form, the more valuable it became. Growers had found all sorts of tricks, such as crossbreeding and cutting the shoots while still young, to coax the plant to follow a desired form. Masters of the art, working with secret knowledge passed down for generations, would on occasion grow true masterpieces with fingers, toes, and even faces and pale white hair.

Of course, such masterpieces fetched the highest prices, sometimes trading on the market for equal weight in rare amber.

Aging was part of the process as well. After the plant was harvested, the interior would start to decompose into a green, pulpy liquid that fermented. Cut open too soon, the contents were still just sugar; too late, and the drink had gone sour. Consuming the liquid was the only infraction of the taboo against drinking that was tolerated in public, and thus was even more valued. To some connoisseurs of the rotting man, it was the bouquet when the plant was sliced open that was worth the price, the drink being merely an afterthought. Elaborate ceremonies had sprung up around the opening of a masterpiece. A full ritual could take a day or more to reach the moment when the knife finally punctured the skin, the invited guests honored beyond measure for the right to attend and inhale what to them was the delectable fragrance.

The samurai around Aldin watched with disgust as a deal seemed to come to completion at a vendor's stall. The haggling had been brisk, with several parties competing for a prime specimen, though not quite of masterpiece status.

Aldin's curiosity was aroused by the sight, and he slowed to watch the results.

The deal was finally struck, and with great ceremony, the successful bidder called over his kinsmen to pick up the coffinlike box that held the rotting man so that it could be borne home for the feast.

The merchant, now following tradition, brought out a smaller rotting man a half meter in length, and obviously of inferior stock. After reaching into the folds of his robe, he pulled out his dagger and, with a flourish, cut the fungi open from head to foot with one quick slice. The plant emitted a soggy, raspy belch as the air within was released. The bidders and their kinsmen leaned forward and, like true connoisseurs, exclaimed their judgments.

"Fine scent, rich and full-bodied," one cried.

"Richly sour. Perhaps aged too far past perfection." Another sniffed.

A faint stir of breeze carried the scent over to Aldin, and with a gag he realized yet another reason why the fungi was called the rotting man.

The merchant turned to a small tray of cups and, after scooping them into the plant one after another, offered a round of drinks to his clients. The pulpy green liquid had a faint iridescent glow of putrification to it, and trying to hide his disgust, Aldin pushed on, the samurai muttering darkly to themselves, while the Gafs laughed at their companions' discomfort, for they felt the entire show had been a display of crudeness equal almost to their own.

Leaving the street of the rotting men, the group turned into a narrow alley where no stalls were open. Mari explained that it was a quicker way to the Seda, bypassing the more crowded sections of the market. She assured Oishi there was no danger, but for a moment Aldin felt as if the bad vid he had imagined earlier had been filmed in this very spot. For indeed up and down the street doorways would come open for a moment, several individuals would peek out and then quickly scurry away with strange bulges under their robes, while others, waiting in side alleyways, would rush out, leap through the open doors, and then slam them shut behind them.

He looked to Mari with a quizzical, raised eyebrow.

"Meat merchants. The only native animal worth eating

looks like a pig and is taboo. The damn things thrive here, living down in the caves. They feed them the cast-off mushrooms and fungi and turn out fertilizer. The meat gets sold here. Everyone eats it, but no one wants an elder or ulla to see them. That's why most of the Shigs eat in secret.

"It's not wise to stare, they might think you're trying to recognize them," she added, and with that, Aldin urged the group to push on.

"We're coming up on the merchants of the Hauchma Sul," Mari whispered, as the group approached a turn in the road.

"The what?" Aldin asked, curious about the sound of disgust in her voice.

"It's rumored that they somehow train a plant to grow over a human skeleton until finally the bones are devoured and only the roots are left."

Aldin tried to suppress a shudder.

"Like the rotting man plants, the Shiga have a near reverence for the things, hanging them as decorations to remind them of their mortality."

Turning the corner of the thoroughfare, the group came to a stop at the frightening sight that confronted them. All up and down the lane hung hundreds of vinelike forms, that appeared to be exact replicas of human and Gaf skeletons. Aldin paused for a moment to look closer, and as he stopped, a merchant came bustling out of a shop, eager to make a sale even if only to a cursed offworlder.

"Finest Hauchma Suls to be found on the Hole," the merchant started. "Every rib in place, look, just look at this one here, even the teeth are there. Count them, this one has all it's teeth."

"How do you make these?" Aldin asked, thinking of what Mari had said.

The merchant looked at him and smiled, wagging his finger.

"The secret of the Al'Shiga," the merchant said. "If I told you, you offworlders would not buy from us."

"Just curious, that's all," Aldin said, and drawing back, he started to leave.

"Surely a small one, a child's form, might be more to your liking?" the merchant asked.

"Sorry, I'm not interested. Just looking."

"Pig spawn," the merchant snapped, spitting at Aldin's feet. The native hurriedly withdrew as the Basaks growled menacingly.

They moved off down the lane and at last came to the open boulevard that led straight as an arrow to their destination.

The Skyhook soared straight into the heavens above them. It could, of course, be seen from anywhere on the Hole, but it was only here on the main concourse that the view was unimpeded—the full magnificence of the First Traveler creation soaring above them.

To Aldin, who had seen many of the strangest sights in the Cloud, from the ringlike Kolbard to the remnants of the great supernova, the sight of the tower still left him awestruck. Like many of the other creations of the First Travelers, it had a permanence to it that transcended anything the Humans and Gafs had so far dared to attempt.

The Gafs and samurai looked at the structure, not able to quite understand its function as Aldin could, but nevertheless convinced that here was something that only gods could build.

"If we're going to make contact," Mari announced, "it'll be someplace around here." Following her lead, the group set out across the vast open plaza that surrounded the Skyhook.

The pavement was of the same material used by the First Travelers to face the Skyhook. However, the brilliant metallic substance was barely visible, for the square from end to end was coated with the remnants of thousands of festivals that had been held down through the centuries. Over the entire square hung the noisome stench of decaying blood, so that Aldin and his samurai companions covered their faces and struggled to hold down their breakfast with each breath.

A faint stirring of wind brought drifting clouds of smoke emitted from one of the clan temples that bordered the square, adding yet another overpowering smell to the fetid plaza.

With a shudder, Aldin looked over to the blocklike structure. A procession was weaving its way up the outside steps, dragging a yellow-robed form along in the middle. The thin, high cries of the victim drifted on the foul-smelling breeze.

Horrified, Aldin slowed to watch, but a cloud of smoke curled down from the top of the temple, obstructing the view; therefore he could only imagine what nightmare was being performed atop the temple stairs.

From out of the interior of the temple came more forms, carrying shroud-wrapped bodies upon their shoulders, and they, too, turned and started up the outside steps. While this drama was being enacted, others were crossing the square on their own business, not even pausing to take a second look, so inured were they to the harsh demands of their cults.

"I think we better push on," Mari whispered, grabbing Aldin by the arm.

At last they reached the base of the Skyhook and ascended the stairs that led to the wide platform that surrounded the structure.

The scene was one of chaos.

Offworld merchants stood behind their temporary stalls, trading with the natives for the precious green amber. Most of the merchants were day runners, as the offworlders who dared to live in the foreign quarter referred to them with disdain.

They'd come down the Skyhook on the morning run, do their trading during daylight, and then hop a car back up to safety at day's end. The Shiga, who hated all foreigners, at least had a small measure of respect for those who dared to live in the foreign quarter, but for the day runners their contempt was outright and without reservation.

Gangs of young Shiga thought it high sport to go down to the Seda and pelt the merchants with offal. Legitimate dealers of the Shiga felt it an act of high humor if, after striking a fair deal, they could still cut the merchant's throat after goods had been exchanged. However, their code did command that it was sinful to kill with intent of robbing, so after a merchant and his guards were dispatched, they would leave their amber in payment for the goods traded, and depart.

Of course, such an act would trigger a near riot, as the dead man's neighbors fell upon his stall. Such activities caused even greater disdain on the part of the Shiga, who would jeer such base activities.

At times the merchants' circle appeared to be the center of a mad feeding frenzy. A merchant would be killed, his neighbors would fall upon the loot lying in the street, and more Shiga would move in to kill the unwary, thus leaving more stalls open, until a bloodbath would be triggered, and the surviving merchants, their deep pockets stuffed to overflowing with green amber, would flee back to the protection of the Skyhook waiting room.

Aldin slowly walked the circle about the tower, the Shiga eyeing him with suspicion. Fortunately no blue robes were in the crowd, as Mari had foreseen, since today was a sacred day for their particular cult and, as such, all were in the temples.

"Aldin, Aldin Larice!" a voice suddenly echoed.

Aldin turned and saw a merchant waving and grimacing excitedly in his direction.

"Will Wedser!"

Shaking his head with disbelief, Aldin motioned for his guards to follow, and warily they edged through the crowd that backed away at their approach.

Wedser motioned for his half-dozen guards to back out of the booth, and as the samurai and Gafs set up a protective ring, Aldin stepped into the enclosure.

Wedser reached for a small lever underneath the table and the guillotine shutters slammed down. There was an angry cry from the samurai outside, but Aldin could hear Mari reassuring them.

With a grin he grabbed Wedser's one good hand. His friend, as usual, looked the worse for wear. It seemed that whenever he'd run into his old school and gambling friend, there was another part of his original anatomy gone, replaced by a shining prosthesis that would be embellished with fine gems or intricate carvings.

The right hand, of course, was a replacement, the original having been lost when the two of them were still students and had gone on a drunken hunting expedition against one of the smaller dragons of Maci.

Both of Wedser's ears were of the finest silver, a substitute for the ones hacked off in a barroom brawl. To Aldin's amazement, Wedser's nose was now made of gem-encrusted platinum, and he couldn't help but stare.

"Ah, yes, the nose." Wedser chuckled. "Remember my Gaf bodyguard Orklon? Well, he bit it off when he thought I'd cheated him on a little wager."

"But I saw Orklon standing outside!" Aldin exclaimed.

"We made up," Wedser said matter-of-factly.

Aldin shook his head, not even bothering to ask for the details.

Wedser, still chuckling, reached into his tunic and pulled out a flask, offering it to Aldin.

"You know, I've got several thousand riding on you," Wedser said while Aldin took a long pull on the flask.

"How the hell did you get into the betting?" Aldin asked. "That's a Koh privilege."

"Not anymore." Wedser chuckled. "The entire Cloud's betting on this one." And then he went on to explain the intricacies of the lottery and the underground futures market that had sprung up around it.

Aldin could only smile and shake his head.

"Seems like you already know about the lottery," Wedser remarked, looking at his old friend.

Aldin only smiled in reply.

"You know, the betting was rather heavy that you'd already be dead."

"Well, I'm sorry to disappoint the mob," Aldin replied bitterly.

"Anyhow, I got in on the beginning when the payoff was over five million to one," Wedser announced triumphantly.

"I hope you at least had the loyalty to bet on me," Aldin said.

Wedser merely shook his head and smiled.

"By the way," Aldin asked in an offhand manner, "is there any rumor as to who got this lottery thing started?"

"Word is around that Zola Koh had something to do with it."

Aldin leaned back, and for a moment a thin smiled creased his features.

"Anyhow," Wedser asked, wanting information far more than wishing to provide some, "any tips for an old friend?"

Aldin, as if coming out of a reverie, looked over at Wedser.

"If you're playing the market," Aldin said, thinking aloud, "sell short."

"What was that?"

Aldin looked over at his friend and smiled. "Care for a little arrangement?"

Wedser smiled and drew closer.

"I'm all ears," he said, chuckling at his own joke.

"Two things then. First, I need a contact with the

Al'Shiga. I need supplies, food, and, most of all, information."

Wedser thought for a moment before replying.

"Funny you should ask," Wedser replied. "There was a Wardi—yellow robe—who came through here not an hour ago, asking for you."

"Oh, really?" Aldin replied.

"Yeah, I told him to look for you in the foreign quarter, but he said he preferred to meet you outside of there."

"Who is he?"

"Didn't give a name, but my guards know who he is."

Aldin nodded his approval, and pulling open the steel shutter, Wedser shouted for Orklon to go find the yellow robe in question.

"And the second part?" Wedser asked.

"Just thought you might be able to find an old friend of mine." Aldin motioned for the shutter to be closed. With a smile he leaned forward and poured a drink for both of them.

"Come, offworlder."

The man before him was obviously a master; the silver trim on his yellow robes denoted his rank. The native was shorter than most, with a powerful stocky build. His face was as rugged and square-shaped as his massive body, his black hair cut even at the shoulders. The first thing that Aldin had noticed about this man was dark smoldering eyes, and he wasn't sure whether they held the look of a terrible purpose or of insanity. About his waist was a broad leather belt; a small sack and scabbards for several blades, which were ornamented with precious amber inlays, hung from his side.

For a second Aldin looked back at Wedser. Could Gablona have gotten through to him and arranged this meeting as a setup?

"He did give the ceremonial head bond," Mari whispered, sensing Aldin's hesitation.

As if hearing the woman's words, the master looked back. "I have bonded my head for your safety, or do you not believe my words?" There was a note of menace in his voice.

"All right then," Aldin said evenly, "we'll go with you."

The Gaf guards gathered around Aldin; the samurai formed

an inner circle, and Oishi, as usual, put himself between Aldin and any possible sources of danger.

The Shiga looked over at Aldin with obvious curiosity over such precautions.

Let him think I'm cautious, Aldin thought. If this master ever thought he could get the upper hand, it would be murder just for the sport of it.

Without a backward look, the Shiga turned and strode through the swirling crowds, with Aldin's party following in his wake.

At the approach, the crowds of Shiga parted before them. After several minutes Aldin realized that they were parting not so much for his armed guards but rather at the sight of the master. All eyes were upon him. The Human Shigas backed up, mumbling to themselves.

The man looked neither to the right nor the left. He didn't swagger as some of the others did, nor did he slink along from doorway to doorway expecting attack at any moment. His stride was self-assured, purposeful, as if he were walking along a country lane without a care or fear.

The samurai mumbled to themselves in admiring tones, sensing the calm self-confidence of the warrior. After crossing the open plaza, they came at last to the tunnellike gate that led into the Wardi quarter of the city.

Without even slowing, he led the way into the darkness. The wide tunnel was packed with a shouting wave of beings coming in the opposite direction. In any other situation Aldin would have called his guards in and waited for the crowd to pass—the narrow confines of the tunnel was the last place that he'd want to be trapped—but the master simply continued on.

Oishi looked at Aldin and then with a shrug realized that they'd have to follow and hope this wasn't a double cross.

As before, however, the crowd parted at their approach, the master moving before them like the prow of a ship cutting through a sea of men.

Suddenly there was a quick flurry of motion, a muffled scream echoed in the semidarkness.

With fluid ease, the master swung about, his right foot catching someone in the crowd full in the chest. There was the dull snap of cracking ribs. Even as he kicked, a blade in his left hand slashed across the throat of another, who fell back howling, fumbling with his hands to stem the pulsing flow of blood.

The action was almost over before Aldin even saw that the two Bengada in green robes had drawn blades in their hands and wore the ceremonial red knots.

The samurai nodded their approval at the display, as the master, still holding his fighting blade, surveyed the dozen or so greens in the crowd with an almost languid disdain.

"Twice today you've tried," he growled. "Haven't you had enough?"

The greens backed up and without a word disappeared back down the tunnel, leaving their two dead companions on the pavement.

"This will only take a moment," the man said. He took the satchel from his belt and knelt by the first body. Aldin turned away as the bloody container received two more heads, doubling the day's take.

After leaving the tunnel, they went on into the city. Most of the travelers on the street were Human yellows, but here and there were small clusters of Gafs as well. Both Human and Gafs nodded at the approach of the master, raising their right hands, palm outward, in a sign of greeting, which he, as an obvious superior, did not return.

Finally he led the way into a small side street and turned at last into a narrow doorway that opened as he neared it. Aldin looked back to see several dozen yellow robes emerge from out of side doorways, cutting the group off from behind. He looked over at Oishi, who merely nodded.

The group stopped at the door, and Oishi pushed ahead and stepped in first. His tension was obvious. If the man had wished to set them up, this would be the ideal place. They were near to the other end of the city; home was almost a league away. Thousands of yellows, who could obviously be aroused by this leader, could be on them in moments.

Aldin looked around at his guards, who were eyeing the building and the alleyway with suspicion. Every nerve seemed to be screaming at him to go back out of here and retreat to the safe house. But he knew that they were backed into a corner. They needed contacts with the Shiga, and if he wavered at all, there'd be a loss of face, not only in front of the Shiga but among his own guards, as well.

After pushing through his guards, Aldin came up behind Oishi, and together they stepped into the ulla's fortress.

He was stunned by the simple elegance of the place. The doorway led into an atrium, lit from above by skylights, the walls hung with bright tapestries, which were either ornately worked script from the Shigas' sacred text or curious representations of star fields and whirling galaxies.

The atrium led into an open courtyard, and he couldn't help but wonder if this was some architectural holdover from a distant past.

The courtyard even had a fountain in the middle, most likely fed by the hot sulfurous springs that welled up at a thousand different locations throughout the Hole.

The man beckoned for Aldin to sit on a low divan and motioned for Zergh, Mari, and Oishi to join them as well, while the rest of Aldin's guards settled down on the floor in the foyer.

"My name is Ulsak," the man said. "And you are Aldin Larice."

Surprised, Aldin looked at the Grand Master of the Wardi. He had heard, through Mari, of this man—most feared of all the masters of the six clans.

"So, you wish an understanding," Ulsak said lazily, even as he pulled the bloody satchel loose from his belt and tossed it to a waiting servant.

"Precisely," Aldin replied, thrown off guard for the moment by Ulsak's directness.

"Why?" And as Ulsak spoke, he fixed Aldin with his gaze.

"Because it could be to both our advantages."

Ulsak threw back his head and laughed. "Little man, little man, there is nothing among the stars you could offer me, yet there is everything that I could offer you. Your life could be one example."

Nervously Aldin looked about the courtyard and into the shadows of the half-dozen corridors that disappeared off into darkness.

"No, no," Ulsak said evenly. "There's no one hiding in the shadows. Such melodrama is for the young, or the inexperienced. But if I wanted you dead now, you would be dead. Such as you are of no account."

"It seems," Oishi interrupted, "that we could kill you now as well."

Ulsak threw back his head and barked out a short grunt of laughter. "Bravely spoken. Would you care to cross your blade to mine, here and now?"

Oishi stood up, ready to accept the challenge, but Aldin shot out his hand, restraining him.

"We're here in peace," Aldin commanded. "You gave your head bond to that. We seek merely an arrangement for trade and information."

Besides, he knew that if Oishi succeeded they'd never get out of the building alive. That was *if* Oishi succeeded. After the display in the tunnel he had doubts that even the best of his swordsmen could match the man in front of them. He looked up at Oishi, motioning for him to sit down. Oishi shot him a glance, and in that look Aldin realized that the samurai had nerved himself to die against the Shiga, all over what was merely an opening insult in the game of words.

"Best listen to him, little man," Ulsak said coldly.

Aldin fixed Oishi with his gaze.

"Another time," he whispered, and finally the samurai relented and sat back down, fixing Ulsak with a cold stare.

Aldin looked back at Ulsak and saw a faint look of approval in the man's eyes at Oishi's behavior.

"If we're done with threats," Aldin sallied, "then let us talk terms."

"What is it then that you can offer me?" Ulsak responded.

"Off this world, I'm a man of substance. When my time here is done, I could arrange exclusive trade to you for the finest metals of sword quality. Whatever luxuries you'd require, I could bring to you. Name the price and the goods and they are yours."

Ulsak leaned back and laughed again. "You offer me gifts and trade from a man who will soon be dead. You offer the promise from beyond the grave. You offer nothing."

"How can you be so sure that I shall die down here?"

"Come, come," Ulsak replied. "This is the world of the Al'Shiga, the brotherhood of the blade. This is our world, and you are merely an interloper here. Don't you think I know why you are here?"

"You tell me then," Aldin replied coldly.

"The games," Ulsak replied slowly, leaning forward and staring at Aldin.

"So you know?"

Ulsak could only shake his head in amazement.

"Then if you know," Aldin replied, "why do you even tolerate this action of those who sail the stars? You hate all of us, I know that. Why, then, let the Hole be a place where the star-rulers play their amusements?"

"Because it amuses us as well," Ulsak replied, a smile tracing his mouth.

"How so?"

"Because what you do here fits our own game," Ulsak replied.

"In what way?"

Ulsak could only shake his head as if talking to a child. "You know that the Ulman, the Great Festival, comes on the last day of your so-called game."

"The double eclipse," Mari said as Aldin turned to her in confusion. "Word of it's been going around the city. Both moons will eclipse the sun at the same time."

"So what does that have to do with us?" Aldin asked.

"You see, I wish to make you and yours an offer."

"Which is?" Aldin asked, feeling suddenly on edge.

"That when the sky darkens you come to me."

"And you'll do what?"

"Why, kill you, of course," Ulsak responded. "What else?"

"Thanks for the offer," Aldin said, "but I think I'll pass."

"You don't understand," Ulsak rejoined. "I like you. I like the way your men showed up the Isma and the look of your warriors. If you come to me, I'll make sure that you suffer not. You'll be drugged for the ceremony and your men will be spared, to be my servants."

Aldin merely shook his head.

"You don't understand," Ulsak replied. "We of the Shiga will not let you leave this place alive. We could kill you at any time."

"Then why not do it now?"

"I have my own private reasons," Ulsak replied.

"Oh, just that you want me to come walking in here like a lamb to the slaughter, that's all." Aldin stood up.

Oishi barked a command, and the samurai accompanying the group rushed out from the foyer to stand by Aldin's side.

Ulsak remained seated on his divan, but from behind him there was a faint stirring, and half a hundred yellows appeared from out of the shadows to stand on the other side of the pool.

"Shall we have it out here and now?" Oishi growled.

"No need," Ulsak replied lazily. "No need at all. I was just trying to be friendly, and you take insult."

"You've asked us to come to you begging for death, but know that we, the forty-seven ronin, will die sword in hand."

"Too bad," Ulsak replied. "Let me tell you your alternative then. Before the sky darkens our ullas shall proclaim that the hour has come and that a new sacrifice must be made. Then shall the hunt begin. As many of you as can be taken will be taken alive. Then shall you be brought to the great square."

He fixed Aldin with his gaze. "The ceremony is really quite simple. You'll be tied with a canvas sack strapped to your shoulders. Into the sack a pipe will be fixed, and with each passing second a drop of water shall fall, and another.

"Oh, it won't seem like much at first, but as the hours pass, liter after liter of liquid will drip in, weighing you down further and further."

"That doesn't seem like much," Aldin replied, and even as he spoke he wished he had not, for he suddenly had a flash of insight.

"Ah, but there is one little detail," Ulsak said dreamily, his eyes half closed.

"You see, you and all your men will be tied over sharpened stakes. Gradually the burden upon your shoulders will be too much to bear and you'll sag beneath the weight. But no, for the stake will jab into you, and you'll straighten up again. But then you'll sag again, and cut even deeper.

"Finally you'll try to nerve yourself, to force yourself down to end the agony. The stake will slide into your body. The hot stab of agony will cut through you, and with a shriek you'll rise back up again. I've seen it before, it's a wonderful show to watch. Some victims try to jam themselves down, but always the flesh rebels, and so they struggle on.

"Oh, and the screams, such wonderful screams, even from

the strongest and bravest," Ulsak continued. "Some just scream, most whimper and beg. We love the beggars. Each cry for mercy is met with howls of derision. It's really quite funny sometimes. The victims will start bouncing up and down on the stake like a toy, trying to jam the stake through to their heart and finish it, but always they pull back, so exquisite is the agony."

Ulsak leaned over from the divan and picked up a fragment of a rotting man. He examined it in a detached manner before placing it into his mouth.

"So it will go for hours, as gradually you weaken and falter, sliding lower and lower, impaling yourself. Until at last the stake drives clear through your body.

"Oh, if it's done right, a stake can cut clear through a man's diaphragm and into his lungs before he finally dies. It's a wonderful thing to watch. You should visit our temples more often."

Aldin struggled to suppress a retch of fear. He was tempted to draw his own blade now, to fall upon the ulla and go down fighting.

"You're thinking of finishing it right now," Ulsak commented. "But I wouldn't do that."

"And why not?" Aldin asked, his voice husky with tension.

"For I need Gablona to die with you," Ulsak replied. "After all, you wouldn't want your fat friend to have the pleasure of dying after you, now, would you?"

"Why? How come the time of our dying is so important to you?"

"I've presented you with an enigma, a mystery." Ulsak chuckled. "Die now and you won't find out. You know that if you fight me now, out of your own fear, it will be cowardice that will condemn all your followers here to certain death."

Aldin spared a quick glance from Ulsak back to his samurai and Gafs and realized that the man was right. If they tried to fight, the alarm would be raised, and in moments everyone with him would die.

"Let's go for him anyhow," Oishi hissed.

Aldin looked back to Ulsak, who still sat unmoving.

"Why not just take me prisoner now?"

"If you were my prisoner now and for the days remaining before the Ulman, it would not be correct. That is for you to ponder. But I did want to tell you about your final reception. After all, it gives me pleasure to know the fear you'll live in. That is why I loitered at the Seda all these days, knowing that sooner or later you and your followers would come looking for information.

"I wanted to tell you this so that you had time to think upon it, and in the end would come willingly to me. It'll be so much easier than having to hunt you down and drag you out to such a painful end.

"There's nothing more to be said now," Ulsak said, putting on a show of being suddenly weary and bored.

"You may go. There is no need to worry now about food. Before you arrive back at your tavern, my people will deliver all the food and drink you require. There'll even be a purse of amber waiting for you, if you should need to purchase anything we have forgotten."

Ulsak saw the suspicion in Aldin's eyes. "Head bond I give that all I provide you with is wholesome."

"Why?" Aldin asked.

"To keep you safe until it is time for my people to fetch you," he replied, smiling. "Know that always my men will be watching you, and the fat one as well. We won't accept any more games between the two of you and shall find a way to warn either of you if something is amiss. I wish to keep you safe until you are needed for the sacrifice."

Ulsak rose from the divan and strode across the room to stand before Aldin.

"It is as if your fate were already ordained," he whispered. "Submit to what I have decreed, and die without pain."

Without a word Aldin motioned for his people to start for the door.

"The game is only beginning," Aldin said, feeling that the line was foolish but that he had to say something.

Ulsak laughed. "Sleep and dream of what I've told you, Aldin Larice. I know a great many things more, and I know, as well, that by the end, the nightmares you will have will bring you to me with open arms, begging for the peace I can bring you, before we drive the stake into your living body and like a broken toy you try to jam the sharpened point into your own heart to end the agony."

* * *

"You did what!"

Vush bowed low before Losa. For an Overseer, the outburst was something unheard of, for theirs was a society where calm detachment was the highest and noblest reaction to almost any news—good, bad, or indifferent.

"As I have just explained, I sold the tickets where either of them lives. We know your plan is reliable, the Shiga will not fail. Therefore, looking at the profit line, I thought it was a useless investment."

"You sold an option on all our tickets that dealt with the two of them or either one living through to the end of the game?"

"There was an aggressive bid for them, with a high profit margin," Vush explained nervously.

"How many did you sell?"

"All of them," he whispered nervously.

Losa turned away in exasperation.

"We both know they don't have a chance of surviving this festival," Vush replied. "Ulsak will see to that, so why waste the investment?"

"That's beside the point. We are dealing with probabilities here. There is a chance, small though it may be, that they might live. We've already soiled our destinies far too much with this venture. If my superior should discover our involvement . . ." He fell silent, not even wishing to contemplate what the council might say about such dealings.

"Who bought them?"

"We're not sure. It was a dummy corporation, and they picked up all five hundred thousand first-day tickets the moment I put them on the trading floor."

"Why did you do it?"

Vush could only shrug what would pass for shoulders. How could he explain that close contact to the game had seduced him as well? At first he'd been detached, but each passing day of watching the board and smelling out the trades had finally hooked him. The sell-and-purchase flurry just before Sigma's death had been the nail in the coffin. He was a market addict. The turning of billions in profits was a game that had become an obsession.

The lower beings had captured him essence and soul with the lure of betting the system and winning. Of course, he no longer even contemplated the fact that wealth held no meaning for an Overseer, since it was meaningless for them to purchase what they could not use or need.

"I saw the chance," he could only say lamely, "to turn five hundred thousand nonviable tickets into cash."

"And what the hell are we going to do with cash?" Losa asked, his voice rising to a shout.

Vush could only stand there, somewhat amazed himself at what he had just done. How could he explain the beauty of the profit they'd just made? An initial investment of a half million k's turned into two and a half billion.

"Let's just hope for your sake they don't live," Losa growled.

Vush showed his shock at such a comment. It was completely against all their training to wish such an ill event upon another being. Even the superior showed some shock at what had just escaped his lips, and he turned away in embarrassment.

"Everything else is at least ready," Losa whispered, changing the topic after his humiliating outburst.

"The moment the game ends, the claims will be presented. The holdings of every company in the Cloud, save for those belonging to the Xsarns and Gaf Koh Bukha, will be forfeit when GGC can't pay off its debt. The total collapse of the Cloud's economy will follow, and we'll be in control.

"The Shiga will be released and all evidence will point to a vindictive act by Gablona's heirs. Chaos will result from that, and in the end, their civilization will turn to us to restore order. Thus there'll be no resistance to our takeover.

"We can comfort ourselves in knowing that it was they who designed it, set it up, and implemented it. Thus we have no shadow on our destiny, and we can bring order to these beings once and for all. Let us hope that what you have done will not affect this."

No problem at all, Vush thought cheerfully, and we'll still make a fascinating profit.

"It's too bad about Gablona and Aldin though," the superior replied. "But of course we'll have nothing to do with their actual passing; that is in the hands of others."

"But of course," Vush said, nodding solemnly in agreement.

Losa turned away from his assistant. The message had come to him this morning from the Arch requesting his presence for an audience. So the old one had found out at last, Losa thought. Well, already it was too late for him to change anything, and lost in thought, he floated from the room.

CHAPTER 11

Sᴛᴜɴɴᴇᴅ, Tɪᴀ ʟᴇᴀɴᴇᴅ ʙᴀᴄᴋ ꜰʀᴏᴍ ᴛʜᴇ ᴛᴇʀᴍɪɴᴀʟ ᴀɴᴅ sʜᴜᴛ
the system down.

So that's what Yaroslav was on to, she thought, having
returned to check once again, still not quite believing the discovery she'd made earlier that morning. The parts of the puzzle meant nothing by themselves, but together they presented
a dangerous picture.

It had been difficult tracing Yaroslav's path, but after several days of poring through his notes, she had at last found his
access code word. From there it became a process of tracing
system after system, looking to where he had cut into the com
link files, since all links were recorded.

Then had come the stunning discovery. Several weeks before the game had started, a front company for the Alma Consortium had purchased fifty aging transport liners from one of
Gablona's shipping firms. The document of transfer was

signed by Gablona himself, while he was still in the reeducation center!

Now, why would Alma be interested in enough transports to carry nearly a million passengers?

And then the realization had come. Bukha had confirmed that the Overseers had invested heavily into the game. But why could they be so certain about some bets, and if so, what guarantees had they offered to make sure that such actions would indeed take place?

She had taken her suspicions to Bukha, and he had thought them to be so wild as to be beyond all logic.

"Granted they're betting on this," he had replied, "but the rest of your crazy ideas? Not even the Overseers would dream of such a thing. In fact, I have just sent a memo to the Arch expressing my curiosity as to their intentions, and he replied that he was just as surprised as we were."

"Do you actually believe the leader of the Overseers?" Tia had snapped.

"No, of course not. But what you're suggesting is wholesale genocide, something beyond the capability of any Overseer. And besides," he had said coldly, "how do I know you're not simply trying to implicate Corbin, or arrange for his disgrace, so that when he regains legal title to the Gablona holdings, you'll be in a position to challenge him?"

"You're playing the game as well. Remember our little purchase together, through that hidden futures market. We'd be fools not to know that it was the Overseers dumping those shares."

"You were sworn to secrecy on that," Bukha snarled, "and damn you, you'd better keep it. I pulled you in because we needed the capital. I find it interesting that you dumped your shares with GGC in order to buy the tickets, but that's your concern, not mine. Now, I don't have any more time for your insane stories."

And he had dismissed her as if she were nothing but a wild-eyed girl who had concocted a fabrication in order to get attention.

Damn them, she cursed silently. Where the hell was Yaroslav?

She knew there was only one action she could take now, since the damned Kohs, who gloried in their superior attitudes, would never listen. Turning the com link back on, she tapped into her office to relay a message to Bukha's private line.

After shutting down the unit again, she looked around the shabby apartment. From out of the half-open closet she could see Yaroslav's cat peering out at her.

Tia walked over to the kitchen alcove, pulled out the heavy bag of food she had just purchased that morning, and poured all the contents out on the floor. After jamming the filthy sink drain closed, she filled it with water.

"No litter for you," she said, looking over at the scrawny cat. "You'll have to find something in the closet, but I don't think Yaroslav will even notice."

The cat looked at her and retreated back into its hiding place.

If something was coming down from the Overseers, there was only one way to intervene now she thought, and walked out of the apartment.

"I tell you this whole thing stinks of fraud," Bukha shouted, looking down the length of the table to Zola, who eyed him nervously.

"My dear Bukha, we agreed to this meeting with you and the Xsarn to finalize the findings of our accountants. The preliminary reports are in at last. In five days all the final documents will be drawn, and all holdings from the Alexandrian game will be back with their rightful owners. That is the topic of this meeting, not your accusations."

The room seemed to be divided in half. Most of the Kohs, all shareholders in the Galactic Gaming Company, at one end of the table, with Bukha and the Xsarn at the other.

Tension had been high all morning, and for most, their attention was scarcely on the accountings of the last game but rather on the climax of the current one.

For over fifteen days there'd been no action. Both Aldin and Gablona seemed to have settled into a siege mentality, their fortresses barricaded, with no attempts made against each other. The Al'Shiga had been strangely quiet; reports came back from the offworld traders that the marketplace was empty, the locals almost in hiding.

For Zola, all was going to plan. The following morning,

the gates would be closed on all further betting, according to the lottery rules. But he was still worried. He was starting to suspect that there were information leaks within his organization, and a large block of tickets could be bought up overnight that could cause a loss to the company.

"Besides," Zola continued calmly, "you're talking about an accomplished fact. GGC Incorporated has taken in over five trillion bets so far, and there's a hell of a lot more yet to be reported into our main computer system. Over ninety-nine percent of them have already become invalid. Of course, statistically we'll have to pay some money back out, but current profit-line estimates run to nearly four trillion after expenses."

The Kohs around Zola nodded among themselves; those nearest to their leader patted him upon the back in an effusive outpouring of goodwill.

Zola leaned back while one of the Gafs next to him bent over to light one of the foot-long cigars he had taken to of late. There was the slightest of nervous twitches as he held his cigar, which he covered with a quick flourish of his hand.

"Shares in the company are now worth a quarter of a billion each per block of a thousand, a five thousand percent increase in investment. The final dividend and payout should exceed the value by over three to one. I therefore think, Bukha Koh, that you are nothing but a fearmonger, trying to frighten investors to a panic and sell out so that you can buy in on the game."

The other Kohs looked at Bukha with scorn, as if he had just made an obscene noise.

Zola turned and looked back at the group with a self-confident smile.

Bukha realized that any further comment was useless, and settled back in his chair.

"Well, there is one other problem," the Xsarn interjected, "which needs to be addressed."

"And that is?" Zola interjected lazily.

"Payment of the accountants and lawyers handling the Alexandrian case."

"I know a good payment." Vol snarled. "Once we're done with them, let's take them all and drop them in the Hole, for the Shigs to take care of."

There was a chorus of affirmations, for as in any age, such

beings were held in disdain by the more honest citizens.

"At least it'll eliminate all those damn vid ads of lawyers asking you to sue after every liner crash."

"Now, now, gentlemen," the Xsarn said, raising his upper and lower arms in an appeal for calm. "I admit to sharing the same sentiments, but it simply wouldn't be practical. They'd all file lawsuits that would keep us tied up for years. After all, they're like Dargonian lice: wipe out one crop and another will spring up to replace them."

"Wait a minute," Zola said, cutting off the debate. "You just said we've got to figure out the payments. I thought that the assets of the three game players would be used in the event that any of them died."

"I did," the Xsarn replied slowly.

"Sigma's dead; his holdings should be more than enough."

"But he had no holdings of any worth, and his legal team has already filed a brief to that effect."

"What the hell are you talking about?" Zola roared.

"It's simply this. I found out this morning that Sigma seems to have outguessed us all. Two days before he was taken prisoner for the game, he filed a document putting all his holdings into a trust for exactly one year. At the end of the year, if he was still alive, the trust would be turned back to him. If he was dead, the trust would be retained by the original holders."

"And who holds the trust?" Zola asked.

"The Alma Consortium."

"The Alma Consortium?" Vol roared. "That's an Overseer front!"

"Exactly. And their lawyers have already filed a brief declaring that all of Sigma's wealth is now theirs."

"This is impossible, it must be a forgery!" Zola said, coming to his feet.

"I've already checked. It's valid, and it predates the signed agreements for this game. Therefore, when Sigma signed the death waiver giving his property over to defray expenses, he was in fact signing away nothing. His money was already locked in a trust fund.

"Which brings me to the point, gentlemen," the Xsarn continued. "The heads of the accountants' and lawyers' guilds seemed to have gotten wind of this complication."

"They would, wouldn't they?" One of the Gafs snarled.

"I called this meeting to inform you that they want payment in advance before delivery of all reports and the legal signing of all documents returning our properties back to the original holders."

"In advance? Who the hell do they think they are?" Zola snapped.

"They've got us by our soft shells," the Xsarn replied. "Without payment, they'll sit on the reports, our companies will languish, and we'll lose billions more."

"The reports are already filed," Vol cut in. "I say we just seize the computers, hire different lawyers, and sort it out on our own."

"You know the code of their guild," the Xsarn said. "They'll never commit an act that could deny a brother of his fees. Every lawyer in the Cloud will be against us."

Zola threw up his hands in exasperation. "All right, how much do they want?"

"The bill comes out to twenty-one billion and some odd change."

"Twenty-one billion!" Zola choked, and for a moment everyone thought he was about to have a stroke. Gasping, he turned to the sideboard, and had to drink a triple brandy before he finally regained composure.

"But I thought it wouldn't be more than ten billion!"

"I've checked," the Xsarn said, shaking his head dejectedly. "They had a fine-print clause for quadruple overtime payments. Of course, they spent more hours on overtime than they did on the standard pay rate."

"Well, this is a hell of a mess," Zola mumbled dejectedly.

"A mess that's got to be solved now," the Xsarn replied. "Every day that the closing is delayed will amount to a loss of billions in trade."

"They want it now?" Zola asked, incredulous.

"In writing; today."

Zola looked around at his companions, who suddenly stepped back or attempted to blend into the walls.

"Then we'll just have to ante up the money from our companies," Zola said.

"But most everything we own is already locked into the

last dispute; the lawyers won't accept that," the Xsarn replied. "But they did have a suggestion."

"And that was?"

"Payment out of the funds of GGC."

Zola sat back for a moment and punched into his com link. The day after the game ended, the company would pay out the dividends based on winnings, and all the company's assets would be gone.

"We can't touch the assets until all bets have been paid off."

"They'll accept that as long as you personally guarantee a payment of ten billion up front and the remainder after the close of the game."

After dealing with the heady sums of the last two months, billions seemed like a paltry sum. At least it would keep the dogs quiet, Zola reasoned.

"Agreed," he said dejectedly. "Now tell those bastards I want the Alexandrian paperwork on our desks the moment the game ends."

The Xsarn nodded in reply and punched the prearranged message to the lawyers waiting outside, who brought in the contracts.

After they had left, followed by a variety of mumbled threats, Vol stood up and motioned for attention.

"Well, there is another alternative," he said quietly.

"And that is?"

"The game still has six days standard to go; Aldin, as we know, has next to nothing, but if Gablona should happen to die, then we'll still be able to attach his assets."

The group looked up to the Xsarn.

"I've checked his accounts," the Xsarn said quietly. "He didn't show the foresight of our dear departed friend Sigma, and all his property is still legally in his hands."

The Kohs fell quiet and looked from one to the other.

"It certainly would be a pity though if good old Corbin should die," Zola said softly, and all the Kohs around him shook their heads and mumbled in agreement.

Bukha looked around at his fellow Kohs. Could Tia have been right? he started to wonder. He'd yet to say anything directly about his concerns regarding the Overseers, for a variety of reasons. But could she have been right?

"I think you're insane, Aldin. Completely insane!"

"Yes," Mari snapped angrily. "Let's just hide here till it's over."

"Hide here?" Aldin could only shake his head in disbelief.

Ulsak's envoys had paid a visit that morning. The leader of the group was finally admitted and handed Aldin a missive from Ulsak, which stated in the politest of terms that the original deal still stood, and warning him as well that with the coming of the next dawn a special eight-day festival would start. The Ulman, the coming of the Great Darkening, had been revealed to the masses the week before, and the city would be packed with celebrants from the other five cities until the climax.

The party had left stacks of food outside the barricaded door and then departed.

Deliveries of food had come at regular intervals, just as Ulsak had promised. At first the samurai had refused to touch it, despite Ulsak's head bond, but Mari had finally reassured everyone that poisoning of food was considered the basest of crimes, fit only for cowards. In fact, what they had experienced was part of Al'Shiga tradition: the sending of food and gifts to one's victim before hunting him. All the natives did it, and great status was attached to the amount of wealth one lavished upon his intended victim.

There was even a rotting man, one that Mari assured them was of the finest grade, fit only for true connoisseurs. The Gafs, as if a challenge to their crudeness had been offered, finally snatched it up and, bearing it down to their quarters in the basement, tried it out.

Half of them had come staggering back up, retching and gasping. Those who endured the ritual swaggered up later, and fell to taunting their weak-stomached comrades, but most of them seemed a bit pale, by Gaf standards, for the rest of the morning.

"Look, Ulsak knows our hiding place, and undoubtedly so do the other groups," Aldin argued. "Ten minutes after the festival starts, we'll be under siege."

"We've been working on this place for weeks," Mari countered. "They could throw hundreds against us."

"My lord does have a point," Oishi replied, coming up to join the two behind the bar.

Aldin nodded to his bodyguard.

"This Ulsak has acted first and foremost to frighten. He hopes then that we shall be like rabbits, frozen in fear, ready to be plucked up and thrown in the sack. That was the meaning of this morning's action and the threats at the earlier meeting."

"What would you do then?" Aldin asked.

"Go on the offensive."

"What!" Mari hissed. "There are only sixty of us; there's a million of them."

"All the more reason," Oishi replied gamely, a smile lighting his features. "For it would never be expected. Always do what your foe does not expect."

"Behind these walls we could last till the game is up," Mari argued.

"They have no doubt thought of a way to get to us, and you have not thought of something else."

"And that is?"

"The game, as you call it, ends shortly. But that is only up there." Oishi pointed upward. "Down here the situation will still remain the same. You'll never get from here to the Sky Tower alive."

"And there is the other problem," Mari countered.

"That is . . ." Aldin ventured.

"Your friend Gablona."

Aldin could only grumble to himself. No matter what his plans, Gablona was still the unknown factor.

"Someone coming," Hideo barked, coming in from the guardpost by the door.

"Now what?" Aldin cursed silently. He could only hope it wasn't more Shiga with their damn rotting men. The whole place still stank from the last one.

Following Hideo, he slipped up to the door and peeked out.

A single form came up the street, slipping from doorway to doorway in the lengthening shadows of early evening.

There was something familiar about the person. Aldin

watched as the stranger suddenly stepped out and started to rush up the street, and then he saw other forms step out behind him.

"Let's go!" Aldin shouted, pulling up the bar to the doorway.

Before his companions even had time to ask, Aldin was out the door, Oishi and Hideo behind him.

The stranger saw him and hesitated.

"Run!" Aldin screamed.

"Aldin!" It was a woman's voice, and she started toward him.

Then the shadows following her closed in, joined by half a dozen more from a side alleyway.

"Ronin, to me!" Hideo screamed, drawing his long sword and rushing forward.

It was over in seconds, before Aldin could even react. The dark-cloaked attackers swept in on the woman, who, seeing the threat too late, tried to rush toward the tavern.

A thin rope coiled out, the weighted end snaking around her. Hideo charged in, but suddenly more attackers materialized. With a vicious cut, Hideo dropped one, and then a second.

Aldin came forward to his aid.

"No!"

A form came up beside him and, with a vicious blow, knocked him to the ground. Aldin, terrified, started to kick out, and then saw that it was Oishi holding him down.

"Hideo!" Oishi screamed.

But it was too late. The old samurai turned and turned again, but in an instant he was swarmed under, and the blades of the assassins flickered as they slashed in the pale light of early evening.

There was the pounding of feet about them, the wild cry of more samurai pouring out of the tavern, the heavier Gafs trying to shoulder their way to the front.

But the attackers were gone, already disappearing into the side alleyways.

Aldin came to his knees. He looked over at Oishi, but already the samurai was on his feet, a look of anguish on his face.

He rushed forward to the body of his friend, a dozen feet away. With a cry, he knelt down by Hideo.

"Oishi made his choice," Zergh said, coming up to help Aldin to his feet.

Dazed, Aldin looked at his old friend.

"He might have been able to save Hideo," Zergh said quietly, "but he had to stop you from rushing in where, if recognized, you would certainly have been killed. He chose obligation over friendship." And then Zergh turned away.

Stunned, Aldin stood in the middle of the street as Oishi came past him with unseeing eyes, bearing the body of his old comrade back into the tavern.

"Why the hell did you rush out like that?" Mari demanded, facing Aldin as he came back through the doorway.

"Because I knew who was out there. It was Tia, my niece."

Startled, Zergh turned around. "What the hell was she doing down here?"

"I don't know, but for her to try to seek me out, it must be important. But now the Shiga have her."

"Those weren't Shiga," Takashi said, the last to return from the foray.

Aldin looked down at what the samurai held in his hands.

It was a strip of black cloth.

Tia was in the hands of Gablona.

"There was a moment when the one called Larice was in danger," the messenger said, trembling before the presence of Ulsak. He had been part of the ceremony that had dispatched the last ulla who had displeased the master, and he had no desire to be the next.

"And?" Ulsak asked, looking up at the man through half-lowered eyelids.

"He was stopped without harm," the messenger continued, not elaborating on who had done the stopping.

"Very good then," Ulsak replied.

"And this offworlder?"

"She was taken by Gablona's men. The one called Larice was obviously distraught—she called his name."

Could it be Larice's lover? he wondered. Perhaps there was a way this could be used.

For days he had contemplated how to take this Aldin and

Gablona unharmed. Gablona was as good as in the net already, but the envoys to Larice had returned with reports of the intricate defenses that had been built. Many would die in the attack. That did not bother him though, he would expend ten thousand of his followers if need be. His only fear was that Aldin himself might die in the process. He had underestimated the man, expecting in the end that he would be resigned to his fate as any of the Al'Shiga would have been. Among his own people, if one realized that a master of the knife was hunting him, more often than not he would simply go to the great square and there await the man.

Tradition demanded then that the deathblow be a painless one, with the sharpest of blades, for one who accepted his fate. To hide would mean that a slower death was permitted. He had expected Aldin to take the painless death.

Killing him now in a tavern fight would not fit his plans at all. After all, Ulsak was the Ema, and a fitting sacrifice must be made to sanctify the moment when the two darknesses appeared. Two lives offered for the two lights—that had to be the way.

"And you say the fat one now has her?"

"Yes, Oh Great One."

Ulsak looked up at the ulla and smiled. All about him had started to call him by that of late. Already they were accepting the revelation of his destiny.

He had learned one thing of this Larice. The man had the foolishness to be compassionate. Ulsak saw how concern for his own men had stayed Aldin's hand. Such a thing was weakness, and perhaps that weakness could be used.

"I want a messenger sent to those who guard Gablona. You know the man in question?"

"Yes, Oh Great One."

"Give me several moments, and then I will summon you."

The messenger, breathing an inner sigh of relief, left the presence of the leader. Out in the hallway the other ullas looked at him with some surprise, expecting that they had seen the last of him when he entered the room.

The messenger saw a stranger in the back of the group, and then had a vague recollection of having seen him before. It was the mad shaman who had suddenly appeared before the Seda some days past.

Two of the ullas, dragging the man between them, went into the audience chamber.

Ulsak looked up at them and cast a curious gaze on the ragged bundle between them.

"Why do you bring this filth into my presence?" Ulsak demanded.

"He has been making a nuisance of himself," one of the ullas said, releasing the old man and pushing him to the floor.

"In what way?"

"We keep finding him prowling about the base of the Holy of Holies, the inner sanctuary beneath the Seda."

Curious, Ulsak looked at the ragged bundle at his feet.

"Then just kill him," Ulsak said lazily.

"We can't. He is a madman, a shaman, and thus protected. Only a master may have a madman killed, and then, only in private," the ulla replied, trying not to sound dogmatic in the presence of his leader.

The old man rose to his knees and gave a long, penetrating look at Ulsak, then immediately fell flat upon his face.

"I have seen the eyes of the Ema, and thus shall I be saved," the shaman cried.

Ulsak, who had been about to order the quiet strangulation of the annoyance, stopped.

"How do you know that?" he asked. Only to those among his inner circle had he revealed his true identity.

"Is not the Seda the way of the Ema? I have come to pray before the Holy of Holies, for soon the greatness of he who shall rise upon it will be revealed," the old man cried.

"Only you as our leader can order his dispatch," one of the ullas whispered. "He's proclaimed that you were the Ema to not only our own but to the other clans as well."

Ulsak smiled softly. Did not the Ema need a prophet to call his name before the arrival? His own ullas could not do it, for it would be suspect.

Ulsak turned to the side table and sliced off the hand of a rotting man.

"Come, old man. You must be hungry." And he held forth the morsel.

The old man looked up at him with ravenous eyes and snatched the delicacy, consuming it with obvious relish.

"Get out of here," Ulsak roared at the ullas. "To think that you would even dream of harming the messenger of the Ema!"

The ullas nervously retreated, and as the door closed, Ulsak leaned over and cut open the stomach of the rotting man.

"Join me for a drink, old one," he said enthusiastically, not even noticing the suppressed retch of the shaman as the smell of the rotting man filled the room.

"So, if it isn't my darling former mistress," Gablona said lazily, looking up at Tia with half-closed eyes.

Tia turned and looked back at Hassan, who smiled knowingly at her.

"I was going to come to you next," Tia snapped, "but I couldn't find where you were hiding."

"Of course, but of course," Gablona said softly, signaling that Hassan could leave.

The assassin stood in the doorway, wishing to hear what was about to be said, acting as if Gablona's command did not matter.

The Koh looked up, and Tia, her eyes shifting from one to the other, said nothing.

"You may leave us, Hassan."

"She could be dangerous," Hassan replied smoothly. "Perhaps a guard should stay with you."

"I said you may go."

There was the faintest of smiles on Hassan's face as he bowed low, the look of defiance still on his face. Tia watched with interest, saying nothing. The door closed behind Hassan.

"I haven't seen you since the end of the Alexandrian game," Gablona said smoothly, picking up a thin sliver from a small rotting man that rested upon a side table. He speared another piece and offered it to her, and she wrinkled her nose in disgust.

"An acquired taste. Turned my stomach, too, at first, but really it's like an aged, full-bodied cheese."

He ate with his eyes closed like a true connoisseur, as if all his senses were concentrated on the repast.

"After this game is ended and I am back in my rightful place, I intend to export this delicacy. I think there's a market for it with some of the other Kohs."

"That's if you survive," Tia said.

"But of course I'll survive," Gablona replied. "I would think, my dear, that given the present circumstances, you should be more worried about your own survival."

"Come now, Corbin," Tia said meekly. "Remember, I'm also part of the Gablona clan. I was merely holding your assets until everything blew over."

"Xsarnfood!" Gablona roared. "You betrayed me to Sigma, and you threw in with that damned uncle of yours. I ought to have your ass dragged down to a Shig temple, but frankly I think I want to kill you with my own hands!"

Gablona stood up, kicking the side table over so that the rotting man fell to the floor with a sickening thump.

Tia struggled to remain calm. "Kill me now and you'll never find out why I came down here."

"Ah, yes," Gablona said. "Of course I was thinking of that as well, so first we'll talk and then I'll kill you, unless your answers convince me otherwise."

But he still remained on his feet, his fat, chunky hands resting on the sword strapped to his waist.

Tia eyed the sword and suddenly found it difficult to suppress a laugh. Somehow the fact that Corbin Gablona had been reduced to wearing a sword seemed totally ridiculous. He was a Koh, a year ago he had hundreds of paid guards surrounding him, and now he was reduced to this. But she could see, as well, the murderous look in his narrow, slitlike eyes, and all thought of making a light comment fled.

"I came to warn the two of you that the game is fixed."

"Fixed," Gablona said, a smile lighting his face, and with a deep chuckle he sat back down.

"Fixed, you say?"

Tia nodded in reply.

"But of course it's fixed," Gablona roared. "Do you think me to be that stupid? I had it fixed from the beginning!"

Incredulous, Tia could only shake her head in disbelief.

"How do you think you fixed it?" she asked softly.

"I promised Zola an even billion up front. I also pointed out to him that if he could make certain arrangements regarding my safety from the Shiga, that such information could help with the betting."

"What could you possibly use to bribe the Shiga?" Tia asked.

"Ah, now that was a fine stroke," Gablona said. "And quite frankly, none of your damn business."

"And I suppose you really trust Zola," Tia said.

"Of course not," he snapped. "But it's more profitable for him if I live than die."

"Not anymore."

"What's that?" Gablona asked, stirring from his complacency.

"Sigma outwitted all of you. You and Zola figured that with Sigma dead, the lawyers would be paid from his estate, and then there'd be no reason for you to be hunted. But Sigma signed his holdings over to a blind trust before he was captured. He died penniless. The Kohs need twenty billion, and if you die, that debt will no longer be their concern."

"The bastards, they wouldn't think of it!"

"If there's a way, they'll do it," Tia said coldly.

Gablona's eyes suddenly grew narrow. "If you knew this, then why were you going to Aldin first? You don't give a damn about me, you never did."

"I was going to come to you next."

"That's a lie," Gablona roared. "There was something you were going to tell your precious uncle, and you were going to keep me in the dark!"

"All right," Tia snapped. "We've got evidence that the Overseers are arranging the game as well!"

Gablona was silent for a moment. "To what end?"

"If certain events came to pass down here, they'd clean up on the bets, bankrupting GGC."

"That's Zola's company, not mine," Gablona growled. "If they bankrupt him, that's fine with me. In fact, I'll cheer them on."

"You don't understand," Tia shouted, frustrated with his self-centered interests. "Almost all the assets of the Cloud have been tied into the company. They agreed to sign a financial liability clause stating that if there wasn't enough money in the pot, that additional winnings would be paid for by the shareholders' personal fortunes."

"So what?" Gablona laughed. "Damn fools were crazy to do it. If the Overseers clean them out, then more power to them."

"But the Overseers are playing the bet that either one of you, or both of you, will die!"

For the first time Gablona looked concerned. For a moment he sat in silence. Turning away, he reached down and yanked one of the feet off the rotting man that lay splattered on the floor and munched the delicacy in a detached, thoughtful way.

"Are they bribing the Shiga then?"

"It's the only conclusion we could reach. They seem to be gearing up for some sort of festival."

"Ah, yes, the festival. Something about an eclipse. One of the blues already told me about it. They'll take Aldin then for the sacrifice, and the game is over! But I've made my arrangement for that as well, through Hassan."

"How's that?"

"Hassan has been my contact to one of the Shig masters; we've got a guarantee. Part of the deal is that one of my men gets to strike the deathblow."

"Why should that matter?" Tia asked wearily, not believing what she was hearing.

"Because, my dear, the biggest betting arrangement in history is being played out. I've brought several hundred thousand tickets and a major block of them call for me to kill Aldin. If Hassan strikes the blow, I get the credit and win several hundreds of billions as a result!"

Gablona actually beamed with pride as he revealed the foresight behind his planning.

"Of course, with Aldin dead, everything will be finished —the game's over, and I go back up the Skyhook to claim my winnings and start afresh. If the Overseers have wiped out my other Kohs in the process, what concern is it of mine? The game will be over, and I'm a free man."

"The game is not going to be over, damn it!" Tia snapped. "This is why I was going to Aldin first. He'd at least listen to logic. The Shigs will take him, and you as well."

"I've already paid them off," Gablona said smugly.

"With what? Money? They don't give a damn about money. It's power only they're after, and somehow the Overseers have offered them far more than you'll ever be able to scrape up."

"First off," Gablona said, "I can outbribe any damn Overseer in the Cloud, I made my deal with them as well. They asked me to sign a trade agreement for some of my ships the day before I was sprung from the reeducation camp. They said it'd be a goodwill gesture of trade between us. You know and I know they don't do business with us. I'll simply threaten to blackmail that bastard Losa with the information that he's dabbling in our financial concerns. I did business with them once, I'll do it again. As for the Shiga, I'll just send Hassan back out and he'll match anything those do-gooders can come up with as a counteroffer."

With a sigh of exasperation Tia sank back in her chair. So the damn fool *had* signed over the ships. He didn't even realize they were going to frame him with it.

"Go ahead," she grumbled, "let them kill you. Frankly, I really don't care at this point. This whole damn thing has gone totally insane."

Gablona eyed her carefully, and Tia, remembering her former days with him, realized that already he was plotting something else.

"What is it?" she asked wearily.

"Oh, something really quite simple. Knowing your uncle, he's a man who places honor and family above most anything else."

Tia suddenly felt a cold chill.

"Look, Corbin dear," she said quickly, "we can work something out between us. After all, you always did say I was the best mistress you ever had."

"Past tense, my dear, past tense," Gablona said. "I was just wondering though what Aldin might say if I offered to meet him in order to exchange you for something else."

"Such as?" Tia whispered.

"Himself."

CHAPTER 12

"THIS IS MADNESS," OISHI HISSED.

Aldin looked at his companion and shook his head.

"She's my niece, I've got to do it," he said.

"I don't care about her," the samurai replied evenly. "It's you I'm responsible for."

"And in the end I'm responsible for her. If you were me, would you do any different?"

"I would remember my obligation to my clan, to those who serve me."

Aldin turned with a smile and, reaching out, rested his hand on the samurai's shoulder.

A faint smile crossed Oishi's lips, and he lowered his head, not able to argue with this man.

"Your men are in place?" Aldin asked.

"Don't worry, we'll still get you out of this," Oishi said gruffly.

"You better," Aldin said, trying to put on an act of bravado.

He started to walk out into the street, but a hand came up, grabbing him by the arm. Turning, he saw that he was looking into Mari's eyes.

"Come, come," Aldin said quietly, "time for us to be off."

The woman drew closer, and Aldin suddenly realized that her hair was freshly washed, a light scent of lavender wafting on the air. Her eyes held his for a moment, and for the first time, he admitted to himself that he was somehow drawn to her. For so long now she had just been Mari, quick to argue with him or anyone else who came near, so that even the Gaf berserkers had learned to give her a wide berth. But now he saw the vulnerability underneath it all. A vulnerability that he realized was caused by him, and the danger he now faced.

They stood silent for a moment, their hands lightly touching. The samurai drew back, while the Gafs coughed and growled self-consciously.

"Take care of yourself, you stupid bastard," Mari whispered.

"Is that it?" Aldin asked with a mild tone of self-pity. "You certainly have a way with words."

"You damned fool." She drew him close, wrapping her arms about him. Aldin felt the lightest of kisses on his neck, and then the brush of lips across his.

"We'll get you out; I'll bash that fat bastard if he so much as touches you."

"Certainly a romantic send-off." Aldin laughed self-consciously.

Mari smiled up at him, her eyes damp, and then abruptly turned away. With a curse she pushed one of the hulking Gafs aside. Zergh drew close to her and she buried her head into his chest.

"Here goes," Aldin whispered to himself, and he stepped out of the alleyway and started for the door. Never had he felt so alone as he did at that moment.

The street was empty, wrapped in shadows and fog. Sound was muffled by the swirling blanket of gray, but still he could hear the deep, steady rumble of the drums, as in the distance the Al'Shiga gathered in the Great Square before the Seda, the drums calling the faithful on this the first morning of the ceremony. The fog had been a help at least. After slipping out of the tavern, Oishi had dispatched the yellow robe that had been watching the back door, and thus they had gotten by the guards unseen, taking out the one who watched Gablona's place as well.

There was a deep, almost primordial feeling to the twilight before the dawn. The fog was all-encompassing, as if the entire world were a grayness, the void before the coming of light, while the drums were not only heard but felt, matching the pulsing of his heart.

The shadows of buildings loomed to either side, and Aldin felt as if from every window slit unseeing eyes were watching, judging, and deciding if here was someone worth the time to kill.

A deeper darkness stood to his left, the walls of the black house reaching above him, and he knew that here there was no fevered imagination stoking his fears. He was being watched. A shadow fluttered in a window and drew away.

Would Corbin simply strike him now? He found himself almost wishing that he would, ending the suspense and the fear. For if he feared anything, it was that after nearly two score days on this world, Corbin had been seduced by its naked brutality and would prefer the techniques of the Shiga to the simpler brand of murder practiced by the Kohs.

The door was open; they were waiting for him.

Aldin realized at that moment that if ever he was performing a courageous act, it was now. But if it was so courageous, he wondered, why was his heart thundering and his legs turning to jelly? Suddenly he was afraid not only of Corbin and what might happen, but also of the far more mundane fact that in another couple of seconds he might lose control of his bladder, or just simply pass out.

Hoping that the cloak he wore to keep off the morning chill would hide his trembling legs, Aldin made for the door.

Ominously the entry corridor was empty. Nerving himself, he stepped inside.

"Bravo, Aldin," a voice called out of the darkness. "Bravo indeed, worthy of a vid performance."

Corbin stepped out of the shadows. "Heroic uncle comes to save innocent niece from the clutches of the villain."

"I've met my end of the deal," Aldin said weakly. Try as

he could, his voice was pitched too high, so that his words sounded like the squeak of an excited adolescent.

"Now, now," Corbin replied, beckoning for Aldin to follow him into the back chambers, "all in good time. But for the moment let me again be the gracious host to my old vasba and my former mistress."

"Let her go now," Aldin replied, trying to sound forceful, "or the deal is off." And he took a step backward.

"I don't think you have much choice," Gablona growled, and he pointed to the door behind Aldin.

An assassin had slipped in from the street behind Aldin. A naked blade in his hand was poised at Aldin's back.

"I think that if you tried to back out, you'd find one more orifice than your body was designed for."

Gablona stopped for a moment, chuckling at his own wit. "Come, I think for health reasons it would be better to follow me."

Aldin felt the blade nick through his cloak. He stepped forward and followed Gablona into the heart of the fortress.

"What the hell is going on?" Zola shouted, punching up the viewscreen. The drink he'd been about to offer his visitor lay spilled upon the floor. He'd expected yet another unpleasant meeting with the Koh everyone had now nicknamed Cassandra, but before their conversation had even started, a paging report had sounded, diverting his attention.

Bukha came around the desk to stand behind Zola.

Zola called in a screen command, and instantly the printed text gave way to a grid coordinate. On the screen were two blips of light side by side.

"Aldin and Gablona are together," Bukha said quietly.

Zola punched in another command and the scale of the screen shifted. Still the two blips were right on top of each other. "Damn it," he said, "they're practically sitting in each other's laps!" He watched the screen and saw no shifting or movement. "Obviously they're not fighting. What the hell is going on?"

"I'd say offhand," Bukha commented lazily, picking up a bottle of muscatel from the sideboard and pouring a replacement drink, "that they seem to be talking."

"Impossible," Zola snapped.

"Impossible, maybe, but nevertheless they aren't moving about, the way they would if there was a fight. But what about the others?"

Zola nodded and punched in another command. The scale of the screen shifted, zooming back to cover an area of several blocks.

"Aldin's guards and Sigma's Gafs seem to be spreading out around the building, but curious . . ."

Zola's voice dropped off.

"What is it?"

"Just that I see only ten guards for Gablona."

"Curious indeed," Bukha said quietly, and walking past the screen, he settled back into his seat.

"Well, I did come here to discuss a certain situation."

Zola, with his eyes still on the screen, merely grunted.

"Do I have your attention?"

"Of course, of course," Zola said absently.

"I just wanted to warn you that from my latest information, you, and in fact the entire economy of the Cloud, will be bankrupt."

"What, what was that?" Zola replied, his attention still fixed on the screen.

"Damn it, listen to me," Bukha suddenly roared, and standing up, he swept the screen off Zola's desk, so that it fell to the floor and shattered in a sizzling shower of sparks.

"Now what the hell did you do that for!"

"You've got to listen to me!"

With a snarl of defiance Zola swung around in his chair and punched the paging button. "My monitor just got knocked out," he snapped. "Damn it, find another one and bring it in here right away."

Releasing the button, he looked up at Bukha.

"My people will bill you for the damages," Zola said briskly. "Now state your business, then get the hell out of here."

Exasperated, Bukha slammed his drink down on Zola's desk, spilling the contents. "You've been had," he snarled. "I don't give a damn about you. But I've got to stop this, otherwise, come next week, the Overseers will control the economic wealth of the Cloud. I'm not tied into it, but if they hold the majority, they'll be able to squeeze the rest into their fists before another year standard is out. And damn it all, it's your fault!"

"What? What are you talking about?" Zola demanded, his attention finally fixing on what Bukha was saying.

"Listen closely," Bukha said with deliberate slowness. "The Overseers are playing your game!"

"Playing the game? You mean the lottery?"

"Exactly."

The color drained from Zola's face. "How?"

"They set up some dummy companies. Now tell me, how many valid tickets are still out there?"

"What kind? There're tens of millions of tickets floating around that can still pay off. Hundreds of billions were sold after Sigma died, but payoffs on those will be low, only in the thousands."

"You don't even know!" Bukha shouted.

"There was never a cause for worry," Zola said defensively. "My probability expert pointed out that the more tickets sold, the greater the chance that the results would fall into the probable average."

"So you haven't kept track of those tickets sold on the first day."

"How could we, there were trillions sold!"

"Well, I'll tell you then," Bukha snapped.

"That's privileged information. Only the stockholders had access and you're not a stockholder."

"But one of your ex-stockholders did some research for me."

Zola sat back in his chair.

"That bitch,"he said. "Well, it serves her right to have sold short. I thought she was a fool selling that stock back to me, and now I know it."

"She's the only one who will ever get any profit out of this venture. Did you ever stop to think *why* she sold short?"

Zola fell silent. He had been gloating that Tia had sold her shares to him for ten billion. She was giving up a dividend of fifty billion as a result. No matter that he had used company assets to pay her—that could be buried easily enough with a couple of false entries about payouts once the game was ended.

"Because," Bukha continued, "in ninety-six hours GGC will be belly-up."

"Tell me," Zola said, his nervousness suddenly apparent.

"As near as I figure, there are still a couple of hundred possible outcomes over the next four days."

"Correct."

"The full payoff will only occur, though, if tickets also show a bet that Sigma would die on day fifteen."

"Of course, of course."

"Well, at this very moment there's a block of tickets out there held by several betting syndicates. These tickets all show Sigma dying on day fifteen."

"How many?"

"In the tens of millions. Now, if your so-called probability norm was followed, there should only be a couple of hundred thousand probable winning tickets still out there."

The reality started to sink in.

"Tell me the rest," Zola said meekly.

"Tia managed to figure out that these syndicates hold blocks of tickets ranging from a quarter of a million up to five million on one of the probable outcomes that could happen over the next several days."

"I think I'm going to be sick," Zola whispered.

"Sick? You better start thinking suicide," Bukha snapped.

"But we've got trillions of katars in assets!"

Despite what he was hearing, Zola could not help but show some pride when he mentioned the amount. It was ten times what any Koh had ever controlled before.

"Well, you're going to need all of it," Bukha snarled. "The syndicates are fronts for the Overseers. If one of several of these probability outcomes occur, the ones the Overseers are betting on, your little firm will owe them an amount ranging from three trillion to ten trillion katars."

Zola sat in the chair with a numbed, glazed-eyed look.

"And remember," Bukha said with an almost vindictive tone, "any stockholder at the time the game ends, or after the seventy-fifth game day, will have his personal assets made liable if the company should not be able to meet its obligations. The Overseers insisted on that clause in agreement not to interfere, and in your rush for money none of you ever thought about the reasons behind it."

"They'll own the Cloud," Zola whispered hoarsely.

Bukha fixed Zola with a vicious stare. "You walked right into their trap."

"If you had told me yesterday, we could have dumped out of the company before the clause took effect."

Bukha was silent.

"Why didn't you tell me!" Zola screamed.

"Because you would have turned it to your advantage and not acted for the benefit of us all."

"What can we do?" Zola asked weakly.

Bukha leaned forward and smiled. "Make sure that the two below live, or die in an unexpected way."

Zola swung about in his chair and punched the pager.

"Get Kurst now!" he screamed. "And damn it, where's my other screen?"

Zola turned back to face Bukha, and already the self-assured look had returned. "Now I guess we should figure out which probability would be best to our advantage."

"Brilliant, absolutely brilliant," Blackie mumbled. Kurst could only beam with pride. The information he had brought was simply priceless. With a smile she rose from her desk and took the short walk down the corridor and out onto the trading floor.

The buy orders were out in seconds. Apparently the market already knew that Aldin and Gablona were together, in the middle of Gablona's lair. Trading was brisk, with six-hour options on first-day tickets calling for Aldin to die by Gablona fetching up to five hundred thousand a share. But when Blackie's order went out, the representatives of the Alma syndicate were nevertheless quick to notice and to counterbuy in turn.

Within minutes, tens of billions in options were exchanging hands on the trading floor.

"So nice of you to drop by," Gablona said, settling into the chair across from Aldin. "Just like old times, Koh and loyal vasba getting together for a drink."

Aldin was silent, nervously watching the assassin who stood to one side.

Gablona, noticing Aldin's discomfort, waved for the assassin to step out of the room.

"So, have you been enjoying our little stay down here?" Gablona asked smoothly.

"Look, Gablona," Aldin said, "get to the point."

"Gablona Koh," Corbin snapped back coldly. "Remember my title and your social rank."

"Corbin," Aldin replied slowly, "the title goes to those who deserve it. For generations the word Koh was linked to men of honor, to men who understood the code that only through integrity could we keep the economic system of the Cloud intact. You've debased it, cheapened it. My father served your father, as did his father before him. But you've changed all that forever."

"Are you quite done?" Gablona laughed.

Aldin suddenly realized to his surprise that his nerves had been steadied by the outbreak. Finally after all these years he'd spoken his mind to Gablona, and the release had made him feel strangely cold, as if detached from what he knew might occur in the next few minutes.

"You realize of course that we're both being played by the Shiga."

"You perhaps," Corbin replied smoothly. "Ever met Ulsak?"

Aldin could only shake his head with disgust.

"He introduced me to their delicacies," Corbin said, "and to some of their other practices as well."

"What did he want with you?" Aldin asked.

"Oh, only an offer. A guarantee, if you will. Deliver you to him, and I get their agreement to leave this place unhindered when the game is finished."

"And you actually believed that?"

"I made it worth his while. Oh, there was quite the bidding for you. Now, my friends the blues are still enraged over that foolish little incident on the first day. I had quite the bidding war going between the two. But finally Ulsak made a little sweetener for the deal."

"Go on, enlighten me."

"He agreed to let me kill you and thus make a rather interesting profit on the side."

"How could your killing me affect . . ." Aldin began, then fell silent.

"Exactly," Gablona said with a grin. "I don't have any tickets with you dying by the Shiga. But I did have someone buy up blocks of tickets with my killing Sigma and then you. Now it's all a question of when. I've only got fifty valid tickets for you dying on this game day or the next. But if I hold off for four days, I'll have a thousand. Hold off till the next-to-last day of the game, and I've got two thousand. And finally I own ten thousand tickets calling for your death on the last day. So, you see, I stand quite an increase in the profit line by keeping you alive for just three more standard days. I'll come out of this little affair with billions in profits, and Ulsak agreed to it all."

Aldin could only look away with disgust.

"So eat hearty, my friend," Gablona said, laughing while pointing out a table spread with a variety of Shiga delicacies. "Ulsak even provided me with some confiscated brandy. Fine stuff. I suggest you make yourself at home. The festival should be starting about now, and our friends will be by to pick you up."

"Release the girl," Aldin said coldly. "At least fulfill that promise that you made to me. You said you'd let her go if I surrendered."

Gablona settled back into his chair, a broad smile lighting his features. "I lied."

"He's been in there nearly an hour," Mari whispered, looking around apprehensively, for the fog was starting to burn away.

"He said not to move till the girl was out," Oishi replied.

Suddenly the distant rumble of the drums fell silent, there was a faint brightening to the sky, and the sun broke through the early-morning haze.

A horn sounded in the distance.

Mari grabbed Oishi by the sleeve. "Damn it, do something, now!"

"Now let me guess," Gablona said. "I don't think that you'd be so stupid as to walk in here without a plan for your people to get you out."

"What makes you think that?" Aldin replied nonchalantly, as he picked about the tray of meats Gablona had offered, trying to find something that didn't look too disgusting.

"It's what I would have done."

"I doubt that. You wouldn't have done what I just did, not even if it was your own mother held prisoner."

"My mother," Gablona barked. "Let me tell you about my mother. If the Shigs had her, within a week she'd have turned them around and been made their queen. But as I was saying, I wouldn't suggest that your people come in here and try to cut you out. For tickets or no tickets, you wouldn't get out of this room alive."

"I assumed that, but what about Tia?"

"Still the girl. The way you're acting you'd think she was your mistress rather than your niece."

"You're disgusting," Aldin snapped.

"I know," Corbin replied, his one-hundred-and-thirty-five kilo frame shaking as he laughed.

"All right, I think it's about time anyhow. Let's fetch her."

Corbin picked up a small bell by his chair and rang it. Seconds later the door behind him opened, and Tia, looking rather worse for the wear, was pushed into the room by one of Corbin's guards.

"I think you better stay," Corbin commanded of the assassin. "After all, we wouldn't want the odds to be two to one in here. Might upset the betting upstairs."

Aldin rose to his feet and went over to Tia's side.

"What the hell are you doing here?" Tia cried, and without being told, she suddenly realized what Aldin must have done.

For the first time since her childhood Aldin saw his niece's eyes start to fill up.

"You stupid idiot," she said, wiping away a tear. "You know whatever he offered would be a lie."

"I know," Aldin said quietly. "But if I hadn't, I never could have lived with myself." And he put his arms around her.

"Did he hurt you?" Aldin asked.

"Who, him? He wouldn't have the guts to touch me."

"Now, now," Corbin drawled. "There was a time when you rather enjoyed the way I touched you."

"Filth," Tia snapped. "I had more fun playing with a block of ice than I ever had with you."

For a second Aldin feared that she had pushed him too far. There was a flaring of anger in Gablona's eyes, but he merely turned away, struggling visibly for control.

"Rather than simply have you poisoned," he said slowly, "I think I'll give you to the Shiga instead."

Aldin felt as if he were going to lose control, that he would simply have it out here and now and, with luck, take Gablona with him. The Koh, as if sensing his mood, stepped back several paces.

Suddenly the doorway that led back out to the front of the building swung open, and one of Gablona's assassins entered the room.

"Ah, my friend." Gablona laughed. "Are the Shiga here for their package?"

The assassin nodded in reply.

"Where's Hassan?"

"Detained," the assassin replied. Suddenly Gablona realized that he did not recognize this man.

The double door was pushed open and a file of yellow Shiga entered the room, all of them cloaked in the robes of their order.

Without a word they surrounded Aldin, pushing Tia aside.

"Oh, take the girl too," Gablona said nervously, not sure of what was happening, still looking at what he thought should be one of his assassins. "Tell your lord Ulsak that she's a gift from me, a little extra dividend to show my friendship."

"You bastard," Tia screamed. "If the Kohs ever hear of this, that a family head murdered me, a Koh in my own right, they'll never forgive you."

"Memories can be erased with enough money," Corbin said, trying to hide his fear. From out beyond the doorway he heard the sound of struggling and a muffled cry in the barbaric tongue that his assassins still used among themselves.

Several of the yellow robes surrounded Aldin and then the girl, while Gablona stepped back into the corner of the room.

Four of the men broke away from the group and started toward Gablona.

"Where are my guards?" he shouted.

"Dead," one of them whispered. "Ten of them were nothing for us."

With a movement so swift that it was almost a blur, one of

the yellows reached to his headband and pulled out a coil of wire. The wire snaked out, looping over Gablona's head.

Screaming with terror, Gablona fell to his knees, desperately struggling to pull the razorlike strand loose from his throat. The steel bit in, the skin about his jugular pulled so taut that the slightest pressure would cause the skin to rupture, spilling out his life.

"You're going on a journey as well," one of the yellows snarled. "It's time we all visited Ulsak."

Aldin and Tia were pushed to the door. Coming past Gablona, Aldin almost felt a touch of pity. The man was half choking, his eyes bulging in their sockets from the strain and the terror.

"I tried to warn you," Aldin said coldly, but before he could say another word one of the yellows cuffed him with the back of his hand, nearly knocking Aldin to the floor.

Down the darkened corridor they were led, and then out into the brightness of early dawn. The air was still cool, faint wisps of morning mist drifting past overhead.

Around them were several dozen yellows, who looked nervously up and down the street.

"Let's move," the one leading Aldin commanded. "The blues still want these two."

At a near run the party started out. Gablona staggered in the middle of the group, his captor having attached a long pole to the garrote handles and then passing his prisoner off to one of his men.

The group made its way down the street. The two yellows leading the way suddenly slowed, as if sensing that something was not right. Several shattered barrels lay in the middle of the alley, the paths covered from one end to the other with the spilled contents. The reek of liquor filled the air.

"These weren't here when we passed," one of the Shiga said cautiously, going over to kick one of the barrels aside.

Suddenly there was a flash of light and a thunderclap roar.

The lead warrior, screaming, staggered back, his robes drenched with flames, half his companions on the ground, writhing in agony.

"Tia, down!" Aldin screamed, diving for the pavement.

As he rolled into the gutter, he looked up and saw his guard turning, blade drawn, coming straight at him.

The man was going to kill him now, Aldin realized, trying to kick himself backward out of the Shiga's reach. The warrior took another step and then was slammed backward as the snap of a catapult was heard. Another half-dozen bolts cracked out from the corner building. With a wild shout the door was flung back, and, with Oishi in the lead, the samurai swarmed out.

Their blades flashed in the morning light, sweeping and cutting as they advanced.

A Gaf berserker leaped over Aldin and, with a backhanded blow, finished off the yellow that had been brought down by the bolt.

There was another explosion, this time to the rear of the column. Aldin sat up and saw a dozen Shiga down on the ground, their shattered bodies pouring blood from half a hundred wounds.

Aldin looked up, and from an upper window another projectile, a heavy, five-gallon jug, arched out, a sputtering fuse marking its path.

"Down," Aldin screamed.

The jug disappeared in a blinding flash, knocking the rear of the column flat.

From out of a side alleyway farther up the street, more Gafs appeared, screaming hysterically, Zergh at their lead.

The narrow street was aswarm with men and Gafs. Aldin felt hands grabbing him by the armpits, and he came back up to his feet, several samurai standing about him, beaming with delight. He saw Tia crawling out from under a Shiga corpse, her cloak and trousers soaked with blood, a dagger in her hand, which she had obviously used. As quickly as it had started, the ambush was finished. The last of the assassins were stunned by the flame, explosions, and surprise, and had died without inflicting a single casualty. One Gad had been lost, but the rest were elated and now danced about, shouting with glee that their blades had tasted blood.

But there was a new component to the plan that he had not thought of.

"Gablona! Get him!" Aldin cried.

The Koh lay in the middle of the street, floundering about like a fish out of water. The assassin who had been leading him lay slumped against a wall, a catapult bolt driven clear through his body.

Seiji approached the Koh and, grabbing hold of the staff, pulled Gablona to his feet. The skin about his throat had been cut from the pressure of the garrote and a trickle of blood started to run down the front of his silken shirt.

Gablona, feeling the warmth, felt about his neck and, with a strangled gurgle of fear, raised his bloodied hands up before his eyes.

Aldin came up before Gablona.

"More than we bargained for," Oishi said grimly, looking with disdain at Gablona.

Aldin was silent, as if making a decision.

"Twist the garrote but a bit more," Oishi said coldly, "and you're rid of him."

Aldin looked from Oishi to Tia and then back to the Koh.

"What should we do, Tia?" he asked.

"I'm tempted to choke the life out of him myself," she replied with a chilling laugh.

Corbin extended his hands, gurgling pitifully.

"I remember Kira, the coward. He had that same look before I took his head," Oishi snarled with contempt.

Aldin continued to stare at Corbin without moving.

"We better get moving," Mari shouted, coming up to join the group. "Takashi just came in and reported that the blues have stormed the tavern, and now they're really mad. They'll be coming here next."

"Do you wish the pleasure of the kill?" Oishi asked, pulling the garrote handles free from the pole. "Or should I twist the life out of him now?"

Tears coursed down Gablona's face, and he held his hands up to Aldin, imploring him for mercy. The act drew jeers of contempt from the samurai. Without a word Aldin stepped forward and took the garrote handles from Oishi. Gablona's breath came in short wheezing gasps.

"It would take but half a twist," Aldin said. "And when I think of what you'd given Tia over to . . ."

He turned the handles ever so slightly, and Gablona let out a half-strangled shriek of fear.

With a snort of disgust Aldin turned away and let the handles drop.

Gasping, the Koh fell to his knees and pulled the garrote free. Sobbing, he fell forward, his breath coming in deep, shuddering groans.

There was a murmur of disappointment from the samurai and Gafs.

"I don't understand," Oishi said in confusion. "He's been trying to kill you down here; moments ago he betrayed you and your niece. And now you do this. It's not wise, my lord, to let such an enemy live."

Gablona looked up at Oishi, his eyes filled with hatred.

"I have my reasons," Aldin snapped. "Now let's move!"

With a barked command, Oishi turned away, pointing the way back to the building that they had taken earlier at sword-point and from which they had launched their surprise attack.

Aldin looked quickly around. The ambush had gone off perfectly. He had counted on the fact that Gablona would betray him and not release Tia. He had counted, as well, on the belief that the Koh would not kill him outright and either sell him to Ulsak or keep him alive for later use. The barrels and bombs were to be used in storming the citadel. What had surprised them all was the arrival of the yellows, but Oishi had obviously adapted the plan to take care of them. In fact they had made it easier by bringing Aldin and Tia out into the open. The broken barrels had been ignited with the first bomb, and the possible retreat backward was shattered with the others.

It had taken days to boil off the hundreds of gallons of sulfurous water for the first ingredient, and digging in the tavern's privy provided the saltpeter. They had used half their stockpile in this the first attack.

They'd broken all the rules of the Hole, using projectiles and explosives to kill Shiga. If they had not been united against them before, they would most definitely be so now. But already he was thinking on that path as well.

"Let's go," Mari shouted, anxiously pulling at Aldin's sleeve.

"Someone's coming," one of the samurai warned, and pointed up the alleyway.

From around the corner a single man appeared, blood pouring from a slash across his cheek.

It was Hassan.

"You damned fool," Gablona roared. "What happened?"

Hassan approached the group, walking right past the samurai, who held their blades up, ready to strike.

"We were betrayed," he said, speaking to Gablona as if the rest were not even there.

"By whom?" Aldin asked.

"Who else? Ulsak. I, and the twenty men you sent with me for a parley, were met just outside the foreign quarter where they jumped us. All my men were killed. I alone fought my way out and tried to get back here to warn all of you."

Aldin looked at the man. "The Shiga use poison blades." He pointed at the wound. "You should be dead."

"Oh, this," Hassan replied smoothly, reaching up and dabbing the blood as if aware of the injury for the first time. "A yellow picked up one of our blades and tried to use it on me."

Hassan looked about the group.

"I guess I should surrender to you," he said evenly, and reaching into his belt, he pulled out his blade and handed it hilt first toward Oishi.

"I'd rather be your prisoner and get out of this alive than wait for the Shiga to get me."

Oishi looked coldly at Hassan, not believing a word he had heard.

"Take him with us," Aldin said. "His skills might be useful. Now let's get out of here." And planting a kick on Gablona's backside, he pushed the Koh.

"For what you've done, the entire Shiga will be after you." Gablona gasped.

"They're after your ass as well," Aldin snapped.

In the distance a horn sounded, and then another, and another. The Shiga would soon find out their sacred laws had been violated, on this, the start of their festival, and Aldin felt a cold wave of fear. If they were worked up before, he could only imagine the frenzy that would come now.

"So this is the price of your agreement?" Aabec of the Isma said coldly, his blue robe fluttering as he gazed about at the carnage.

Ulsak was withdrawn, almost distant, as he walked among the corpses of his followers. After rolling one over with his foot, he squatted down to examine the wounds.

"Blast wounds," Ulsak said softly.

"How?" Tores Ser of the Bengada sect shouted. "We've never allowed explosives on the Hole, everything coming down is monitored in agreement to that. We train without such things in order to prevent those above from ever suspecting or learning to fear us."

"They made it themselves," Ulsak replied.

"And look at this," Aabec stated, pointing to the catapult bolt that protruded from a Gaf body.

Ulsak nodded grimly. "They've brought their little game down here and brought their own rules as well."

"Our followers will ask questions," Aabec whispered, coming up to the other rulers. "They've been taught that such things bring instant death."

"We'll think of something," Ulsak replied, and the others nodded. After all, wasn't that what their religion was all about, a game of deception to keep the faithful in line?

"Then we agree on the rest?" Ulsak asked.

The others fell silent.

"You should have just killed them out of hand," Aabec suddenly stated, and the others nodded in agreement. "We could have had them both dead a hundred times over."

"But I did not want it so," Ulsak snapped in reply.

"And why not?" Tores Ser inquired.

"Because the two could not die until the final ceremony."

"I suspect you haven't told all," Tores Ser said menacingly.

"Suspect all you want, but in this we must be united."

Tores Ser said nothing, but Ulsak could see the suspicion in his eyes—a suspicion the others obviously shared.

"We've heard the ravings of this shaman," Aabec said coldly, looking over at Ulsak. "Heard a rumor as well that you actually met with him and did not stop his mad ramblings."

"Tell me," Nargla of the red Sutar sect asked quietly, "do you intend to call yourself the Ema?"

Ulsak merely looked at the other masters and smiled.

"Follow me in this. Soon I can reveal the rest to you. I asked you to hold back your men from killing the offworlders, and you agreed as we always have when a master makes a request of another," he said evenly. "If there is failure, I shall take the blame."

There was a murmur of interest from the others. They had

their various rivalries for power, to be sure. But the tradition of a hundred generations had shown the masters that it was through cooperation with each other that their own power was maintained in balance. But Ulsak had been different, trying to somehow grasp for something more.

They all shared the same thought—undoubtedly this man was going to proclaim himself as the Ema, and as such demand their allegiance to him. But of course such a thing was impossible, since only a madman would dare to claim the title.

The other masters looked one to another and then back to Ulsak, and nodded in reply.

"We start the hunt at once," Ulsak stated, fixing each in turn with his gaze.

"I shall section off the foreign quarter first, and then the city around it. Your people are to be pulled out of here and back to your own cities. I then want a cordon set up completely around the outer edge of the wild jungle region, so that if they try to slip out, they can't get past you and then on into the cultivated regions beyond. We haven't much time, they must be found before the Ulman."

"There're a million places they could hide in this city alone," Aabec replied.

"If need be, I'll burn the entire region to the ground," Ulsak snarked. "For in a brief time none of us shall have need of it, ever again."

And those around him looked back and forth to each other. So the rumors were true; perhaps there was a way off the Hole, after all. He had asked their cooperation with a vague promise of power undreamed of, but if he could indeed get them off, then that meant he was the Ema, and they in turn would have to submit.

One by one the masters turned away without further comment until only Ulsak stood alone gazing at the corpses about his feet.

CHAPTER 13

Aldin CAME UP TO THE WINDOW AND LOOKED OUT TO WHERE Oishi was pointing.

It was a scene out of a nightmare. The night sky was illuminated from horizon to horizon with flames. From their vantage point overlooking the great square, streams of foreign refugees filled the side streets, their few possessions lashed to carts, wagons, and overladen wheelbarrows. Others staggered beneath the weight of their packs, struggling to move forward.

The flames that had started late the day before in the foreign quarter had quickly spread even into the yellow section, but the inhabitants, if anything, seemed to revel in the destruction. Aldin had actually seen some of them, carrying torches, toss the burning brands into buildings in their own quarter.

The air was rent with the roar of the conflagration; explosions, as houses and fortresses burst into flames; and the high, thin screams of the terrified merchants.

There was an insane randomness to it all. Groups of merchants would finally work up the nerve and rush out from the shelter of an alleyway about to be engulfed in flames. Approaching the perimeter of yellow Shiga, they would slow. Shiga warriors would surround the group. After several minutes most would pass. But others would be cut down on the spot, while still others were herded away.

Some groups of merchants would try to charge through, but none ever made it to the Skyhook, a trail of bodies the only sign of their passing. Perversely, as quickly as they fell, other merchants would fall upon their bundles of goods, even as their comrades were being dispatched.

"Anyone they even suspect of being us is singled out," Oishi said.

"I never thought it would ever sink to this," Aldin whispered.

"Gablona, come here and look at this," Aldin hissed, and stepping back, he pushed the Koh up to the window.

Gablona was silent, his pale face drawn with fear; he had yet to recover from the fright of his capture and the subsequent chase.

The route Aldin had planned for their escape into the countryside had been blocked. They'd nearly been trapped when a group of yellows picked up their trail. It was almost like a hunt. The group that stumbled upon them sounded a horn, and it seemed as if from every alleyway bands of assassins came pouring out to close the net.

Mari had led them on a mad dash, leaping fences, crawling over refuse heaps, and skulking in abandoned buildings until finally they had shaken off the pursuit—a feat that had cost the lives of two more samurai, who without Aldin's knowledge had stayed behind to slow the searchers.

Rather than heading for the outer edge of the city, Mari had led them inward toward the center, reasoning that such a path would throw off the yellows. For the moment it had worked, and finding an abandoned warehouse next to the great square, they had crept in, to wait out events.

"This is your fault," Gablona said, looking back at Aldin. "If you had come along quietly, none of this would have happened."

"And you'd be dead, too," Aldin snapped back in reply.

But still the words hit hard. Aldin looked back out to the

square. Hundreds of innocents were dying out there, and the entire city seemed to be given over to an insane pillage as the yellows appeared bent on destroying it all from one end to the other.

Mari, as if sensing how deep Gablona's words had hit, came up to Aldin's side.

"There's more to it than what we think," she said soothingly. "Even the Shigs wouldn't destroy their own nest unless they had a reason. They could hunt for us just as easily without this. It's as stupid as rioters burning down their own homes and shops to protest some imagined grievance. Once they're done with this, no merchant will ever dare to live down here again. Without the merchants the supply of metals will dry up overnight. This place will be worthless. It's almost as if the Shigs are burying everything, since they no longer need it."

"Damn it all, that's what I came down here to tell you about," Tia said, coming up to join the group by the window.

"What's that?" Aldin asked. They had been so busy with their escape, he hadn't even found the time yet to ask her why she had taken the risk to come down to this madhouse.

"Remember, I'm still the acting Koh of the Gablona holdings," she stated.

Corbin turned and fixed her with an icy gaze but said nothing.

"It's just that I found a report that fifty of my dear lover's heavy passenger transport ships had been contracted from one of the shipping firms our family still held."

"So what's so important about that?" Gablona asked. "I already told you about that."

"I thought it to be rather curious, since all the ships were hired without a filed port of destination, with an open-ended contract."

Gablona fell silent.

"So what does that have to do with this?" Aldin snapped, pointing back out toward the destruction outside the window.

"The ships turned up in orbit around the Garn system. I found the information on Yaroslav's files just before I came down here. That's why I came. I felt the only way to stop this was to get to you two and hope to arrange a truce. If you two live, it throws off all their plans. The Overseers won't win, and most likely they'll just leave the Shiga alone then. It seems at least that my coming here kind of worked anyhow," she said almost in a self-congratulatory manner.

"What's the Garn system?" Mari asked.

"Just a worthless hunk of real estate, the next star over from here," Tia replied. "By jump, it's not even an hour away. There's nothing there, no resources, no colonies, nothing, just a scorched rock orbiting a dying star. We only found out because even as I was tracking down those ships, one of our prospecting vessels that was in the Garn system reported the ships as they jumped in, then all contact was lost.

"Here are fifty ships," Tia continued, "worth millions a day in leasing payments, orbiting in the middle of nowhere."

"As if waiting to pick something up," Aldin said slowly.

"As if waiting for something to happen here," Tia replied.

The enormity of it was stunning.

"Why didn't you tell the Kohs?" Aldin asked.

"I tried, but Bukha wouldn't listen. The rest of the damn fools were so caught up in their game, they wouldn't have believed me anyhow, figuring I was just out for my own gain."

"The Shiga are destroying all this because they no longer need it," Aldin said, astonished. "They'll be leaving, on Gablona's ships. By the heavens, they're planning to get off this planet, and somebody is helping them!"

Gablona backed up from the group, which turned to face him.

"I had nothing to do with it!" he squealed.

Aldin grabbed hold of Gablona and started to shake him.

"I ought to throw you out there to the mob. If the yellows don't kill you, the merchants will!" he screamed.

"I didn't do nothing! The Overseers wanted the lease, I gave it to them, that's all," Gablona cried.

"So that explains all of it. The archaic tactics, the destruction of everything they own. You were going to bribe them with transport off in exchange for your miserable hide. The Shiga have been preparing all along to leave this world and spread their cult throughout the Cloud, in service to their dark and hungry God."

"Honest!" Gablona shrieked. "I had nothing to do with it! I

promised them some modern weapons, that was it!"

"I hate to say it," Tia said, "but I think for once he's telling the truth. It was Alma money, and they were going to frame Gablona as the fall guy!"

"That's it!" Gablona gasped, looking gratefully at Tia. "That's it, they were framing me!"

"Shut up, all of you," Oishi said.

Aldin looked over at the samurai who had crouched back from the window. As if dropping a piece of trash, Aldin let go of Gablona, who fell back gasping, and, bending low, came up next to the samurai.

"All your arguing drew some attention," Oishi whispered.

Ever so cautiously Aldin crept up to the window slit and peered out.

Directly beneath them a group of yellows stood, looking up straight at the window.

Aldin quickly ducked back down.

"Damn it all," he cursed, "I thought we'd be safe here for a while. Let's get the hell out of here."

"But where?" Tia asked.

"This is a warehouse for a food merchant," Mari replied. "I was checking it out; down in the basement I saw a door that must lead into the catacombs beneath the city."

Turning, they scurried out of the room and down the staircase to the ground floor. Before they had even reached the landing, there was a pounding on the door.

"Let's go," Oishi barked, and the rest of their companions, who had remained hidden on the ground floor, fell in behind Mari's lead.

The pounding on the door behind them ceased. Suddenly there was a splintering crack, and the door bulged back on its hinges.

Oishi, Seiji, and Ura fell to the rear of the group, letting the others push past.

There was another crack, one of the hinges was ripped out of its mount, and the door leaned back. The last of the group cleared the steps to the basement.

"Fall back!" Oishi ordered, but the two with him refused to budge.

Another crack and the door crashed inward. Half a dozen

Shiga standing on the other side dropped the heavy beam they were using for a ram and started to rush in.

Oishi leaped upon the door, his sword arching out, taking the head off the first attacker. With a backhanded flourish he swung his blade up on a diagonal cut, slicing the second yellow open from hip to shoulder.

Ura waded into the fray, his two-handed axe raised high, dropping the third yellow who had turned and was coming in low beneath Oishi's guard.

The three stepped back from the door, as if taunting the remaining attackers to press in.

The three remaining yellows hesitated. One of them barked a command and then, turning, ran back up the street.

"Coward!" Seiji screamed, and pushing through the door, he closed with the remaining natives.

"Don't," Oishi shouted, but Seiji, taken up with battle lust, ignored him.

Seiji feigned with a stab and a quick sidestep. The first yellow jumped to one side, while the second came straight in.

Recovering, Seiji slashed low and then, in imitation of Oishi, attempted a backhanded sweep upward that caught his opponent in the same way that Oishi had.

The assassin to his side closed in, and his dagger sunk home into Seiji's back, even as the young samurai shouted in triumph.

Wild with rage, Oishi leaped over the falling body of his nephew and, with a downward slice, finished the last assassin.

"That's them!"

A group of frightened merchants stood across the alleyway, having witnessed the entire fight, and now, screaming, pointed at the three. The one remaining yellow, who had broken away, was already out in the square, screaming for help.

His vision blurred with tears of rage, Oishi looked around and barely noticed Ura grabbing him by the shoulders, pulling him back through the doorway.

"Now they've seen us!" Ura roared.

"Seiji!"

"Forget him, he's dead," Ura shouted, and grabbing Oishi by the arm, he dragged him back into the warehouse and toward the basement door.

Aldin, along with several of the samurai, noticing that

Oishi had stayed behind, were coming back up the stairs in search of him. Ura, bellowing for them to move, pushed Oishi into the group.

"Where's Seiji?" Takashi asked.

"Dead," Oishi said weakly. "I failed, I should have stopped him."

Stunned, Takashi stood on the stairs and then with a wild cry started back up.

Aldin reached out and grabbed him.

"It's too late, my friend, your son's dead," Aldin cried. "Now stay with me!"

Tears of anguish formed in Takashi's eyes, and he was torn between service to his master and to his son who lay in the doorway.

"You must live for me!" Aldin cried.

Oishi, forgetting his own anguish, came up to Takashi's side and, grabbing hold of him, looked into his eyes.

"He's gone," Oishi whispered, "but we must still live."

Trembling, Takashi nodded in reply, and, turning, they started down into the darkness.

Stumbling down the stairs, Aldin urged the group forward.

Aldin gagged as he stepped into the basement and covered his mouth with his sleeve.

The room was a long, deep cavern, sloping downward into the dark. Mari was right. It was a food storage room, a room filled from one end to the other with rotting men. Hundreds of coffinlike containers lay on the floor, each of them filled with the human-shaped fungus in various states of decomposition. Hundreds more of the rotting men were stacked like cordwood along one wall. The stench was overpowering. It was even too much for some of the Gafs, who were joining a number of the samurai who had staggered off to one side, retching.

The only light was a single lantern up ahead, which cast long wavering shadows so that the corpselike forms seemed to shift and waver, as if hundreds of decomposing bodies were twitching and jerking.

Aldin looked around and saw in an instant that no one was moving. With an angry shout he pushed his way through to the head of the column.

"What's wrong here?" Aldin shouted. "How come we're not moving?"

"Because the bloody door's locked, that's why," Mari snarled.

"Locked? What the hell do you mean, it's locked!"

"Look at my lips," Mari said slowly, "and listen. I said that the door is locked. The catacombs are on the other side; a lot of merchants lock their entry, afraid thieves might slip in."

"You mean you led us down here into a trap?"

"I knew we couldn't trust her," Hassan said, his voice icy with sarcasm.

Aldin wanted to turn and lash out, but there wasn't time. "Can we knock it down?"

"How? Throw rotting men against it?"

"Well, let's blast it then!" Tia suggested.

"It might look good in the vids, but not in real life," Zergh replied. "That door's solid iron. You'll need something on this side to contain the blast, otherwise it'll just blow away from the door and destroy everything in here."

"Then we gotta get back out of here," Aldin cried, suddenly overwhelmed by a terrifying wave of claustrophobia.

The sound of footsteps echoed above them.

"They're in the building," Zergh whispered.

"Then we'll just fight our way out," Ura said, patting his bloodstained axe.

"They'll just swarm us under," Aldin said, hs voice edged with desperation. "Get out in the street, and even the merchants will riot against us."

"Then it is time to chant our death songs," one of the Gafs said, an almost dreamy quality to his voice.

"Yeah," Tia commented coldly, "in a couple of days though we're gonna look like these damn plants."

"That's it!" Aldin shouted.

"I think it'll be over any minute now," the Xsarn said, looking at the display screen that dominated the far wall.

One-half of the monitor provided a sensor-implant reading, showing Aldin, Gablona, and their companions clustered close together. The second half of the screen showed a close-up shot from one of the sensor mounts on the tower. It was zoomed straight in on the warehouse, and showed hundreds of yellows swarming into the building.

"We can't let word leak out," Vol shouted. "Remember,

there's the other market as well. The stock market's taken a bad enough beating as it is. The day after the Alexandrian fiasco went public we took a twenty-two percent loss. If word gets out the Overseers are planning a hostile takeover, it'll go insane."

"From what we're seeing on the monitor, it won't matter in a couple of minutes," one of the Kohs remarked. "They'll own the companies anyhow, and damn it, we can't even get our assets out!"

Several of the Kohs were in near-catatonic states. The crowd that had at one time so eagerly gathered around Zola had now abandoned him, the seating having shifted to the opposite end of the big table, so Zola now sat alone, while Bukha had a circle about him.

"It's Bukha's fault," Zola shouted. The logic was so outrageous that immediately the room fell silent, ready to hear what he had to say.

"Bukha himself admitted that he suspected this trick, as early as game day thirty. Why didn't he say anything then? If he had, we could have dumped our stock, or . . . or . . ."

"Rigged the results," the Xsarn interrupted.

"Exactly."

There was a low murmur of agreement from the assembly.

With a smug look Zola sat back.

"Because I still only suspected," Bukha replied coldly. "In this volatile a situation, even a rumor could have set off a panic."

"We're businessmen," Vol said. "We would have approached it like businessmen."

"And panicked," Bukha snapped.

"Now it's too late," Zola replied. "They're only three and a half days standard, or seven gaming days, left. You said earlier that there were alternatives. What are they?"

"By your own admission, there are nearly fifty million tickets covering the bets of Sigma dying on day fifteen, and Aldin and Gablona dying by the natives some time in the next seven days."

"Damn Gablona and Aldin both," the Xsarn said, a cold anger in his voice, so that those sitting next to him backed away. "They've both had the chance to kill each other for the last day, and neither one has acted. If they had, the Overseer bets would have been worthless and we'd be out of this mess."

The rest of the Kohs growled in agreement.

"What held them back?" one of the Kohs asked.

All of them could see where Aldin and Gablona were huddled together, within inches of each other. Just the flick of a dagger from one or the other, and the Overseers' plot would be ruined!

"Damn it, Aldin, kill him," Zola hissed, "before the Overseers win it all!"

"Do we have any other alternatives?" the Xsarn asked, looking at Bukha.

"There is one," Bukha said slowly. "If either Aldin or Gablona dies by a source other than the natives. The Overseers' holdings of bets in those areas is next to nothing."

"So we'll still get the profit!" Zola cried.

"There are one or two possible outcomes that could prevent that, since a large block of tickets is still outstanding on both surviving."

"What's the best payoff?" Zola asked eagerly.

"One dies by the other, or by Sigma's Gafs, since a kill by them would still be credited to Sigma."

"Is there any chance to arrange it?" the Xsarn asked.

"But that would be against the rules," Zola said with an innocent smile.

"By the way," Vol asked, looking around the room. "Where's Tia?"

"Oh, went back home, something about family business, I heard," Bukha finally replied.

"This is horrifying," the Arch whispered, looking first at the two Overseers who stood before him and then back to the screen.

"It is a destiny that is now beyond our intervention," Losa replied softly.

"A destiny that we are aiding nevertheless. The Al'Shiga are killing hundreds of innocents."

"Innocents? I think not," Losa responded. "They are of the merchant classes. By its very nature the merchant class must exploit to derive this thing they called profit. Profit is derived at the loss of that whom you deal with. Therefore they have taken from the Al'Shiga, building upon their debt to existence, and now the Shiga vent their rage at this, their first act of rage upon all who live in the Cloud. We must try to understand their violence and hope to be able to help them better relate to themselves."

"But we are helping them nevertheless."

"We are merely letting the balance return," Losa stated. "First, they are about to wreck them economically with this lottery. In a very short time, and by their own rules, we shall have control of their economic system. Second, the Shiga shall be loose. Such a movement will sweep across the Cloud for years, until there is nothing but chaos. We are letting the natural forces play themselves out, as we should have done when the three races first arrived, rather than intervening and stopping their war."

The Overseers fell silent. The action they had taken once before was still a source of controversy to them. They had been appointed as guardians by the First Travelers, to hold the Cloud until such time as their unseen lords return. Never had they expected the onslaught by the other beings.

What they had done was nothing more than a bluff, a bluff that had stopped the wars, before one power had become dominant and unified the Cloud. Thus had a status quo been maintained.

Their one demonstration of power had awed the primitives, but never had the primitives realized just how tenuous the Overseers' hold over them really was. For the world-shattering demonstrations had in the process destroyed the very machinery that brought them about, and the Overseers had no idea how to re-create the mechanism, since it was a First Traveler device.

"Whether the decision was right or wrong," the Arch said, "still I made it, and it has at least kept us in a semblance of power. But now you have taken it upon yourself to force the issue."

"And force it I have," Losa said coldly. "We will soon have control over their economic system. If we had attempted to take that alone, they would have rebelled directly against us. The Shiga are the other ingredient. The day their game ends and it is announced that we own most of the assets of the Cloud, the Shiga will break out."

"But it will be chaos," the Arch replied.

"And it will ruin our own economic ventures," Vush said, an edge of panic in his voice. "The profits we will lose will be astronomical!"

The other two turned and looked at their companion with disdain.

"It seems, friend, as if you have been seduced by these outsiders!" the Arch commented.

Vush fell silent and looked sullenly at his two companions.

"We are not concerned with economic systems," Losa said, "but rather with controlling these vermin. If we merely took their economic system, there would be shock at first, but rather quickly the Kohs would unite against us, and in any such confrontation we would be quickly eliminated. Do remember we are not more than several hundred in number, while they have tens of billions."

"So, the Shiga?" the Arch asked.

"The day the game ends, the Shiga will be allowed off their planet. The Kohs have only a mechanical security system there, no living being wants the job. It will be easy for us to bypass them with our own system.

"The fifty ships I mentioned earlier will arrive at that time. They belong to Gablona, and it will be made to look as if Gablona bribed the Shiga to save himself. Each of those ships can carry twenty thousand. That first wave will spread out— in fact, it will hit the planet that is the economic nerve center of the Cloud and where the Kohs are currently meeting. That wave will then be followed later by others. They shall be like an epidemic, spreading from planet to planet.

"The chaos resulting from our control of their economy will paralyze the resources of the Cloud, and we will merely say that what we now own cannot be used for violence.

"Within half a dozen years, the Cloud will be in anarchy. The people will blame the Kohs."

"But could not the Shiga themselves become a threat? You yourself have had contact with them. Could they not then point to us and tell the people what we have done?"

"We have had contact with only one of them. He alone knows the full extent of our involvement. It would indeed be unfortunate if his ship should meet with an accident, and thus he could not speak. He is their unifier, and with him gone, the rest will merely spread like chaff in the wind. The center lost, the Shiga will play themselves out. If another unifier rises up, we can arrange for him as well."

"You are talking about murder," the Arch said coldly.

"Your definition, from another time," Losa replied.

Losa looked up at the Arch, who hovered before him. The Arch was old, with a memory stretching back eons before the barbarians had come. And his ways, too, were old. From this confrontation the others would see that the Arch had not met what needed to be done, that he was not willing to risk the path of his destiny for a higher good—the preservation of the Cloud. After this was done, the consensus of the others would shift away from the oldest and come to rest on someone else, and Losa knew who it would be.

"It is still intervening too far."

"When the Shiga have expended their energy, reducing the remaining spacefaring worlds back to primitive states, it shall be complete. The barbarians will be trapped on their planets; the few that are left, we can control, and thus we will have done what the First Travelers asked.

"Through holding their economic forces in check and letting the violence of the Shiga play out against it, they will render each other impotent."

"And if this fails?" the Arch said evenly.

"Then you will still be the Arch, and I—" Losa laughed smoothly "—well, then I shall be in your hands for punishment. I did this on my own. If successful, it will be my success; if it fails, then I am sure you will be quick to blame."

The Arch looked down at Losa, his features creased with a look of contempt. Losa had played the game all too well. There was nothing the Arch could do. If he tried to stop it, the involvement of the Overseers would be revealed, and then the barbarians would unite.

"But what about my profits?" Vush cried.

The other two ignored him even as he turned and floated from the room, lamenting the possible destruction of his new-found game of economics.

"I do not know whether to thank you or to curse you," the Arch said coldly.

"If what that screen indicates is true," Losa replied softly, "the Al'Shiga will soon have them, and then there'll be time enough for thanks."

"They must have gotten through the door and locked it from the other side," a Shiga shouted.

"They couldn't have," Ulsak whispered. "I think they're still here." He gazed about the room of rotting men. Somehow his prey was near, very near.

He looked again at the iron door. The heavy locks would take time to smash. To open them would have required a key; the scum must have had one and gotten through.

He again looked about the room. A thought started to form in his mind when a shout came from the end of the corridor.

"My lord, some of our men have set fire to the building. We'd better get out!"

"Damn them all!" Ulsak roared. A day and night of uncontrolled arson was starting to take its toll on discipline, and some were now burning anything they could set a flame to.

With a curse he turned away.

"Is there another way in there?" he roared, pointing to the door.

"There should be another entrance in the next building, behind this one," a yellow answered.

"Let's go then and send a party out through the back alley, in case they got out that way. Then find the man who set this building aflame. I want him tied to the door frame and left as an example."

With a cold snarl Ulsak turned and started for the exit. He stopped in the doorway for a moment and turned in hesitation. He looked to the corner of the room, where the thousands of rotting men were stacked, and then stormed back up the stairs.

There was a stirring in the corner.

Gagging, Aldin tried to push away the rotting man that lay on top of him. His hand went straight into what would be the stomach, and the foul gases within escaped with a soggy rasping sound, the slimy green-brown juice within cascading in a gurgling torrent straight into his face.

With a groan of disgust he pulled his hands out, now covered with a slimy brown-green coating.

Not now, he thought, struggling to control his stomach. He

pushed up again, this time grabbing the plant by the throat. The head came off in his hands. Kicking out, he pushed the rotting man aside, the head still in one hand, and stood up.

The room was alight with the faint phosphorescent gleam of the plants, giving a strange, eerie glow to the cavern. Overhead there was the sound of crackling flames—the yellows had put the building to the torch.

His heart was still pounding with fear. The act had been one born of desperation and several minutes of hard arguing. The Gafs had wanted to storm back outside, and the samurai were in agreement, stating their desire to at least die out in the open. Finally he had convinced them, and they had crawled into the pile of rotting men, pulling the plants over and around them.

"It's clear," Aldin hissed.

All about him, it seemed as if corpses were rising up from their graves, to suddenly be shaken aside, revealing the slime-covered fugitives beneath.

As one, the entire group started to cough and gag, kicked the plants aside, and reassembled in the middle of the room. Aldin nodded with approval toward Ura, who had stayed with Hassan throughout. If there had been trouble with that man, having the Gaf's hands on his shoulders would have stopped it. Hassan might be useful yet, he thought, but that did not mean he trusted him.

Only Gablona, out of the entire group, seemed calm as he absently munched on the remains of a rotting man. What was worse, it instantly became obvious that Gablona was drunk, having swallowed a good portion of a liquid meal from at least one of the plants.

"Now we're even worse off than before," Gablona said, his voice slurring. He pointed straight overhead. The growing sound of the conflagration was clearly audible.

"This whole building will collapse in on us," Tia cried, her voice edged with panic.

Aldin looked around at the group. The samurai and Gafs were not pleased at all, and he could feel their anger.

"Better to have died in the open," Ura growled, "rather than be roasted like sholts in a flame."

"What are we going to do?" Tia shouted.

Without comment Oishi unsheathed his sword and started

for the exit, but even as he reached the opening, a flaming beam collapsed across the doorway.

Wide-eyed, the samurai turned back to face the group.

"I have no intention of dying by fire," Oishi said softly, coming back to Aldin's side. "It's not the best of ways to go; I've seen it before."

Aldin looked straight into Oishi's eyes.

"Let me do it for you," Oishi said softly, "and for Tia and Mari as well. One of the others will take the fat man, but I wish the honor for you. It will be painless."

Aldin had brushed with death so often in the previous days that he thought he would be used to it. But still he could not control his trembling. And he realized now, as well, the courage of the samurai around him, who had willingly faced death not only for him but also for their dead lord, three thousand years ago.

"At least your killing us will ruin the betting," Aldin said, trying to force a chuckle.

What an irony, he thought, turning away. In this madness of betrayal and counterbetrayal, it would be an act of loyalty and compassion that would ruin all the plans of the powerful Kohs. Whatever happened, Zola would likely make hundreds of billions out of it, he thought, shaking his head.

Aldin looked back at Oishi, and trying to force a smile, he merely nodded in reply.

"Give me a moment," he said softly.

"We don't have long." And as if to add force to the argument, there was an explosive roar. The far end of the cavern caved in with a shower of sparks and a wave of smoke and searing heat.

Aldin stepped over to where Mari and Tia stood huddled against the wall.

"Oishi asks to help us leave here," he said softly, taking the two with either hand.

Tia buried her head into Aldin's shoulder, crying.

Mari looked down at Aldin, trying to force a smile. "Damn it all, Larice, I was hoping to bed with you at least once." And leaning forward, she gave him a passionate kiss. Pulling back she wiped away her tears and smiled.

"Let's go," she said softly.

Aldin looked back at Oishi, who stood with drawn sword,

and nodded. Taking the hands of the two women, Aldin went to his knees, facing the wall, Mari and Tia to either side.

"The Basak die fighting!" Ura roared defiantly.

Screaming with rage, the berserker ran up to the iron door and slammed his axe against it.

He stepped back to give another blow.

Almost on the edge of hearing, Aldin detected the faint jingle of metal striking the floor before him. As if in a dream, he looked down.

A key was lying on the floor.

"Wait!" Aldin screamed.

With a surge of terror he looked back. Oishi had already started his swing on Tia. The blade came to a stop, inches from the girl's neck.

"It's the key, the goddamn key!" Aldin screamed.

He reached forward, snatched the cold metal object up in his trembling hands, and came to his feet. Fumbling, he stepped to the door and stuck it into the latch. He turned it as he held his breath.

The door clicked open.

Laughing hysterically, he looked up and pointed to the sill above the door.

"It was resting on top of the doorsill! Ura's blow must have knocked it down."

"Well, let's get moving!" Ura roared, looking around triumphantly as if he had somehow reasoned out their escape, rather than stumbling upon it in a blind rage.

Grabbing hold of the door, the berserker pulled it open.

Aldin held his breath. Ulsak had ordered his men to enter the catacombs through the next building. Were they already in there and waiting? Even if they were, Aldin reasoned, at least now he could go down fighting.

The door swung back. Silence.

Ahead there was the phosphorescent glow of yet more rotting men, but nothing else.

With a shout of joy the Gafs rushed forward, the samurai falling in behind.

Oishi came up to Aldin's side, and the two stopped for a moment to gaze upon each other; nothing had to be said, for both understood.

CHAPTER 14

"WHICH WAY DO WE GO?" OISHI ASKED, LOOKING BACK AT Mari.

"How in hell am I supposed to know?" she snapped back. "This is my first time down here, same as you. All I know is the catacombs go for kilometers beneath the entire foreign quarter. Rumor is it even leads into the other cities."

"But you lived here, I thought you'd know," Oishi replied, trying to be patient and deferential to the person he now considered his lord's chosen lady.

Ahead lay a narrow corridor, with an immediate branch off to the right. The party stood in silence, still stunned by the narrowness of their escape, as the rest of the building caved in behind them with a shuddering roar.

"Do you hear something?" Aldin asked after a moment.

Directly ahead there was a distant, rhythmic pounding.

"Ulsak's boys trying to get in, I think," Tia whispered.

"Well, that settles it then," Aldin announced, and pointed to the right.

Holding the lantern rescued from the cavern, Oishi took the lead and the group set out behind him.

The tunnel went on for several hundred meters and then doglegged to the left, where several turnouts greeted them.

"Now what?" Oishi asked.

"Like I said, how the hell am I supposed to know? Where we're going, they don't give road maps."

"We could be running in circles then," Gablona announced.

"Better than frying to a crisp," Aldin retorted.

"Why not simply hide down here?" Zergh asked. "It'd take them days to find us."

Several of the samurai turned about at that suggestion, and more than one nodded his approval.

Aldin shook his head. "Two reasons. First off, we don't know this place. They undoubtedly do. If ever we are discovered, they'll call in their friends, and that's it."

"And the second reason?" Oishi asked, watching Aldin closely.

"Old military axiom. 'In open country, do not bar your enemy's way; on dangerous ground, press ahead; on desperate ground, fight.'"

"Sun Tsu," Oishi announced, a look of admiration crossing his face.

Aldin merely nodded. "We are on desperate ground. Our enemy expects us to run, to hide. He'll never expect us to attack, and I plan to take the offensive. If we don't, not only will we lose our lives, but the Cloud will sink into chaos. They know we're in the catacombs; they'll expect us to hide here. So let's give them a surprise—let's move and get out of this city."

He looked at the choices ahead of them, did a quick mental toss of the coin, then pointed to the right.

Another hundred meters brought them into another cavern, and the party came up short.

It was a garden of rotting corpses, and for the first time, those not of the Al'Shiga discovered how the plants were grown.

The entire corridor was filled with garden beds, and from

each a dozen or more of the plants sprouted. Gablona took one look, paled, and dropped the remnants of the rotting man he had been so blithely munching on.

The rotting men were fertilized with Human corpses.

Bodies filled the garden beds, covered only with a scant layer of dirt, their outlines clearly visible. Here and there the soil cover had been washed away, so that cadavers in various states of decomposition stared out at them, the fungi growing out of foreheads, sunken chests, and protruding limbs.

The stench was overpowering. Trying not to look to either side, Aldin strode down the middle of the cavern, his companions nervously following.

When they reached the end of the cavern, a corridor curved off to the left, and there another horror awaited them.

Now they could see, as well, where the baskets of men came from. Skeletons hung suspended down the length of darkened halls, illuminated only by the faint glow of the plants growing in their fertilized beds. Each of the skeletons was encased in a filigree web of vines that traced about the bones, feeding off their calcium and finally crumbling them to dust, leaving nothing but the outline behind, encased in wood.

"Pull half a dozen of those things down," Oishi commanded. The men looked at him in confusion but complied.

Leaving the corridor of baskets behind, they met another three-way junction. The group stopped for a moment to rest.

"We could be going in circles down here," Gablona repeated drunkenly.

"Well, do have any damned alternative?" Aldin snapped.

The Koh merely smiled and shrugged his shoulders.

"Noise to the right," Ura hissed.

Aldin looked up. Suddenly there was the faint glow of a torch in the distance. "Move!"

They pushed straight ahead.

"They're on to us," Ura shouted, and from behind all could hear the shouts of pursuit.

"Keep moving!" Aldin cried. "If we stop to fight, they'll get word out to block us."

The group took off at a run. Oishi fell to the back of the column and ordered his men to stack the baskets. Sticking his lantern into the middle, he waited till they were ablaze before withdrawing the lamp and racing to rejoin the group. Within seconds the tunnel behind them was engulfed in fire, the baskets looking like writhing skeletons in the flames.

Shouts of rage echoed behind them as they raced on into the darkness.

Horror after horror was passed: fungi shimmering with green phosphorescence; hundreds of baskets, which Oishi knocked down, torching them as he passed; and pens of blind, white sholts, which the party drove out of their cages to further confuse the pursuit.

Twice more they ran into search parties, one running straight into them from a side corridor. The fight was sharp but brief, leaving three yellows and two Gafs behind. One enemy survived, and with a shout disappeared into the darkness.

For nearly a day and a half they pushed on, no longer taking the time to stop, until finally two Gafs had to carry Gablona between them, lest the overweight Koh slow them in their desperate retreat.

At last Zergh, who was at the head of the column, signaled a halt.

"There. There, do you smell it?" he whispered.

So long had they been breathing the stench of the catacombs that Aldin felt as if the reek of decomposition had seeped into his very soul. He came up to stand by Zergh.

"What?"

"There. Smoke."

Then he smelled it. Smoke from a wood fire and, mingled with it, the scent of fresh air.

"To the right!" Aldin cried.

The party pushed after him, desperate to breathe clean air. There was a faint light in the distance, glowing red. The group rushed forward and spilled out into the forest.

It was nearly as bright as day, though overhead the stars shone dimly. To their left the city was in flames, a firestorm that swept from end to end. The pall of smoke, roiling low, dipped down in vast eddies, cloaking them in its choking darkness, then rose back up again.

The wind roared about them, sucked in toward the vast heart of the inferno.

"Now where do we go?" Oishi asked.

"To stir up some trouble," Aldin replied, looking about.

"How?"

"If I know Ulsak, he's lost tremendous face already by allowing our escape. There'll have to be a hunt for us out here, and he'll be under pressure; there must be less than five of their days to go now. By now he must have figured we've gotten out of the city, and there's just too much territory to cover without the help of the others. Let's clear the city and see what we can stir up."

The group stopped for a moment and looked back again at the city, the Skyhook rising up out of the flames, reflecting the firelight so that it looked like a pillar of fire rising into the heavens.

"They're insane, totally insane," Mari shouted. "There'll be nothing left but ashes."

"Perhaps they wish it that way," Tia replied softly.

"We think they made it out of the city, master."

"You think? Did I hear you say you think they made it out?"

Ulsak turned on the messenger, his features contorted with rage.

The messenger bowed low before the master ulla.

"I want an answer; I cannot act on assumptions, on 'I think.' Did they or did they not escape?"

The messenger, trembling, raised his head from the floor.

"They escaped, tracks were found leaving a hidden entry between the west and north gates," he whispered.

"Did your men do what I told them? Seal off every possible entry, and then search corridor by corridor?"

"It was impossible," the messenger cried. "The catacombs run for dozens of kilometers, with half a hundred known exits, and perhaps as many unknown. They must have stumbled on an unknown path and followed it out."

"If I recall," Ulsak said softly, "not less than a month ago I foresaw the chance of this happening and suggested that you prepare for such a likelihood. Did you?"

"To the best of our ability," the messenger replied softly, not daring to say that such a conversation had never happened.

"Your ability is lacking," Ulsak said, and then turned away to face his aides.

"They must be between us and the whites," Ulsak said, looking to his staff. "Send a messenger over to them now, I want the other four sects alerted immediately. We've got to find them and kill them with all proper ceremony, otherwise our plans are for naught. And let my commanders tell every man that if they slip by again, all who are responsible will suffer as much as the two we plan to capture."

Ulsak turned and looked back at the man cowering on the floor.

"Impale him," he said, the slightest of grins lighting his features. "Make sure it's the slow way."

"Will the traitor come through for us?" an ulla asked, coming up to Ulsak's side, even as the condemned ulla was dragged out of the room.

"He knows what to do," Ulsak replied coldly.

"We did find one man down in the catacombs though."

"Who?"

"Just that mad shaman. He was by the door of the ancients, peering about and shouting incantations."

Ulsak stopped for a moment, half wondering.

"Should I bring him to you?"

"I don't have the time. Whip him out of the city and tell him to go live with the Sutar. I have no further need of him. He has been my prophet, but now the time of phophecy is at hand."

The ulla bowed low and scurried away.

About the doorway of the ancients? Why and how could that old madman have found his way down there? But there was no time now to dwell on such matters, and he pushed the thought out of his mind.

The starlight barely silhouetted their target, who rested easily against the tree.

Aldin felt an almost wolflike thrill. Since coming down to this place, he'd been the prey, with all the disadvantages of the defense. No matter how vigilant, one was still gripped with fear, not knowing when or where the attack might come. For a day and a half since emerging from the catacombs, they had been hunted by the Shiga, but now the tables were about to be turned.

A twig snapped directly behind him, and turning, he saw

Hassan freeze in midstride. The samurai accompanying him mouthed a silent curse at the assassin, who looked about as if embarrassed by his mistake.

Instantly the guard was alert, dagger drawn.

Aldin froze, watching the man from the corner of his eyes. If the man shouted, they'd really be in it.

Oishi lifted his head up from the ground, and cupping his hands, he gave the call of an owl, a signal they had noted was used as communication between the Shiga guardposts.

The guard relaxed and started to lean back against the tree.

He never saw, and barely felt, the blade that a second later slashed his throat open.

Takashi grabbed the body and quietly lowered it to the ground.

The attack party swept forward, Aldin staying back with the reserves at the edge of the woods.

The enemy encampment was plainly in view.

Oishi tied his own sword behind his back and swept up the blade from the dead sentry. He looked about at his men.

The sky to the east was starting to brighten, so that the pale yellow robes they had taken from the last group they surprised were barely visible.

"Ready," Oishi whispered.

The dozen men nodded.

"Now!"

The dozen samurai rushed forward and within seconds were in and about the first campfire. A dozen of the whites were slain before the alarm was even given, but by then the samurai had already turned about and were rushing back into the woods.

"Ulsak, Ema Al'Shiga!" Oishi roared, waving a bloody head in his hand as the party melted back into the woods.

The reserve of samurai and Gafs were already pounding down the trail, rounding the first bend. They reached the first of four warning stakes tied off with a red cloth and gave the trail a wide berth; as they ran deeper into the woods, they passed the three others.

The samurai dressed as yellows rushed behind them with Oishi in the rear. When he reached the first stake, he pulled it from the ground and flung it into the woods.

The pursuit was closing fast.

After turning the next corner, he pulled at the second warning stake as he had the first.

From behind he could hear the shouts of rage. There was a thunderous crack, and the screams of rage turned to cries of terror and pain as the first man tripped the spiked deadweight that swung down from an overhanging branch.

Laughing grimly, Oishi pushed on into the woods, the pursuit left behind.

Stopping at last, the group fell to the ground, breathing hard from the exertion and excitement.

"Well, that ought to stir things up a bit," Aldin said grimly. "No matter what Ulsak says, some of the white Shiga will still think that the old ways haven't been given up, and some yellows have gone off to hunt a couple of heads."

While they talked, Takashi scrambled up to the top of a tree to gain a better view. Minutes later he was back down.

"What'd you see?" Oishi asked.

"They're still drawing the net, keeping a continuous line all the way about the five cities, closing in at a slow, steady pace."

Aldin sat in the dust and drew a circle in on the ground.

"A good five hours of light left," he said quietly. "They'll most likely close half the distance into the city by then. We've got to keep stirring things up and hope for the best. If we can punch a hole and get out, or, better yet, turn them against each other, we'll make it through the next three days. And then Bukha can get us out of here."

Aldin looked over at Gablona, who sat quietly, and as Aldin's gaze turned upon him, the Koh smiled softly.

"But of course," Gablona whispered, and Hassan, by his side, merely nodded his approval.

"Let's move across the whites and hit the blues next," Aldin said, and the samurai growled their approval at the mention of the blues.

As the sun crossed the zenith, the group settled down along the edge of a marshy stream and waited. They could clearly hear the beaters, pushing closer, and the excited shouts of the Shiga racing up and down the line as the men shouldered their way through the brush.

Suddenly, not twenty meters away, the dense undergrowth parted and a face peered out.

Aldin froze and raised his hand to those waiting on the opposite slope, signaling that the enemy had arrived.

More and more appeared along the edge of the stream and hesitated.

Finally, what appeared to be an ulla pushed forward and with a hearty curse stepped into the stream. Within seconds he was nearly neck deep and, with feeble strokes, beat against the lazy current. All up and down the riverbank the men started in after him. The ulla finally reached the other side, and dripping mud, he slipped and splashed up to the edge of the riverbank. His hand reached up to grab a root, in order to pull his way up onto dry land.

"Ulsak, Ema Al 'Shiga!" Oishi rose up out of a bank of rotting leaves. The ulla's head flipped from his body, and with a wild shout, Oishi snatched it from the side of the bank before it tumbled back down into the stream.

For a moment the blues stood there stunned, all eyes turned on the yellow-robed warrior, only his eyes visible; about his head the red cord of the Mukba. With a wild shout, Oishi turned and scrambled up the slope, a dozen more yellow-robed samurai rising up, some striking at those who had drawn close to the bank, the rest simply falling back, taunting the blues.

They all disappeared over the hill.

With shouts of rage at such base betrayal, the blues surged forward, eager for revenge. After reaching the bank, they started up; one, then another, and suddenly a score fell in the high grass. The grass-covered traps were only a half-meter deep, but it was enough to drive the sharpened stakes clear through the foot of a victim.

As Aldin and his companions disappeared down the trail, pulling back from the closing circle, they could hear the shouts of the blues in the distance—and the name of Ulsak screamed with rage.

"But I tell you, my men had nothing to do with it!" Ulsak roared.

"That is beside the point," Orphet of the white snapped back in reply. "My men are convinced that your people have everything to do with it: that you yellows have not put down the dagger of the ritual, and are taking advantage of the hunt to harvest some more heads, and that this is part of your plan."

"That's madness. Do you believe that?"

"Of course not," Orphet replied evenly, but Ulsak and those around him could see that the answer was more diplomatic than truthful.

"Well, do you doubt my word?" Ulsak roared.

"For two thousand years we've lived with the dream," Tores Ser of the greens replied. "The dream of returning to the stars, of ending our exile and purifying the Cloud to the One Faith. Now today you've told us that you, Ulsak, shall make the dream come to pass. That the tower shall be open, that ships await, and we can sweep out to the stars. Only the hidden Ema can have such power. Do you therefore intend to claim before all that you are the hidden Ema?"

Ulsak looked about at the other leaders of the Shiga. They would see—in three days they would see him as he was meant to be revealed.

"Yes, I claim that title. I am the hidden Ema of the Al 'Shiga, sent to liberate, to guide us on our destiny to the stars!"

His claim was greeted with stunned silence.

"And by what signs do you thus reveal yourself? For the Ema shall have the power to unlock the tower, to guide his people upward, where the ships of God shall await us, so that we shall do His bidding and slay all who oppose Him," Nargla of the red Gafs stated.

The others looked at him. Though the inner circle knew that what they taught to the masses was merely legend, Nargla had not rejected his faith when raised to the inner ranks.

"Bring to me the two that are hunted," Ulsak replied. "They must be brought to me no later than the night before the Ulman. Upon the square they shall be staked, and the moment that is done, the doors shall open wide for us."

"The doors open for any man or woman," the leader of the white Janinsar sect replied, "but only those from above may return. If the Shiga dares to enter the tower, then he is cast back down."

"But by that you shall see," Ulsak announced, "and thus it

will be revealed that I am the hidden prophet. From above I shall watch the sacrifice, and when it is complete, and I have not been cast down, you shall see that the way is open for all. I have been promised that, by those called the Overseers."

"You're mad," Nargla said coldly. "You are no hidden prophet. If we gain the tower, it should be by the hand of the Unseen One, not by these politics. We are doomed here, and nothing more. We all believe that, at least we who rule should."

"You shall see. Perhaps this is how what you call the Unseen One has decided it shall be, through the foolishness and greed of those we wish to overthrow," Ulsak said, a distant look to his eyes.

"But it all rests on these two," Orphet replied coldly. "That means to me that you don't have this power of the Ema unless those are delivered."

"It is the sacrifice," Ulsak stated quickly. "With their blood I promise you the stars."

"Our own people don't understand this. They don't understand why you burned the foreign city, and even your own homes, they think you've gone mad. It was to be a time of taking heads and general festivities. Instead you've called us to merely hunt these two. Our people have always been taught that only when the Ema comes will the six tribes be again united as one, answering then to the tribe that has raised up the Ema."

"You fools," Ulsak roared. "All I want is those two alive; nothing more. Then you shall see that what I speak is the truth. If not, I offer you my own head in sacrifice."

The other ullas fell silent.

"You offer your own head?" Orphet asked craftily.

"Yes! Just tell your people that the attacks upon them are not by my men, that it is a deception. Tell them that the two must be taken alive and brought to me. My head I shall then offer as debt, along with the heads of my entire clan, if what I say does not come to pass."

The masters looked from one to the other and smiled.

"Then your word is bond," Orphet replied softly, and turning, he strode out of the room, all but Nargla following.

"And if these two are not captured?" the old Gaf said softly.

"They will be. But remember, I want them alive."

"Why? If you simply want them dead in payment, then we should kill them on the hunt and be done with it."

"No!" And Ulsak turned away.

He wanted those above to see that it was he, Ulsak, who did the kill, not someone else who might then claim to have been the bringer of the liberation.

He turned and looked back at Nargla. "Because they have offended me. And those above demanded that their deaths not be hidden, but out in the open, in the great square for all to see."

It was a lie, but Nargla could not know any different.

"The circle was half closed today; tomorrow by sundown your people shall be to the walls of the city. My own have formed a perimeter about it. The only ones in between are those we hunt, once you and your escorts return to your men."

"But if they are not captured . . ."

"They must be," Ulsak said, and in the strain of his voice Nargla understood what was to be done. The kill would be his before the night was over, but it would not be the kill Ulsak expected.

"There. The only spot not covered by watch fires," Aldin said, pointing off to the south.

"A part of the red sector," Mari said quietly.

In a broad arc from horizon to horizon the fires of the Shiga surrounded the city, the noose drawing in ever tighter. Aldin looked back over his shoulder. Parts of the city behind them still burned, the outline of the town now marked by another circle of flame, the watch fires of the yellows, preventing return back into the catacombs.

"Why is that one spot unlit?" Aldin asked, thinking out loud.

"It could be a trap to lure us in," Mari commented.

Aldin looked back at the city and judged the distance back out to the outer perimeter.

"Damn, if only we had one more day. Damn it all." He lowered himself down from the tree limb from which he and Mari had been watching the position of the hunters.

"Is that one spot still dark?" Oishi asked, coming up to join them.

Aldin nodded.

"It's worth a try. Could be our little strikes of today had their effect and some of the Shiga are dropping out of the hunt, leaving a hole open. If we could break through, we'll be out on the other side and can run them all the way to the escarpment. By then your game will be over, and hopefully your so-called friends will pick you up."

"I still don't like the smell of it," Aldin said.

"Do we have any alternative?" Oishi asked softly.

Aldin realized that the samurai was right and could only nod his head in reply.

Within the hour they were off, moving single file down the narrow trail that one of the Gafs, scouting ahead, claimed moved straight toward the darkened area. As the stars wheeled overhead, the party pushed forward, wary of any traps that might be set, not knowing that now there was no one between the two perimeters, so nervous were the six clans of betrayal by the other.

As they drew close to where they felt the position to be, the group slowed its advance. Ground that could be crossed in a minute at a pleasant walk now took a long, agonizing hour to cover as samurai and Gaf scouts drifted ahead, signaling to the rest when all was clear. They'd move up a hundred meters, then wait until the next hundred meters were cleared.

It was during one such wait that Ura crept up to Aldin's side and whispered the news. "Hassan is gone."

"What! I thought your people were watching him and Gablona."

"We were," the hulking Gaf said lamely.

Aldin felt as if he were about to burst with rage, but realized that Ura was mortified at his failure—no reproach could make him feel any worse. "Gablona?"

"Still here. Claims he knows nothing."

"Damn him, I almost wish I *had* cut his throat."

"Can I?" the Gaf asked, his features lighting.

"Damn it, no," Aldin snapped. "Now go back and keep an eye on him at least."

Crestfallen, the Gaf disappeared back down the trail. When Oishi came back to report the next sector cleared, Aldin broke the news.

"Damn him, I wanted to kill him and you wouldn't let me."

"I know, I know," Aldin said, cursing himself for not following his instincts.

"We'd better move," Oishi announced. "For whatever reason, he left. It can only hurt us."

Following Oishi's lead, the party quickened its pace.

"They're heading toward the red perimeter." Hassan gasped, still out of breath from the run through the forest. He'd nearly met his end at the city wall, when a yellow, nerves on edge with rumors that the whites were out hunting heads, had taken a swipe at him, and only through instinct had he managed to roll beneath the blow even as he shouted that he was a friend.

"Where?" Ulsak asked.

"The darkened position."

"Damn him. Nargla is offering them a way out, I know it!"

"Let's move," Ulsak ordered.

"There's the line," Oishi whispered.

"It just isn't right," Aldin replied. "No fire, no guards, just a gaping hole waiting for us to walk through."

"Or into."

"Or into," Aldin echoed softly. His heart was thumping like a trip-hammer. If this is what men talked about, the thrill of the ambush and the stalk, he resolved never to step outside a building again after dark should he get out alive. He felt as if every bush had eyes; that this was a dark, foreboding whirlpool, sucking them in to certain destruction. Through the brush, a couple of hundred meters to either flank, they could see the roaring blaze of the perimeter, but here it was as dark as the grave.

"What shall we do?" Aldin asked.

"Draw swords and move straight in," Oishi replied. "The only alternative is to sit here till dawn, which isn't too far off, or retreat back into the net they're drawing closed around us."

The word was passed down the line. Sheathed weapons were drawn and shimmered softly in the starlight.

Oishi stood up and started forward.

"Drawn blades aren't necessary, offworlders" came a voice out of the darkness.

Oishi froze. Startled cries of alarm echoed down the line.

"I said, drawn blades aren't necessary!"

A single torch burst into flame not a dozen meters ahead. Oishi, lowering his blade, stepped before Aldin.

"If we wanted a fight, my people would have taken you long ago." A single figure stepped forward.

Aldin put his hand on Oishi's shoulder. If this was a trap, they'd walked straight into it. At least delay might give them time to find a way out.

"Who are you?" Aldin shouted.

"Nargla, Master Ulla of the Sutar."

"Mari!"

The column behind Aldin parted as Mari pushed her way forward.

"He claims to be the master of the reds," Aldin said as she came up to his side, not daring to take his eyes off the Gaf who stood on the trail before them.

"It's him," she whispered.

"I wish to strike a deal," Nargla said.

"A deal for what?"

"Safe passage through for you."

Aldin didn't know whether to shout with relief or order Oishi to attack in the hope that at least they could take a Shiga leader down with them.

"I know you don't believe me," Nargla said.

"And why should I? I'd be mad to trust what you say."

Nargla barked softly. "Well said."

"Then what is it you propose?"

"If I wanted you dead, I would have simply ordered an attack on you, without this parley."

"We might have caught him by surprise, and he's stalling till his people move up," Oishi hissed.

"Also well said. That is how I would react."

"Enough of the compliments. Get to the point," Aldin snapped.

"I want some answers first, before I let you through."

"And that's it?"

"That's it. There's no love lost between Ulsak and me.

You're the path to his goal. If I can eliminate the path, then I have hurt my foe. Ulsak wants you taken alive, for a sacrifice. I intend to wreck his plans."

"And eliminate us in the process," Oishi argued.

"Is that it?" Aldin asked, motioning for Oishi to be still.

"But first there are some things I need to know," Nargla replied.

"Ask."

"You have my honor as an ulla of the Shiga. You have my head as debt if I betray you."

Mari mumbled a surprise at this.

"It's a bound oath," she whispered.

"I merely ask that we talk first, then the path will be cleared."

"We can talk just like this," Aldin replied, his mind on edge with caution.

"Our shouting will only draw attention," Nargla reasoned, "and things that will be said are best not heard by even my own. I merely want you and the fat one to come to me. We'll sit and talk and then you are free to pass my lines, as I have sworn."

Aldin hesitated.

"You are free to come into our lines," Oishi called.

Nargla laughed harshly. "I am the one offering life. I have the power but to shout, and my men on the other side of the stream will swarm over like flies to carrion. If there is any walking to be done, it will be done by you two, not I."

Aldin looked first at Mari and then Oishi.

"Don't, my lord," Oishi begged.

"It might be the only way," Mari reasoned. "He gave his oath on his head. It means that if he lied, any of our clan is free to claim it without retribution at any time. It also means he can't call one of his clan to harm you."

Aldin still hesitated.

"Oishi!" he shouted in a voice loud enough for Nargla to hear. "You still have that bow that you made down here?"

"Yes, my lord."

"Then nock an arrow. Draw it straight on that Gaf. If he moves to harm us, kill him."

And then he looked back at the Gaf for a reaction.

Nargla stood still, a slight look of disdain lighting his features.

"The weapon of cowards," he barked. "But draw if you will, I won't harm you."

"Bring up Gablona," Aldin shouted.

A minute later the Koh was at the head of the column squealing with fear when he realized what Aldin was proposing. After drawing a dagger, Aldin nicked Gablona in the back, pushing him forward.

"So you are the two," Nargla said almost matter-of-factly, looking each of them over closely as they drew closer.

"If you mean the ones that have avoided capture by the entire Shiga nation," Aldin said, "then the answer is yes."

"A successful avoidance of capture is successful only when the hunted is safely beyond pursuit. If I were you, I would not be so boastful," Nargla said softly.

"Still, we've given Ulsak and his friends a run," Aldin said.

"For what reason is all this madness?" Nargla asked.

"You wouldn't believe it all if I told you," Aldin replied wearily.

"Most likely I would not, coming from the lips of an unbeliever."

"Then why are you bothering to talk with us?"

"Because I wish to know why your death will bring Ulsak power. For if what he said is true, then the Seda will be opened at midday the day after tomorrow when the sky grows dark. Who would be so mad as to allow us off this world merely for the sake of killing you two?"

Aldin shot Gablona a look of contempt, and the Koh tried to avoid his gaze.

"It's a long story," Aldin replied.

"Don't move!" Nargla suddenly hissed.

There was the crack of a twig to Aldin's left.

Turning, he looked off into the darkness beyond the light of Nargla's single torch.

There was the sound, as if someone had blown on a pipe barely heard. Something nicked his shoulder.

Stunned, he looked down. It struck him as almost being too absurd to be believed. He'd been hit in the shoulder with a dart the size of his finger, the sharpened point already stinging his shoulder, as if he'd been jabbed by a bee.

"Ulsak!" Nargla shouted, throwing his torch to the ground.

As if he were suddenly looking down the length of a long, dark tunnel, Aldin started to turn. Everything seemed to be happening in slow motion.

He heard Oishi's bow snap and the sound of impact as the arrow lifted Nargla off his feet, smashing the heavy Gaf to the ground.

Gablona staggered before him, looking somehow comical with several darts sticking out of his fat stomach, his face contorted. The terrified Koh was shouting, but Aldin could hear no sound.

Suddenly forms leaped past him; around him, dozens of them.

Distantly he saw two faces peering down at him. One was Hassan; the other, Ulsak. He tried to scream even as he fell away into darkness.

CHAPTER 15

"ARE YOU SURE ABOUT THE INFORMATION?" BLACKIE ASKED, still not quite believing what she was hearing.

"I had it from Zola himself. The rest of the Kohs are in total panic. It seems that there's a block of two million tickets calling for the death of Aldin and Gablona on the last day, which starts in just another six hours standard."

"Two million," Blackie whispered, sitting down across from Kurst. "And these are first-day buys?"

"Exactly."

"That comes out to a payoff in the trillions," she whispered. "GGC will be completely wiped out."

"There's more," Kurst said softly. "In the papers of incorporation for GGC they waived the liability clause. If GGC can't pay off all debts, the stockholders must forfeit all personal assets. In other words, a majority of the corporate assets of the Cloud will go to the winners."

"Who holds the tickets?"

"Alma," Kurst replied. Several days ago he hadn't even heard of them, but now he could think of little else. The Overseers were to everyone but the Kohs a vague entity of semilegend. If the game was merely going to be ultimately a transfer of funds from one consortium to another, it would be of no concern. But as the news leaked out, a tremor was felt throughout the marketplaces of the Cloud. If the Overseers owned everything after tomorrow, what would happen?

"Surely they can't allow this," Blackie said.

"Certainly not. Zola and some of his friends are talking of open rebellion, refusing the transfer of funds, and planning to keep right on running things."

"But these Overseers—legend has it that they have awesome power in their control."

Kurst could only shrug. "As long as the social order stays intact, there isn't much that can be done. Surely these Overseers won't start smashing entire worlds just to gain their winnings."

"Let's hope, but what is your information?"

"There's still a plan afoot. I overheard Zola's conversation with another Koh. Really, as this thing gets worse, they're getting more and more slipshod in their security. Anyhow, Zola's claiming that he still has someone down there, and an arrangement for Sigma to kill Aldin and Gablona."

"What! But Sigma's dead, his Gafs going over to Aldin."

"But if one of Sigma's Gafs kills those two, then the credit still goes to Sigma, even though he's been dead for nearly a month."

Blackie looked away from Kurst and punched up the latest market flow on the screen.

Trading had slowed off significantly the last five days. Options on some tickets had been running at almost full payoff value, five million katars for what had originally been a one-katar investment. All tickets regarding the death of Aldin and Gablona by the natives had vanished from the market days ago, their holders now hanging on for the final payoffs.

"There aren't many tickets out there," Blackie said.

"Buy them," Kurst snapped. "Zola's been right so far. This is the final insider move."

"They're going for fifty-three thousand a ticket right now for a full option till the end of the game."

"Buy 'em all," Kurst replied.

"Look, we've made several hundred million," Blackie argued. "Let's keep what we've got and get out before this market collapses."

"Several hundred million can buy over six thousand options," Kurst said, quickly running the calculation in his mind. "We could turn that into thirty billion with this kind of information. We'd be Kohs if this works out, think of it!"

Blackie looked up at Kurst, amazed at the transformation. A month before he had been an archetypal professor, locked up in his probability studies, playing his imaginary numbers games. But now he was as rabid as any shark on the trading floor, smelling yet one more deal, the final big one that could bring him all that he ever dreamed.

"I still don't feel good about this," Blackie said softly.

"Do it!" Kurst shouted. "Do it and we'll be Kohs, with wealth beyond imagining."

Blackie sat back, looking at him closely. Finally, with a quiet nod, she got up and left for the trading floor. Within minutes the shares of a Sigma kill had climbed to sixty thousand, and kept on rising.

Oishi sat alone, bathing his wounds in the gently swirling water of a stream. The field about him was a riot of color covered with deep orchidlike flowers as wide across as a man's reach, the scent an intoxicating fragrance that made him think of the cherry blossoms of home. The early-evening light drifted across the sky, as if taking the red of the flowers and using it to paint the clouds.

But he did not see it. Alone, lost in thought, he cleaned each of the cuts and then, rising, returned to the riverbank. Taking up a thread and a needle that one of his men had carried, he set to stitching the long dagger slash that had laid open his shoulder.

The pain was barely noticed; long ago he had learned to control such things, turning his thoughts to something else. But what he thought of cut far more deeply than the sting of the needle.

He had failed his lord.

He had stood ready, bow drawn, and watched his lord walk straight into the trap that he feared. With the snap of the first twig, he'd tensed the bow, aiming straight at the red-robed Gaf's heart.

The onset had been stunning and complete.

One moment, the path was empty except for the two off-worlders and the Gaf. The next moment, half a hundred yellows had swarmed out, engulfing Aldin and Gablona. In that first instant he thought that in spite of Mari's comments about head bond Nargla had betrayed them anyhow. But Nargla never had a chance, Oishi had seen to that.

With a cry of rage he'd fired, then, tossing aside his bow, raised the others to charge, with the desperate hope that still the situation might be saved.

But maddeningly, the path was blocked by a squad of yellows who seemed determined to do but one thing, to die so that the others might escape.

Oishi's full attention returned to his wounded shoulder. The last rough stitch went in. He twirled a knot into the line and bit the thread.

When that first blade had hit, he thought himself dead, for surely the poison would bring him down. That first cut drove him to a wild frenzy, and he waded through the yellows, bellowing with rage, slashing again and again with his long sword.

Yet the yellows did not give back before him. As quickly as one died, another leaped to fill the gap. And all the time, over the heads of the assassins, he could see the knot of men dragging Aldin and Gablona off into the darkness.

At last, with a wild shout of rage, he downed the last assassin, the man's blood splashing into his eyes as he took off his foe's right arm with a single upward slash, and then kicked the screaming yellow to the side of the path, for the rest of his men to finish off.

Coming up to Nargla, he stopped.

Aldin and Gablona were gone. Off to his left he could hear the captors crashing through the bushes in retreat, and with a shout he ordered his men to pursue, expecting that at any second he would fall at last to the poison, not only from the first wound but from the half-dozen other slashes he had picked up in his wild, frenzied attack.

To his right he could hear shouts of alarm as well; the reds were stirring from their hiding place and coming up to the rescue of their leader.

There was one last act to perform, he thought, his mind suddenly cleared from the first wild, explosive rage.

He turned back up the path and, grabbing the first yellow body, he carried it up and dropped it next to Nargla. He put his foot on the Gaf's chest, yanked the arrow out of the ulla's heart, and then, taking the dagger out of the yellow's hand, he plunged the blade back into the hole. At the very least it would give the reds something to think about. Then turning, he crashed into the woods, even as the first red assassins appeared on the trail, racing to the rescue of their master.

He paused in his thoughts and, leaning over, examined the still-oozing wound on his thigh. Then he set to work on that one as well, the needle rising and falling, stitching the gaping cut together. It was funny, he hadn't even noticed that one until they'd finally given the pursuit up within sight of the city walls.

Every step of the way it seemed another yellow had leaped out at them. It would only take a moment to dispatch the assassin, but each moment put Aldin another step farther away, and finally the pursuers no longer even heard them, but could merely follow the trail until at last it had come to the clearing. The shattered city was before them, the gates shut. He was tempted to give over to his rage and simply charge straight ahead, but it was Mari who stopped him.

"He's already in the city," she whispered, her voice choked with tears. "We'll simply be throwing our lives away without any hope of saving him."

Trembling with exhaustion and despair, Oishi agreed, and the group had retreated back into the woods and camped by the small, flowing stream.

More than half were injured, four more samurai and five Gafs dead, ironically leaving him with exactly forty-seven warriors, including Mari and Tia. Gradually they had come to realize that the enemy had not been using poison blades. Most likely out of fear that one might accidentally be used on Aldin or Gablona, so intent was this Ulsak on capturing them alive. Without the poison, the assassins had fought at a disadvantage, accustomed to a fight where even a scratch was as good as blow to the heart.

Finished at last with the wound, Oishi stood up and stretched. The dark red sun was on the horizon, sinking faster than what he was used to, on wherever his own world now was.

Standing, he looked along the bank. Several of his men had been doing the same as he, cleaning their wounds, tending to their weapons, or simply sleeping the sleep of exhaustion.

Sentries were posted, but somehow he knew there was little need for that now. The circle had advanced no farther, for what they had sought was taken. A day ago, all those with him had assumed that they would fight, and fight well, before going to their deaths. Now, but a day later, they rested along the quiet riverbank, knowing that after tomorrow, the game would be ended. Already Tia had promised them wealth, titles, and what could be called the ranks of daimyos for their loyal service to her uncle.

The sun's disk flattened out and disappeared. The seventy-ninth day had ended. With a sigh Oishi realized that if they so desired, this time tomorrow they would be free to leave.

And Aldin would be dead.

After putting his loincloth back on, he picked up the tattered robes of his old uniform he had once worn in service to Asano. The sleeves were caked with dried blood, the stains already set into the silk. He looked at the garment closely. Mingled somewhere in there were the stains of Kira's blood as well. How far away was it really from that world? Oishi wondered, looking up at the sky. He could remember the night when Aldin had taken him up to the roof of their hideout and pointed to the swirling light that sparkled in the midnight sky, and told him that there was home, the world that but months before had been the only world he'd ever known.

With a sigh he searched again for that speck of light. Where was Asano, his old lord? For by now he had come to realize that where he now walked was no spirit world, this was a world of living, breathing men, and other creatures as well. And like his own world, it was a realm with all the deceits, all the betrayals that men carried in their hearts. All except for Aldin, who in so many ways reminded him of Asano, right down to the gentle laugh and the desire to treat others with honor. So out of date, Oishi thought sadly, out of date even in my world, for what did honesty in his refusal to bribe Kira get his lord but betrayal, humiliation, and death?

Oishi put on the bloodstained robe and reached down to pick up the two blades that he had laid out on the grass. Replacing the weapons at his waist, he smiled inwardly at their touch. They were living things, his companions on the road of the samurai, with a lineage dating back to the great master Matsumasi, who had forged them with his own hands, imbuing them with his sense of honor and truth.

There was a faint cough behind him. He knew it was Takashi, who always did this when he wished to speak but did not wish to interrupt Oishi in his thoughts. He turned to face his brother and could see the grief in Takashi's eyes as well. The loss of the warrior's only son had cut into his soul, but he would hold his mourning in check till this was over.

Till this was over, Oishi thought. Zergh had lied to them, that fact Aldin had finally revealed. Even if they had survived there was no going back to their own world ever again. It was a world thousands of years past, and others had died, in their place. But somehow that didn't seem to matter at the moment.

"I was speaking to Tia Koh," Takashi said, and as he spoke Oishi looked past him to see that the other samurai had drawn about him, the Gaf warriors standing on the edge of the circle.

"And?" Oishi asked softly.

"She said that we shall be named daimyos in her kingdom, with an entire world to call our fiefdom. She blames us not for Aldin's capture and says that it is senseless to do more."

Oishi merely nodded, and saw Tia standing on the edge of the group, Zergh at her side. She smiled wanly at him, the anguish of what she had been through still written on her features.

"As she said to me as well," Oishi replied.

Takashi was silent.

"So why are you telling me what I already know?" Oishi asked.

"For though honored, I must respectfully decline."

"To do what instead?" Oishi asked, looking at his brother who, though older, still acknowledged Oishi as the leader.

"I shall die with my lord Aldin," Takashi announced.

"But there is no way we can possibly reach him in there," Oishi said.

"Nevertheless, I swore to protect him. I have failed. At

least I shall die sword in hand, and in the next world my lord Aldin shall greet me, standing beside Asano, and both shall know that I died a samurai—with honor."

Oishi felt tears in his eyes, and looking to the others, each of them nodded in turn. For once the Gafs did not bellow in their crude way but instead silently lifted their axes on high in agreement.

He watched as Tia gazed in amazement, and bracing her shoulders back, she nodded to him as well, Mari at her side.

"Then I shall not die alone," Oishi whispered. "I could not ask this of you. But know that yet again the forty-seven ronin are one. And though our lord will see us not, still in the end he shall know he did not die abandoned."

The group relaxed, as if they had already passed the great barrier, and now that it had been crossed, they hid their fear, choosing to enjoy the last moments of comradeship. Several of the men and Gafs fell into light banter, patting their weapons and boasting of accomplishments past and to come.

Tia came up to stand by Oishi's side, and nervously she reached out and took his hand.

"Why?" she asked.

"Because I am samurai," he replied, as if that simple statement explained all.

"You must not go with us," he said, looking her straight in the eyes.

"Sexist," she snapped, a smile tracing her features.

"What is that?"

"Never mind," she replied, and from her look he knew there was no sense in pushing the point any further. "When do we go?"

"I was thinking in the middle of the night. We'll get into the city, push as close as we can to where this Ulsak lives. If we can get through, we'll get Aldin out."

"But you don't believe that for a moment, do you?" she whispered.

He knew there was no sense in lying. "They made a mistake once, and thus we escaped. Such a commander as Ulsak will not allow it again. He'll have thousands of guards out, but at least they shall know we tried—and died as samurai."

Oishi sat down on the grass by the riverbank, and kneeling down, Tia joined him, her hand still in his. Around him the other samurai had drifted away, some to sleep, most to talk with old friends or new friends found among the big furry Gafs whom they still deferred to, remembering the old edicts of their emperor. Others, like Takashi, simply sat by the bank of the river, watching the reflection of the starlight as they inwardly prepared to say good-bye.

"Tell me of your worlds," Oishi said softly. "And how all this came to be."

"Ah, where do I start?" Tia laughed gently.

"Wherever you wish."

With a sigh she drew closer, her lips close to his.

"How you came to be here, I'll start there, and then tell you of the history of men, back to a place once called Earth," she whispered.

Smiling, she looked into his eyes.

"There is a legend that has been carried across ten thousand worlds," she said in barely a whisper, her eyes gazing into his, "to all the worlds where men have walked. Across three thousand years still it is remembered, the story of the forty-seven ronin, who would die for their lord, already dead . . ."

So the stars wheeled in their course, the great Magellanic Cloud, in all its splendor, lighting the sky above them like a silvery band.

"I hope you go first," Gablona said weakly, looking across the room at Aldin, who stood chained to the opposite wall.

"Pleasant of you," Aldin replied. "And considering what they plan to do, I must say that I agree."

The door into their cell creaked open and Ulsak strode in, his face alight with an evil grin. Stopping in the doorway, he looked from one to the other, gloating over his catch.

"I must say, your hospitality is not quite as good as the last time," Aldin snapped, pleased with himself at his defiance. He'd been planning the line for hours, feeling that it was certainly better than groveling before the man who was about to bring about his death.

"Ah, yes, the accommodations," Ulsak replied, looking about the cell. "One of the few buildings spared the conflagration just so happened to be my private dungeon."

"How convenient."

"Yes," Ulsak replied, playing along with the game. "You

see, my personal fortress was caught in the fire when an errant breeze blew some embers on the roof."

"How sad," Aldin retorted, happy with the momentary diversion the banter provided.

"So I thought it best to house you here, with a safe roof over your heads till dawn."

"Which is how long away?" Gablona cried.

"Oh, the night passes slowly for you, does it? How callous of me. It is near the middle of the darkness. But for your convenience I'll have a guard come to you every quarter of the hour for the rest of the night to inform you of how much time you have left.

"Have a pleasant evening, my friends." Ulsak laughed, and turning, he strode from the room.

The two were silent for a moment, until finally Gablona raised his head to look at Aldin.

"I hope you suffer worse than me," the Koh screamed.

"And then Aldin said good-bye to Alexander, known as the Great . . ."

Oishi reached out and touched her lightly on the cheek.

"I think it's time we started," he said softly.

She stopped, self-consciously, and laughed gently.

"I wish this night could go on forever." Tia said, and sighed.

"But in a short time it will," Oishi replied. "And then you can tell me yet more, for as long as we wish."

Before he even realized what he was doing, he leaned forward, his lips brushing against hers.

Eagerly she sought him out, her hand still held by his.

Finally he pulled back, their one kiss fading away. The two smiled like children who had kissed for the first time in a darkened corner.

Oishi came to his feet, and as if knowing that he was again the leader of his comrades, she released her hold on his hand.

"It's time," Oishi said, and all about him the others stirred, coming out of their reveries, their quiet thoughts, or the final snatches of forced bravado shared with comrades who understood what in fact each was trying to hide.

"What is your plan?" Ura asked, coming up before Oishi, his Gafs forming up in a knot behind him.

"Plan?" Oishi lowered his head and started to laugh. "Plan, you ask? Find a low spot or break in the wall, go through it, and then head into the city."

"What about the catacombs?" Mari asked.

Oishi shook his head. "It's a miracle we ever found our way out of them. We could go in there and be lost for days."

The others nodded their agreement.

"Then let's go," Oishi announced, and drawing his sword, he held it up to the starlight.

"Bravo. Bravo, I say," a voice called from out of the shadows. "I wish I could have a social realist painting of this moment, I'd call it 'the forty-seven ronin march again.' Absolutely heroic!"

The group stopped, weapons lowered.

"Who is it?" Oishi shouted.

"Lower your voice, my good man. Please lower it, or they'll hear."

The shadow drew closer. Beneath the starlight, a bent, wizened form took shape; leaning on a staff, a man stepped before the group.

"What the hell do you want, old man?" Mari snapped.

"Just a little talk between friends."

"No tricks from you, old one, or we'll cut your throat and be done with you," Ura growled.

"You Gafs, always such a bloodthirsty lot."

"I know that voice," Tia snapped, and pushing through the crowd, she came up to the old man.

"Well, I'll be damned," she said with a laugh. "Yaroslav!"

"Yaroslav it is." The old man chuckled, and extending his arms, he threw aside the staff and danced in a circle.

"Had all those bastards fooled, did it for weeks. Got a little flogging in the end, but at least they didn't impale me. Shows you what can come from being a good anthropologist. I was their mad shaman, and they ate up every word I said, like Xsarns in a shit bowl!"

"You know this man?" Oishi asked, coming up to stand by Tia.

"Ah, yes, you and Tia," Yaroslav said, wagging his finger at the two. "Been watching you for some time, really quite touching."

"You old goat," Tia snapped, even as she hugged Aldin's old friend. "You mean you were watching us?"

"Watching you. Damn my eyes, the moment I heard that Aldin had been taken, I knew I had to find you before you folks ran off and did something rash and got yourselves killed. I have a little trick up my sleeve. There was a small chance I could pull it off alone, but with your help the odds are increased. Some good detective work on my part, to be sure, but I figured you'd be near the gate where Aldin was brought in."

"You know where they have him then?" Oishi asked hopefully, his features alight with joy.

"Nope."

With a sigh Oishi turned away.

"Then step aside, there's something we have to attend to," the samurai said sadly.

"Now wait a minute," Yaroslav said, rushing up to the head of the group and standing before Oishi. "This whole thing is ready to crack open. Whatever trick you played against the other clans had it's effect. Those young bucks of theirs are hot for some yellow blood, their ullas are barely holding them back."

"That's no concern of ours now," Oishi announced.

"Why, the reds are in an absolute frenzy, claim that Ulsak murdered their ulla to get Aldin. Even the discovery of one of your men dressed in the yellow didn't quite persuade them; they think Ulsak dressed the body up as a ruse."

Oishi smiled at that one.

"Ah, I thought your hand might have been in it. Not even Ulsak would kill another ulla—a bad precedent for masters to kill masters. The only thing that's keeping them together is the sacrifice of Aldin and the promise of what comes later."

"You mean their getting off this world?" Tia asked.

"How did you find that out?" Yaroslav shouted with surprise.

"A little deductive reasoning, that's all. Gablona tried to make a deal for his life, the Overseers manipulated it, and fifty ships are now slated to dock at the tower tomorrow. Why the hell didn't you tell me before you left?"

"Girl, there's hope for you yet," Yaroslav announced. "Sorry I couldn't say anything, but to be frank, I still wasn't sure of you. Blood is thicker than water, they say. You are only Aldin's relative by marriage."

He paused for a moment and looked at her again. "I guess I was wrong.

"But anyhow," Yaroslav continued, looking back to the rest of the group, "we can still have our say in this thing."

"By trying to turn the clans against each other?" Mari asked.

"I thought of that. It could help, but there's more important business to be done. I plan to bring down the whole damned thing, but I need you people to help me bring it about. You can run about and raid if you wish, but the damage has already been done, and in the few hours remaining, you won't do much more. Now, come dawn, the gates will be opened, then all the Shig fighters from the other five clans will march in, all of them hot already. There'll be more than a million of them there in the great square. The slightest spark ready to set them off. Now if Ulsak delivers as promised, all will be forgotten. But if he fails . . ." And his voice trailed off as he looked around excitedly, bursting with anticipation for what he had planned.

Oishi hesitated.

"We were going to die in the name of our lord," he said quietly.

"When all this hits, you most likely will," Yaroslav stated.

"What are you thinking then? And be quick about it," Ura demanded.

"First, back to the catacombs."

"What? To crawl about down there, while our lord dies above?" Oishi shouted. "Never!"

"Just trust me," Yaroslav said excitedly. "I'll try to explain what we need to do on the way. With your help I'm sure of getting past the guards Ulsak has set up."

Oishi looked over at Tia, realizing that she alone out of the group knew this insane old man.

"He's Aldin's closest friend. Him and Zergh," she said quietly. "I'll go with you, Yaroslav."

Oishi looked at the man closely and could see the excitement, and also the pleading, in his eyes.

"All right then," Oishi announced, "but this better be a damn good reason."

"Oh, it is, it most certainly is." Yaroslav began to cackle. "Why, it'll be the biggest damn display in history. Now let's go."

And following the old man, the party disappeared into the darkness.

CHAPTER 16

THE ROAR OF THE MULTITUDE THUNDERED OVER THEM, SO deafening that Aldin could not even hear the screams of terror from Gablona, who was standing right next to him.

A million voices cried out in anticipation, their factional differences forgotten for the moment, united at the thought of watching the death of those whom Ulsak had promised.

Aldin looked over his shoulder to where Ulsak stood above him on the dais. The ulla looked out upon the multitude with arms extended, a glint of savage delight in his eyes. For a moment his gaze dropped to Aldin.

The old vasba turned away. The Shiga leader was completely mad, one could see it in his eyes, and Aldin trembled inwardly with the thought that in a few short hours that madness would be unleashed across the Cloud.

"Hear me, O my people!" Ulsak screamed, but his voice was carried away, like the cry of an infant before the thunder of a maelstrom.

Four guards stepped up to Aldin's side, and grabbing his chains, they pulled him forward. Together they stepped off the high dais and started down the steps to a lower platform that was constructed so that all in the great square could see.

No matter how hard he had tried to nerve himself for this moment, Aldin felt his knees go to jelly when he saw the sharpened spike rising up from the platform floor.

Swooning, he sank to the ground, so that the guards had to drag him forward.

At the sight of his collapse, the howling of the Shiga rose to a thunderous pitch, and Aldin felt as if his ears were about to burst.

With rough shoves and curses the Shiga dragged him to the stake. Trembling, he looked up from the ground. The steel spike glistened evilly in the morning sun. Aldin turned his head aside and vomited, which caused the crowd to roar once more with delight.

Lying on the ground, gasping for breath, he saw Gablona rolling on the platform beside him, his shrieks for mercy carried away by the roar of the crowd.

Rough hands grabbed Aldin by the shoulders and pulled him to his feet. Another hand forced his mouth open and pushed a flask between his teeth. Cool liquid poured down his throat, and he drank, thinking that this would be the last time he would ever do so.

Seconds later he felt a tingling in his fingers and his heart started to race, as if he had suddenly downed half a dozen jolts of coffee.

"It'll keep you from passing out," one of the guards shouted in his ear. "We wouldn't want the fun to end too quickly."

Suddenly the crowd started to fall quiet, their faces uplifted toward the heavens.

"The smaller darkness," a guard shouted, and Aldin looked up toward the pale red sun.

The edge of the sun's disk, partially obscured by high thin clouds, showed a thin sliver of darkness, as if the edge had been nibbled off. A hush fell. After the thundering roar, the silence was almost as frightening.

The sea of faces gazed upward and then looked down to where Ulsak stood. Aldin looked over his shoulder and saw that Ulsak had walked up to a high pulpit constructed atop the dais.

"Hear me, O my people," Ulsak roared. His voice echoed across the plaza. Farther out, criers mounted small platforms scattered throughout the crowd, and hearing Ulsak's words, they shouted them once again so that even in the farthest corner of the square the words of the leader could be heard.

"Today is the day of the Ulman," Ulsak shouted. "And now I reveal to you all what shall come to pass. Today shall be the day of uniting. Our six clans shall become one."

His words echoed away, and a low murmur arose, so that Ulsak held his hands up even higher to call for silence.

"For the uniting has been prophesied since our beginning. By the sacrifice of these two, the Unseen One has decreed that the time has come.

"Now at last I am allowed to reveal to you who I am."

He paused with a dramatic flourish, and as his words were carried out, an ugly murmuring rose from the crowd. The yellows fell silent, as if in anticipation, for if their ulla was raised up, then the Wardi would be the first within the one clan.

"Hear me, O my people. At last I may reveal all. For I am the lost Ema, sent to guide you back to the stars!"

A wild shout went up from the assembly, the voices raised up in either triumph or rage at such sacrilege. Around the base of the tower dozens fell to the circle of yellows, as some of the reds, driven by wild fanaticism, drew blades and rushed forward. For a moment Aldin thought that a general riot was about to break out, and for the first time in years, he silently prayed.

But suddenly an awed hush fell over the crowd as again they looked to the sky. For the first time in their two thousand years upon the Hole, the inhabitants saw the beginning of a double eclipse.

The shadow advancing to the right had already slipped farther in, but to the left of the sun the thinnest sliver of another shadow had appeared, moving in the opposite direction.

Hushed with awe, the crowd looked back to Ulsak.

"This is our sign. The two shadows, represented here by the two about to die. At the moment the two horns of light disappear, they shall die, and the Seda shall be opened to you, my people, and together we shall go to the stars and kill in the name of the Unnamed!"

His words were met with stunned silence—which held a power as frightening as the thunder of the multitude.

"In promise to you and as a sign, I go now, to above— there to cast open the doors. Look to the Platform of the Fallen, and there you shall see me. And when I fall not, then you shall know that I am indeed the Ema revealed. And when next you see me face-to-face, we shall be among the stars."

With a dramatic flourish Ulsak turned from the pulpit and strode down the stairs. A dozen Wardi warriors stood at the base, a platform held high, covered with the finest of yellow silks. Ulsak stepped upon it, and shouldering their burden, the twelve carried their leader across the dais and to the entry of the tower. One last time Ulsak turned to face the Al'Shiga, and then he disappeared through the entryway and on into the tower.

"Impale them," an ulla commanded, coming up to the guards.

The four men picked Aldin up, and after moving forward, they positioned themselves about the upraised stick. Then, ever so gently, they lowered him down. Aldin's feet touched the ground, and as they did so he felt the nick of cold steel slice through between his legs. Instinctively he rose up on his toes, and at the sight of his struggling, laughter rang out across the square.

The guards grabbed the four chains that were hooked to a steel belt about his waist, extended them out, and hooked them to four curved spikes extending up from the platform floor.

Ever so gingerly Aldin tried to move. The steel belt held him in place, and try as he could, it was impossible to move himself off the deadly spike scant inches beneath him.

He heard something being rolled up behind him, and turning his head, he saw a large copper urn, a single spigot extending out from the container that was hooked into the canvas bag on his back.

The ulla came up to the spigot and then looked up to the sun, as if judging the time. He turned the flow open and leaned forward to look inside the bag.

"That should bring you down just as the horns disappear,"

the ulla said with a grin, and then he turned to the guards.

"If either of them are still standing by then, just push them down and finish it." He looked back at Aldin, the same merciless grin still lighting his features.

"You're lucky. The water flow is quick, and you'll be dead in a couple of hours. Usually we take a full day to finish the job."

"Your mother takes carnal pleasure from pigs," Aldin snapped.

The ulla's face darkened with rage, and Aldin started to laugh hysterically. After all, there wasn't anything worse the swine could do to him now.

Several of the guards turned away with smirks as the ulla stormed off the platform.

Aldin looked over at Gablona, who stood just three meters away.

"This is a fine mess you've gotten us into, Larice," Gablona cried.

"I've gotten us into? You cheated on the last game; you even tried to fix this one. You made Ulsak that deal. You're insane."

"Well, at least those bastard Kohs up there'll have nothing left after I'm gone," Gablona cried.

"Just shut up and leave me alone," Aldin said.

He stretched up on his toes again and then, ever so slowly, lowered himself down. The edge of the blade nicked him again.

The crowd before him had fallen silent, except for occasional taunts and jeers. He gazed out over them. A million madmen, he thought, shaking his head. Their women and children back in the cities, almost as insane. The Cloud would become a charnel house when these people were let loose. For two thousand years there'd been no organized military, so there would be little if any organized defense. The wolves before him would slaughter with glee.

He shifted his shoulders slightly. Already he could feel the first faint tug of weight as the canvas pack on his back started to fill with water.

He lifted his gaze up. A most incredible sight, he thought

wistfully, a double eclipse, and he watched as ever so slowly the sun began to disappear.

"We've lost all contact with the Skyhook," Vol shouted, bursting into the room.

"We know," the Xsarn screamed. "It went down ten minutes ago."

The Kohs were in wild confusion. All afternoon there'd been a funerallike despair. Aldin and Gablona were obviously in the hands of the Shiga, and the vid hookup had shown the preparations—and the impaling platforms. Throughout the entire Cloud all commerce had stopped. Here and there a lucky ticket holder sat in a tavern or in the public square, watching the printout reports, already counting the millions he'd win if he was lucky enough to have bought the winning combination on the first day, not knowing the disaster that was in the making.

One of the minor Kohs of GGC had already been found dead in his office, a liter bottle of poison in his hand.

"Zola, is this a repeat of last time?" Vol screamed. "Switch the vid signal, then tell everybody something different happened."

Zola could only shake his head. His hoped-for agent was lurking somewhere down there in the catacombs, hundreds of meters away from the two. With that mob it would be impossible now for him to get through.

He looked up at Vol.

"Are you mad?" he whispered. "The only com link directly to the tower is down. All signals from the game, however, are still being routed through."

"Then why?" Vol roared.

"Because, my fellow Kohs, I think the Overseers are about to pull something else that they don't want us to see."

Suddenly by Bukha's desk a paging signal flashed on. Picking up a headset, he hooked in, and all about him fell silent.

A quiet moment passed, and a look of stunned disbelief crept over his features.

He dropped the headset.

"So, Tia was right after all." Bukha gasped.

"What? What about Tia?" Zola asked.

"She tried to warn me, but I simply wouldn't believe it."

"Warn you of what, for heaven's sake?"

"I just had two reports come in. The security system on the tower was shut down an hour ago, when a dozen Overseers boarded the structure. The damn thing's wide open."

"And what's the other?"

"It was just reported that fifty primary transports just down-jumped and are in orbit around the Hole, already maneuvering to dock with the tower."

"Fifty ships?" the Xsarn asked, still not comprehending, and then the truth finally dawned.

"I think I'm going to be ill," the Xsarn whispered, and rising, he staggered from the room.

"That's it," Yaroslav whispered.

Directly ahead they could see a half-dozen yellows standing in the open corridor, and beyond that, what appeared to be a door, made from the same substance as the Skyhook.

"We're directly under the foundation of the Skyhook," Yaroslav whispered.

"Be quiet, old man," Oishi whispered. He'd heard what was planned but still could not quite believe. But there was nothing else that could be done but to follow through with this madman's folly.

The party approached the six yellows and slowed.

"You're relieved," Yaroslav announced, drawing up to the guards. "My men here have been sent down to replace you."

"By whose orders?" one of the yellows growled suspiciously.

"By my orders."

"You're the mad shaman. You can't order us."

"Oh, yes, I can," Yaroslav roared, waving his hands about as if drawing up a mystical curse.

The six stepped back slightly but still refused to move away.

"Leave us now."

"When our ulla tells us and not before," one of the yellows barked defiantly.

"Oh, that's it?" Yaroslav snapped, and he started into waving his hands in earnest while drawing up next to the leader.

The guard pushed Yaroslav back with a curse and then doubled over with a grunt, a dagger sticking out of his chest.

Oishi flung aside his yellow robe, and in the same movement his sword snaked out, catching the second yellow before his look could even change from astonishment to pain. The rest of the samurai closed in and finished off the others.

"A good kill," Oishi announced, clapping Yaroslav on the shoulder.

"Still have the old touch. I told you I would," Yaroslav snapped.

He strode up to the door and gazed about.

"Seven keys," he said softly, and his fingers traced out the outline of seven squares set into the wall.

"Took me a while to even figure that out. I was down here for days prowling around, right under their noses. They thought I was mad, and after meeting with Ulsak, they left me alone. Then heaven knows how many hours I spent on these keys. Pushing them, and pushing them. Figured that a certain sequence would do the trick to let us in. But by Jove, which seven? Finally stumbled on it a couple of days back, and then it was 'open sez me.'"

Yaroslav stood up on his toes and touched the seven inlaid squares.

Nothing happened.

"Now don't tell me I've forgotten it," he mumbled crossly.

Exasperated, Oishi turned away to avoid screaming with rage.

"Now let's try it again, one, two, four, six, three, five, seven."

There was a faint click and the doorway opened.

"Figured those First Travelers would have a logic to the sequence, otherwise I'd still be out here punching. Well, what are you waiting for?" Yaroslav snapped, looking back at his companions, and he strode into the room.

Oishi waved, and from the darkness at the end of the corridor, the rest of his party appeared, each of them laden down with earthen jars that Yaroslav had directed them to pick up earlier.

As Oishi stepped through the door he fell silent with awe. The room gleamed with the same strange whiteness of the tower. Overhead, lights without flame, like those he'd seen when aboard the sky ship, snapped on dimly, so that several of the men gave startled cries.

"Quickly now, quickly," Yaroslav called, guiding them onward.

Down the long corridor they followed the old man until at last the pathway broadened into a single room.

"Stack the jars along that wall," he commanded.

Momentarily confused by what he was seeing, Oishi went up to the wall Yaroslav had pointed out.

Strange lights glowed along the length of the room, while here and there strange figures danced across boards of glass. And then one of his men screamed.

From out of the far corner it emerged. It towered twice the height of the startled samurai—a strange metallic-looking thing with a hundred arms that wavered back and forth as it approached, floating as if suspended by invisible hands.

"I'd like to introduce you to a First Traveler," Yaroslav announced, pointing to the creature that hovered before the terrified group.

"Quite harmless actually," Yaroslav announced. "Let's you wander about, do what you please. I don't even think it's aware we're here. Just busy with doing its job, that's all.

"When I finally broke in here, its presence confirmed what I'd suspected of this room. Figured that such a location would have to be down on the planet, since being located in space made it vulnerable to all sorts of mishaps. Quite ingenious of them, really. Any seismic activity, the sensors pick it up, a dampening system switches in, cancels it out before anything can go wrong. It even compensates for the solar wind fluxes, with tiny rocket bursts.

"Now we got a wonderful moment here. Two large moons aligning sets up quite a tidal force, along with that huge sun above us. Oh, quite a gravitational pull indeed. These controls here should dampen it out, since the force is not distributed equally, with a greater pull farther up the line than down here."

Yaroslav looked over at the samurai and saw he'd lost them.

"Oh, never mind. Just put those jars there. Carefully now, nitro and ammonia nitrates are a bit finicky, not like your black powder. Took me days to make the stuff."

The last jar was finally placed, and Yaroslav looked around the room.

"I think you better get out of here," he said, a smile on his face as he stuck a roll of fuse into the single jar of black powder and then placed it into the middle of the explosives.

Stepping back, he grabbed a torch from one of the Gafs. For a moment he hesitated, looking closely at the warrior, and then he turned away.

"Let me do it?" Oishi asked. "The rest of you get out of here."

"Not on your life," Yaroslav roared. "And give you all the fun? Now get the hell out of here!"

The samurai looked at the old man, and with a nod he turned and raced from the room, following the others.

Yaroslav looked up at the First Traveler that hovered impassively above him. It had created itself to build, to maintain, but in its world, a concept to defend had never occurred, and so it watched and did nothing.

"Sorry, old man," Yaroslav whispered. He touched the torch to the fuse and with a wild shout of glee, like a boy who'd just let off a firecracker in school, he turned and raced out of the room.

Most of the sun was gone now, and the pack dug into his shoulders. Beads of sweat ran down his face, the salt stinging his eyes.

As the sun slowly disappeared between the closing disks of the moons, a low chant had started from the yellows, which gradually had built and swelled, the plaza echoing with the noise.

"Al'Shiga, Al'Shiga, Al'Shiga!"

Maddeningly it was timed to the beat of his heart, each word a thundering roar that pulsed as the blood thundered through his veins.

He tried to shift the weight, and as he did so, his knees buckled and the steel slipped ever so slightly into his body.

With a grimace of pain, he straightened, and his agony was apparent, so that the Shiga roared the louder.

Finally he decided. He would do it. In one cold thrust he'd simply lift his feet and fall. It could certainly be no worse than this. For surely it would come anyhow; to draw it out, for even another minute, was madness.

Shaking his head, the sweat fell away from his eyes. He wanted somehow to scream a curse at them all, but knew they could not hear.

And then he raised his head up, to gaze at the wonder in the sky, the two horns starting to form between the closing disks, the Skyhook bisecting the sun now as it rose to the midday sky.

All this he was leaving, he thought almost wistfully, while another part of his mind steeled him for the fall.

He raised himself high onto his toes, to add the extra inch or two, as if it would help to speed him into oblivion.

Good-bye to it all.

He let his knees buckle, and he tried to drop.

With a wild shriek of pain he shot back up. For a moment he felt off balance, as if he were going to fall again, and he tottered, still shrieking, knowing that the blade had cut in not more than a centimeter at most.

Down he started to slip. Desperate, he fought to regain his balance and shot back up on his toes. His balance wavered and he slipped downward again, the edge of steel slipped into the now-open wound.

In his mind he remembered Ulsak's taunt—how the impaled would bob up and down like a toy, screaming their anguish. He looked over at Gablona and saw the Koh was doing the same, and for the first time in weeks he felt pity for the man, even while shriek after shriek was torn from his own lips.

Suddenly he heard the taunts and chants die away to a hushed silence. Thousands of arms were pointed toward the tower. Steadying himself, Aldin looked up, and there, far above, on the side of the Skyhook, was a tiny yellow dot.

For a moment he thought he felt the ground beneath him buck, and he danced for balance, bobbing up and down again, and then the tremor died away.

Soon the horns would close, the north and south ends of the sun shrinking away to nothingness, and at the thought of what was coming, Aldin shrieked with pain and rage.

The platform trembled beneath his feet, so that with a fearful gasp, he stepped back. Wide-eyed, Ulsak turned and looked to the Overseer.

"It is nothing," Losa whispered. "The tower moves because the moons draw upon it. But there is nothing to fear."

Trying to control his rising terror, Ulsak turned back and stepped out.

For millennia, whenever a Shiga had attempted to escape back up the tower, he was met here, three hundred meters above the square, where all passengers going up were checked before continuing their journey to the stars. Those of the Accursed then stepped back into the cars of glass and ascended. The faithful were dragged to this doorway and thrown out, to fall back onto the Hole.

But never again, Ulsak thought triumphantly, mastering his fear.

He stepped to the edge and gazed out.

Below him, filling the city, were his people. And suddenly, as if on a distant wind, he could hear them calling, chanting.

"Ema, Ema!"

Beaming with triumph, he stood there for long minutes, basking in the adulation of the multitude.

Craning his neck, Ulsak gazed up the long length of the Seda, which now pointed like a needle straight into the eye of the disappearing sun—the horns growing smaller and smaller.

It was all his; he would soon be master of the stars.

And then his eyes narrowed.

The needle was no longer straight!

He saw the faintest of bulges, like a ripple running down a string held taunt. The bulge loomed larger, racing downward.

With a startled cry, Ulsak leaped back into the room behind the platform. A growing rumble, a creaking and groaning, snapped through the Skyhook, and like a ship riding a wave, the tower shifted, slamming Ulsak into the wall.

Wide-eyed, he looked at the Overseer, and even on such an alien face, he thought he saw fear.

Another ripple snapped them yet again; the two were tossed against each other.

With a cry of alarm, Ulsak stepped back out onto the platform. A wave was racing straight up, returning back to the heavens, but another was rippling down, twice as big as the first. The tower shuddered. A dull rumble barely on the edge of hearing echoed through the room, growing louder and louder. The floor bucked up to meet him, then instantly dropped away.

Crawling, Ulsak dragged himself back to the platform, and sticking his head out, he peered up. Wave after wave was rippling downward, each one bigger than the last.

"It's falling," Ulsak screamed. He turned, with blade drawn, to confront the Overseer. But the room was empty.

"I forbid it!" Ulsak cried. "As the Ema, I forbid it!"

He dragged himself out onto the platform and stood erect. Below, the multitudes shifted and moved, as if he were gazing down upon insects beneath his feet.

"I am the Ema!" he roared to those below, and to the heavens above. "Stand and believe, for I command it!"

A thundering roar echoed louder and louder.

He turned his gaze upward once again, and as he did so, the horns shimmered and disappeared in the clear noonday sky. A blazing red crown engulfed the dark spot where the sun had been, while from horizon to horizon the stars shone out in all their splendor.

"It is the time that I foretold!" Ulsak screamed.

The thunder grew louder and a wave of darkness came racing down from above.

"I am the Ema!"

And as he screamed, the platform fell away beneath his feet.

Suddenly Aldin was aware that the roaring of the crowd had died away.

All faces were lifted upward, and in his agony, he raised his eyes.

For a moment he thought his vision had deceived him: the Skyhook had a bulge in it.

Amazed, he watched as the wavelike motion raced ground-ward, growing larger and larger. A distant rumble slapped through the soles of his feet as the wave snapped into the ground. Instantly it recoiled and raced back up the other side of the structure.

A deadly hush fell over the Shiga.

Another wave came down, and as it passed the first one going back up, the two seemed to combine, doubling the bulge for a moment, so that it looked as if the entire tower should snap in half.

"Aldin, what's happening?" Gablona cried.

"Something wrong with the tower. It's setting up a wave motion."

The second wave hit the ground and Aldin felt the ground shake beneath his feet, so that he struggled for balance.

"Here comes another one," Gablona cried excitedly.

"The damn thing's going to collapse!" Aldin shrieked.

His words drifted out over the crowd, and an excited murmur started to rise.

Aldin realized the moment had to be seized.

"Ulsak blasphemed!" he screamed. "He is not the Ema, our deaths displease the Unnamed One!"

A wild shout went up from the reds closest to Aldin.

The fourth wave hit and, rebounding back up, rose past the fifth traveling downward. A thundering crack echoed across the plaza.

Aldin looked up and at that moment the sky darkened as the eclipse went total. He drew in his breath, for he should already be dead.

He looked to the guards about him. Three of the men stood back, their eyes wide with terror, but the fourth one strode forward and, reaching out, grabbed Aldin by the shoulders and started to push down.

"Ulsak!"

A roar went up from those nearest the platform.

The guard, who had been looking into Aldin's eyes with grim hatred, turned his gaze upward and stepped back with a startled cry.

Aldin looked back up.

In the half-light he saw a shadow racing down, robes fluttering in the wind.

With a sickening crunch, Ulsak hit the pavement, his body bursting open by the gate into the tower.

"Death to the Wardi, they have blasphemed!" a voice rose up from the reds.

The guard turned away from Aldin and fled, while all about the dais a wild frenzy of killing erupted. Another wave hit, with a mind-numbing roar.

Aldin watched gaping in amazement as wave after wave

raced up and down the length of the Skyhook, so that it tossed and turned like a ship upon a storm-driven sea.

A light rain drifted down around him, and confused, he suddenly realized that it was flecks of material wrenched off from the tower. The rain turned into a shower, and then into a torrent, as larger and larger chunks of facing ripped free, plummeting into the crowd. First one man fell, then another, and then two or three went down as chunks several meters in width fell upon the crowd.

Amazed, Aldin found himself laughing.

"Looks like the choice is impaling or being crushed," he roared, looking over at Gablona, who stood open-mouthed, gazing at the crumbling tower.

Suddenly he felt hands upon his shoulders, and in a flash of panic he braced himself, knowing that some enraged yellow still wanted to finish him off.

There was the tearing of canvas, and the water sack behind him ruptured, the weight splashing away so that he felt as if he were floating.

In the semidarkness, a Gaf stood before him, a man in a tattered samurai robe by his side.

"Pull these chains up!" Oishi roared.

Fumbling, the men around him fell to with a will, and Mari broke through the press, throwing herself into Aldin's arms with a scream of relief, so that he momentarily sagged.

"I'll be damned if I'm able to sleep with you now!" Aldin shrieked, struggling for balance.

The chains fell away and gingerly he rose up on his toes and stepped back.

A samurai came up to either side and prevented him from collapsing.

"What about me!" Gablona screamed.

Aldin looked over and saw that the Koh was still chained to the spike.

"A billion katars," Aldin roared.

"Anything, anything," Gablona pleaded.

"Tia, you witness as fellow Koh!"

"Done," she cried, coming up to Aldin's side.

"Anything, I'll make it one point one billion. Just let me out!" Gablona screamed.

Aldin nodded and several Gafs pulled Gablona loose.

"How do you like my show?" Yaroslav cried with glee, coming up to Aldin's side.

"Magnificent, how did you do it!"

"Later . . . but right now, let's get the hell out of here."

Yaroslav waved for the group to follow, then started back toward the tower.

"Back there?" Aldin screamed.

"It'll be an hour or more before it really starts to come down, and there's no way we'll get across the square alive. Let's head for the catacombs and get out of this madhouse. There's an entry down through the tower."

Aldin looked back over his shoulder.

Beneath the eerie light of the eclipse, the Shiga were falling upon each other in a wild frenzy of murder and revenge. Color surged against color, while those closest to the tower desperately tried to claw their way out from the hail of doom raining down from above.

"You're all fucking crazy!" Aldin roared, and following Yaroslav, they raced into the tower entrance.

"We're still too close," Tia shouted, gasping for breath as they climbed a low hill outside the city walls.

"We could walk for a week and not get away from the debris," Yaroslav announced. "That thing's forty thousand kilometers up. The top parts will simply go into orbit, lower sections in decaying orbit, while the rest will collapse back in on the world. You could be a thousand kilometers away and still get hit."

"Anyhow I did some rough calculations as to how it would fall and found a cave just ahead where we could get some cover and still watch the show."

"Hope your math isn't too far off," Aldin said anxiously as he turned his gaze heavenward.

Just below the crest of the hill they found the shelter Yaroslav had been leading them to. Beneath the lip of the cave, the group turned to watch the madness in the city below.

From every gate, the Shiga poured out, different color robes mingling together, slaughtering each other on the way— the general pogrom against the yellows giving way in minutes to an all-out frenzy against all other sects. Few yellows seemed to be left. Here and there they could see knots of them holding off against several other sects, and as soon as the yellows went down, the comrades of moments before would turn against each other.

"Look at that wave," Tia cried, pointing back to the tower.

A massive pulse came racing downward, clearly illuminated now by the hourglass-shaped sun that had crossed into the western sky.

"This might be the one," Yaroslav whispered. "Once that imbalance started, it would just keep feeding on itself, growing and growing till it came to this."

The air about them rumbled, as if from an approaching storm.

With an earth-shattering jolt, the wave hit the ground. The tower started to torque from the effect. A loud crack echoed across the Hole, and ever so slowly, the tower twisted in its moorings.

Another even larger wave hit as the tower base was still twisting from the previous blow.

To everyone's stunned amazement, the structure actually lifted into the air, ripping free from its foundation. For long seconds it hovered fifty or more meters in the air, pulled up by the momentum of its mass rising upward. And then a downward pulse hit, smashing the Skyhook into its foundation with such force that the entire city seemed to leap from the impact, so that for a moment even the Shiga broke off their frenzy of killing and lay upon the ground, wailing in terror.

"It's snapped!" Gablona cried, pointing upward.

Aldin looked up and saw where the tower had parted, kilometers above, so that it seemed like a mere thread had been cut.

"Twenty, maybe thirty kilometers up." Yaroslav chortled. "Oh, this is going to be simply marvelous. And I did it, I did it!" The old man danced with glee.

For a minute or more it seemed as if the thread had barely moved, and then ever so gradually, it started to shift, racing out eastward, the narrow filigree line broadening out.

A faint shriek filled the air, growing in volume as it dropped in pitch.

Louder it grew, and closer the line came toward the ground. The base, again resting on the ground, leaned over, the angle dropping lower and lower. A plume of dust rose up from around it, and then the structure started to hit.

It was as if one long string of explosives had been laid out in a line from the center of the city, all the way to the edge of the Hole and beyond.

With a thundering roar, the tower smashed downward, the explosive impact rippling straight across the city, sending rubble hundreds of meters back into the air, to rain down again and cast up yet more destruction.

The ground shook beneath their feet as the line of impact swept past, not more than a kilometer away, and then thundered off into the distance.

"And look at that!" Ura screamed, pointing up.

A section of tower, several kilometers or more in length, was plummeting straight down like an arrow.

"Magnificent!" Yaroslav shouted, still capering about.

It hit the south edge of the city, the three-kilometer-high length telescoping in on itself, sending out a deadly plume of debris that soon covered the entire city beneath its pall.

The Gafs roared with delight, joining Yaroslav in his mad dance.

"Thousands, tens of thousands of servants for our brothers in the next world," Ura exulted. "We'll be the most famous Basaks that ever lived and died!"

They watched as the sun drifted away before them, until finally only a small span of sky separated the hourglass-shaped disk from the horizon.

"You know, I wonder whatever happened to that bastard Hassan," Gablona said, coming up to stand by Aldin's side.

"Knowing him, he'd survive even this," Aldin replied, feeling almost good-natured toward his old employer.

"You weren't serious about the billion, were you?" Gablona asked, as if joking with an old friend about a half-forgotten debt.

"One point one billion, to be precise," Aldin replied with a tight-faced smile.

"Well, at least we've survived. In another couple of minutes it'll all be over."

"Aldin!"

Something slammed into him, and he staggered back and rolled.

Looking up, he saw the Gaf named Kolda lying on the ground, a samurai blade in his chest.

Takashi stood over the body, a strange look of detachment on his face, and then he fell away, his stomach sliced open from hip to hip.

With a cry of panic, Aldin crawled up to the fallen samurai.

"The Gaf came up behind the two of you and drew his blade, but I stopped him," the samurai whispered. "Something about that one's been bothering me for days."

Yaroslav and Oishi came up and knelt by Takashi's side.

"Can you help him?" Aldin cried, looking at the old man.

Yaroslav looked at the wound and shook his head.

The samurai looked up and smiled.

"Ah, what a fight it was today, best battle I ever saw. My son shall enjoy hearing of it," he whispered, and then he fell away.

Horrified, Ura came up and looked at what one of his comrades had done.

He turned to Oishi, an imploring in his eyes. "Kolda was a traitor. May he never gaze upon his brothers in the next world. May he be the servant of demons, to torment him ever after."

"And of the blood debt of my brother?" Oishi asked coldly, snapping his blade half-way from its scabbard as he stepped before Ura.

"He shall be the servant of your brother in the next world," Ura said evenly, eyeing Oishi's blade, "but if you want more, you are welcome to try."

"My brother is dead," Oishi roared, swinging his blade free and raising it on high.

From around the group, weapons were leveled as humans and Gafs came to the support of their leaders.

"Damn it, hasn't there been enough?"

The two sides hesitated.

"Hasn't there been enough killing?" Aldin asked again, his voice a choked whisper as he stepped between Ura and Oishi. Turning, he looked into Oishi's anguished eyes.

"Your brother is dead," Aldin whispered, "he died with honor to save me. Your brother's blood debt is upon me as well." And as he spoke tears started to course down his face.

"He was my brother as are you and I ask you, let there be no more killing."

Aldin looked over his shoulder at Ura, who stood with blade held high.

"As you are my brother as well."

The Gaf lowered his blade and turned away.

Aldin looked back again to Oishi and held him with his gaze.

"My friend," Aldin said softly, "I will help you to bury our brother."

Oishi's shoulders started to shake, and, as tears ran down his cheeks, he slowly sheathed his blade and went to kneel by his brother's side.

Aldin looked over to Gablona, who merely shrugged.

"That is honor," Aldin snapped. "He took an oath and died by it. While to you, you think honor is something to be bought and sold."

Gablona looked at him with silent contempt.

"You didn't learn anything, did you?" Aldin said.

Gablona didn't reply.

"That's what all of this was about. That's why the Shiga failed, that is why you failed." He turned away to look back at Takashi.

"And that is why he died," Aldin whispered as he stood up and walked away from the group.

The sun was touching the horizon, and as he watched, it slipped away and disappeared.

"The game's over," Yaroslav said softly, coming up to Aldin's side. "It's over."

Gablona came up to Aldin, and the old vasba looked at him with contempt.

"Why did you save me?" Gablona asked.

"Business," Yaroslav said with a smile. "You see, Aldin and some of his backers have several hundred thousand tickets riding on the two of you coming out alive."

"You bastard," Gablona roared, "and here I thought you were saving me out of loyalty to an old employer."

"Correction," Aldin said softly, looking up at the Koh. "When we're done collecting our winnings, maybe I'll be offering a job to you."

"Better I died back there than to suffer this," Gablona roared.

"Oh, we can still arrange that," Tia said, joining the group. "I'm sure Oishi would love to escort you down to what's left of the Wardi."

With a bellow of rage Gablona strode away.

"What'll you do with your winnings?" Yaroslav asked.

"Pay off some old debts, I guess," Aldin said softly. "I guess some of them I'll never be able to pay off though." As he spoke, he looked first at Takashi and then at the Gafs and samurai who stood around the body of their fallen comrade.

"Saved. I don't know how, but we've been saved," Zola cried, collapsing back in his chair.

All about him the other Kohs were in wild celebration, raising toasts to good old Aldin and Gablona for having been such sensible fellows and coming through the game intact.

"Ah, gentlemen," Bukha shouted, pounding on the table to get attention.

"What is it now?" Zola laughed. "Old doom and gloom. I told you we'd come through it."

His disappointment about the failed assassination of Aldin and Gablona was almost forgotten. The seduction of the one Gaf had been a plan within a plan. It'd been easy enough, taking the berserker aside before the trip down, impressing him with a little flashy trickery, a levitation or two with lift beams, and then the promise of undreamed-of wealth. Anyhow, the Gaf was now conveniently dead, so no one would ever know, even if the botched attempt had lost him billions.

At least the Overseers hadn't wiped him out, and he could only guess at how much GGC had won.

"Gentlemen, please," Bukha said. "I have one question."

"Go on, what is it?" Zola asked.

"Are all the stockholders of GGC present in the room?"

Zola looked about and did a quick count.

"Not counting Petir, he was a little too quick with the juice."

And the other Kohs shook their heads and laughed at the foolishness of their old friend.

"Good then," Bukha said smoothly. "There are two orders of business left to attend to, then we can adjourn this council and return to our worlds and the business of business. The reason for calling this extended council has been fulfilled as of this morning. All our properties tied into the Alexandrian game have been sorted out, all our lawyers and accountants have accepted the findings, and the paperwork needs only our signatures. But let us discuss the more pressing concern first."

"And what, pray tell, is this pressing concern?"

"First off, we can start to arrange the payout of winnings," Bukha announced softly.

"Yes, the winnings," Zola said offhandedly.

Several of the Kohs fell silent. So intent had they been upon the threat the Overseers presented that the other possible outcomes had become secondary.

"Fine, then," Bukha said, and he nodded to the Xsarn.

The Xsarn rose up to his full three-meter height and looked over the room. "Two hours have passed since the setting of the sun on the Hole, officially closing game day eighty. I therefore officially decree, as moderator of this contest, that all tickets bearing the bet Sigma dead by Gablona game day thirty-one, Aldin and Gablona survive, are winning tickets, paid at odds as represented on said tickets."

"Right, go on, then let's get this over with. There's only a hundred thousand first-day tickets with those combinations throughout the entire Cloud." Zola chuckled. "I've already checked."

"Then you officially accept those results?" the Xsarn asked.

"I do."

"And attest to them as chairman and majority shareholder of GGC?"

"I do," Zola replied, and leaning forward, he pressed his thumb to the monitor before his desk, and the scanprint was taken, officially marking the document the Xsarn had called up.

"Excellent," Bukha said.

"Why are you so enthused?" Zola asked.

"It's just that there are other blocks of tickets," he replied smoothly. "You were so intent on first-day buys with full odds that you never bothered to check out tickets bought between the fifth through thirty-fifth days. It seems as if there is a block of over a million tickets purchased on those days, and all held by one firm. Oh, some of the tickets had been held by others, but they were bought up on, shall we say, a little side venture."

Zola paled.

"I've taken the liberty of running some calculations," Bukha continued. "Of all possible winnings on your officially accepted results. You'll see them on your screen now."

Zola squinted at the screen, and then, with a scream of anguish, he stood up, knocking over the chair.

"They got it all!" he shrieked. "There's only nine billion left after payout!"

"Exactly," Bukha said softly, a self-satisfied grin lighting his features.

"Who did this?" Vol asked, collapsing in the chair by Zola's side.

"Oh, a little holding company—a bit of venture capital some people pulled together."

"Who?"

"One of the shareholders is coming up now. One of my ships just picked him up, and he'll be here in a couple of hours to claim his earnings. An old vasba friend of mine."

He neglected to mention that he had been one of the major venture capitalists, but they'd find out soon enough.

"Aldin Larice?" Zola whispered.

"The wealthiest man in the Cloud," Bukha roared, pounding the table as if he had told the funniest joke of his life.

"Busted, completely busted." Kurst groaned. The massive display board had gone dark; the trading floor was empty. Around him the servobots swept by, sucking up the thousands of pounds of shredded paper and broken bottles, and carting away the occasional suicide found beneath all the trash.

Kurst cradled the Erik 10 in his hand and tried to nerve himself to look down the barrel. "Three hundred million lost. We could have been Kohs!"

Three hundred million, all of it gone. The downpayment on the new ship was as good as gone, the mortgage on his time-share pleasure world cost more in a month than his old salary could pull down in ten years. There was a half million outstanding on his credit. All of it gone.

He cocked the Erik 10 and brought it up to his temple.

"At least let me step out of the line of fire before you pull the trigger."

Kurst looked up.

"Hi, Blackie," he whispered, suddenly feeling rather foolish. It was like a bad vid, the girlfriend coming to talk the fallen financial king out of finishing the job.

"Just leave me alone for a couple of minutes, will you?" he asked, his voice shaking.

"You know, the genius who thought up this venture shouldn't be wasted," she said soothingly.

Kurst groaned in reply. If only he hadn't gone out for a drink with that crazy old man, he thought wistfully. He never would have heard about the game or have been given the idea for the lottery, and none of this ever would have happened. Damn that Yaroslav, he thought darkly.

"Well, all I wanted to do was show you something before you pulled the trigger," Blackie said.

"What?"

She knelt down by his side. She fished through her pockets and pulled out a creased, coffee-stained slip of paper, holding it up for him to see.

He held the paper up in the dim light, looked, and then started to hand it back to her.

With a startled cry he suddenly snatched it back and looked at it again.

"It's a winning ticket, a first-day winning ticket!"

"Used to have five hundred of them, but sold the option on four hundred and ninety-nine. But for the hell of it, I figured I should hang on to one, just in case."

"You're a wonder, Blackie." And dropping the pistol, he grabbed her by the arm and started for the door.

"I've been thinking on some probabilities!" he said hurriedly. "This last lottery thing could be just the beginning. Now listen to this idea . . ." And the door swung closed behind them.

The Arch floated into the room, the dozen Overseers already assembled bowing low at his approach.

"Are you all satisfied?" he said, the slightest trace of anger rippling through his voice.

The others were silent.

"Can we control the damage?" he asked, looking over at Vush.

"Already done," Vush said in reply. "There are no written records, no evidence. The story of the juice heads who originally brought the tickets will hold. The ships were officially contracted through Gablona's company, so that lead is closed, and already they are making their way back to port."

"And Losa?"

"Dead, along with the dozen others who went with him. The security system on the tower has been deactivated and then went down with the tower. Losa and the others tried to escape, but the car was knocked off its tracks and fell back into the Hole. All possible evidence was destroyed when the tower went down."

"A dozen dead," the Arch whispered. "Nearly five percent of our numbers." And shaking his head, he looked out over the assembly.

"The case then is closed. If need be, we shall have to cover any traces of evidence as they come up. Oh, the Kohs know, to be sure, but they won't dare to say a thing, since their reputations are on the line as well. But I tell you this, the next time we shall have to be subtle, far more subtle." And with a nod of dismissal he floated out of the room. No one would ever know, he thought. No one would ever suspect that he had been aware of it all from the very beginning. So those under him took the blame, and he, as was fitting of any leader, could always prove his innocence.

Finally only Vush was left. The others might be downcast, but he most certainly was not. Dumping the Sigma killing Aldin and Gablona options had netted him a fortune, and if he had hands he would certainly have rubbed them with glee as he floated out of the room, contemplating what investments to play with next.

Showers of debris still rained down, the sky above traced with brilliant streaks of light as sections of the tower, some of them hundreds of kilometers in length, dropped into the atmosphere and fell white hot on the blasted landscape below.

Wild shouts of rage and anguish still echoed in the streets of the doomed city, but he did not hear them.

Stepping over the mounds of dead, he traced his way up to

what had once been the Seda, the focus of veneration that had been their doom.

Kicking through the rubble, he searched, guided by the flames about him and the broad streaks of light in the heavens above, as if the sky itself was being torn asunder.

The street bucked beneath his feet, slapping him to the ground, and long seconds later a distant rumbling boom washed over him, the blast sucking the breath from his lungs.

He turned and looked to the west. Over what had once been the city of the reds a massive fireball, thousands of meters high, raced skyward, its top already spreading out in a dark, malevolent cloud.

He pushed on into the rubble, and then at last he found what he sought.

The head was gone, smashed beyond recognition most likely, or carried away by someone still taking trophies. Most likely by a red, he reasoned, it'd give them some comfort. But from the cut of the robes, he knew who it was.

He spat upon the corpse.

"You were not the Ema," he hissed coldly, "for never did you have the cunning."

And Hassan looked out over the ruin, and then raised his eyes upward.

"But some day I shall be!" he whispered coldly.

CHAPTER 17

"I WISH YOU COULD HAVE SEEN THE LOOK ON HIS FACE."
Bukha laughed and poured himself another goblet of sparkling
muscatel.

"Here he is, barely recovered from the shock of finding out
our little company had snatched all the winnings. So he's settled down a bit on that thought.

"'After all,' he said," Bukha whined, giving a fairly good
imitation of Zola, "'we still won nine billion out of it,' and
then in walks the lawyers' and accountants' guilds, handing
him a bill for twelve billion, wiping him out and leaving all of
them in debt besides. Then, it turns out, he borrowed from the
company as well, to buy out Tia. And now he's even deeper in
debt than before!"

Roaring with laughter, Aldin lay back on the silk divan and
took another drink from the tray that the servobot offered.

"I think you've had enough," Mari announced, taking the
goblet from his hand.

"Enough, is it?" Aldin shouted, a mischievous smile lighting his features. "My dear, you are talking to one of the richest beings in the Cloud." And he nodded deferentially to Tia and Bukha. "If I want a drink, I shall have it."

"Doctor's orders," she replied, handing the goblet back to the servobot and shooing it away.

"Your little injury still isn't healed, and you heard him say 'no alcohol and plenty of rest for a month.'"

"Which ends tomorrow," Aldin announced defiantly.

"And then your payoff to her as well." Yaroslav laughed.

The two looked over at the old man, and both reddened in self-conscious embarrassment.

For the evening's festivities Yaroslav was again wearing his shaman outfit. Ever since their return, he could hardly refrain from again describing how he'd brought down one of the largest structures in the Cloud, and given the slightest excuse, he'd quickly launch in to a full technical rundown on the forces involved, his hands waving back and forth to show how the mounting oscillations finally tore the tower apart.

"I heard Gablona gave you a call. What did that bastard want?" Tia asked.

"Yes, yes. What did the old fox want now?" Bukha interjected.

"I still can't believe this," Yaroslav responded. "A short time ago Aldin and I were being hunted from one end of the Cloud to the other. Through Bukha we planted the idea for this game, feeling it was our only hope of living out the year and getting Gablona off our backs. Oh, we threw in a few flourishes—the lottery, for instance. And now Gablona's actually calling you!"

"That part with the Overseers though," Bukha countered. "You must admit that was a close one. We never expected that."

"But still we came out of it all right," Yaroslav replied.

"Barely," Aldin said, his voice not more than a whisper.

"Anyhow," Bukha asked, looking over at Aldin, "what did that man want?"

"The usual, can't pull the working capital together to pay off his debt."

"So what did you say?"

"I offered him a job," Aldin said, laughing. "And the damn

thing was, he actually hesitated for a second before telling me to go to hell! But he did have an interesting counterproposal."

"And that is?" Bukha asked, suddenly alert.

"He's interested in a game," Aldin replied matter-of-factly.

"By heavens, a game," Bukha roared, slamming down his drink.

The group fell into a fevered excitement, and within seconds Yaroslav was holding forth on an interesting part of the ringlike Kolbard that held potential.

With a sad shake of his head, Aldin rose to his feet and slipped out of the room.

As he walked down a broad open corridor, the doors at the end parted.

Before him was his favorite spot on his new yacht, which he had named *Gamemaster*, in memory of his old trade.

From one side to the other the forward hull was transparent, revealing the entire Cloud in all its splendor, the starry heavens a vast sea of light sprinkled across the darkness of space.

And he saw the one he was looking for, standing alone, gazing out upon the universe.

"Thought I'd find you here," Aldin said softly, coming up to his friend's side.

"Ah, my lord," Oishi replied, bowing low.

Aldin came up and put his hands on Oishi's shoulders, forcing him to rise up.

"Oishi, I am not your lord. I never was."

The samurai smiled, shaking his head. "It gives meaning to what I am, a samurai in service."

"If that is how you wish it," Aldin replied. "But in service to a friend, in the same way that I shall forever be in service to you."

Oishi was silent.

Aldin's hands still on the samurai's shoulders, he looked into the man's eyes. "Do you miss them?"

Oishi nodded his head ever so slightly.

"Takashi, and Seiji, and all the others," Oishi said softly.

Aldin could only nod.

"But they died as they wished, as warriors," Oishi quickly said, turning back to look at the stars.

"They died for me, for all the foolish vain reasons that

brought us together. And the burden is more than I wish to bear."

Oishi looked back at Aldin.

"You tried to explain how we came to this strange place," Oishi said. "It is hard to understand, but what I think it means is that if you had not, I and those of us who are left would already be dead. So in that you gave us life. You did lie to us in the beginning, for I have heard it is impossible now for us ever to go back to the exact time that we left."

Aldin was silent.

"So I shall not die for Asano," he said quietly. "And I met the lady Tia instead." And a smile creased his face.

Aldin nodded. The two had been inseparable and he felt nothing but pleasure with the Tia he now saw, who in the presence of Oishi was at last carrying herself with the dignity befitting a Koh. And for the first time he saw her truly happy as well.

"I am glad of that, and thankful," Aldin replied softly, "but still the others haunt me."

"Then perhaps you did not learn, as you said Gablona had not learned," Oishi continued. "For some rare people honor is above all else. I pledged my honor to help you. I pledged it first not knowing who or what you were, believing something else. At first I felt cheated, but honor held me to my sworn course. But then I came to see the honor within you as well. That you would give all, including your life, for the sake of a friend. That you treated others with respect, expecting nothing less in return.

"Oh, such actions often as not can bring deceit from men of no honor. But after all, Aldin, to speak in terms your world understands, life is nothing but a game, and it is not the winning of it but the playing of it with honor that counts in the end.

"Those who died for you believed that. If you wish to honor them in turn, then live as they would live and mourn them not."

Aldin gazed at Oishi and smiled with a sad, wistful look in his eyes.

"And, yes," Oishi said softly, "I am honored to call you my friend."

"Larice, where are you?"

The two turned around and saw Mari towering in the doorway.

"Come on back in here, Yaroslav's cooking up some great ideas."

"Coming, dear," Aldin said, and turning, he suddenly winced with pain.

Oishi, a look of concern in his eyes, came up and took his friend about the shoulders.

"Your wound! Are you all right, Aldin?" Oishi asked.

Aldin could only look to the doorway where Mari waited.

"I hope so," Aldin said softly, "I sure do hope so."

And together, arm in arm, the two friends left the room, rejoining their friends as the *Gamemaster* soared into the sea of night.

ABOUT THE AUTHOR

William R. Forstchen, who makes his home in Florida, was born in 1950. Educated by Benedictine monks, he considered the calling of the priesthood but decided instead to pursue a career in history. Completing his B.A. in education at Rider College, he went on to do graduate work in the field of counseling psychology.

William was a history teacher for eight years and currently devotes his time to writing, educational affairs, and the promotion of the peaceful exploration of space.

William's interests include iceboating, Hobie Cat racing, sailing, skiing, pinball machines, Zen philosophy, and participation in Civil War battle reenactments.